CYBERFICTION

CYBERFICTION
AFTER THE FUTURE

Paul Youngquist

CYBERFICTION

Copyright © Paul Youngquist, 2010.

First published in 2010 by
PALGRAVE MACMILLAN®
in the United States—a division of St. Martin's Press LLC,
175 Fifth Avenue, New York, NY 10010.

Where this book is distributed in the UK, Europe and the rest of the world,
this is by Palgrave Macmillan, a division of Macmillan Publishers Limited,
registered in England, company number 785998, of Houndmills,
Basingstoke, Hampshire RG21 6XS.

Palgrave Macmillan is the global academic imprint of the above companies
and has companies and representatives throughout the world.

Palgrave® and Macmillan® are registered trademarks in the United
States, the United Kingdom, Europe and other countries.

ISBN: 978–0–230–62151–0

Library of Congress Cataloging-in-Publication Data

Youngquist, Paul.
    Cyberfiction : after the future / Paul Youngquist.
        p. cm.
    ISBN 978–0–230–62151–0 (alk. paper)
        1. Science fiction, American—History and criticism. 2. Science
    fiction, English—History and criticism. 3. Cybernetics in literature.
    I. Title.

PS374.S35Y68 2010
823′.087609—dc22   2009030404

A catalogue record of the book is available from the British Library.

Design by Newgen Imaging Systems (P) Ltd., Chennai, India.

First edition: March 2010

10 9 8 7 6 5 4 3 2 1

For the sci-fi geeks and dreamers of Engl. 191:
travel the spaceways

CONTENTS

ILLUSTRATIONS

FIGURES

TABLE

PREFACE TO APOCALYPSE

Little Boy fell from the sky on August 6, 1945, unleashing the heat of a homemade sun. Its light still blinds the world.

The story of the detonation of the atomic bomb over Hiroshima has become iconic: the city of 245,000 strangely spared from fire-bombing that had touched hell to 66 others; the lyrical approach of three B-29 Superfortresses, one of them (the Enola Gay flown by General Paul Tibbets) bearing a payload of a single "special" bomb; the silent flash, the crushing concussion, the winds of fire and crisping flesh; the pillar of ash rising 40,000 feet and billowing into a baleful mushroom; the immediate incineration of 80,000 Japanese civilians, Korean forced laborers, even a few American POWs; the lingering deaths of another 60,000 people from the corrosive effects of nuclear radiation; the confusion, the rubble, the carnage; the military victory and the moral outrage. Hiroshima was an atrocity of sublime proportions. It changed the world. As the dust settled and the fallout dissipated, it would change the future too.

This is a book about that change. It claims that the future also died at Hiroshima. Since the arrival of cybernetics and info-technology, the future has become harder and harder to imagine. Science fiction provides the best barometer for this change. As a literary genre, science fiction usually produces speculative visions of future. It extrapolates from contemporary social and scientific conditions to imagine new possibilities—utopian, dystopian, or just plain strange. Doing so presumes, however, that the future *is yet to come*. What if it is not? What if all the bold tomorrows of a thousand pulp fantasies are obsolete? What if the future is no longer so distant as those luminous tomorrows? One might expect science fiction to notice. And indeed, in much science fiction since Hiroshima the future ain't what it used to be. Rockets, aliens, and atom blasters are out. Info-tech, cyberspace, and the genome are in. Outer space implodes, cyberspace proliferates, and the future obsolesces. Hiroshima is a death knell.

Why Hiroshima? World War II had no shortage of atrocities on all sides. The Japanese were hardly humanitarian during their Imperial romp through East Asia. The Americans firebombed every major city in Japan before dropping Little Boy. In a single night (March 14–15, 1945) they killed nearly 80,000 civilians during a raid on Tokyo—to say nothing of the European theater with its Coventry, its Dresden, its Holocaust. And yet among all those atrocities, Hiroshima takes the measure of humanity's future. If the Holocaust is the conscience of contemporary culture, brute testimony of past horror, Hiroshima is a prophet. It prognosticates catastrophe yet to come. Or rather, Hiroshima *is* that catastrophe, one that augurs the arrival of a posthumous future.

What is the calculus of horror? Interestingly, it is not numeric. Though many human beings died that night in Tokyo as were obliterated instantly in the atomic blast, nobody remembers that horror. What distinguishes Hiroshima from the Holocaust (in numbers the palm goes to the latter), is the stunning *speed* of mass destruction. In a few searing seconds everything in a six-mile radius from ground zero—buildings, bridges, plants, pets, women, men, and children—turned into ash. The atom bomb was a bolt from above, delivered by a B-29 with a mother's name. Contemporary documents tell the story best. In a statement following the detonation of Little Boy, President Truman made this baleful promise to the Allies' stubborn enemies: "If they do not now accept our terms they may expect a rain of ruin the like of which has never been seen on this earth" (Kort 232).

It was no idle threat. The vice chief of the Japanese Army General Staff, Torashiro Kawabe, noted in his journal on August 7 that "the whole city of Hiroshima was destroyed instantly by a single bomb" (68). Instantly. The horror of the atom bomb sleeps in the malign speed of its destructiveness, as Japan's formal protest against atomic weapons three days later attests: "American airplanes released on the residential district of the town of Hiroshima bombs of a new type, killing and injuring in one second a large number of civilians and destroying a great part of the town" (326). In one second. Such an efficient incinerator does not distinguish between military personnel and noncombatants: "men and women, old and young, are massacred without discrimination. [...] Consequently there is involved a bomb having the most cruel effects humanity has ever known" (Kort 326). This new weapon was so swift a sword that it spelled instant annihilation. Emperor Hirohito was quick to draw the inevitable conclusion, described in the Imperial Rescript of August 14: "Should we continue to fight it would not only result in an ultimate collapse and obliteration of the Japanese nation, but also it would lead to the total extinction of human civilization" (330). Cross speed with totality and what happens?

Apocalypse.

Not without a lot of effort, of course. The only atomic bombs to see deployment, Little Boy at Hiroshima and Fat Man three days later at Nagasaki, were the strange fruit of an intense, dispersed, and highly organized blitz of military research and development. The Manhattan Project got its name from the Manhattan District of the Army Corps of Engineers (early nuclear research took place at Columbia University), but its component parts were strewn across the United States. There was the Metallurgical Lab in Chicago, Illinois, the uranium separation facility at Oak Ridge, Tennessee, the plutonium production facility at Hanford, Washington, and most famously the bomb design and development laboratory at Los Alamos, New Mexico. The diverse labors of these facilities came together—literally—on a small island in the South Pacific called Tianen, from which the United States launched myriad sorties of Superfortresses carrying incendiaries against the Japanese people, as well as those two planes loaded with a single "special" bomb each. Tianen was a miracle of military economics. Hap Arnold, commanding general of the Allied Air Forces, called it "just one large airport" (Gordin 69), which it was. The coordinated labor of a global workforce allowed it to operate with lethal precision.

Tianen consolidated the dispersed ingenuity of the whole Manhattan Project. Uranium, plutonium, electronics, casings, precision-machined parts, engineering charts: an array of components came from far-flung locations to Tianen for final assembly into atom bombs. In a strangely literal way, Tianen was Manhattan in miniature: its size and shape resembled the New York island enough for its architects to mock familiar arteries: Broadway and Wall Street, 42nd Street and Canal. If Manhattan is a global city today, a major node in the network of global capital, Tianen was its prototype. World War II was, after all, a *world* war. The labor that coalesced on Tianen was global in scale. The design, production, and assembly of atomic bombs peculiarly resembles the design, production, and assembly of consumer goods. Assembling the atomic bomb, in other words, was a kind of dry run for globalization, with this difference of course: in this case the final product obliterated its target market.

The implications for a global economy of this coordination of distributed agencies appear clearly in President Truman's description of the marvel of the atom bomb's production:

> the greatest marvel is not the size of the enterprise, its secrecy, nor its cost, but the achievement of scientific brains in putting together infinitely complex pieces of knowledge held by many men in different fields of science into a workable plan. And hardly less marvelous had been the capacity of industry to design, and of labor to operate, the machines and methods to do things never done before so that the brain-child of many minds came forth in physical shape and performed as it was supposed to do. (Kort 230)

President turns prophet as Truman details the complexity of the *economy* of the bomb's production. Its global scope and intellectual diversity augurs an economy to come whose dispersed agencies coordinate with military precision.

Assembling the atom bomb was not, however, primarily an economic enterprise. It was a military objective whose means were conceived and executed by an avant-garde of contemporary science. J. Robert Oppenheimer and company constituted a cadre of the leading scientific minds of the mid–twentieth century. Their dreams of reason bred nightmares in the name of peace and freedom. "Now I become Death, destroyer or worlds," Oppenheimer said famously quoting the Bhagavad Gita at Trinity, site of the first successful test of the implosion bomb. Not Vishnu but theoretical physics brought this particular death into the world. In 1945 the atom bomb was the crowning achievement of Western science, a discovery so potent as to transform the world in a flash. Truman understood the monumentality of the Manhattan Project's success: "What has been done is the greatest achievement of organized science in history" (230)—this from his "Statement on the Bombing of Hiroshima." Those directly involved also understood the magnitude of their contribution. A petition signed by 69 scientists raised a cautionary voice against their own history-making discovery. "If after this war a situation is allowed to develop in the world which permits rival powers to be in uncontrolled possession of these new means of destruction, the cities of the United States as well as the cities of other nations will be in continuous danger of sudden annihilation" (218). With victory comes responsibility. For the signatories of this petition, the greatest achievement of contemporary science raises the grim possibility of sudden annihilation— "after this war."

That is a crucial qualification. One should not forget that the development of the atomic bomb was a military objective. It is easy in retrospect to evaluate its use in strictly—and reductively—moral terms. That judgment saddles Truman with a burden of personal deliberation that led ultimately to the decision to deploy nuclear weaponry against a civilian population. Would that things were so simple. The documentary record proves more complex. Secretary of War Henry L. Stimpson sums it up in a press statement two days after Hiroshima: " 'I will say this at this time, that in my opinion and that of General Marshall and his associates, the bomb, from a military standpoint, is merely another weapon much more powerful than any of its predecessors" (Gordin 57). Militarily considered, the atom bomb is just another bomb—more than others, but sharing their strategic purpose.

The point here is to acknowledge that the choice to drop Little Boy and Fat Man was a military decision. Difficult as it may be to accept in the context of liberal democracy, where the rational individual remains supremely accountable for any and all decisions, especially the ugly ones, dropping the atom bomb was at the time a matter less of moral accountability than military strategy. That doesn't make it right. More horrifically, it makes right beside the point.[1] Documentary evidence proves too that military strategy anticipated not one or two or even three atomic bombs (the infamous Third Shot that never dropped), but a whole campaign of nuclear savagery. Perhaps democracy, under the right conditions, finds military violence much more congenial than it likes to admit.

Science fiction—the fiction of technoscientific culture—since World War II has taken such possibilities seriously. It comes as no surprise that such fiction would respond to the horrors of Hiroshima with the gnashing of teeth and the pulling of hair. But the effects go much further. The sheer speed and destructiveness of nuclear weaponry utterly transforms the genre. After Hiroshima science fiction turns gradually into cyberfiction, and the futures it envisions.

But that would be telling. What can be said at this point is not merely that the future is changing, but more chillingly that it has been permanently tainted by fallout from Hiroshima. Instantaneous annihilation remakes humanity. People need faster reflexes if they are to survive such catastrophes, surer mechanisms of moral and military response. The future withers as a court of appeal for the ultimate value of human life. In its place comes another kind of speculation, peculiarly suited to life in the wake of Hiroshima and best depicted by J. G. Ballard in his brilliant, brief compressed novel *The Atrocity Exhibition* (1970). Ballard's protagonist, whose name shifts like the "x" in an algebraic equation, imagines (or calculates) a series of thirteen possible futures. In different ways, through different combinations of variables, these futures redress a psychotic cultural present made insufferable by memories of Hiroshima. The trick, if the protagonist could work it, would be to contain the force of catastrophic violence in a conceptual sequence that would absorb it: the death, for instance, of his wife at a weapons range plastered with massive images of Elizabeth Taylor's face. Ballard's book is a death kit, a set of scenarios for redistributing instantaneous and total violence. The futures it imagines are speculative alternatives that establish a statistical rather than causal connection to the present. All are possible. None is true. And if that is the case, the future is fungible.

There is more to say about such possibilities. To see how they inform science fiction since Hiroshima, however, it proves useful to approach the genre historically: Where does cyberfiction come from? Where is it going? What is the future of its speculative futures?

ACKNOWLEDGMENTS

These are the generations of tomorrow. To them I commend my everlasting gratitude and hope:

William Stotler begets Michael Minneman. Ian "Jesus" Stanford begets Ben Ogrodnik. Jeffrey Nealon begets Rich Doyle. Cecil Giscombe begets Julia Kasdorf. James Morrow begets Samuel Delany. Henry Giroux begets Eric Weiner. Billy Joe Harris begets Aldon Nielsen. Andrew Pilsch begets Julius Lobo. Hannah Abelbeck begets Katie Tune. Cory Holding begets Kristin Shimmin. Moura McGovern begets Nancy Cushing. Dustin Kennedy begets Geffrey Davis begets Adam Hayley. Ed Ballock begets Brian Tuttle begets Mark Wochner. Natasha Hoffmeyer begets Erika Polson. Manolis Galenianos begets Karl Davidson begets Jorgé Sofo. Megan Rickards begets Caitlin Rose.

Thanks to the editors of the following journals for publishing and then permitting republication of material in this book: *Postmodern Culture, Cultural Critique, African American Review,* and *the minnesota review.* Thanks deluxe to Marilyn Gaull, whose wiles and wit gave *Cyberfiction* a future.

I am unspeakably indebted to these dear friends for their love, their cooking, and their kindness in reading drafts: Jeffrey Cox, Sajay Samuel, Samar Farage, Thora Peace Brylowe, Talissa Ford, and Grégory Pierrot.

Finally the soundtrack, without which life would be a mistake: Wes Montgomery, Grant Green, James Blood Ulmer, John Scofield, and Marc Ribot.

1

Yesterday's Tomorrows

1

SPECULATIVE FUTURES

ORIGIN OF THE SPECIE

no!

Science fiction starts with *Frankenstein*, a morbid tale of bioscience gone bad.[1] The book's lurid longevity attests to its virulence. Its author's gender and her story's strangeness make *Frankenstein* an instance of subversive writing, and not simply because Mary Shelley was intimate with subversives: a posse of English expatriates that included Lord Byron and her husband Percy Bysshe Shelley. Her book challenges the foundations of liberal civil society. As others have shown, that challenge arises from—and advances—a feminist perspective.[2] I would like to suggest that *Frankenstein* advances an economic agenda too, one that strikes to the heart of the liberal politics that makes science fiction possible. Mary Shelley not only anticipates that genre by over a century, but also reveals a killing contradiction at the heart of liberalism between money and life. Shelley's infamous monster incarnates the economic problem of trying to substitute undying specie for matter that decays.

Think of Frankenstein as the ultimate body builder. The monster he creates in the dark of his lone garret is buff beyond words—strapping, swift, and eight feet tall. Frankenstein's motives for creating him resemble those of many a member of civil society, if a bit overblown: he wants to accumulate life's abundance, produce a breed from barren matter, bring life out of death. Driven by an extravagant, scientific devotion to the life of the physical body, he seeks to realize its full potential. "The structure of the human frame, and, indeed, any animal endued with life" attracts his fascination (Shelley 51). He studies physical bodies meticulously with no nostalgia for spirit. As he puts it, "I became acquainted with the science of anatomy: but this was not sufficient; I must also observe the natural decay and corruption of the human body" (51). The life of the human body *includes* death, and Frankenstein's devotion to enhancing it is a lot like that of liberalism, which has been called the politics of possessive individualism. Both seek to maximize the quality and value of bodily life in the face of its inevitable decay: an old spoilage problem rendered in new scientific terms.

Frankenstein performs a thought experiment on the liberal solution of accumulation. What if matter itself could provide a permanent fix to the problem of spoilage, decay, and death? Frankenstein's research into the arcana of corruption ultimately yields a transfiguration of dead matter into *more life*!

> I was led to examine the cause and progress of this decay, and forced to spend days and nights in vaults and charnel-houses. My attention was fixed upon every object the most insupportable to the delicacy of the human feelings. I saw how the fine form of man was degraded and wasted; I beheld the corruption of death succeed to the blooming cheek of life; I saw how the worm inherited the wonders of the eye and brain. I paused, examining and analyzing all the minutae of causation, as exemplified in the change from life to death, and death to life, until from the midst of this darkness a sudden light broke in upon me—a light so brilliant and wondrous, yet so simple, that while I became dizzy with the immensity of the prospect which it illustrated, I was surprised, that among so many men of genius who had directed their enquiries towards the same science, that I alone should be reserved to discover so astonishing a secret. (52)

With all due respect, Frankenstein was not the first to make such a discovery. A hundred years earlier John Locke had discovered the secret solution to death and decay, albeit in an economic not anatomical idiom. It was money.[3] Perhaps Frankenstein's rediscovery of "the cause of generation and life" is simply the physiological equivalent of an economic solution. When he declares that he himself became "capable of bestowing animation upon lifeless matter" (52), he may be saying little more than any good liberal who turns lifeless matter into money and reanimates his own life by the golden measure of endless accumulation. Life from death. Something from nothing. For all his anatomical expertise and existential élan, Frankenstein discovers little more than Locke did before him.

There is this difference, however: Frankenstein *incarnates* the logic of accumulation. He gives it a physiological form. His monster embodies the capacity to transcend decay and transfigure spoilage. It might be interesting, therefore, to view the monster as a form of money. Not a pretty form either, but that is Shelley's point. The monster is to money as the portrait is to Dorian Gray: the grotesque double of the logic that sustains proprietary self-interest. There is much in the book to back this view. Consider for starters the name of the monster's creator. It is surprising how little attention has been paid to the name "Frankenstein." By British standards it is doubly other: obviously German (the Franks were Goths who in the sixth century invaded the territory now known as France) and maybe Jewish. Franken-stone. Goth rock.

There is even more to it. The name also has an economic register. The *Oxford English Dictionary* defines the verb "to frank" as follows: "to superscribe (a letter, etc.) with a signature, so as to ensure its being sent without charge; to send or cause to be sent free of charge." A letter qualifies for sending when marked, stamped, posted, *franked*. Franking authorizes its free physical movement from person to person, place to place. It pays or cancels the cost of communication. The signature, mark, or stamp that works this grace turns an economic into a semiotic transaction, or more precisely occludes the economic conditions that authorize communication and mobility. Strange as it seems, Frankenstein does something similar when he endows his monster with life. He cancels the cost of creating and sustaining it—morally as myriad commentators contend, but economically too. By abandoning his creature, he disavows any direct connection between the logic of accumulation (something from nothing) and the value of life. He franks an empty letter and sends it away for nothing. He turns an economic problem into a moral one. The results are disastrous.

Bodies pile up like fast food wrappers. But why? Psychological explanations aside (the monster enacts Frankenstein's buried hostility; he is a Doppelgänger that cannot help killing; he is eros in an egoistic world), maybe it is because he embodies the logic of accumulation; in other words, it is because he is money. The monster reveals what is limited about Locke's use of specie to solve the problem of spoilage. Like the monster, money animates dead matter. Both substitute what persists for what spoils. But the fix is temporary. In both cases that substitution remains *physical*, the (re)incarnation of carnal decay. Is money somehow more alive than meat for not spoiling? For that matter, is the monster? The death he proliferates suggests that the logic of accumulation, the melioration of money, remains too intimately tied to matter to compensate spoilage. Its permanence is all too temporal, its perpetuity merely material.

What after all is the monster's biggest complaint? His ghoulish physicality: "I was," he says, "endued with a figure hideously deformed and loathsome" (120). Embodying the logic of accumulation *deforms* it, materially limiting its potential. Frankenstein stamps into life a logic that destroys it. He coins new specie and sends it into the world to move freely. The monster's mobility may exceed human potential, but it remains materially constrained. Under such conditions, the logic of accumulation circulates death in the name of life. That is Shelley's response to Locke's valorization of money. Specie provides only a partial solution to the problem of spoilage. Money reduced to matter limits the logic of accumulation. Gold circulates with the speed of physics, but accumulation is, at least potentially, perpetual. The monster's tragedy is to live out this contradiction. The physical limits of specie deform the exorbitant possibilities of accumulation, and the monster responds with violence: "I declared everlasting war against the species" (136). When money compensates decay, human life turns monstrous. Specie spoils species. Little wonder, then, that "money" and "monster" share the Latin root "monere" (to warn, admonish). *Frankenstein* posts a warning: a monster stalks life, a monster called money.

Is the first science fiction novel a critique of capital? In a limited sense, yes: it allegorizes the contradiction between specie and accumulation. Money cannot accumulate perpetually. It cannot accommodate the *logic* of accumulation. Specie-being is subject to a hideous physicality. If like the monster all it really seeks is to circulate and reproduce, the materiality of money remains an obstacle to its greatest possibilities. Shelley's novel becomes a kind of gold-standard tragedy, staging the harrowing human costs of capital accumulation, a logic that destroys the material life it was meant to sustain. But that is not the end of the story. The monster never dies, only disappears—perhaps to return in another place, at another time.

Shelley's time, the early decades of the nineteenth century, relates to our own as a kind of prehistoric era. Ask what is missing from the quaint old world of *Frankenstein*. No airplanes, no Internet, no credit cards. It is a world not yet gone global, a slower world without transatlantic flights or telecommunications. Now ask how Frankenstein's story would become different with the simple addition of a telephone. Frankenstein himself would have a lot of explaining to do about why he never answered when his beloved Elizabeth called to inquire about his health. He could phone ahead and warn his family that a walking corpse was heading their way. Police and other public officials could coordinate a strategy for tracking the gruesome giant. A few calls to the right people might obviate the need for torches and pitchforks. The monster could whip out an iPhone and twitter away, avoiding the rejection that so frequently comes with face time. In short, the story of Frankenstein and his hideous progeny would be a failure in the context of telecommunications. Part of its lasting appeal arises from the nostalgia it inspires for a world where monsters are still possible because no one hears about them in advance. The telephone spoils all that. It is an information angel. *then are monsters in world w/ tech — also — Dracula?!*

Frankenstein may be the first "science fiction" novel, but only anachronistically. Hugo Gernsback would not coin the familiar phrase for a hundred years. It takes that long for this new form of writing to emerge as a genre with its own rules. Mary Shelley writes *no!...ted sci-fi Gothic ghost story* in a genre that did not exist in 1819, an achievement stunning in itself, but all the more so considering that her novel criticizes economic conditions necessary for the emergence of "science fiction." The cursed physicality of her monster—his specie-being—marks a limit that neither accumulation nor communication could exceed when she wrote *Frankenstein*. The monster's tragedy is his inability to transcend substance (the materiality of money). His creator's is his inability to transcend isolation (the materiality of message). Both illustrate the foolhardiness of aspiring to exceed such physical limits. A science such as Frankenstein's that would assist in doing so turns suspect, the twisted creature of human hubris. But what if one really could accumulate more than specie allows? Or communicate faster than the speed of ink? What if science made such transgressions not just possible but familiar? What if science fiction were to develop in such a way as to disqualify Shelley's tale from the genre? *speculating about speculations, are we?*

A USER'S GUIDE TO SCIENCE

Gernsback introduced the term "science fiction" in 1929 in his magazine *Air Wonder Stories.* A formal definition of "science fiction" soon followed. In the editorial statement of the inaugural issue of another of his magazines, *Science Wonder Stories,* Gernsback declares, "It is the policy of *Science Wonder Stories* to publish only stories that have their basis in scientific laws as we know them, or in the logical deduction of new laws from what we know." Gernsback submits fiction to the rule of scientific law, which remains both faithful to precedent and open to change. That is the McGuffin of the genre, the gimmick without which writing does not qualify as "science fiction." Unicorns are out, time machines are in. Wizards are out, scientists are in. With a sentence Gernsback draws a line, perpetually blurred but perfectly visible, between old world fantasy and a new kind of fiction whose plausibility derives from the rules of science.

But what is science anyway? Gernsback presumes it to be a system of laws that establishes a foundation for truth sturdy enough to ground realistic extrapolative fictions. One interesting thing about this presumption is how effortlessly it dispenses with competing explanatory frameworks. Scientific laws and not religious beliefs, psychological principles, or even human values set the terms for the plausibility of this new kind of fiction. And indeed, for many Westerners science in Gernsback's sense and not religion, philosophy, or art makes life possible. It has become easier to live without God than without science and its ubiquitous technologies. Flick a switch in a cathedral and God falls into the grid. In an age of incandescence, the declaration "Let there be light" loses spiritual force. Science in Gernsback's sense so completely characterizes life that now it illuminates the world.

Or so Gernsback implies: scientific laws set the terms for reality and its (science) fictions. It does not take a rocket scientist, however, to wonder whether the laws of science are actually true. Put another way, one could ask whether those laws are *given* or *produced*. If science is a closed system that works by way of a few given laws, then one can disregard that question and go about the business of proving what is true by simply applying those scientific laws and verifying correlative certainties. But Gernsback's definition, perhaps in spite of itself, also raises other possibilities. Consider the word "scientific," the adjectival form of the word "science," which derives from the Latin word "scientia," meaning *knowledge*. Science is knowledge. True enough, but this definition has a curious history. In its earliest stage (fourteenth century), the word science means roughly and simply "the state or fact of knowing" (*OED*). Note that this definition makes no claims to truth, only to awareness and comprehension. Not until much later does the word "science" acquire the familiar connotation of being, in the words of the *Oxford English Dictionary*, "a branch of study which is concerned either with a connected body of demonstrated truths or with observed facts systematically classified and more or less colligated by being brought under general laws, and which includes trustworthy methods for the discovery of new truths within its own domain." This definition of science does not become standard until well into the eighteenth century—a surprisingly recent development!

The historical question these definitions beg is exactly how science, a state of knowing, becomes science, the state of knowing *truth*. Michel Foucault hardly overstates the historical case when he notes that contemporary science has "traversed absolutely the whole of Western society" to the point that it has "become the general law for all civilizations." For Foucault, science achieves this authority, however, not because it is true per se, but because its truth arises through "ritualized procedures for its production" (*Power/Knowledge* 66).

Science in Foucault's sense *produces* the knowledge it vindicates. It combines an imperative to discover truth with procedures that guarantee it, a circumstance not so different from religion except that it works without a divinity to define it. In Foucault's limber description, " 'Truth' is to be understood as a system of ordered procedures for the production, regulation, distribution, circulation and operation of statements" (133). Science produces truth by producing knowledge through a system of ritualized and institutionalized procedures. Its laws, the scientific laws that ground Gernsback's editorial policy, are true to the extent that they—and new laws they give rise to—conform to these procedures. By approaching science as such a system, Foucault makes its truth a function of historical imperative and, more ominously, institutional power. But he also opens it to change. New information can give rise to new results—transforming science itself and its honorific procedures for producing truth.

Foucault offers a surprisingly similar description of liberalism as a political strategy, one that suggests how it relates to both the procedures of science and the rise of science fiction. He views liberalism in terms of not ideological content but (surprisingly) *procedure*:

> Rather than a relatively coherent doctrine, rather than a politics pursuing a certain number of more or less clearly defined goals, I would be tempted to see in liberalism a form of critical reflection on governmental practice. [...] The question of liberalism, understood as the question of "too much government," was one of the constant dimensions of that recent European phenomenon, having appeared first in England, it seems—namely, "political life." (*Ethics* 77)

Foucault turns away from the self-proclaimed content of liberalism, its stated values and goals, and looks instead at what, in view of science, might be called its procedures for producing the truth. Those procedures are quite specific in operation and effect. Foucault says they produce a reflection on the practice of government and an evaluation of its *performance*. Liberalism is performance politics. It measures, adjusts, and corrects toward the end of political *efficiency*: the question of too much government turns into the problem of making the most out of life politically.

Foucault calls this strategy "biopolitics," the political administration of the production and reproduction of life.[4] Liberalism advances biopolitics through procedures of political efficiency. Notice the sweet compatibility of this description with science considered as a system of procedures for producing truth. This compatibility is not incidental. Like science, liberalism is flexible. It advances governance through

procedures of observation, evaluation, and modification. Its preoccupation with "too much government" puts change at the heart of
its political project. As with science, change is part of the procedural
repertoire of liberalism. Admittedly, liberalism often miniaturizes
that capacity, subordinating change to the easier project of policing
"too much government." Even so, its attention to performance and
efficiency keeps it open to new possibilities. Like science, it adapts.
This procedural compatibility makes liberalism the preferred politics
of science and science the preferred method of liberalism.

Science fiction is their literary brainchild, a dreaming in science
that produces new possibilities for politics. The exemplary genre of
liberal technoscientific culture, science fiction exploits new kinds of
knowledge in order to change the world. What if one really could
accumulate more than specie allows? Or communicate faster than the
speed of ink? What if science made such transgressions not just possible but mundane? What if material conditions were to change in such
a way as to render Shelley's tragedy obsolete? Between Mary Shelley
and Hugo Gernsback a social formation develops that makes science
fiction possible, not because it fulfills the visionary possibilities of
Frankenstein but precisely because it does not. Shelley's identification
of accumulation and destruction, money and death, while perennially
pertinent, occurs under social conditions that predate globalization.
That too is part of the novel's charm. But by the time Gernsback
stakes his generic claim over the literary territory of science fiction,
things have changed. New practices emerge that push past the limits of Shelley's critique. Regency England and modern America are
historically incommensurable worlds, asynchronous times. If by the
early twentieth century science fiction becomes a culturally dominant
popular discourse—literary software for a technoscientific culture—it
is only because of these practices. So what are they?

POSTOPIA

The cultural practices that make science fiction possible are myriad.
I cannot map them all. But I can examine two that seem to me necessary for the rise of science fiction and its heir cyberfiction: telecommunications and finance capital. When Gernsback solicits "stories
that have their basis in scientific laws as we know them, or in the
logical deduction of *new* laws from what we know" (my italics), he
troubles the temporality of traditional science, turning it toward the
future. Science as a set of procedures for producing truth becomes

the prophet of possibility, evangel of worlds to come. Science fiction in turn becomes a vernacular discourse for imagining those worlds. Such developments are not just conceptual. They arise out of specific technological and economic practices. Gernsback unites the cultural authority of science with the imaginative force of fiction and makes the future a court of appeal for the hopes and dreams of civil society gone technoscientific.

This sense of the future has a history, of course, associated with secular and religious practices of prophecy. It also develops historically in a way even more germane to science fiction but usually overlooked. The future becomes an *economic* practice when assimilated to the logic of accumulation and the kind of time associated with money in civil society. The perpetuity of accumulation redeploys the future as investment strategy. Literally. This prophetic practice turns economic when it becomes the means with which to calculate and administer the fruits of accumulation. Cumulative time is the *future of money*. Neither event nor idea, the future becomes a logic, an algorithm, an equation that administrates the present by way of economic possibility. From religion to economics: the future changes from something people do into something that *does people*—determines their possibilities, administrates their lives. As an economic practice, the future monetizes tomorrow.

This is the history of the future that gives rise to science fiction, which is why critical attempts to assimilate it to the European literary tradition of utopia do not get very far.[5] Admittedly, some science fiction seems utopian (the works of Isaac Asimov and Ursula K. Le Guin come to mind), but its futures arise less from a philosophical than an economic imperative. Utopian writing antedates the emergence of science fiction by some four hundred years. The Idealism inspiring it (the refusal of this world driving the thought of a better one) partakes of a general European tendency to devalue material life in favor of something better, some conceptual beyond. While offering a powerful critique of a debased social reality, this tendency (Nietzsche calls it *nihilism*) remains allied with a religious or prophetic practice of the future. *Eurotopia* as I like to call it musters only a partial explanation of science fiction, one that is anachronistic to the social and economic conditions of its emergence. Utopia remains too idealist to fathom the phantasmagoria of an economized future. To do that requires examining specific cultural practices without which, as Shelley's prototypical novel attests, science fiction does not quite happen. It is too hideously the progeny of economic circumstance.

but economic SF is not the only kind ...

A PATIENT WAITER IS NO LOSER

Those practices, historically speaking, are just around the corner from *Frankenstein* (1819), but they configure a whole new world. In 1837 simultaneously in Great Britain and the United States patents were sought for a device that would transform communication: the electrical telegraph. Telegraphy had long been the dream of political and commercial visionaries who experimented with new ways of sending messages during the years immediately preceding and following the publication of *Frankenstein*. In France, inspired in part by Napoleon's military ambitions, the Chappe brothers developed a system of optical relays radiating from Paris that could transmit a message to the Rhine in six minutes (Sterling 1.A). In England semaphore systems arose for sending messages overland from London in all directions: east to Deal, north to Yarmouth, south to Portsmouth, and west to Plymouth. These systems were optical and mechanical, depending for success on good weather, manned beacons, and very simple encryption. The real breakthrough in communications, the development that would enable global flows of information, came when William Fothergill Cooke and Charles Wheatstone strung a mile and a quarter of wire along the London to Birmingham railway and proved the possibility of instantaneous electronic telegraphy. It was pure magic: communicative action at a distance. Rail as a medium for delivering messages was fast but physical. The wire above the tracks was sublime, dematerializing the time of transmission. In 1838 Samuel F.B. Morse, the granddad of American telegraphy and inventor with Alfred Vail of the famous code that bears his name, sent the first message in dots and dashes across two miles of wire at Speedwell Ironworks in New Jersey. Within twenty years telegraph cables crossed the American continent and the Atlantic Ocean. Within a hundred and fifty years they would wrap the planet in fiberoptics and conjure the World Wide Web.

The point may be obvious, but it bears repeating: telegraphy transfigured communication by dissociating matter and message. Before instantaneous transmission, messages moved with the speed of the fastest available messenger. Postmen, pigeons, ponies, sloops: the material conditions of communication remained tied to transportation. The telegraph changed all that. Messages now moved with the speed of light, or as close to it as impedance would allow. Send a message on the first commercial telegraph, thirteen miles of wire running from Paddington to West Drayton, England. Send it the exact moment the fastest train departs. Which arrives first? There is no contest. The disembodied message moves faster than all messengers. Telegraphy is spectral. By severing material ties between transportation and communication, the electronic telegraph dematerializes messages. This is not to say that communication occurs without material infrastructure. On the contrary, a complex grid of wires, generators, relays, and transformers develops to sustain them. But this extensive infrastructure turns transparent with regard to the messages it transmits.

When transmission replaces transportation as the material condition of communication, life breeches physical limits, at least when it comes to messages. Writing becomes *information* and begins to circulate with electrifying speed. That is what *Wikipedia* implies when it describes telegraphy as "the long-distance transmission of written messages without physical transport of letters." Distance all but disappears when writing dissociates from matter. Worried there is a monster on the prowl? Alert the family, send a cable. The instantaneity of telegraphic communications makes information potentially ubiquitous, eliminating certain gruesome surprises in advance. Hitherto unknowable futures become knowable on the basis of the best available information. Speed and mobility eclipse time and space as conditions of life and value where communications are concerned. With the telegraph begins the forced and speedy march of culture toward a global network of information flows.

When Corn Was King

James Carey argues that "in a certain sense the telegraph invented the future as a new zone of uncertainty and a new region of practical action" (118). It opened a cultural and imaginative space that science fiction would fill with visions of worlds to come. But this new communicative practice is not the only cultural condition of those visions. Carey points out that the telegraph instantly articulates with another practice, the social effects of which are even more profound: it was no "mere accident that the Chicago Commodity Exchange, to this day the principal American futures market, opened in 1848, the same year the telegraph reached that city" (118). The futures market, quite literally, economizes the practice of the future. The telegraph utterly transforms the market for agricultural commodities, introducing a way of managing its unpredictability. It solves the old spoilage problem in a new way, one that frees property from both physical substance *and* its specie equivalent. It dematerializes accumulation, allowing it to proceed at the speed, not of the transportation of goods, but of the transmission of information. It is no accident that science fiction, *the* vernacular discourse of the future, emerges fully only after the consolidation of a market for futures. With the telegraph, the futures market provides a practical precedent for imagining futures with a payoff.

Here is how it works. A farmer grows corn for delivery in October. The time between planting and harvest makes the value of his commodity hard to predict. A disaster could intervene—a drought or a strike—reducing the market value per bushel of corn to less than what he needs to make a profit. If he could contract in advance to sell his grain at a price that would assure gain for his labor, he could take some of the unpredictability out of farming. Contracts develop for just this purpose, technically called forward contracts because they stipulate the delivery of a particular commodity at a particular date in the future. Such contracts are in themselves not new. The East India Company used an early version of them called "warrants" in the first half of the eighteenth century, and in the seventeenth the Dutch traded grain, herring, even securities for future delivery (Carey 118, Williams 309). What the telegraph enables is the development of a *market* for trading forward contracts, which thereafter become known as "futures." It levels the playing field between sellers and buyers, or rather eliminates it altogether, transmitting information about market value to distant places instantaneously. If one could consolidate this information and manage the relationship between current and future market value of commodities, one would create a situation in which differences between those values becomes an occasion for capitalization.

This is exactly what happens with the development of a futures market. Instantaneous communications dematerializes trade. It eliminates distance between seller and buyer (disabling *arbitrage*, the transportation of goods to exploit uneven pricing in different markets) and turns commodities into contracts (driving *speculation*, the trade not in corn but corn futures). What matters now is not *matter*, the physical substance of corn or specie. The contract is everything, and it flies between buyers with the swiftness of electrons. With the futures market, says Carey, "space was, in the phrase of the day, annihilated, [and] once everyone was in the same place for purposes of trade, time as a new region of experience, uncertainty, speculation, and exploration was opened up to the forces of commerce" (119). Trading futures on an open market makes it possible to imagine futures in science fiction.

In two ways. The futures market inaugurates two different economic practices of the future, related respectively to the sellers of commodities and the buyers of contracts. The material motive for such a market originates with a seller, say our farmer, who wants to minimize the risk of growing corn in advance of knowing its market value. A futures contract allows him to hedge his bets—minimize his risk—by fixing a price in the present for corn delivered in the future. Here the future is a straight line that runs from the moment of contractual obligation to that of delivery, guaranteeing a foreseeable return on the costs of production.

But there is another way of practicing the future economically, and without it a futures market would be inoperable. Our farmer can secure his contract only through a buyer willing to front money against the possibility of making more. A hedger requires a speculator to advance the funds that minimize risk. The speculator is willing to do so only because changes in market value can produce gains that exceed the terms of the contract. So the contract becomes a new commodity, traded to accumulate profit that our farmer was unwilling to risk his harvest to reap. Here the future is a series of recursive loops that cycle among the contract's buyers and sellers. Where the future of hedging is singular and stable, those of speculation are multiple and probabilistic—subject to the vagaries of market value. In actual practice a clearing-house manages them all, initially advancing funds for the contract to the farmer and squaring its ensuing trades on a daily basis. But the real point is that the futures market that develops first in Chicago in the mid-nineteenth century gives rise to two ways of practicing the future, one a straightforward narrative of remuneration and the other an episodic series of variable returns.

SPECULATIONS

Science fiction is the creature of these practices. It builds futures out of them. They arise around an armature of economic exchange, specifically the sort that takes time as the medium of capital return. I am not saying it is impossible to imagine the future without futures contracts. But I am saying traditional efforts proceed along philosophical or religious lines. In science fiction as a vernacular discourse, the future is an economic practice—or an array of them. Only after the telegraph opens time to commerce and the futures contract makes it a medium for profit does science fiction appear, practicing the future in a manner continuous with speculation. It takes more than science, in other words, to make science fiction possible. Sure, the procedural truth production of science underwrites the fictions of extrapolation that Gernsback calls for and that have since become a hallmark of the genre. But without futures to anticipate in relation to the present, extrapolation would remain a conceptual operation rather than a culturally relevant procedure. Economized futures relate the present to what is yet to come. More importantly for science fiction, they involve a *return* to the present, existentially in so far as the moment of profit is always *now*, but economically too because that profit *is the return*. This notion of return sustains the futures of science fiction, configuring a relation to the present that gives the genre its critical force. Like futures contracts, whether for hedgers or speculators, science fiction makes the present the destination of foresight. The return it imagines is less utopian than economic, a world made better for the investment—or worse.

History backs me up here. Science fiction as a distinct genre does not arise until well after communicative and economic practices converge and reorganize culture accordingly.[6] There are, of course, authors who anticipate these possibilities. Most obviously Mary Shelley. Or Edgar Allen Poe ("The History of One Hans Pfall," for instance). Jules Verne in France writes a kind of inverted historical novel that takes the future rather than the past as a medium of cultural memory. Works like *20,000 Leagues under the Sea* (1874) and *From the Earth to the Moon* (1865) extrapolate a future from available scientific and anthropological knowledge. They practice the future in the manner of a hedger, along the straight line of minimum risk and maximum predictability. In this Verne sets forth a lineage of science fiction that runs through the American pulp magazines to some of its greatest practitioners: Isaac Asimov, Robert Heinlein, Ray Bradbury, Ben Bova, Kim Stanley Robinson. These and other familiars are best bet imagineers whose futures yield plausible returns.

It would be easy but unwise to identify science fiction solely with this lineage. There is another lineage more powerful and culturally pertinent, that appropriates the practice associated with the other side of the futures contract, that of the speculator. It is a beautiful historical coincidence that the willfully avant-garde wing of science fiction in the 1960s tried to rechristen it *speculative* fiction. Or is it a coincidence? The move, even if inadvertent, pushes science fiction toward the speculative side of economic practice. Speculative fiction. The fiction of speculation—not only in a philosophical sense (cognitive estrangement and all that) but in an economic sense too. And indeed, the most lively and disturbing lineage of science fiction emerges where its futures and its returns are unpredictable and risky, in the full fiscal sense *speculative*. Science fiction not as bargain but gamble: its futures fungible, not given.

This lineage too has its precursors and luminaries. Maybe the best way to identify it, given its economic heritage, is through the way it practices its futures. If the future of the hedge is a straight line to tomorrow, those of speculation are recursive loops of variable return. Futures work differently for the speculator and the hedger. For the former futures are not stable. They freight a *return* to the present—for better or for worse. A science fiction commensurable with this practice would exploit not simply *futurity* but also its fungibility. Not futures but their *movement* would be its medium, forward *and* back. Speculation always returns—maybe many times during the life of a single futures contract. The movement of speculative futures is bidirectional. It flows backward as it returns to the present. A fiction that exploits this fungibility would flow too, from now into the future, from the future back to now. It would be the fiction of time travel, a speculative fiction of anticipation and return.

Stories of time travel, then, most clearly illustrate the relationship between science fiction and the futures of speculation as an economic practice. Broadly conceived, science fiction comes into its own during the historical transition from industrial to finance capitalism, roughly the turn of the twentieth century. The practice of the future typical of speculation is fundamental to this transition. That is why H.G. Wells looms so large as a progenitor of the genre. In his hands time travel produces *value*—cultural value that accrues through an imaginative journey into a questionable future that ends with a return to the present. *The Time Machine* (1895) moves from a Victorian present some 300,000 years into the future—*and returns*, adding value to that present by the measure of future's fungibility and the decadent social conditions it reveals. This narrative strategy is not entirely without precedent. Charles Dickens anticipates it in *A Christmas Carol* (1843) when Ebenezer Scrooge receives his troubling visitations from the spirits of Christmas past, present, and future. It is revealing in this regard that Scrooge's future involves a vision of enslavement to capital. His old boss Marley remains eternally shackled to the practice of double-entry accounting. Bookkeeping is a bad investment if hoarding specie is its only return. Scrooge returns to his present a changed man ready to defy the logic of accumulation. Dickens anticipates the use of time travel to promote speculative futures and profitable returns. Wells takes the next step. In *The Time Machine* the future flows back into the present thanks to nothing more spiritual than a machine made of brass, leather, and crystal.

"CAPITAL TIMES"

I stole that heading from Eric Alliez. It's so *gnomic*. It crystallizes the point I want to make about science fiction and finance capital.

Paraphrasing Marx, Alliez says that finance capital represents "the *form* of capital emptied of its *content*" (xviii, italics in the original). It is the apotheosis of speculation, the shape capitalism takes once emancipated from the shackles of specie and the commodity. The futures contract works the semiotic miracle of dissociating exchange from material substrate, whether goods or gold. It is like currency only more so. Trading futures in corn does not require its physical transfer. The only exchange that matters is semiotic, the transfer of a contract from seller to buyer. This transfer can occur myriad times between the moments of our farmer's initial contract and the delivery it stipulates. To illustrate: 2004 saw eleven times as much money made trading corn futures as actual corn. The big money, the *real profit*, is in speculation, not commodities. When this principle usurps production as the impetus of exchange, industrial capitalism cedes to finance capitalism as the dominant form of economic activity.

That move begins in earnest by the late nineteenth century, and without it science fiction would not have become a dominant genre in the century to come. It is no coincidence that the years between 1894 and 1914 saw the publication of three major symptoms of this shift: H. G. Wells's *The Time Machine* (1894), Albert Einstien's "On the Electrodynamics of Moving Bodies" (1905, the famous relativity paper), and Rudolf Hilferding's *Finance Capital: A Study of the Latest Phase of Capitalist Development* (1914). These works consolidate culturally what speculation advances economically. The first two, in vastly different ways, illustrate as they enact the fungibility of futures. Wells's time traveler moves ahead and returns through *time*, with the correlative result of increased knowledge—an accumulation of information. Einstein's moves ahead and returns through *space*, with the relativistic result of enduring youth—an accumulation of time itself. Both time travelers add value to the present as a return on the fungibility of their futures. Hilferding's neglected masterpiece explains why such practices acquire cultural force when they do.

They are commensurable with finance capital. I'm not saying that finance capital makes possible stories of time travel and theories of relativity, not exactly. I *am* saying that the speculations of popular culture and science both proceed under economic conditions that invest them with legitimacy. I doubt that Einstein could have developed his special theory of relativity under the conditions of mercantile capitalism. I'm sure Wells could never then have written *The Time Machine*. Both require a familiarity with fungible futures, which economic speculation advances and normalizes. Hilferding shows how pervasively speculation sets the terms for the economics of finance capitalism. Stocks dissociate ownership from property, dispersing it among far-flung investors. Production shifts accordingly from family owned industries to professionally managed corporations. Stock exchanges arise to manage speculative investments. Profit accrues now not merely from the sale of goods, but from the exchange of stocks, bonds, futures, and other derivatives. Idle capital gets reinvested in myriad ways as the market gobbles up liquidity to maximize flows of exchange, to the point that the whole system floats free from its material foundation in labor and interest follows investment with an angel's inexplicable swiftness. Here is the crucial passage:

> The magnitude of property seems to have nothing to do with labour; the direct connection between labour and the yield on capital is already partially obscured in the rate of profit, and completely so in the rate of interest. The apparent transformation of all capital into interest-bearing capital, which fictitious capital form involves, makes any insight into this relationship impossible. It seems absurd to connect interest, which is always fluctuating and can change regardless of what is happening in the sphere of production, with labour. Interest seems to be a consequence of the ownership of capital as such, a *Toros*, the fruit of capital which is endowed with productive powers. It is fluctuating and indeterminate, and the "value of property," a category, fluctuates along with it. This "Value" seems just as mysterious and indefinite as the future itself. The mere passage of time seems to produce interest. (150)

When the simple passage of time—not labor, not exchange of goods, not accumulation of specie—produces interest, speculation rules the day. Under such conditions, which involve large-scale social practices such as stock markets, corporations, international banks, and a global communications network, the future is no longer simply time to come. It becomes economized, the means of maximizing profit beyond the physical limits of goods and specie. Oh brave new world! Finance capital makes futures the condition of persistence, growth, and possibility. No wonder science fiction comes into its own just as Hilferding publishes his masterwork. It is the representative fiction of finance capital.

As if to prove the point, Philip Wylie and Edwin Balmer publish *When Worlds Collide*, a doomsday sci-fi fantasy from 1933. It speculates on what might happen were earth to be obliterated by an errant planet—two planets, actually, which proves a happy circumstance, since one misses and provides safe haven for the remnant of humanity. The hero of the tale is one Tony Drake, handsome WASP

What about Twain?

stockbroker. Wylie and Balmer are writing during the dumps of the Depression, so it is not surprising that a market crash augurs global disaster. But when worlds collide stocks crash for good, and with the end of the market comes *the end of the future*. Scientists form a secret "League of the Last Days" to anticipate the coming crisis. In the words of one headline, "SENSATIONAL SECRET DISCOVERY: World Scientists Communicating in Code" (16). As word leaks out that disaster approaches, Drake worries about his career as a trader: "How would it affect the stocks? Would the Stock Exchange open at all?" (26). Open it does, but without providing the usual comfort of fungible futures:

> The Stock Exchange, I see, is going to be open today. In fact, it undoubtedly is open now. And I am not at my office watching the ticker and buying A.T. and T. on a scale down, and selling X—that's United States Steel—whenever it rises half a point, for somebody who wants to go short from lack of faith in the future. What am I talking about? Where is the future? What happened to it? (40)

The proof that the future has died is the pointlessness of futures trading. Approaching doom spells financial disaster, which robs the future of fungibility and promise. In *When Worlds Collide, finance is futurity*, and without it the world can scramble only to serve the interests and save the lives of a lucky few.

Granted, it takes time for finance capitalism to develop to the point that it, drives the global economy. Its effects were mostly local— Euro-American—in the 1930s (only rich white people survive Wylie and Balmer's coming collision). Commentators date the moment of the arrival of finance capital on the world stage to the early 1970s, when Fordism gives way to flexible accumulation, manufacturing cedes to service, and deregulation frees up capital flows.[7] Maybe the representative event here is Richard Nixon's decision in 1971 to cut the U.S. dollar, the standard of value for foreign currencies, free from gold. The old Bretton Woods system, which fixed rates of exchange and restricted capital flows, fell apart as foreign governments uncoupled their currency from the dollar, allowing the market to determine its value. These are the circumstances that David Harvey associates with the emergence of a global economic system dominated by the operations of finance capital:

> The formation of a global stock market, of global commodity (even debt) futures markets, of currency and interest rate swaps, together

with an accelerated geographical mobility of funds, meant, for the first time, the formation of a single world market for money and credit supply. (161)

"For the first time," says Harvey. While in a sense he is right—never before the 1970s were these particular means in place to assure the domination of finance capital over the global marketplace—it is important not to conclude they were wholly without precedent. In retrospect, much of the initial effusion over globalization and its cultural correlative, postmodernism, partook of the delirious 1990s discourse of the New Economy. From Harvey to Jameson, from Baudrillard to Bauman, the horror or happiness of a globalized economy augured a Whole New Era described by words like postmodernism, neoliberalism, simulation, the spectacle.

While it is pointless to disagree, it might be worth heeding Doug Henwood's admittedly glib claim that "'globalization' isn't as new as it is often thought." He confesses to coming "dangerously close to arguing that 2003 is essentially 1913 plus fiber optics. It's not, of course" (174). No, it is not. But for our purposes it is worth emphasizing that the economic practices, particularly those of the future, which multiply to become the worldwide tangle of the global economy are also those that allow science fiction to gain ascendancy early in the twentieth century. Speculation makes this new kind of fiction possible in advance of the economy that fulfills its possibilities. In this science fiction is, culturally speaking, well ahead of postmodern theory, perfectly positioned to reflect upon the cultural prospects that open up with economized futures. That is why Fredric Jameson sells the genre short when he insists that it positions the present as the past of an extrapolated future it can only fail to realize. Jameson's allegiance here to Adorno (the last Eurotopian, albeit in a negative mode) blinds him to the *return* that the futures of speculation produce in the present. The whole point of a futures contract is to add value to the present, predictably for the hedger, exponentially for the speculator. Science fiction returns the value of its speculative futures to the present, not to confirm its stasis, *but to change it.* Linear or recursive, the futures of science fiction promote the possibility that this present moment, this historically determined world, will be different—or already is, by the measure of speculation.

That at least is the hope of what we might call the *desire of futurity*: the logic of accumulation with a happy face, set free to realize its disembodied dreams. But there is a dark correlative to this desire, a demon that haunts this angel's flight. The very practices of the future that produce value and promote difference come ultimately to limit both. The situation somewhat resembles Harvey's description of finance capital "becoming ever more tightly organized *through* dispersal," a kind of incarceration of money in its own flow (159, italics in the original). That would explain the shrill quality of Harvey's work and related cultural critique. Science fiction also tracks this perverse effect of the future's fungibility. Its speculative futures anticipate the future of speculation: the eradication of the future as a zone of possibility and difference. *how?*

FUTURE SCHLOCK

A brief illustration will clinch the claim that science fiction, at least in America, is the child of finance capital. It has often been noticed that sci-fi is the progeny of pulp magazines.[8] Several material developments in the early twentieth century interact to animate a mongrel genre that crosses scientific knowledge with popular entertainment: the joint-stock company, the linotype machine, the internal combustion engine, a distribution network, a mass readership, and most crucially, cheap paper. Pulp makes science fiction possible. And not only because it is cheap. Affordability means mass production, which opens up the prospect of profit increasing incrementally with unit sales. As a creature of the pulp magazine industry, science fiction was born of money. The point of its existence was to make more. Beyond any literary genre (with the possible exception of Romance), science fiction in America was a business. There is no separating science fiction from its commercial heritage. That is part of its charm—and cultural force.

There would be no science fiction without finance capital to give it life—the sweet, tawdry life it acquires in the pulps. Financing magazines is tricky business, and in some ways sums up economic conditions of cultural production in a corporate context.[9] Unlike many commodities, magazines have two sources of profit: purchasers of individual copies on the one hand, and advertisers on the other. A magazine publisher sells two products at once: a magazine (in this case full of science fiction stories) *and its readership* (the audience for those stories). As a commodity, the magazine does double-duty: it sells stories to readers and it sells readers to advertisers. That makes the economics of magazine sales complex. Its cost to readers can fall below its cost of production if circulation produces a large enough audience that advertising revenues exceed sales revenues. And with advertising comes speculation, the investment of ad dollars up front

to secure large profits in the long run. Magazine economics reenact
the split conditions of futures trading. Individual buyers and subscribers are a publisher's hedge against investment. But the real money
accrues through speculation as the number of magazines sold drives
advertising revenues to greater heights. No wonder science fiction
eventually gets called speculative fiction. The futures it promulgates
are as much a function of economics as imagination. *fair enough.*

The history of science fiction during the Golden Age of the
pulps, roughly 1930–1950, illustrates the economizing of its futures.
Gernsback may have been the granddad of the genre in America, but
for all his boosterism he was businessman too, hawking his new sense
of what fiction could do in an array of magazines with titles like *Air
Wonder Stories* (1929–1930), *Science Wonder Quarterly* (1929–1933),
and *Scientific Detective Monthly* (1930). The most famous and influential of these was, of course, *Amazing Stories* (1926–1929). It was
a large format magazine printed on an unusually heavy pulp paper
that Gernsback chose especially for its publication. Across the bot-
tom of the garish front cover of every issue, starting with the first
in April 1926, ran a banner proclaiming its heritage: "Experimenter
Publishing Company, New York, Publishers of Radio News—
Science & Invention—Radio Review—Amazing Stories—Radio
Internacional." Gernsback was eager to promote science fiction, or
rather *scientifiction* as he first called it, as a commodity produced by a
company in the business of marketing marvels for quick consumption.
In an early editorial he defends his decision to avoid any mention of
science in the magazine's title: "After mature thought, the publishers
decided that the name which is now used was after all the best one to
influence the masses, because anything that smacks of science seems
to be too 'deep for the average type of reader'" (483). From the start
Gernsback conceived of *Amazing Stories* as a mass-market publication
for a mass audience.

It took awhile for the economics of pulp publication to mature.
Gernsback financed his magazines primarily through sales and sub-
scription. The 25 cents price per issue was not cheap (especially during the Depression) and ads were few. A typical issue of *Amazing
Stories* was mostly typed in dense double columns. It would carry a
full page plug on the inside front cover for another of Experimenter's
magazines (*Science and Invention* for instance) and ads for jobs in
chemistry, electricity, or bookkeeping on both sides of the back cover.
Advertising between covers was close to nonexistent, mostly of the
"opportunities in radio" variety placed in the back. Gernsback made
money, or tried to, by keeping production costs to a minimum. He

was notoriously stingy, filling his pages where he could with "classics" whose copyright had lapsed and offering contributors of new stories somewhere between half a penny to a penny per word. His habit of deferring payment until those stories were actually published rather than upon acceptance did not endear him to writers whose financial needs were often desperate. He managed to alienate some of the best, and the quality of *Amazing Stories* soon fell short of the promise of its title. As the Depression set in Gernback's hands-on approach to publishing proved increasingly untenable, and he was forced to cover mounting losses by selling the magazine.

Even so, Experimenter Publications established the basic format and formula that a later generation of pulp publishers would tweak and perfect. One innovation in particular is worth mentioning because it became a staple of science fiction publishing, a source of its longevity. Gernsback actively cultivated the loyalty of his readers. *Scientifiction* was as much their genre as his, and he urged them to participate in its production. Words like the following were typical: "The Editors wish it to be understood that this is *your* magazine in all respects; they will always be guided by the wishes of the majority. We will publish from time to time a sort of voting blank in which you may show your preference as to the type of stories published in the various issues" (*Amazing* 483). Fan participation was avid and earnest. Every issue of *Amazing Stories* included letters from readers. They debated scientific plausibility, artistic integrity, even authorial intent. They performed cultural critique in a vernacular idiom. Through the feedback loop of fan letters Gernsback involved readers in producing the dreams they consumed.

When the magazine went belly-up in 1929, it was purchased by Tieck Publishing, a less visionary company than Experimenter but financially solvent. Issues appeared with uninspired regularity. It was not until two major publishing houses bought the best of the science fiction pulps, however, that they really took off. In 1933 Street and Smith, one of the biggest firms in the business, acquired *Astounding Stories*, *Amazing*'s main rival for king of the pulps, and in 1937 Ziff-Davis, a publisher based in Chicago, bought *Amazing Stories*. Call it the era of Dreams, Inc. Publicly traded publishing companies ran the trade in future fantasies. Street and Smith is the great example here. The firm has been described in terms that make it an ancestor of the Disney empire: "One of the largest and oldest of the pulp magazine publishers, Street and Smith was among the premier mythmakers in American popular culture" (Tymn and Ashley 62). As the title of a book celebrating its centennial proclaims without irony, Street and Smith was *The Fiction Factory* (1955). Its heritage spans back to the mid-nineteenth century. Its roster of successes is stunning: weeklies, paperbacks, magazines, hard-backs, comics—with names like *Ainslee's Magazine, Sport Story, The Shadow, Doc Savage, Pocket Detective, Chelsea House Books, Super Magician Comics, Buffalo Bill.* Street and Smith published them all. And made piles of money. *Astounding Stories* appeared first in 1930, published by Clayton Magazines of New York. When it moved to Street and Smith, it gained that golden lease on life any magazine could envy, "a large solvent publisher with good access to distribution outlets and display space" (Tymn and Ashley 64). *Astounding Stories* quickly became the industry leader. It slashed its cover price to 20 cents (*Amazing Stories* would follow suit). It paid its writers the magnificent sum of 2 pennies a word—and paid upon acceptance. When John W. Campbell took over as editor in 1938 he inherited a flourishing venture that allowed him to develop his own vision for science fiction: "it was his magazine as long as it made money" (Tymn and Ashley 65). He changed its title to *Astounding Science Fiction*, justifying the switch in an editorial that set a very particular agenda for his sense of the genre: "Those who can, and are wiling to think of the future, are the ones we can, and want to, appeal to with *Astounding*. Science is the gateway to that future; its predictions alone can give us some glimpse of time to come. Therefore, we are adding '*science*' to our title, for the man who is interested in science must be interested in the future, and appreciate that the old order not only does change, but *must* change" (March 1938 53, italics in the original).

Science plus fiction equals *change*. Associating science with the future, Campbell charts a specific course for science fiction. For him it is a genre concerned less with technological innovation and wonder than more simply—and socially—with change. *Astounding Science Fiction* gains something like a social conscience under Campbell's editorship. New futures require new pedagogies and new pulps to work their magic: "That curiosity about the future is so seldom developed, even when it exists, because there are so few publications for its developmnt [*sic*]. Far more than the change in title, the aid of readers is needed. You can reach those who would enjoy the magazine, with a little training in the exercise of that dormant future-curiosity" (53). Notice again the call for reader participation that Gernsback made a mark of the pulps. Campbell extends its reach, urging his readers to join not only in producing science fiction, but more profoundly in producing the future. By exercising "that dormant future-curiosity" his readers will grow accustomed to change, maybe becoming bold practitioners. They might *make the future happen*, participating in the imperative of science that the old order not only does change, but must. For Campbell, *Astounding Science Fiction* is public pedagogy, and the futures it promotes are transformative.

It is hardly irrelevant that such claims come in a magazine whose main purpose is to make money. Campbell's rhetoric of change cannot be disentangled from that purpose. The content of *Astounding Science Fiction* accommodates its commercial function and distributes the future as an economic practice. I'm less interested in evaluating that practice morally than simply noticing how it works. A fan buys a magazine for less than it costs to produce and reads a bunch of stories that inspire visions of different worlds to come. That describes a practice that neatly fosters a subjectivity open to and capable of the kind of speculation associated with finance. Content alone does not achieve that end. It takes money too. After the big publishers acquire science fiction pulps they up the number of ads per issue significantly. That is how they can afford to cut the cover price.

With Ziff-Davis, *Amazing Stories* acquires many more ads than it ever had under Gernsback: around three pages of them before the masthead, with color ads on the inside front and back covers ("Charles Atlas!" or "Make Your Own Will"). In later issues ads migrate to side columns on back pages and plug gaps between stories. The *kind* of ads the pulps carry changes too. In Gernsback's day most of them hawked jobs—futures of a personally improving sort. But in the era of Dreams, Inc., self-improvement gives way to self-satisfaction and commodities come to the fore. The June 1938 issue of *Amazing Stories* carries ads for Ex-Lax, Star razor blades (4 for 10 cents), Cremo Cigars, Yello-bowl pipes, pimple medication, and other goods. The familiar exhortations to careers in bookkeeping, electrical engineering, and automobile repair are still there, but now they accompany full or half page ads for other Ziff-Davis publications, *Popular Photography* or *Popular Aviation*. Thankfully for many a confused suitor, the inside front cover carries consoling news: "Sensational Scientific Tests Prove Listerine Cures Dandruff." Imagine that. "First science discovered the dandruff germ...then...Listerine kills it!"

Street and Smith publications were even more savvy—or venal. In March 1938, the first issue of *Astounding Science Fiction* featuring Campbell as editor, Listerine graced the inside front cover with a photo of a loner in a fedora over the caption "Often the Best Man— Never the Groom." Bummer. The back cover bore a full color photo of a joyous young couple zipping along on a red sled, both miraculously smoking. "Chesterfield!" The word alone was enough to convey joys of nicotine. Inside were more than four pages of ads for name-brand merchandise: Luden's cough drops, Lee union-made Jelt denim overalls (with cartoon testimonial), Harley Davidson motorcycles ("Be King of the Road!"), Old American Whiskey, and, of course, good old Cremo Cigars and Star razor blades (4 for 10 cents). There were products for health and hygiene ("Piles: don't be cut until you try this"), opportunities for fame and fortune (Raise Giant Frogs), and promos for exotic knowledge (Female Beauty 'Round the World: World's Greatest Collection of Secret Photographs). What gorgeous goods!

Campbell's pedagogy of the future happened in several ways at once in *Astounding Science Fiction*. While its stories promoted versions of change, its advertisements prompted visions of satisfaction. Both produced the future, or more precisely enabled it to be practiced as an economic and social possibility. Neither stories nor advertising would have been possible without money—and not merely the 20 cents ponied up by the reader. Advertising was big bucks sent after bigger profits. It often came from corporate sponsors and financed the costs of corporate publishing. Science fiction and its amazing futures flourished in a thick atmosphere of finance capital. The dreams it induced materialized around the fiscal armature of finance: funds from advertisers, from investors, from bankers, even from individual subscribers, whose increasing numbers meant spiking advertising revenues. The pulps promoted practices of the future commensurable with the economized futures of speculation. Imagine a world to come, then measure change in the present accordingly. Speculate and collect. Make an investment and take the return. Read. Dream. Buy. The pulps distribute visions to the masses. They democratize the fungible futures of finance.

THE POSTHUMOUS FUTURE

As a vernacular public pedagogy, I'm trying to suggest, pulp science fiction teaches readers how to imagine futures. It was by no means the sole medium for teaching that lesson, but for a generation of young men (its main readership) aspiring to better themselves during the Depression in the Land of Opportunity, those futures promoted social and fiscal fantasies of progress. That such fantasies have economic motivations is obvious, but that they emerge in part from economic *practice* is the lesson of another of Campbell's wide-eyed editorials. In a column entitled "NOT THE BUT A" appearing in the May 1938 issue of *Astounding Science Fiction*, Campbell introduces

an advance in the conceptual possibilities of stories about time travel:
"the earliest supposition was that if the machine went forward in Time
it went to *the* future. It took science fiction nearly a quarter of a century to change that "the" to an "a"—to realize that time-travel would
lead a man to *a* future, perhaps, but not to *the* future" (107). During
that quarter of a century, Einstein's paper on relativity appeared, as
well as Hilferding's tome on finance capital. Between them they consolidated, scientifically and economically, the plausibility of fungible
futures. *The* to *a*. Science and economics both assert the multiplicity
of worlds to come, futures doubly different: from the present, but
from equally plausible alternatives too. *The* to *a*:

> A tiny thing? A mere grammarian's distinction? Yet on it—because
> it was actually a vastly important change—a whole new literature of
> time-travel and time-concept is founded.... If the future can follow
> either of many paths—and that, I feel, must be so, if our modern sci-
> ence is reasonably sound—then there is a new possibility. In the year
> 5938, for instance, either of two civilizations *might* exist. A time-trav-
> eler going down the paths to Tomorrow might reach either one or the
> other. (107)

Such civilizations, Campbell goes on to say, might struggle against
each other to inherit a birthright from the present. Or alternatively,
the present might struggle to produce one future and not the other.
By raising these possibilities Campbell ups the speculative ante for
the futures of science fiction. They function less as a passive gamble
than an active investment. They intervene in the very outcomes they
project. Campbell makes science fiction the cultural equivalent of
insider trading, imagining not *the* future but *a* future most congenial
to speculation. That is a fairly complicated way of relating the present
to its futures. They *will be different*, but the point of science fiction,
or at least its new-fangled stories of time travel, is to adjudicate among
them—as returns on cultural investment in the present.

But who or what can predict the future? As any investor knows,
speculation is legalized gambling. Consider the fate of the pulps
for proof. Their Golden Age dawned in the 1930s and died in the
1950s, a victim of economic forces beyond their control. The collapse of a major distributor in 1952, American News Company,
meant issues piled up unread in warehouses. Television arrived and
offered snappy home entertainment for the one-time price of a set.
Paperbacks got cheaper and served up adventures that spanned galaxies in two hundred pages, offering a more economical delivery
system for dreams than bulky periodicals with their multiple authors

and expensive ads. But it was World War II that did the most to pulp the pulps. Paper shortages meant that all but the most robust went the way of the Dodo. After the war they took the shorter, smaller form of the digest—about the size of a trade paper back, slim and slick. Magazines like *Galaxy* and *Science Fiction and Fantasy* aspired to coffee table legitimacy and wanted to look the part. The old pulps were too *vulgar* for the bungalow. Their polychrome babes and aliens reeked kid stuff. The war matured America, apparently, and science fiction followed suit.

Or did it? World War II not only wrecked the economics of pulp publishing. It also produced conditions that would qualify the giddy prospects of fungible futures. By the 1950s those futures were dying. Telecommunications and finance capital made them imaginable, but during and after the war new practices come to administrate dreams. Campbell's celebration of multiple tomorrows becomes increasingly difficult to sustain. Stories about space ships, bug-eyed aliens, time travel, and laser blasters still got written and published. But after Hiroshima something happened to science fiction. Outer space fell into cyberspace and futures lost their fungibility. The fallout of Hiroshima yet lingers in the transparent militarization of contemporary culture.

2

CYBERFICTION

(handwritten margin notes: "what is this? too close terminologically to cyberpunk." and "according to?")

REQUIEM FOR HUMANITY

World War II militarized America. Or maybe it just took the wrappers off the war machine liberal democracy requires for stability. World War II certainly gave a military tweak to the fungible futures of finance and science fiction. The difference between the stock market and a war zone, if there is one, is the finality of their futures. The financial speculator calculates price movements and bets. The military commander calculates troop movements and fires. They are strangely similar activities, except that the consequences of the latter can be lethal—or should be, if the point is to kill the enemy. War raises the stakes significantly. The game of loss and gain becomes a calculus of life and death. Historically speaking, something happens to warfare in the twentieth century that resembles what happened to finance in the nineteenth. If the telegraph made communications instantaneous, promoting the capitalization of time by turning futures fungible, the advanced military weaponry of World War II made war *fast*. Not merely in that *blitzkrieg* way where tanks flatten every obstacle in their path. The decisive innovations were even faster: diabolically swift aircraft streaking across the sky at inhuman speeds. They dropped infernal payloads from bamboozling coordinates. They filled the skies with signs of a new covenant—this time from hell.

(handwritten margin note: "+ this happened in Crimea, WWI, ...")

They were Valkyries of the air, the sinister weaponry of the pulps come to rain terror on civilian populations. The military aircraft of World War II and the big ballistics to come changed warfare dramatically and with it the organization of civil society. For all the contemporary critical talk of globalization, postmodernism, neoliberalism, and corporate power, strangely little attention gets paid to the military antecedents of these developments. If as Foucault suggests, politics is war by other means, if civil society needs a war machine to maintain stability, then political awareness begins in acknowledging liberalism's constitutive military practices. Chief among them for society after World War II is the capacity to destroy enemy aircraft. That makes Norbert Wiener, prodigious mathematician and cooriginator of the systems science called *cybernetics*, a major if unacknowledged architect of contemporary civil society—or rather Imagineer. Wiener gives postwar liberalism the capacity to imagine futures with precision and speed.[1]

Not just any futures, of course. As a brilliant mathematician with an interest in calculating machines, Wiener put his mind during the war to the tricky problem of attack aircraft: they flew too fast to destroy easily. Think of those old World War II movies where brave American bombers fly over Deutschland, each carrying a payload of incendiaries with names chalked on their nosecones. The air around them is full of artillery bursts that blossom into death. The dashing squadron leader presses a button on his mike: "Careful men. We're taking a lot of flak." The sky buzzes with junk the Germans hurl up hoping those enemy planes will *fly into it*. In the early years of the war, air defense was less a matter of shooting planes *down* than scattering nuts, bolts, and ball bearings in their way. It was about as efficient—and effective—as fighting wolves with water balloons. Wiener puts the problem more succinctly:

> Even before the war it had become clear that the speed of the airplane had rendered obsolete all classical methods of the direction of fire, and that it was necessary to build into the control apparatus all the computations necessary. These were rendered much more difficult by the fact that, unlike all previously encountered targets, an airplane has a velocity which is a very appreciable part of the velocity of the missile used to bring it down. Accordingly, it is exceedingly important to shoot the missile, not at the target, but in such a way that missile and target may come together in space at some time in the *future*. We must hence find some method of predicting the future position of the plane. (5, my italics)

The sheer speed of enemy aircraft makes precision kill all but impossible because it exceeds human capacities of calculation and response. Brains and reflexes are no match for such swift targets.

But machines are. Wiener's solution—to automate computation—removes the human element from the calculus of mortality. One might think this gives the advantage to a living pilot who can evade incoming missiles with freak maneuvers—the "evasive action" of so many movies and TV shows. Not so. Automating the computation of air defense means eliminating the human element on *both* ends of the encounter. Since evasive action occurs under conditions limited by

the speed and physical tolerances of man and aircraft, those conditions can be calculated in advance, effectively eliminating the pilot as
an independent variable in the equation of air defense: "an aviator
under the strain of combat conditions is scarcely in a mood to engage
in any very complicated and untrammeled voluntary behavior, and is
quite likely to follow out the pattern of activity in which he has been
trained" (6). See what Wiener does here? He removes the human variable completely from the equation of air defense. Machines do a better job than people of calculating lethal trajectories at blistering
speeds. When it is a matter of kill or be killed, a gunner's Noble
Human Heritage is so much nostalgia. It draws fire. Victory, which is
to say life, requires jettisoning humanity—and fast.

   Put another way, shooting down planes is a constitutive act of contemporary culture. Calling that culture "postmodern" or "post-
structural" obscures this military heritage. The much-ballyhooed
"death of the subject" is more a military objective than a theoretical
effect. Wiener erases human subjectivity from the calculus of mortality, preferring statistics to consciousness as the best means to coordinate agencies among computing machines. For him it makes no
difference whether the machine in question is human or mechanical.[2]
Eliminating the priority of human agency in favor of a probabilistic
description of interplay among communications subsystems is his
great contribution to contemporary culture, and in this he anticipates
familiar post-structuralist innovations. I'm not suggesting that post-
structuralism is the theoretical wing of the military-industrial complex, not exactly. But it *works* as critical analysis partly because its
basic theoretical assumptions (discursivity, relationality, distributed
agency) arise out of strategic military practices (communications,
command, control) that became prevalent during and after World
War II. Post-structuralism and cybernetics fit hand in military glove.
The postmodern culture that emerges after the war has a cybernetic
heritage. If the cyborg is a privileged symbol—or symptom—of this
culture it is not, as some commentators suggest, because a cyborg
commingles flesh and metal, but because a cyborg *assimilates them
statistically.* Flesh and metal interact because a code coordinates their
agencies—the way software allows humans to interact with computers. Not technology but communication is what constitutes a
cyborg.

   In this sense any interface among machines (as independent operating systems) creates a cyborg. As a military tactician Wiener works
to maximize command and control among them. Military objectives
involve not what the cyborg *is*, but what it *does*—and when. Wiener's

tactical aim is to kill enemy aircraft, and this aim requires "some method of predicting the future position of the plane." It requires practicing the future so that plane and missile intersect in a fireball. Such an orientation toward the future resembles that of economic speculation, with this difference: where the speculator tries to exploit the future's fungibility, Wiener tries to manage it, eliminating as much uncertainty as is commensurable with an assured kill. From a strategic perspective, the future belongs to command and control.

The emergence of cybernetics during and after World War II promotes a powerful strategy for managing the fungibility of futures toward maximum predictability. In a sense cybernetics is the philosophy of instantaneous communications.[3] Its main assumption is beautifully simple. Society is a system of messages. They circulate among senders and receivers, producing stability in the whole system. Because what matters is the message, it is of no particular import whether sender or receiver is in a traditional sense human—or even alive. The simple capacity to communicate sets the terms for cybernetic "life." It would be sentimental from this perspective to believe that society is an exclusively human order. Dogs, cows, cats, plants, computers, automobiles, televisions, and now even toasters all send and receive messages. The interesting question for cybernetics is whether they do so in a way that enhances their persistence. If such entities *are*, in a sense, the messages they emit, then they are better understood as patterns of information than as organisms in any traditional sense. "Life" is a pattern of information that communicates patterns. It persists in and through messages. Society is a complex system—or rather network of systems—that sustains myriad such patterns of information.

Cybernetics studies *how*, which is where the future comes in. Shooting down a plane is an extreme example of the problem of persistence. The crux of the problem is the ability to predict the manner in which particular patterns interact. That in this instance one persists and another does not illustrates that messages circulate force. The system of messages that *is* society is a weltering field of forces. To persist under such conditions is to manage patterns in advance. That is why command and control are central to Wiener's sense of cybernetics. Persistence requires futures to be subject to predictability and regulation. It is as if Wiener were trying to find a way of minimizing the risks of speculation while exploiting the investor's sense that futures bring a return. Wiener is a master of the statistical hedge. The best possible return is persistence, which offers little in the way of capital gains, perhaps, but communication nevertheless continues and life goes on.

The way this return accrues is both the glory and the bane of cybernetics. The central notion here, a notion whose social significance increases as cybernetics becomes culturally pervasive, is *feedback*, which Wiener defines as "the property of being able to adjust future conduct by past performance" (*Human Use* 33). A thermostat is a simple feedback device, recording changes in temperature and adjusting furnace operation accordingly. A human, he argues, is a highly complex feedback device, or better yet an assemblage of such devices, interacting to adjust future stability by past performance. Human beings are built that way physiologically: "The central nervous system no longer appears as a self-contained organ, receiving inputs from the senses and discharging into the muscles. On the contrary, some of its most characteristic activities are explicable only as circular processes, emerging from the nervous system into the muscles, and re-entering the nervous system through the sense organs" (*Cybernetics* 8). Wiener assimilates the future to the human nervous system. The physiology of feedback is recursive, and it enhances bodily life in a way strangely similar to that of economic speculation. Its futures involve a *return to the present* that modifies its value. Where the gains of speculation are financial, those of feedback are in a simple sense physiological, producing the persistence of patterned behavior.

So far the way feedback works sounds pretty functionalist, and the downside of cybernetics is that it can be susceptible to this description. But Wiener takes great pains to build flexibility into his systems science. A pattern that purely repeats in the long run communicates very little. In accordance with the Second Law of Thermodynamics, such a pattern advances *entropy*, the statistical increase of disorder in any closed system. The first time someone hears about the priest, the rabbi, and the evangelist, it is funny. But the third time? Wiener points out, however, that interaction among feedback patterns, especially in a communication system as complicated as society, will open many of them to change and mutation. *Information* registers that difference because information communicates something new: "the information carried by a set of messages is a measure of its *organization*" (*Human Use* 21). In an unexpected way, then, information negates entropy. It counteracts the statistical increase of disorder in closed systems by opening them up, organizing and circulating unanticipated patterns.

Wiener recuperates the humanism his systems science otherwise rescinds by ascribing to human communications this capacity for variety. I'd like to avoid that move by emphasizing instead the *ahumanism* of cybernetics. One of the problems that science fiction since

World War II confronts is the coming of a cybernetic society whose complexity wildly exceeds human capacities for cognition and communication. At issue is the social deployment of feedback as a recursive logic of command and control, one that practices the future as a function of past performance. The problem here is perilously simple. Will such futures remain fungible? Or will that recursive logic capture them, enclose them, colonize them in the name of performance and efficiency? _This is a linguistic fault line._

What, to put it bluntly, is the future of the future? Will it remain a zone of possibility, a practice of *difference* (and I mean that in the full French sense of *différance*)? Or will the futures of speculation articulate with those of feedback to configure a cybernetic society that administrates, with maximum efficiency and profitability, the production and reproduction of life? Michael Hardt and Antonio Negri, Paul Virilio, Gilles Deleuze, Giorgio Agamben, and Foucault all anticipate the coming of such a society, one that maintains homeostasis on a systemic scale by converting fungible futures into predictable outcomes—and incomes. Ready, aim, fire. Kill or be killed. Speed dictates decision. When the ballistics fly, smart machines crunch or crash. There is no human choice in the matter. As a zone of possibility, the future becomes a thing of the past.

INTO THE NET

Western culture came out of World War II different than it went in. Lots of terms describe this difference: globalization, transnationalism, neoliberalism, postmodernism, the list continues. They register a tremor. They mark a tectonic shift. They signify a rupture between two worlds, one defined by industry and consumption and the other by information and finance. That there is something ambiguous, however, in this historical demarcation is the lesson of that once randy patronym, "postmodern." The OED's second citation for its use teaches a surprising historical lesson. The adjective "postmodern" comes from A.J. Toynbee's magisterial *Study of History* of 1939, which blithely announces that "Our own Post-Modern age has been inaugurated by the General war of 1914–1918." Maybe Toynbee got his wars wrong. But no, he means World War I. If postmodernism has its roots the operations of finance capital, as Jameson suggests, Toynbee's timing is on the money.[4] Trends under way early in the twentieth century took awhile to develop fully. World War II finished the trick. In another OED entry, this one from 1966, postmodernism names a *Zeitgeist*, clearly visible in architecture, which launched "a

new style, [...] the legitimate style of the nineteen-fifties and nine-
teen-sixties." Postmodern here is postwar, the architecture that comes
after hostilities put International Modern and its utopian fantasies to
the torch. Postmodernism is the stylistic signature of this historical
passage and its (simulated) cultural effects.

If postmodernism names a *cultural* dominant, then what term best
characterizes the concomitant *social* formation?[5] "Empire" has been
suggested to describe the gradual emergence of "a new global form of
sovereignty" (Hardt and Negri xii). The main proponents of the term,
Hardt and Negri, see a new form of sovereignty taking shape on a
global scale that works to regulate life at the most basic levels of its
occurrence. They call it "Empire," and it encompasses the globe, or
aspires to, and would fix world affairs in perpetuity. Unlike old-school
imperialisms, Empire is neither territorial nor expansive but rules by
creating the world it controls. How? "Empire manages hybrid identities, flexible hierarchies, and plural exchanges through modulating
networks of command" (xii–xiii). Empire *produces* the social circumstances it regulates by configuring lines of communication that determine life's production and reproduction. If that sounds familiar, that
is because Hardt and Negri use a vaguely cybernetic model to describe
the way this new world order works.

Witness their baleful preoccupation with "control," a logic of communicative constraint they adapt from Deleuze, who lifts it from
William Burroughs. Control scripts social agency so completely
because, in Delueze's words, it "extends well outside the structured
sites of social institutions though flexible and fluctuating networks"
(Deleuze, *Negotiations* 23). Control regulates life not only in close
quarters but even more effectively out in the open, ensnaring it in
preestablished networks of prescribed agency. That is why what Hardt
and Negri call "biopower" is *the* creeping evil of Empire's rule.
Biopower "regulates social life from its interior, following it, interpreting it, absorbing it, and rearticulating it" until it sets total terms
for the production and reproduction of life: "The highest function of
this power is to invest life through and through, and its primary task
is to administrate life" (Hardt and Negri 23–24). Not, of course,
intentionally. Biopower scripts life without human say-so.[6] As
Burroughs might say, "No more Stalins, no more Hitlers." As Wiener
might say (exposing the conceptual heritage of Hardt and Negri's
theoretical model), biopower is entropy.

Social entropy. Hardt and Negri advance the grim fantasy of a new
world order consolidating operations as a closed system. There is little
in Wiener to justify this prognostication, as in fact there is little in

Hardt and Negri to corroborate it. I'm not the first to point out that they are long on conceptual critique and short on material analysis (see Poster). Wiener would argue, as he does quite openly in *The Human Use of Human Beings,* that the sheer variety of communicative systems keeps society from becoming a closed system. Wiener's confidence may be naive, but it has the virtue of theoretical coherence, since *information* counteracts entropy by communicating something *new.* Entropy is repetition. Information is repetition with a difference. Hardt and Negri offer few detailed descriptions of either one. That may be why *Empire,* for all its theoretical savvy, falls on deaf ears as a useful discourse for diagnosing a new world order.

That may also be why many commentators prefer the more benign discourse of the "network society." The work of Manuel Castells is representative here. In rich detail Castells describes the emergence of what he calls "informationalism," a new technological paradigm wherein "what is specific to our world is the extension and augmentation of the body and mind of human subjects in networks of interaction powered by microelectronics-based, software-operated, communication technologies. These technologies are increasingly diffused throughout the entire realm of human activity by growing miniaturization" (Castells, *Network Society* 7). For Castells this new order is less the function of a dominant logic than of the material practices that install and sustain it, most decisively those of microelectronic info-tech. Where Hardt and Negri gesture toward such practices, Castells describes them minutely and examines their social effects. Networks "are self-reconfigurable, complex structures of communication that ensure, at the same time, unity of purpose and flexibility of its execution by the capacity to adapt to the operating environment" (4). They emerge historically out of the "microelectronics revolution" of the 1940s and 1950s, which is to say in the wake of World War II, and they install communications at the heart of society. The network society, then, is a new world order configured by electronic communications.

It probably goes without saying that such a description owes its terms to cybernetics. As Steven Shaviro points out, "Our current understanding of networks dates from the development of cybernetic theory in the 1940s and 1950s" (10). He also says that "A network is always a nested hierarchy. From the inside, it seems to be entirely self-contained, but from the outside, it turns out to be part of a still larger network" (10). This interplay among networks allows them to produce and proliferate information that counteracts the entropy of any given system. Multiplicity maintains openness. Castells can write with sweet optimism that "the culture of the network society is a culture of protocols of communication between all cultures in the world, developed on the basis of a common belief in the power of networking and the synergy obtained by giving to others and receiving from others" (40). Communication among cultures produces information, counteracting social entropy. This process occurs materially, as people all over the planet exploit innovations in communication technology to exchange messages within and among networks: "networks have their strength in their flexibility, adaptability, and self-reconfiguring capacity" (5). As cybernetics asserts, through feedback and information, networks self-organize and adjust to new conditions. The new messages they circulate disrupt their own tendencies toward closure.

Empire or Network? Biopower or informationalism? The choice seems decisive, like a choice between constraint and freedom. But like so many choices, this one is a ruse. Both options owe their descriptive force to cybernetics, however much their affective registers may differ. If I resist both Empire and Network as names for a new world order, it is because they basically *name the same thing*, which is to say the emergence of a social formation whose dominant legitimating discourses and practices are cybernetic. The society that dawns globally with the convergence of finance, military command and control, and info-tech is a cybernetic society. Its futures may succumb to biopower. Or they may multiply with networks. Either way, such prospects owe their possibility to the descriptive force and practical effects of cybernetics.

CYBEROPOLIS

It would be perilous to doubt the social efficacy of cybernetic discourses and practices. Enough ink (or code) has been spilt about the Internet to persuade the dourest Luddite that info-tech is here to stay. Celebrate its prospects or excoriate its exclusions, but the World Wide Web guarantees the social prestige of cybernetics. Users do not just reach out and touch the Internet, after all. They *access* it through a computer—a quintessentially cybernetic operation. Access coordinates messages among different communications systems, only one of which is in a traditional (and trivial) sense human. A human sender interfaces with a laptop, say, that translates typed symbols into digital code and in turn interfaces with other systems (routers, servers, fiber-optic cables, computers, etc.) to circulate messages among receivers. Some of those receivers might be human too, but a lot of them are not. They are machines that send and receive messages with the effortlessness of e-mail. The Internet is a vast, complex, and open cybernetic system, or rather network of systems, whose performance exceeds human tolerances and whose multiplicity works against closure.

That, anyway, is the hope. Rather than approaching the Internet as *the* representative instance of the way networks operate, however, one should acknowledge that the Internet is just one among many cybernetic systems that have emerged to reshape social life since World War II. The way these systems interact will determine whether the future—as a cultural practice—has a future. The development of the Internet, then, is part of a larger history of microelectronic communications. The Internet took shape in the 1960s under the auspices of the Advanced Research Projects Agency (ARPA, renamed DARPA in 1972 by adding the word "Defense") as an initiative to improve communications among big research computers at different locations. The widespread belief, endorsed by Hardt and Negri, that the Internet arose as a way of preserving information in the event of nuclear attack is an urban myth. The Internet's Defense Department heritage is not, however. Military applications were part of its purpose from the start, and DARPA's mission statement makes their strategic value clear: "DARPA's original mission, established in 1958, was to prevent technological surprise like the launch of Sputnik, which signaled that the Soviets had beaten the U.S. into space. [...] Today, DARPA's mission is still to prevent technological surprise to the US, but also to create technological surprise for our enemies" (http://en.wikipedia.org/wiki/DARPA). Such statements conflate the strategic value with the scientific advantage of efficient communications among computing centers. As computers the world over linked up to the Internet, military applications spun off into their own separate system (MILNET). By 1990 DARPA released its communications network from government constraint, freeing it to weave a global web of information and commerce.

Other aspects of the history of microelectric communications are worth considering too. A second network emerged alongside the Internet having equally important implications. The Global Positioning System has fast become the navigational familiar of overnight delivery corporations, scavenger hunters, and soccer Moms. Its military heritage is unequivocal. The U.S. Department of Defense developed GPS out of grounded radio navigation systems used in World War II. The addition of satellites allowed the system to go global, boosted into orbit by the Sputnik surprise. The first satellite navigation system was called "Transit," and was used by the U.S.

Navy in the early 1960s. It mobilized a limited array of five satellites to provide a navigational fix on ships. With the addition several years later of highly accurate clocks, an orbital satellite network began to take shape, eventually named NAVSTAR GPS. It now comprises 24 satellites, distributed around the globe in six orbital planes of four each. At any given moment from nearly any location on earth, at least six GPS satellites are orbiting within sight (http://en.wikipedia.org/wiki/GPS). Ethereal muses of navigation, they wrap the planet in an invisible net of information.

Their specific omniscience—*position*—is military Intel, of such strategic value that it was initially classified. Cybernetic command and control goes global with GPS. The capacity to determine the position of friend or foe anywhere on earth with speed and accuracy gives an enormous advantage to military strategists. Targeting missiles and air strikes becomes a cinch. So the U.S. military has mapped the world. When that little unit on the dashboard says, "please turn right at the first opportunity," it transfers military data directly into a driver's vehicle, ears, and nervous system. A trip to a soccer game becomes a domestic military exercise.

One might wonder why a mere civilian should have access to information that could as easily navigate a cruise missile as a minivan. The U.S. military is not known for its generosity with Intel. Here too the answer involves shooting down an airplane. Although originally a military application, GPS went public in the wake of an airborne tragedy of mistaken identity. In 1983 MiG interceptors flying near Sakhalin Island fired upon an unidentified aircraft that breeched Soviet airspace. It turned out to be Korean Air Lines flight 007, which fell in pieces into the sea along with 269 passengers. Because GPS technology would have averted the tragedy, then president Ronald Reagan directed that the system be made available free as a common good for civilian use when it became operational. Twenty-five years later GPS is a simple fact of life that has applications in navigation, science, and commerce. GPS is practically everywhere and plays an important part in calibrating and sustaining life in cybernetic society.

Consider only one of its commercial applications. GPS has quietly revolutionized the transportation industry. Any industrial economy is only as profitable as its transportation of goods allows. Distribution sucks huge cost from profit, particularly where it involves static storage: the warehouse. If the warehouse could be eradicated, eliminating standstill in the circuit that links production to consumption, the efficiency of the industrial economy could be amped to the limit of physical mobility. Thanks to GPS that ideal is almost within reach. The cabs of eighteen-wheelers now come rigged with GPS receivers. Synced with the Internet, they allow deliveries to be scheduled with ballistic precision. A trucker picks up a load. GPS logs it and plots destination and delivery time. When by legal mandate she pulls over to log hours, GPS makes it as easy as pushing a button. At the point of delivery, GPS records the transfer with a digitized bill of lading. And that is only in the cab. GPS receivers in the trailer can monitor gross weight, offload time, even tire pressure. The blitz of distribution can be conducted by data exchange. Deliveries of goods get calibrated precisely to the demands of retailers, minimizing the need to store them. *Warehouses travel at 75 m.p.h.* (or thereabouts—GPS monitors that too). Transportation parlance calls it "goods in motion," and one secret to economic success is to keep the whole flow of commodities moving at maximum speed. The material economy begins to resemble the finance economy with the difference that the former moves at the speed of law, not light. But *move* it must. What the Internet coordinates, GPS monitors: the system of pickups and deliveries whose speed and efficiency maximizes the profitability of the industrial economy. The alternative, as recent economic events illustrate only too clearly, is economic gridlock.

Nobody does distribution better than Walmart. Sam Walton's sprawling discount retail chain has seen such harrowing success thanks partly to its cybernetic command and control over goods in motion. While outrage may be the only acceptable response to the way Walmart mistreats employees, to evaluate its social function solely from that perspective may be missing the point. The plight of the wage laborer fits uneasily into Walmart's communications landscape, so little has old-time labor to do with the distribution of goods the sprawling retailer administrates. Walmart employees are less wage earners in the classic sense (renting the property of their bodies for pay) than nodes in a network of distribution, bipedal communications devices for transmitting messages between producers and consumers. Their big blue and white badges say it all: "Hello, my name is Sharissa." Hello Sharissa, where can I find the Nintendo Wii? "Right this way. Follow me."

Sure, these workers move boxes, stock shelves, perform traditional *labor*. But little in their activity is productive. Their main economic effect is communication. They are to consumption what laptops are to the Internet: machines for managing the interface among communications systems, only some of which are human. Consumers comprise such a system. So do producers. So do myriad trucks, truckers, truck stops, EZPass sensors, hi-way repair detours, traffic signals, docking queues, product locations, cash registers, and other such means involved in distribution. Walmart's command and control of its supply chain coordinates interaction among these systems with baleful efficiency, and Walmart employees calibrate the operation at the consumer interface.[7] Of course, these people deserve decent pay and benefits—but not because their labor resembles the centralized agency of factory workers. It does not.

Economic theory has not fully addressed the transformation of labor in cybernetic society, although notions such as "the service economy" and "flexible labor" amount to a start.[8] That Walmart is on the leading edge of this transformation is the upshot of Jameson's strange, oracular suggestion that Walmart today is

> the very anticipatory prototype of some new sort of socialism for which the reproach of centralization now proves historically misplaced and irrelevant. It is in any case certainly a revolutionary reorganization of capitalist production, and some acknowledgement such as "Waltonism" or "Walmartification" would be a more appropriate name for this new stage than vacuous terms such as "post-Fordism" or "flexible capitalism," which are merely privative or reactive. (*Archaeologies* 153n)

The reorganization of production that Jameson notices here arises from configuring distribution in cybernetic rather than merely material terms. Instantaneous communications eliminate much of the drag that slows transportation of commodities. Supply chain distribution is capitalist command and control. None of it would be possible without the Internet to coordinate orders for goods and GPS to administrate their pickup and delivery.

Jameson is right to suggest in his premonitory way that Walmart illustrates the emergence of a new social formation, one I would call cybernetic for the pervasiveness of its investment in info-tech. As the instance of Walmart indicates, it is by no means clear that this social formation will be egalitarian and free, as antiglobalistas, myself included, insist it must. The Internet is an interactive network, and GPS will be soon. GPS monitors and administrates communication in ways difficult to evaluate with traditional moral and economic tools. Its massive capacity for command and control suggests that as goes GPS, so goes the future. Waltonism is so effective an economic strategy because it so thoroughly controls the vagaries of distribution—which is to say it *eliminates uncertainty in advance*, or tries to, in the interest of maintaining the homeostasis and managed growth of its economic network. The question GPS raises theoretically, the problem Walmart presents practically, is the function of the future as an economic and cultural *practice* in a cybernetic social formation. Will "tomorrow" become a simple matter of calculation and calibration, a button on a GPS receiver with the word "future" beneath it? ("please turn right at the first opportunity"). Or will its fungibility remain an important means of circulating *difference* among the networks that configure society? Does Waltonism advance entropy or, in Wiener's sense, information? Is cybernetics giving birth to a society that comes *after the future*?

SCI-FI TO CY-FI

Questions, perhaps, for cybernauts—or to use a more traditional moniker, creative writers. What kind of fiction would be commensurable with cybernetic society? The easy answer would be *science* fiction, since cybernetics claims to be systems science. But the game has changed since 1929 when Gernsback defined science fiction as "stories that have their basis in scientific laws as we know them, or in the logical deduction of new laws from what we know." Cybernetics is less concerned with laws than probabilities. Its extrapolations are a function of statistical outcomes rather than physical principles. Cybernetics adapts systems to circumstances and vice versa. The whole purpose of feedback is to modify the operation of a given system through communication with others. Gernsback's science fiction, while open to change, operates on the Newtonian premise that universal laws set the terms for truth and science simply verifies or extends them. What would be a science fiction equal to the statistical predictions of cybernetics, a sci-fi not of law but of probability, a fantasia not of physics but of communications?

Call it *cy-fi*: the popular fiction of cybernetic society. Such fiction need not concern itself explicitly with cybernetics to qualify as cy-fi. It is simply the fiction of a culture—increasingly a global culture—in which cybernetics configures everyday life. Obviously such a culture is unevenly distributed around the world. But the penetration, say, of cellphone technology in developing countries is just one indication of its pervasiveness. I'm not trying to argue here for the emergence of a unified global culture grounded in and perpetuated by cybernetics—a global motherboard called America. But I am trying to describe a historically distinct form of fiction that takes cybernetic practices for its premise and responds accordingly. Cy-fi isn't American or British or French or Polish, even if its practitioners are. If I refuse nationality as the ideological condition of this fiction, that is because the nation plays a less important role in defining culture today than it once did. Cy-fi constitutes the first true genre of globalization.

My guide here as in so much else is J.G. Ballard, a better-qualified observer of contemporary culture than a whole academy of Marxists. In his Author's Introduction to the French edition of his technoporn masterpiece, *Crash* (1975), he describes what it was like to write fiction in the cultural context of the late 1950s: "a world where the call sign of Sputnik I could be heard on one's radio like the advance beacon of a new universe" (3). It was like awakening to a world in which all the old fictions turned suddenly obsolete: "if it were possible to scrap the whole of existing literature, and be forced to begin again without any knowledge of the past, all writers would find themselves inevitably producing something very close to science fiction" (3). But not, Ballard is quick to add, Gernsback's old-school sci-fi of rocket ships and alien encounters. "I was dissatisfied with science fiction's obsession with its two principal themes—outer space and the far future" (3). Ballard's preferred subject is what he calls "inner space," the domain "where the inner world of the mind and the outer world of reality meet and fuse" (3). That's a cybernetic formulation, at least conceptually. No meaningful distinction exists between inner and outer. The old subject/object opposition gives way to a circuit of communication, or rather a variety of such systems. Fiction maps their interactive function, as Ballard's does in novel after novel.

Ballard wants—and writes—a cybernetic fiction for cybernetic society. His writing has been called *hyperreal*, but that description misses its social force.[9] Ballard's fiction simply rescinds *mimesis* as the condition of literary engagement. Representation collapses into the real to reveal their interchangeability through message, code, pattern, and probability. Here's Ballard on contemporary culture:

> The main "fact" of the 20th century is the concept of the unlimited possibility. This predicate of science and technology enshrines the notion of a moratorium on the past—the irrelevancy and even death of the past—and the limitless alternatives available to the present. What links the first flight of the Wright brothers to the invention of the Pill is the social and sexual philosophy of the ejector seat. (*Crash* 2)

This passage is vintage Ballard. The new cultural condition of unlimited possibility—call it the death of consequence—detaches agency from causality and makes probability a better guide to life than morality. A person has a one in eleven million chance of dying in a plane crash, a one in one hundred chance of conceiving on the Pill. With numbers like those, who needs morality to determine behavior? For that matter, who needs Great Literature? "In a sense, the writer knows nothing any longer," Ballard writes. "He has no moral stance. He offers the reader the contents of his own head, he offers a set of options and imaginative alternatives" (5). He drafts probability scenarios. He trades in fungible futures. Cybernauts pattern possibilities that replicate patterns.

They write cy-fi. Not all fiction written in a cybernetic society is cy-fi and not all cy-fi confronts cybernetics. Of Ballard's many stories and books only a few mention computers. Yet he is one of cy-fi's literary masters. Nor is Ballard alone in responding to the postwar society with a new kind of science fiction. The great progenitor of such writing is Alfred Bester, who in 1956 published a brilliant novel called *The Stars My Destination*. It retells in a twenty-fifth century setting the old story of *The Count of Monte Cristo*, but that is not what makes it interesting here. *The Stars My Destination* turns out to be one of the first novels of globalization. Bester earned his living as a writer for TV, acquiring an insider's understanding of the home entertainment industry emerging in the 1950s. Like any traditional science fiction story, *The Stars My Destination* is set in a future dominated by heavy ballistics, interplanetary travel, and advanced weaponry. But Bester blasts away from that tradition in pursuit of a more pertinent future for the world to come after World War II.

His first innovation crosses science fiction with economics. Bester's twenty-fifth century world is distinctive not primarily for amazing technologies, although there are plenty of those, but for economic domination. Monopoly capitalism sets the terms for human life on Earth. A handful of corporations dominate global society and coordinate an economy of production and consumption as big as the solar system. Among them is Clan Presteign, a transplanetary corporate dynasty with a fleet of rocket transports and an empire of 497 retail franchises that distribute—well, it's not exactly clear. But they are successful enough to assure CEO Presteign of Clan Presteign enormous economic influence and social prestige. Bester grounds his fiction in a finance economy gone global whose *éminence grise* puts more stock in *stocks* than laser pistols: " 'Report on Clan Presteign enterprises,' the Equerry began. 'Common stock: High—201 1/2, Low—201 1/4. Average quotations New York, Paris, Ceylon, Tokyo—' " (46). Global capitalism meets Captain Future in this tale of corporate betrayal and revenge. The real question Bester asks is how the operations of Clan Presteign affect everyday life.

Betser tests the legitimacy of capitalism against the lives of the laborers who make it possible. Gully Foyle is one of those laborers, lowest of the low, the working dregs of corporate capitalism, as his personnel report attests: "*A man of physical strength and intellectual potential stunted by lack of ambition. Energizes at minimum. The stereotype Common Man. Some unexpected shock might possibly awaken him, but Psych cannot find the key. Not recommended for promotion. Has reached a dead end*" (16, italics in the original). Bester depicts the classic betrayal of labor by a management that sucks his muscle and tosses the husk. But Foyle awakens to his situation when, stranded in space on a dead wreck called *Nomad*, another ship called *Vorga* turns tail at his distress-flares and runs: "The key turned in the lock of his soul and the door was opened. What emerged expunged the Common Man forever" (22). Foyle comes alive by being abandoned. He doggedly pursues revenge against the ship that forsook him, which he learns is, like *Nomad*, owned and operated by Clan Presteign. His is a story of personal transformation through violence, a sustained meditation on the logic of terror.

Such themes do not make *The Stars My Destination* a new kind of writing, however. The book is much more than *The Count of Monte Cristo* in a space suit. Bester retro-fits the revenge tale to the conditions of life in an emerging cybernetic society. The fundamental social fact of that life is *speed*: humans have acquired the ability to teleport instantaneously over distances up to a thousand miles. The new ability is called "jaunting." A researcher named Charles Forte Jaunte discovered it when a lab experiment turned deadly and he found himself instantly transported out of danger. How it happened he could not say, but research soon revealed that the trick could be taught, and pretty soon people the world over were "on the jaunte." In the words of one expert at a press conference, "nobody knows how we can teleport [...], but we know we can do it—just was we know that we can think. Have you ever heard of Descartes? He said: *cogito ergo sum*. I think, therefore I am. We say: *cogito ergo jaunteo*. I think, therefore I jaunte'" (10–11). Bester replaces subjectivity (*sum*) with teleportation (*jaunteo*)—a stunning transposition that registers a huge cultural shift: from interiority to exteriority, epistemology to communications, physics to cybernetics. By pondering the social implications of instantaneous movement across distance, Bester invents cy-fi, the fiction of cybernetic society.

It is easy to read jaunting as an anticipatory allegory of the Internet. The teleportation Bester's characters experience has since been realized online. One can log on in Chicago and be instantly "in" Tokyo,

at least virtually. Perhaps there is not much difference between physical and virtual teleportation. Wiener doesn't think so: "the fact that
we cannot telegraph the pattern of a man from one place to another
seems to be due to technical difficulties, and in particular, to the difficulty of keeping an organism in being during such a radical recon-
struction. The idea itself is highly plausible" (*Human Use* 103–4).
Bester's fantasy of teleportation fulfills in one swoop the most distant
promises of instant communications. That television does something
similar was not lost on a man as deeply involved in the entertainment
industry as Bester.

He records in advance several changes that attend the microelectronic communications revolution, particularly the way it transforms
the physical world. Jaunting, like the Internet, *deterritorializes space.*
It takes the jaunter across borders and around the world in the blink
of an eye (or better, an "I"). Jaunting dissociates space from location.
No longer a physical *place*, space in this sense turns into a point of
transmission, or rather a series of them, multiple nodes in a teleportation network. Speed and mobility become the values best suited to
life in this space. So pervasive are corporate powers like Presteign,
however, that they are always already everywhere. In effect they *own*
deterritorialized space and thus set the terms for speed and mobility.
Common men (and women) like Foyle remain marooned in the material world.[10] Conflict of haves with have-nots becomes inevitable: war
between the Inner and Outer planets of the solar system erupts over
control of the postjaunting economy.

One of the fascinating—and timely—aspects of *The Stars My
Destination* is its examination of terror as a predictable response to
corporate domination. Gully Foyle's vicious pursuit of revenge turns
him into a terrorist. He tries everything to avenge his abandonment
(he names rape, murder, and genocide among his crimes) until he
realizes that the totalizing violence of his hatred aligns him with his
enemies. Both move logically toward mass destruction, figured in the
novel by a substance called PyrE, a "pyrophore" whose chief property
is instant combustion by psychokinesis. The usefulness of PyrE to
both sides in the war effort is obvious, but unknown to Gully, the
pyrophore is in his possession, and the ethical dilemma he eventually
faces is how to dispose of this weapon of mass destruction. Like
Charles Forte Jaunte before him, Gully also evolves a new capacity to
teleport, this time through deep space. He can space-jaunt throughout the universe along the flexible scaffolding of time.

Hence his dilemma: " 'Am I to turn PyrE over to the world and let
it destroy itself? Am I to teach the world how to space-jaunte and let

us spread our freak show from galaxy to galaxy through all the universe? What's the answer?'" (250). Bester has one, and it comes from a strange source: "'The answer is yes,' the robot said, quite distinctly" (230). Foyle has trouble accepting advice from a robot. But that a cybernetic servant should proffer wisdom to a cybernetic society makes a certain amount of sense: "'A man is a member of society first, and an individual second. You must go along with society, whether it chooses destruction or not'" (250). The robot gets the last word because it too participates in "society"—not through some essential human *qualitas*, but through its ability to communicate. Like its human interlocutors, the robot bartender is a cybernetic machine, and the message it communicates leads Foyle to distribute PyrE to the very common men and women deemed unfit for life in cybernetic society. Foyle says "let them learn or die. We're all in this together" (255). Bester's challenge to cybernetic society is clear: communicative inclusion or else. All must have access not only to the values of speed and mobility, but also to the practices that make them possible. All must jaunte. All must communicate. All must live. All must participate in the psychokinesis that is—or is not—mass destruction. One function of fiction in a cybernetic society is to promote such possibilities.

Cy-fi in this sense picks up where traditional science fiction leaves off. It affirms the fungibility of the future and examines tendencies in contemporary society directing futures toward control, whether through mass domination or destruction. Bester's novel is a polemic against control—and the terror it will produce. *The Stars My Destination* is less interested in positing *the* future in terms of the "laws of science" than in positing *a* probable future—and speculating on the return it offers to present culture.

There are a host of cybernauts who do something similar, cy-fi artists in the best sense who promote speculative futures and exploit their fungibility. Here is a brief, biased, noncanonical, incomplete, random list: Samuel Delany (*Dahlgren, Stars in My Pocket Like Grains of Sand*), Philip K. Dick (any of his thirty-six novels will do), William Burroughs (*Nova Express, The Ticket that Exploded, The Soft Machine, The Wild Boys*), Kurt Vonnegut (*The Sirens of Titan, Slaughterhouse Five*), Joanna Russ (*The Female Man*), Stanislaw Lem (*Solaris, The Cyberiad, The Futurological Congress*), Octavia Butler (*Lilith's Brood*), Kathy Acker (*Empire of the Senseless*), William Gibson (his whole *oeuvre*), the cyberpunks in general (Bruce Sterling, Pat Cadigan, Paul Di Filippo), Neal Stephenson (*Snowcrash, The Diamond Age, Anathem*), Jonathan Lethem (*Gun with Occasional Music*), Justina Robson

(*Natural History*), M. T. Anderson (*Feed*), Charles Stross (*Accelerando*, *Singularity Sky*) and, of course, J. G. Ballard. To say they all write science fiction would not be wrong, exactly, but not science fiction in the traditional sense.[11] They write probability fictions whose futures offer a value-added return to the present, speculative fictions for a culture of speculation, cybernetic fictions for a cybernetic society: cy-fi.

PROBABILITY MEMBRANE

One of the symptoms this fiction examines is the obsolescence of the future as a cultural practice. A grim effect of biopolitical control is a future that collapses into the present. Cy-fi registers this tendency toward *futurity compression*, a situation in which the distance between today and tomorrow narrows to the point of singularity. Futurity compression appears in J. G. Ballard's condensed serial novel *The Atrocity Exhibition* (1970), in which media images and architectural styles preempt human capacities for change. It surfaces over the course of the career of William Gibson, whose early cyberpunk novels of the near future (*Neuromancer* [1983], *Count Zero* [1986], and *Mona Lisa Overdrive* [1989]) fade into austere fictions of global cyberculture (*Pattern Recognition* [2003], *Spook Country* [2007]). Futurity compression also characterizes the work of self-appointed prophets for globalization or the end of history such as Thomas Friedman (*The World Is Flat* [2003]) and Francis Fukuyama (*The End of History* [1995]). If the past is dead, is the future dying too? Has the membrane separating today from tomorrow popped, producing a perpetual present?

In his stylish way, William Gibson ponders these questions from very the beginning of his career. One of his earliest stories, "The Gernsback Continuum" (1981), advances a devastating critique of traditional science fiction that opens up new possibilities for cybernauts. In this context, "The Gernsback Continuum" is about as serious as writing gets. Here is the set-up: editor Dialta Downes hires a hipster fashion photographer to shoot the future—one that never materialized but nonetheless looks suspiciously like that of Gernsbeck's pulp magazines. The project's working title is *The Airstream Futuropolis: The Tomorrow that Never Was*. This particular future faded into the history of popular culture, but not without leaving remains behind: "ephemeral stuff extruded by the collective American subconscious of the Thirties, tending mostly to survive along depressing strips lined with dusty motels, mattress wholesalers, and small used-car lots" (26). The detritus of Gernsback's future lives on in low-rent consumer zones, an antique future gone kitsch for being commodified. Part of the fun here comes from acknowledging the poor staying power of Gernsback's technoscientific clairvoyance. " 'Think of it' Dialta Downes had said, 'as a kind of alternate America: a 1980 that never happened' " (27).

The fun does not last, however. In hot and exhausting pursuit of that alternate America, Gibson's hero goes over the edge: "one day, on the outskirts of Bolinas, [...] I penetrated a fine membrane, a membrane of probability...." (27). And what happens? He sees (or hallucinates) "a twelve-engined thing like a bloated boomerang, all wing, thrumming its way east with an elephantine grace, so low that I could count the rivets in its dull silver skin, and hear—maybe—the echo of jazz" (27–28). A Gernsback fantasy of transatlantic luxury air flight hangs in the sky above California, flown loose from the probability continuum of its 1930s future. A "semiotic ghost," says a friend: cultural imagery that has taken on a life of its own. The camera monkey isn't so sure. Later, fatigued by stress and amphetamines, he drives toward Tucson and things get even kinkier: "Semiotic ghosts. Fragments of the Mass Dream, whirling past in the wind of my passage. Somehow this feedback-loop aggravated the diet pill, and the speed-vegetation along the road began to assume the colors of infrared satellite images, glowing shreds blown apart in the Toyota's slipstream" (30). Under the influence of these images, their patterns shifting his perception, the photographer sees into the life of things. In fear. The future, apparently, does not disappear. It persists into the present. There on the road in front of him loom up Gernsback's children of tomorrow:

> They were blond. They were standing beside their car, an aluminum avocado with a central shark-fin rudder jutting up from its spine and smooth black tires like a child's toy. He had his arm around her waist and was gesturing toward the city. They were both in white loose clothing, bare legs, spotless white sun shoes. Neither of them seemed aware of the beams of my headlights. He was saying something wise and strong, and she was nodding, and suddenly I was frightened in an entirely different way. Sanity had ceased to be an issue; I knew, some-how, that the city behind me was Tucson—a dream Tucson thrown up out of the collective yearning of an era. That it was real, entirely real. That the couple in front of me lived in it, and they frightened me. (32)

Gernsback's futuropolis persists not as a dead but a living dream. And that dream is real, as real as anything on the cameraman's continuum.

Gibson refigures the future as an alternate present, separated from this one by a membrane of probability. He disrupts the linearity that determines the futures of traditional sci-fi and aligns them in series. On one continuum, Gernsback's heterosexual blonds preside over metropolitan Tucson. On another a lone photographer ekes out a living shooting futuristic kitsch. Call the first Reagan's 1980s. Call the second Gibson's. They persist simultaneously in the present as probability continua. And here's what is disturbing: the membrane separating them is permeable. Obsolete futures live on as alternate presents, and probability, not causality, determines which prevails. Futures haunt the present like hallucinations.

The photographer recovers from his encounter with Reagan's America by immersing himself in popular culture on his friend's advice. " 'Really bad media can exorcize your semiotic ghosts' " (33). So he plunges immediately into a dark cinema to watch *Nazi Love Hotel*. Media beats memory any day. His visions persist, but with fading intensity: "I spotted a flying wing over Castro Street, but there was something tenuous about it, as if it were only half there" (35). Images from an obsolete but *real* future still configure perception in the present. That is why they are so frightening. Those images set the terms for what the photographer sees—or does not. Artifacts from Gernsback's obsolete future structure perception in the present. Maybe the photographer sees a semiotic ghost. But maybe he *perceives* what he sees in terms of culturally obsolete images. What if this kitsch hunter sees something real, but misidentifies it as an antique illusion? What if he sees a real flying wing, but perceives it as a luxury airliner flying out of Gernsback's future past?

The setting is, after all, California in the early eighties, dawn of the largest Defense Department spending spree in American history. Perhaps, stoned and frazzled, the photographer *sees* a B-2 Stealth bomber prototype, built and tested at secret airbases in California and Nevada, but *perceives* it as a Gernsback-era luxury-liner. The flying wing design of the B-2 goes back through the P-59 of World War II straight to the pages of Gernsback's *Air Wonder Stories*. Artifacts from the Gernsback continuum not only persist into the present, but also *configure its perception*. If Gibson's hero *sees* an early B-2 prototype but *perceives* it as an obsolete flying wing, the sight blinds him to certain facts of the world he inhabits. A war machine looks like a quaint old luxury airliner. For all his facility with a camera, this photographer does not perceive the militarization of the world around him. The real danger, then, of obsolete futures is their continuing capacity to configure perception long after they fade away. Gernsback's future lives on in the misperceptions it inspires, even in those who, like Gibson's photographer, are hip to its illusions. Those images of flying wings, avocado cars, and blond couples impede the perception of a militarized present.

CALLING ALL PARTISANS

were they ever not in play?

Gibson's cy-fi at least tries to open people's eyes. It puts speculative futures back into play to recover their fungibility. If speculation frames the relation between today and tomorrow, if probability and not causality determine their connection, then *alternatives persist*—even if imagining them is a gamble. As the fiction of cybernetic society, cy-fi beams messages to a world where messages script life. Cyberfiction *is* this communicative function, circulating messages among communications systems (technological, biological, economic) that can modify the operations of those systems. Cyberfiction is broadband literary communication to a world wired to receive and circulate it. That does not mean cy-fi has to be *about* the Internet. On the contrary, cy-fi simply accepts the fact that cybernetics sets new terms for contemporary culture and imagines accordingly. Cy-fi sends messages to all open receivers. It disrupts preestablished patterns of behavior and maximizes the fungibility of futures. Cyberfiction *is that disruption*, the strategic consequence of communications after the future.

I get the distinct impression you haven't decided what you mean...

2

OTHERSPACE

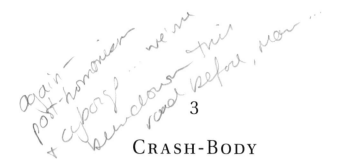

3

CRASH-BODY

CRASH!

One catastrophic instant can change life forever.

J. G. Ballard's *Crash* reveals the destiny of the human body in a world wired by cybernetics and catastrophe: a new crash-body, ungodly offspring of technology and signs. Set in the concrete mediascape of cybernetic society, the novel views the world through a wide angle lens that deprives it of depth, rendering it an interminable surface. Ballard's prose is that of a camera—flat, mechanical, omni-detailed, "hyperreal"—and shows that to write in a technoscientific culture is to represent its technologies of perception. The hyperreality of Ballard's style is the representational effect of photography, the afterimage in another medium of a pervasive perception technology. That is why Vaughan, the sinister hero of *Crash*, is not a writer but a camera-monkey; the writer in the narrative, portentously named Ballard, takes up a position subordinate to the photographer, who becomes the subject of writing, the condition of narration: "Vaughan died yesterday in his last car-crash" (1). From its first sentence to its last, *Crash* pursues the image of Vaughan, its narrative alpha and omega. And that image is photographic, both product and producer of other images. Vaughan is defined by the technologies of photography that condition his perception, as in the following moment of recognition:

> The tall man with the camera sauntered across the roof. I looked through the rear window of his car. The passenger seat was loaded with photographic equipment—cameras, a tripod, a carton packed with flashbulbs. A cine-camera was fastened to a dashboard clamp.
>
> He walked back to his car, camera held like a weapon by its pistol grip. As he reached the balcony his face was lit by the headlamps of the police car. I realized that I had seen his pock-marked face many times before, projected from a dozen forgotten magazine profiles—this was Vaughan, Dr Robert Vaughan. (63)

Handsome is as handsome does: technologies of photography become
the condition of all that Vaughan does and is. Identity is an effect
of the photographic image, which is always already a technological
representation, capable of being reproduced and disseminated, today
photoshopped and e-mailed. Photography is the a priori of (re)cogni-
tion in the cybernetic society of *Crash*. Ballard's prose double-exposes
this function. With the disinterestedness of a camera, it reveals the
operation of the lens in the language of the hyperreal. Stylistically
and analytically, Ballard's book is photo-Kantian.

Its world becomes a surface. One of the effects of the lens upon
representation is to flatten it out, reconfiguring the image in a space
of two dimensions, a surface without depth. Contiguity, mark of the
metonym, regulates relations in such a space. As a result things lose
substance. Boundaries lapse and features merge. Where difference
once distinguished, contiguity now associates, deferring the identity
of *things*. Where a boundary once ruled, as between humanity and
machine, a blur now occurs, creating unprecedented relations and
new possibilities. Consider the effects of Vaughan's camera upon the
all too human act of love:

> Vaughan stood at my shoulder, like an instructor ready to help a prom-
> ising pupil. As I stared down at the photograph of myself at Renata's
> breast, Vaughan leaned across me, his real attention elsewhere. With
> a broken thumbnail, its rim caked with engine oil, he pointed to the
> chromium window-sill and its junction with the overstretched strap
> of the young woman's brassiere. By some freak of photography these
> two formed a sling of metal and nylon from which the distorted nipple
> seemed to extrude itself into my mouth. (102)

Photography breeds freaks by reconfiguring things. Boundaries that
would assert substantive differences—between metal and flesh, for
instance—fall to new associations through the intervention of the
lens. Vaughan's camera registers a world where a breast is as much
an automotive as a female accessory, where sexuality plays upon a
surface that unites the material and the organic. This surface extends
as far the images it reproduces: to the white border of the photograph proper and to the ends of perception of a lens set on infinity.
Representationally speaking, it is both terminal and interminable.

What most interests Ballard is the life of the human body on this
surface. A body without depth ceases to be an organism in the traditional sense. If to have a body means to inhabit a suit of flesh or
possess property in person, organic substance sets the terms for life,
its aims and its ends. But in Ballard's world, the cybernetic world

of technoscientific culture, semiotics subsumes substance. The vital, active organism gives way to the conceptual, abstract image. The body becomes conceptualized, and life turns into signs. So it is for Elizabeth Taylor, "real life" film actress, appearing in Vaughan's apartment and on the novel's opening page in image only:

> The walls of his apartment near the film studios at Shepperton were covered with the photographs he had taken through his zoom lens each morning as she left her hotel in London, from the pedestrian bridges above the westbound motorways, and from the roof of the multi-storey car-park at the studios. The magnified details of her knees and hands, of the inner surface of her thighs and the left apex of her mouth, I uneasily prepared for Vaughan on the copying machine in my office, handing him the packages of prints as if they were the install-ments of a death warrant. At his apartment I watched him matching the details of her body with the photographs of grotesque wounds in a textbook of plastic surgery. (7–8)

The body, in this instance the celebrated body of Elizabeth Taylor, is no longer an organism. Technologies of photographic representation (re)produce images that usurp its priority and reconfigure its integ-rity. The resulting body conceptual can be interminably manipulated: enlarged, reduced, bisected, rearranged, transcoded, transported, and most importantly, transposed. Once conceptualized, the body is transposable to any homologous geometry. Elizabeth Taylor's body conceptually assimilates the textbook wounds of other anonymous bodies. And because proliferation of conceptual equivalence can dis-tribute such a body over the whole extent of the world as surface, life itself, once an organic matter, becomes a cybernetic effect.

In the context of cybernetic society, the old organic model of the body is vestigial of an earlier age, a pastoral moment in cultural his-tory when nature at its most benign could serve as trope for life at its most general. All that has changed. The body has become a conceptual phenomenon (an appropriately peculiar designation). The nearness of the flesh may persuade us daily to live in the faith that we inhabit a vital organism. But in Ballard's novel such faith proves to be, cultur-ally speaking, habitual nostalgia. His characters no longer animate an organism. Rather a conceptual body animates them. Flesh becomes its afterimage and lives within the semiotic horizon of the world as surface. Such a body in such a world has no substance, no interior opposable to an exterior. As with graphic images generally, it is two dimensional—even to its vital depths, a point made strikingly by the cover of *The Atrocity Exhibition*, Ballard's apocalyptic fractal-fiction of

1970 reissued in 1990 by *RE/SEARCH* (figure 1). The body conceptual stands revealed in its full glory as an image that collapses vital depths of substance onto a surface both self-contained and culturally continuous. An image of neither the inside nor the outside of a body neither living nor dead, it reconfigures those old organic oppositions to represent the new form of life characteristic of cybernetic society. As a cultural historian of the body, Ballard documents this sublation of the organism.

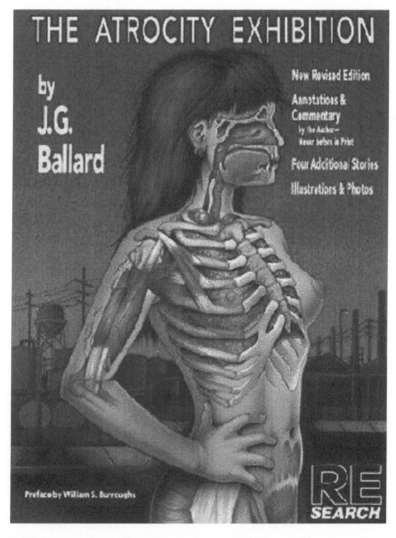

Figure 1   Cover image from *The Atrocity Exhibition*.
Image copyright © Re/Search Publications (Illustration: Phoebe Gloeckner).

VEHICULAR HOMICIDE

Conceptual bodies inhabit the world as surface less as human individuals than abstract integers. Cybernetic technologies invented to
enhance life have reinvented it, transforming the human into a cipher
in a technological horizon. Viewing the world from the verandah
of his apartment, Ballard's hero Ballard remarks in *Crash* that "the
human inhabitants of this technological landscape no longer provided
its sharpest pointers, its keys to the borderzones of identity" (49).
That landscape, so obviously technoscientific, bears no essential relation to the human as either end or origin. As an end, the human has
ended, and in its place has arisen technology itself, or more specifically the image technologies that in fact provide the keys to identity in
this landscape. If the condition of (re)cognition in cybernetic society
is the photograph, the condition of agency is the automobile. *Crash*
plots the remarkable logic of an unremarkable observation: that the
car sets the terms for life as we know it. Life has ceased to be an
organic phenomenon, and the automobile, as "a total metaphor for
man's life in today's society" ("Introduction" 6), plays a decisive role
in its transformation.

The car materializes the body conceptual. The photographic image
may disseminate that body, but the automobile produces it. A body
in a car becomes the prosthesis of a speed machine. As organism, it
dies into the life of motor oil and steel, losing human substance and
assimilating conceptually to an entity neither animate nor sentient in
the traditional sense. And yet life and even passion persists. Witness
Ballard's increasing sense of connection with the car he drives, super-
seding even passion for his young lover:

> The aggressive stylization of this mass-produced cockpit, the exagger-
> ated mouldings of the instrument binnacles emphasized my growing
> sense of a new junction between my own body and the automobile,
> closer than my feelings for Renata's broad hips and strong legs stowed
> out of sight beneath her red plastic raincoat. I leaned forward, feeling
> the rim of the steering wheel against the scars on my chest, pressing
> my knees against the ignition switch and handbrake. (55)

Built for the average buyer, the interior of the car (mass)produces
a conceptual body assimilable to the material geometry of instrument panel and steering wheel. The condition of such a body's
agency becomes the automobile itself. Life in cybernetic society turns
autotelic.

The impact of the automobile upon the organic body is thus to
transform it. Literally. The body becomes a surface in relation to the

car's stylized cockpit, a surface which, like that of the photographic image, lacks opposable interior and exterior. However counterintuitive it may seem, the body *in vehiculo* loses organic substantiality. Consider the logistics of automobility. A driver places her body *inside* a car. The exterior of her organic substance confronts the interior of the vehicle. But since that interior is outside her, it turns her, so to speak, inside out. In the cockpit of a car the body loses organic interiority, becoming part of a conceptual surface that assimilates it— materially. The interior of a car is more like a fold in flexible material than an inner space with an outer edge. Once inside, the body unfolds, becoming a surface without vital depth. The boundary between interior and exterior disappears as body and machine unite conceptually and materially on this surface. It is in this sense that Ballard can describe an automobile with the tender phrase "my own metal body" (113). The lesson of his own violent confrontation with a car's interior is that his body shares its life, not as organic substance but as conceptual surface:

> As I looked down at myself I realized that the precise make and model-year of my car could have been reconstructed by an automobile engineer from the pattern of my wounds. The layout of the instrument panel, like the profile of the steering wheel bruised into my chest, was inset on my knees and shinbones. (28)

Wounds here are not organic traumas but abstract signs that refer body and automobile to a surface that assimilates them both, autoreferentially. The car, in its brute materiality, transforms the human body into a semiotic function.

The passage above continues suggestively: "The impact of the second collision between my body and the interior compartment of the car was defined in these wounds, like the contours of a woman's body remembered in the responding pressure of one's own skin for a few hours after a sexual act." The automobile resexualizes as it reconfigures the body. The result is a "new sexuality born of a perverse technology," one liberated from both eros and desire. The sexuality of the body conceptual is less libidinal than semiotic. With the end of the organism comes the release of its semiotic function onto a surface that assimilates body and machine. Libido turns semioerotic on such a surface, the occurrence of not physical urge but conceptual equivalence. Because such equivalence is abstract it as easily embraces an automobile as a lover. Hence the place of the car in the sexuality of cybernetic society. It is less as erotic object than semioerotic signifier that it stimulates the body conceptual. Witness the encounter between Ballard and Helen Remington, wife of the man killed in a crash with his car:

> The volumes of Helen's thighs pressing against my hips, her left fist buried in my shoulder, her mouth grasping at my own, the shape and moisture of her anus as I stroked it with my ring finger, were each overlaid by the inventories of a benevolent technology—the moulded binnacle of the instrument dials, the jutting carapace of the steering column shroud, the extravagant pistol grip of the handbrake. I felt the warm vinyl of the seat beside me, and then stroked the damp aisle of Helen's perineum. Her hand pressed against my right testicle. The plastic laminates around me, the colour of washed anthracite, were the same tones as her pubic hairs parted at the vestibule of her vulva. The passenger compartment enclosed us like a machine generating from our sexual act an homunculus of blood, semen and engine coolant. (80–81)

The automobile is more a sexual signifier than an object, a condition of conceptual equivalence between body and technology that breeds a new form of life.

The autoeroticism of *Crash* is thus thoroughly *disembodied*. Ballard documents the rise of "a new sexuality divorced from any possible physical expression" (35), a disembodied eroticism that lacks passion even as it multiplies sexual possibilities. Sexual acts themselves—and *Crash* is full of them: genital, oral, anal, manual, material—confirm no intimacy, communicate no love, proliferate pleasures that are purely formal. Liberated from the organic body, they become "conceptualized acts abstracted from all feeling" (129). The posterotic sexuality that Ballard describes in such dispassionate detail recapitulates what he elsewhere calls the "death of affect" characteristic of cybernetic society. Disembodied, dissociated from affect, sexuality plays semiotically upon the world as surface, celebrating the conceptual equivalence of body and machine. Or so Ballard concludes, watching his wife Catherine and his friend Vaughan at it in the back seat:

> this act was a ritual devoid of ordinary sexuality, a stylized encounter between two bodies which recapitulated their sense of motion and collision. Vaughan's postures, the way in which he held his arms as he moved my wife across the seat, lifting her left knee so that his body was in the fork between her thighs, reminded me of the driver of a complex vehicle, a gymnastic ballet celebrating a new technology. His hands explored the back of her thighs in a slow rhythm, holding her buttocks and lifting her exposed pubis towards his scarred

mouth without touching it. He was arranging her body in a series of
positions, carefully searching the codes of her limbs and musculature.
Catherine seemed still only half aware of Vaughan, holding his penis
in her left hand and sliding her fingers towards his anus as if perform-
ing an act divorced from all feeling. (161)

Such is the new sexuality that *Crash* documents: a formal reenactment
of conceptual equivalencies, a disembodied ritual without affect, a
semiotics without meaning. Do you know the
DMB song "Crash"?

SEX DRIVE
Your puns are
annoying me and I love puns

Without meaning? Isn't the function of signs, even sexual ones, to
signify? Not in the world as surface. The semioeroticism of its new
sexuality serves the purpose not of representation but dissemination.
It distributes conceptual equivalence over the whole semiotic horizon
of cybernetic society. Sexuality becomes the function of a transcul-
tural system of signification and not vice versa. Desire is no longer
a biotic urge impelling an organism that gets represented in private
fantasies but a systemic function structuring an equivalence that
gets disseminated in public reenactments. In *The Atrocity Exhibition*
Ballard makes the canny suggestion that "Freud's classic distinction
between the manifest and latent content of the inner world of the
psyche now has to be applied to the outer world of reality" (98–99).
That "outer world" has acquired the semiotic function Freud ascribed
to the Unconscious. It disseminates sexuality over the whole world as
surface. is This Modernity, or the cyber world?
    Elsewhere Ballard describes the function of the cybernetic system
that disseminates this new sexuality: "Just as the sleeping mind extem-
porizes a narrative form of the random memories veering through
the cortical night, so our waking imaginations are stitching together
a set of narratives to give meaning to the random events that swerve
through our conscious lives. A roadside billboard advertising something or other, to TV programmes or news magazines or the radio
or in-flight movies, or what have you" (*Mississippi Review* 31). The
system that disseminates sexuality is not psychological but cybernetic.
It includes billboards, TV shows, magazines, movies. It goes by the
familiar name of "the media" and stitches together a set of narratives
that structure the otherwise random information circulating throughout cybernetic society. But the "meaning" this semiotic system (re)
produces is not "meaningful" in the traditional sense, since it is always
a reenactment of a purely conceptual equivalence: between her face

and that of the movie star, between my body and that of the automobile, between our sexual postures and those of the porn magazines. It is in this sense that "sex," as Ballard describes it, "has become a sort of communal activity" (*Mississippi Review* 32): the behavioral afterimage of a semiotic system that disseminates sexuality without "meaning." Photography is the means of its dissemination and the automobile the place of its reenactment. Car and photograph, the cultural a priori of this new sexuality, condition the operation of this cybernetic system. Without Vaughan's photographs the sexuality of the body conceptual would be inert, for these photographs advance the logic of equivalence latent in the limbs of the human organism:

> His photographs of sexual acts, of sections of automobile radiator grilles and instrument panels, conjunctions between elbow and chromium window sill, vulva and instrument binnacle, summed up the possibilities of a new logic created by these multiplying artifacts, the codes of a new marriage of sensation and possibility. (106)

These codes are not biological but cybernetic, the function of a semiotic system that disseminates sex as a set of gestures, postures, behaviors, positions. The media lifts sexuality out of the body and onto a surface determined by a new mimetic logic. Specific sexual acts become reenactments of images that pervade the semiotic horizon, which is why the car plays so central a role in this sexual *mimesis*. It is the vehicle of our dreams, and the site of our communal equivalence.

Vaughan imitates in his sexual behavior the imagery that pervades the world as surface and by doing so assimilates himself conceptually to the only transcendental available to such a world: the semiotic system itself. The automobile is simply the site of a conceptualized salvation: *imitatio vehiculi*. Hence Vaughan's curious, compulsive need to imitate the imagery of vehicular homicide. It confirms the possibility of a sexuality wholly liberated from the life of the organism, so completely a semiotic function that it includes even postures of violent death. So observes Ballard observing Vaughan:

> Often I watched him lingering over the photographs of crash fatalities, gazing at their burnt faces with a terrifying concern, as he calculated the most elegant parameters of their injuries, the junctions of their wounded bodies with the fractured windshield and instrument assemblies. He would mimic these injuries in his own driving postures, turning the same dispassionate eyes on the young women he picked up near the airport. Using their bodies, he recapitulated the

deformed anatomies of vehicle crash victims, gently bending the arms of these girls against their shoulders, pressing their knees against his own chest, always curious to see their reactions. (145)

Photograph, automobile, imitation: such are the means to a semiotic transcendence of the life—and the death—of the organic body. Vaughan is the weird messiah of this new salvation.

And the crash is his crucifixion. If the body conceptual is produced and disseminated by means of a semiotics that has the camera and the car as its material conditions, the automobile accident reveals the way that system works. It is the technological equivalent of apocalypse. As its title suggests, *Crash* is not primarily about technology or even sex. It is about catastrophe, a sudden and violent shock to the system that interrupts and illuminates its function. Metal crumples, flesh tears, fluids squirt, signs multiply: CRASH. The word is onomatopoeic of disaster. A car crash enacts the banal apocalypse of the body conceptual, revealing its status as a semiotic, postorganic entity. After his auto wreck, Ballard awakens to a new perception of his body:

> The week after the accident had been a maze of pain and insane fantasies. After the commonplaces of everyday life, with their muffled dramas, all my organic expertise for dealing with physical injury had long been blunted or forgotten. The crash was the only real experience I had been through for years. For the first time I was in physical confrontation with my own body, an inexhaustible encyclopedia of pains and discharges. (39)

Ballard's crash jolts him out of the organic world and into the cybernetic. His body ceases to be a vital organism and becomes, in its most physical experience, a conceptual lexicon, and inexhaustible *encyclopedia* of pains. Trauma to the body reveals the whole system that produces it. Only when something breaks—a tool, a car, a body—is its function fully revealed. Heidegger makes this observation in regard to the broken tool, which illuminates a whole system of relations that remains otherwise unrecognized: "for the circumspection that comes up against the damaging of the tool, [...] the context of equipment is lit up, not as something never seen before, but as a totality constantly sighted beforehand in circumspection. With this totality, however, the world announces itself" (105). For Heidegger as for Ballard, this world is conceptual, since reference, the relation of one sign to another, serves as an "ontological foundation[...]constitutive of worldhood in general" (114). Is it mere coincidence Heidegger's example of the sign constitutive of such a world is an automobile blinker? A failure to signal could mean catastrophe. The broken tool illuminates a totality of relations. The crashed car lights up a system of references. Both reveal a world less substantial than cybernetic, one in which the body is a systems function. Such at least is Ballard's posttraumatic conception of the crash-body. His accident unveils his body's semiotic status in a system as wide as the world as surface. Ballard's metaphysical lust for Catherine shows how far that system extends the body conceptual:

> Every aspect of Catherine at this time seemed a model of something else, endlessly extending the possibilities of her body and personality. As she stepped naked across the floor of the bathroom, pushing past me with a look of nervous distraction; as she masturbated in the bed beside me in the mornings, thighs splayed symmetrically, fingers groveling at her pubis as if rolling to death some small venereal snot; as she sprayed deodorant into her armpits, those tender fossas like mysterious universes; as she walked with me to my car, fingers playing amiably across my left shoulder—all these acts and emotions were ciphers searching for their meaning among the hard, chromium furniture of our minds. A car-crash in which she would die was the one event which would release the codes waiting within her. (180)

Catherine's every move models in its geometry some other aspect of the system, disseminating the body conceptual throughout the world as surface. The shock to this system that the crash inflicts reveals the worldhood of that surface even as it assimilates, in one final, fatal catastrophe, the human organism. This transfiguration is as close to salvation as cybernetic society can come, and Vaughan is its messiah. Its immanence is what makes him so angelic and so appalling, an "ugly golden creature, made beautiful by its scars and wounds" (201). He is the alien evangel of some new semio-gnosis and his crash-body is its risen Christ.

CATASTROPHE AND CRUCIFIXION

Vaughan bears comparison to the old messiah. For nearly two millennia Western culture wound a web of signs around the body of Christ crucified. It is clearly an overstatement, but one worth pondering, to say that this brutalized, broken body set the terms for representation in the culture of the Christian West. Hanging limp from a wooden cross, the body of God was the *locus Christus* of signification. Alpha and Omega, all signs began and ended there. How different

in terms of creating a new semiotic lexicon,

yes ... this is NOT what you've said, though.

the effect of this image of somatic catastrophe from that of Ballard's crash-body. If the latter reveals, in its trauma, its status as semiotic function, the crucified body of Christ asserts instead its own empty organism. Vaughan's is a semiotic body where Christ's is physical. The latter grounds representation in a dead substance that solicits transcendence. Representing the dead substance of the organic body, Christ crucified transcendentalizes representation. It is after all God's body that hangs from the cross. The world that announces itself with the broken body of God is not a semiotic but a sacred totality. The catastrophe of Crucifixion reveals only one meaningful relationship, that between death and Life, us and Him. Through the representation of the body crucified, then, catastrophe effects transcendence.

The myriad images of the Crucifixion that still permeate Western culture disseminate this effect. A brief look at one of the most famous should illustrate the point. The Isenheimer Altar, painted by the mysterious master Matthias Grünewald sometime between 1512 and 1516, presents an image of Christ crucified that has become renowned for its horror. Never has the body of Christ appeared so gruesome (figure 2). As if suspended between the ground below and an unfathomable abyss above, it hangs from a cross, flanked by Johns (the Baptist and the Beloved) and Marys (the Mother and the Magdalen), awaiting a proper burial. Christ's body is unnervingly inert, unambiguously dead. And not merely dead—but rotting. Fingers splayed with *rigor mortis*, toes dripping congealed blood, it bears the viscid signs of impossible suffering. The skin is pierced in a thousand places by thorns that gouged and broke. The wounds have begun to fester, peppering the entire torso with putrid spots. The flesh beneath is cold and sallow, as if hung on a hook to drain. In the hollow just below the ribs on the left gapes an oozing laceration—a new orifice, voluble with blood. Above it the head of Christ drops earthward in decay. Impaled not crowned with thorns, it bows to gravity, a dead weight. The mouth that spoke in cure and parable now grimaces in silence. Its teeth and tongue frame an inner dark; its lips are thick and blue. Grünewald's body of Christ crucified succumbs to putrefaction. It signifies its own inertia: the materiality of a dead and meaningless letter. The pale moon that shines above illuminates only a palpable absence. Christ's body cries in its silence to heaven for restitution.

Hence the cultural function of its representation: to ground transcendence in bodily trauma. A dead and rotting organism needs a meaning that will heal it. Such is the problem that bodily suffering presents: it inspires an absolute solution. As Nietzsche said, not

Figure 2 Panel from the Isenheimer Altar by Matthias Grünewald, closed.

suffering but meaningless suffering is the curse that plagues humanity. The body crucified offers up a meaning that mitigates the curse.
It grounds a transcendence that suffuses and redeems its emptiness.
In this regard it makes perfect sense that the Isenheimer Altar stood
originally in a church that was also a hospital, a place of solace for
those suffering the boil-plague of St. Anthony's fire. Itself a medi-
cament, Grünewald's painting treats the suffering it depicts. As pil-
grims identified their pains with those appearing in the dead flesh of
Christ's body, they awakened to the prospect of divine restitution.
Grünewald's Christ is a subjectivity-machine, redeeming sufferers as
subjects of transcendence. The Isenheimer Altar (re)produces a subjectivity conducive to higher meaning for human suffering, which it
then legitimates by means of a narrative of salvation.

The painting unfolds a story that adds depth to its dismal surface—
literally unfolds, as its panels open to reveal this salubrious meaning
(figure 3). Erupting with movement, light, and color, it confronts the
sufferer with a narrative that opens from within the empty body of
Christ crucified to subsume it in a higher presence. At the center of
the narrative is that body, appearing palpably in three different forms:
newborn, cadaver, and risen Christ. It instantly becomes clear that

Figure 3   Panel from the Isenheimer Altar by Matthais Grünewald, open.

the rotting flesh of Christ crucified amounts only to a static moment in a larger movement that would explain it. Inside Grünewald's Crucifixion hides a metanarrative of salvation. That this metanarrative includes the sumptuous episodes of the Annunciation, Birth, and Resurrection of Christ shows it to be underwritten by the Word of God. But the role of Christ's body in substantiating this Story of stories is what is remarkable here. Its three incarnations center in its substance a logos of transcendence. If for Ballard the body becomes a semiotic function, here it makes semiotics possible. The body crucified grounds the circulation of signs in this metanarrative of salvation. Its putrefying flesh is revealed to be the condition of a semiotics that moves dialectically from birth to resurrection. What at first appeared a dead cadaver signifies instead the antithesis of Christ's thetic birth, the reversal of a body-logic that reaches fulfillment in the resurrection. It doesn't take a Hegel to see that these three bodies substantiate a dialectical logos that subsumes organic suffering. Even their placement—the dead body beneath the newborn, the risen body above both—enacts the logos of the body crucified. This body is not a *function* of signs but their *foundation*. *[handwritten: or ... overstatement]*

And the operation of its logic reproduces a subject of transcendence. As *[handwritten: much?]* Grünewald's painting unfolds, it opens up a higher perspective—again literally. Part of the confusion involved in contemplating this particular Crucifixion comes with the multiple perspectives that swirl around it. Christ on the cross appears directly opposite and lit from above while other figures are lit from the front and appear from various perspectives: John the Baptist from the side, Mary Magdalene from on high, and such others. This multiplication of perspectives deprives any one of absolute authority. Death disrupts the subject as it rots the body. With the opening of the triptych, however, two alternatives emerge. The tableau of Mother Mary all but lacks perspective, a surface in high medieval style ordered by the faint but imperious image at the upper left of God. All is coherent here, but in a condition of innocence prior to the Crucifixion. It is in the dialectical movement to the image of the risen Christ that a new perspective emerges. Its all but unbearable brightness of being brings to the space of the final tableau an unprecedented depth, which the foreshortened postures of the fallen guards beneath only exaggerate. This is a space wholly structured by the subject of transcendence. Here appears in all its glory the ultimate solution to the problem of meaningless suffering: a higher and undying perspective from which to view the body crucified. The Isenheimer Altar reproduces in its viewers this subject of transcendence, to the healthful end of healing bodily miseries with higher meaning.

And what of bodily delight? The subject of transcendence views sexuality from on high, radically devaluing its substantial pleasures. The logic of the body crucified subsumes them in its upward movement, identifying human sexuality with death and promoting a higher, postsexual life. Archetypal unwed mother, Mary holds in her arms the tender body of the infant Christ, the fully developed image of which lies dead and decaying in the tableau immediately beneath her. The organic body fulfills its possibilities only by dying. Brief, then, and lethal are the joys of bodily love. Christ's livid cadaver attests to it loudly, demonstrating that a sexuality *of* the body dies *with* the body. Only when delight originates in not the body but the life above does it lead to something better than a corpse. The Isenheimer Altar conveys this sublimation of organic sexuality by locating high above Christ's limp loincloth a glowing image of God the father, holding in his radiant hands a Sceptre and a Globe. Good sex is God sex. When the life of the body originates above, it transcends the dying animal. In the world of Grünewald's masterpiece, as in the culture of the Christian West, an organic sexuality breeds an ontology of death. The subject of transcendence that the painting reproduces, however, subsumes it in the postsexual perspective of a risen life.

VITAL SIGNS

According to Ballard, all has changed. If the trauma of the body crucified lights up this transcendence, that of the body conceptual reveals its collapse into signs. A postsexual perspective is not possible in a world where the body has been reborn as a semiotic function. Sexuality becomes a matter no longer of life and death but of dissemination. Sown over the whole surface of cybernetic society, it reproduces signs of desire. And because its medium is not organic but semiotic, this sexuality cannot die; it lives persistently as signs. Ballard's crash-body reveals a new alternative to the old transcendence, an eschatological semiotics coextensive with culture. Where once the rotting body of the Crucifixion contained the play of signs, now the ruptured body of a crash multiplies it. Vaughan, the weird messiah of this perpetual resurrection, inhabits a strange new cultural space beyond both the opposition of life and death and the organic body that substantiates it. From his perspective, human life has outlived these distinctions, as Ballard observes through his eyes: "I looked out at the drivers of the cars alongside us, visualizing their lives in the terms Vaughan had defined for them. For Vaughan they were already dead" (137). Already dead because never alive, not in the traditional sense. Theirs is an existence made real by not body and blood but speed and steel. Sexuality sustains such an existence by reproducing appearance rather than substance. Hence the high eroticism of a crash: it releases a sexuality of signs that supercedes the organism: "This pervasive sexuality filled the air, as if we were members of a congregation leaving after a sermon urging us to celebrate our sexualities with friends and strangers, and were driving into the night to imitate the bloody eucharist we had observed with the most unlikely partners" (157). This new Eucharist transignifies where the old one transfigures, resurrecting the sexuality of signs in the catastrophe of a crash.

Crash thus documents the obsolescence of transcendence, its collapse into a sexual semiotics driven by cars and cameras. In the mediascape of cybernetic society, the new transcendental is the media, sexuality its Paraclete, and Vaughan its only begotten son—at least for now. The body crucified has finally died and in its place has arisen the body conceptual. Vaughan's genius—and his dark example—is simply to give his life over to the semiotic system that produces and disseminates it, working ultimately to unite them. No subject of transcendence emerges to meliorate a suffering body. Signification assimilates both, rendering misery superfluous. What matters to Vaughan is total equivalence between the body conceptual and a semiotic system that disseminates the life of signs. It falls to Ballard, the accidental apostle, to witness this transignification. He sees that Vaughan's life is irreducible to the organic: "Vaughan's body was a collection of loosely coupled planes. The elements of his musculature and personality were suspended a few millimetres apart" (198). Ballard sees too that such a life fulfills itself, not in some higher meaning, but in the system of signification itself.

His infatuation with Vaughan unfolds incrementally according to the logos of that system, as Ballard recognizes in retrospect: "Thinking of the photographs in the questionnaires, I knew that they defined the logic of a sexual act between Vaughan and myself" (137). Because "for Vaughan the motor-car was the sexual act's greatest and only true locus" (171), Ballard's initiation into the mysteries of the body conceptual can only occur in transit, the car serving as a signification module, a steel bower less of sexual than semiotic intercourse: "His attraction lay not so much in a complex of familiar anatomical triggers[...]but in the stylization of posture achieved between Vaughan and the car. Detached from his automobile, particularly his own emblem-filled highway cruiser, Vaughan ceased to hold any interest" (117). Only when reconstituted conceptually by the interior of an automobile does Vaughan's body seems appealing—that is, only when assimilated to the sexuality of signs. Then it can circulate throughout the semiotic system and the world as surface.

The epiphany of this system and thus the body conceptual that it disseminates comes in the LSD apocalypse that consummates Ballard's liaison with Vaughan. Like a car wreck or a crucifixion, hallucinogens crash the subject. The benign catastrophe they inflict also lights up "a totality constantly sighted beforehand in circumspection." Where the catastrophe of the Crucifixion reveals a compensatory transcendence, this one reveals its collapse into the world as surface:

> An armada of angelic creatures, each surrounded by an immense corona of light, was landing on the motorway on either side of us, sweeping down in opposite directions. They soared past, a few feet above the ground, landing everywhere on these endless runways that covered the landscape. I realized that all these roads and expressways had been built by us unknowingly for their reception. (199)

These angels herald not the risen Christ but his latest avatar, the disseminated Vaughan. In this acid-driven vision of the world as surface Vaughan has become coextensive with its totality, as Ballard will as well through their semiosexual union. Vaughan *excarnates* the system that disseminates the body conceptual: "I was sure that the white ramp [of the motorway] was a section of Vaughan's body" (205). Assimilated to the world as surface he achieves the perpetual resurrection of signs: "The spurs of deformed metal, the triangles of fractured glass, were signals that had lain unread for years in this shabby grass, ciphers translated by Vaughan and myself as we sat with our arms around each other" (200). When Ballard finally fulfills the sexual logic of their liaison, he experiences with his new messiah this resurrection without transcendence, this rebirth of a crash-body neither living nor dead:

> Together we showed our wounds to each other, exposing the scars on our chests and hands to the beckoning injury sites on the interior of the car, to the pointed sills of the chromium ashtrays, to the lights of a distant intersection. In our wounds we celebrated the re-birth of the traffic-slain dead, the deaths and injuries of those we had seen dying by the roadside and the imaginary wounds and postures of the millions yet to die. (203)

With the collapse of transcendence into a culturally pervasive semiotic system comes new life everlasting—*in haec signi.*

This, then, is the mediascape of cybernetic society according to Ballard: a world as surface continuous with the semiotic system that reproduces it. In such a world the human body is transformed, best revealed by the banal, pervasive catastrophe of a crash. The crash serves cybernetic society as the Crucifixion served the Christian West, its images circulating to sustain the possibility of another life. Ballard's crash-body cannot die. It revives with every traffic fatality. Ballard sees in Vaughan's example the life of signs, even after Vaughan's "death": "I thought of Vaughan, covered with flies like a resurrected corpse, watching me with a mixture of irony and affection. I knew that Vaughan could never really die in a car-crash, but would in some way be re-born through those twisted radiator grilles and cascading windshield glass" (210). Vaughan lives in the myriad crashes that resurrect the life of signs. What is the death of the organic body to this system of signification? A superfluity, a nostalgia. Among contemporary artists Andy Warhol best understands that the crash is our crucifixion the crash-body our alpha and omega. *White Burning Car III* (1963) captures the logic of an atrocity that transignifies. Crash!

CODA: PRINCESS DIE! STOP. IT,

It was in a strange state of surreality that I awoke to the sound of a bereaved radio reporter quietly announcing the death in a car crash of Princess Diana. Was it a sick if inevitable joke? A pirated BBC broadcast of Ballard's latest atrocity fiction? For a few peculiar moments I felt I had been translated onto the pages of some hyperrealist sequel to *Crash*. The scene was all too familiar: the crumpled Mercedes, the oozing fluids, the broken body of a celebrity known to everybody, with peculiar intimacy, through media images. And the photographers, the real makers of the immortal Princess Di: brutes clutching pistol grips and training their cameras on her corpse. The suggestion that they were responsible came as a supreme banality. Of course. The logic of the life of signs requires their participation in this sacrifice. The surprise is not that Princess Di is dead, or that she died in a car crash, or that photographers had a hand in it. These are the simple facts of semiotic life. The surprise is how perfectly Ballard documented it all twenty years in advance. He is the prophet of the new life of signs, the *vita nuova* of crash and camera. The remaining question, the darker question, is how the death of Princess Di will affect our sexuality. Are we, with Vaughan, at one with her in the cockpit of that fated Mercedes?

4

SCORE, SCAN, SCHIZ

"But that's why I started on drugs," Gloria said.
"Because of the Grateful Dead?"
"Because," Gloria said, "everyone wanted me to do it.
I'm tired of doing what other people want me to do."
Philip K. Dick, *Valis*

Drugs are a fact of life in cybernetic society. Who can survive without them? Recreational or medicinal, scored or prescribed, drugs allay all kinds of physical and spiritual dis-ease. No one describes their cultural function with greater acuity than Philip K. Dick. In novel after cy-fi novel, Dick examines the role drugs play in a culture increasingly colonized by technologies of simulation and surveillance. This preoccupation reaches tragic proportions in one of his truly great books, *A Scanner Darkly*. Published in 1977 and set in 1994, it tells the story of an undercover narcotics agent given the odd assignment of keeping *himself* under surveillance. *A Scanner Darkly* restages the tragedy of Oedipus in a cybernetic setting, where the imperative "know thyself" turns tricky because there is no self to know, only roles and representations, profiles and simulacra. Under such circumstances the future collapses into the present: the chronological distance in Dick's novel between 1977 and 1994 seems negligible, rendering the latter less a movement beyond the 1970s than their repetition. The 2006 screen adaptation of *A Scanner Darkly*—in trippy rotoscope—provides an occasion for raising questions of drugs and identity yet again, in another decade and a new millennium. While the film lacks the novel's tragic force, it testifies nonetheless to the pervasiveness of drugs in cybernetic society and the opportunity they create for policies of surveillance and control. Released during the second administration of George W. Bush, the film *A Scanner Darkly* revives the critical pique of Dick's novel. If the Bush administrations solidified terms for contemporary drug policy, Dick responds with baleful clairvoyance over thirty years in advance.

MARKET FORCES

What happened to the war on drugs? In a word or rather a number: 9/11. With the declaration of a war on terror, the United States, the world's only superpower, discovered the perfect, perpetual enemy. Drug lords and junkies could take a backseat to cagey brown-skinned terrorists everywhere and nowhere, the ultimate threat to national security.[1] The war on drugs was not won so much as reinvented as social policy. It still rages unabated, but transparently. In fiscal year 2009 the Bush administration requested $14.1 billion dollars to fund it, an increase of $459 million over the amount allocated in 2008, constituting a spending rate of almost $600 per second (*2009 Budget Summary* 1). The money piles up invisibly, eclipsed to public awareness by the high cost of conventional military adventures in Iraq and Afghanistan (www. drugsense.org/wodclock.html). If dollars are any measure of social menace, however, drugs remain an enemy of lurid proportions. That is how President George W. Bush describes their danger in his statement to Congress accompanying his 2008 National Drug Control Policy:

> My Administration published its first National Drug Control Strategy in 2002, inspired by a great moral imperative: we must reduce illegal drug use because, over time, drugs rob men, women, and children of their dignity and of their character. (iii)

As a moral menace, drugs present a clear and present danger to the American people. That this danger, although not conventionally military, remains highly organized and aggressively violent is the lesson of the *National Drug Threat Assessment of 2008* prepared by the National Drug Intelligence Center of the U.S. Department of Justice. There drugs present a menace as mortal as it is moral:

> The trafficking and abuse of illicit drugs are a great burden on citizens, private businesses, financial institutions, public health systems, and law enforcement agencies in the United States. These burdens are manifested and measured in many ways; however the most striking evidence of the impact of drug trafficking and abuse on U.S. society is the thousands of drug-related deaths (overdoses, homicides, accidents, or other fatal incidents) that occur each year. (iii)

By the blunt measure of body count, drugs present a greater threat to American life than those devious terrorists.

Fortunately for us all, the Bush administrations made great strides in combating this scourge, at least by its own testimony. Its 2002 National

Drug Control Strategy promoted a new approach to the problem, shifting emphasis away from the war on drugs and toward a less ostensibly militarized strategy, described as "a balanced approach to reducing drug use in America focusing on stopping use before it starts, healing America's drug users, and disrupting the market for illegal drugs" (*National Drug Control Strategy* 1). This three-pronged approach set ambitious goals: a 10 percent reduction in youth drug use in two years and a 25 percent reduction in five. Those years have passed, and the good news is that National Drug Control Strategy is proving effective: "Results from the *Monitoring the Future* survey for calendar year 2002 would reveal a downturn in youth drug use after a decade in which rates of use had risen and remained at high levels. Six years later, this decline in youth drug use continues at a rate almost precisely consistent with the Administration's goals" (1). Uncanny prognostications! In his address to Congress, President Bush celebrates this impressive achievement:

> We have learned much about the nature of drug use and drug markets, and have demonstrated what can be achieved with a balanced strategy that puts resources where they are needed most. Prevention programs are reaching Americans in their communities, schools, workplaces, and through the media, contributing to a 24 percent decline in youth drug use since 2001. (iii)

Drug use is down among America's youth, the population most at risk for long-term debility and even death. Stop drug use before it starts and you choke the market by eliminating consumers.

It would appear that the Bush administration's Drug Control Strategy is less military than economic. Market trends in consumption are down, bolstering arguments for regulation. But like any market analysis, this one is only as good as its numbers. Take that 24 percent decline, for instance. It turns out to be painfully hard to verify. The graph that illustrates this trend entitled "Current Use of Any Illegal Drug Among Youth" claims the *Monitoring the Future* survey as its source, a study designed and conducted by the University of Michigan (available at www.monitoringthefuture.org). The small print indicates that the decisive numbers derive from "special tabulations" that are "calculated from figures having more precision than shown" (1). Crunch the numbers from *Monitoring the Future*, and the result is indeed a 24 percent decrease in drug use *during the previous thirty days* among eighth, tenth, and twelfth graders—a commendable achievement.

But if one reads the numbers vertically rather than horizontally a quite different result emerges (Table 1). While overall drug use among

Table 1 Trends in Lifetime Prevalence of Use of Various Drugs for Eighth, Tenth, and Twelfth Graders

	2000	2001	2002	2003	2004	2005	2006	2007
Eighth Grade	26.8	26.8	24,5	22.8	21.5	21.4	20.9	19.0
Tenth Grade	45.6	45.6	24.5	41.4	39.8	38.2	36.1	35.6
Twelfth Grade	54.0	53.9	53.0	51.1	51.1	50.4	48.2	46.8

Source: *Monitoring the Future*, 2007 (www.monitoringthefuture.org).

high school students declined, the relative percentage of new users *actually increased*. The Bush administration's National Drug Control Strategy may have decreased the total number of users in high school, but it appears perversely to have produced an increase in the relative number of new users between grades eight and twelve during the same period. Even given the overall gains made by National Drug Control Strategy, proportionally more students tried drugs between eighth and twelfth grade in 2007 than 2001. Peculiar. A general reduction in drug use obscures an increase in new users. But success is success ("What was once an escalating drug problem has been turned around" (*Strategy* 5), and the Bush administration credits its tough Drug Control Strategy.

Measured in dollars, "Stopping Use Before It Starts," the least important part of that three-pronged strategy, would cost $1.5 billion in fiscal year 2009. "Healing America's Users" would require $3.4 billion. By far the biggest chunk of the Drug Control Strategy budget, however, was requested for "Disrupting the Market": $9.2 billion. A shift in rhetoric accompanied these requests. The Bush administration would not conduct a *war* on drugs—after all, it had more pressing military adventures to manage. It would instead disrupt the *market* for drugs. What was once a military has become an economic campaign. Or so the language suggests. However, methods of economic disruption are perilously similar to those of military intervention: interdiction, capture, and eradication, through violence if necessary. Market disruption mobilizes a whole range of enforcement agencies that combat local consumption and global production. The frontline of the operation comprises cops on any city street: success "is due in large part to the tireless work of the 732,000 sworn State and local law enforcement officers throughout the Nation" (*Strategy* 37).

They work tirelessly but hardly alone. They are part an archipelago of Intelligence and Security agencies whose duties are complimentary and whose reach is global. The Drug Control Strategy Budget names twelve in all and clearly if chillingly details the way the prevention of drug production, distribution, and consumption serves as the occasion for militarization of these agencies in the name of domestic security.[2] With the emergence of terrorism as global threat, this move appears increasingly justifiable, as drug production comes to be seen as a means of financing terrorist activity. In the words of the *National Drug Control Strategy*, the United States views

> the global drug trade as a serious threat to our national security because of its capacity to destabilize democratic and friendly governments, undermine U.S. foreign policy objectives, and generate violence and human suffering on a scale that constitutes a public security threat. [...] The drug trade also serves as a critical source of revenue for some terrorist groups and insurgencies. (34)

Local drug use articulates with a network of production and distribution that is worldwide and deleterious to democracy. To discourage drug use at home is to disrupt drug commerce abroad.

Local and global security become mutually constitutive—and justifying. With the emergence after 9/11 of the notion of "narcoterrorism" (defined by the 2005 reauthorization of *the Patriot Act* as "the knowing contribution of ill-gotten drug gains to terrorists or terrorist organizations" (http://thomas.loc.gov/cgi-bin/query/F?c109:6:./temp/~c109jyxIgb:e110467), market disruption shades into the war on terror. Or as the *Drug Control Strategy* puts it, "In a post-9/11 world, U.S. counterdrug efforts serve dual purposes, protecting Americans from drug trafficking and abuse while also strengthening and reinforcing our national security" (34). Perhaps that accounts for an interesting pattern in Drug Control Strategy funding between the years 2002 and 2009. Numbers unabashedly indicate that funding for "Total Prevention" has steadily fallen as that for "Supply Reduction" has increased. In 2002, Prevention consumed 45.6 percent of the Drug Control Strategy Budget, Reduction 54.4 percent. Things change drastically by the 2009 request, with 34.8 percent of total funding going to Prevention and 65.2 percent to Reduction. That is a hefty 10 percent increase in funding devoted to market disruption—with a complimentary decrease in money marked for prevention and treatment. Even as it lauds a 24 percent reduction in drug use among youth at home, the Bush administration quietly but steadily increased funding for operations to disrupt drug markets locally and globally. Beneath this rhetoric of market disruption flourishes a funding pattern whose purpose turns patently military when it combines with those of an interminable war on terror. Market disruption by any other name would be war, begun in part by narco-terrorists and waged by the alliance of security and intelligence agencies funded by the National Drug Control Strategy Budget. Thus militarized, economic disruption becomes an armed strategy of interdiction, capture, and eradication, a permanent and burgeoning budget item for a perpetual war on terror. There is muscular cause for national confidence: "The Administration's first *National Drug Control Strategy* was based on a simple truth: when we push against the drug problem, it recedes. [...] we have pushed back hard—and the drug problem has indeed receded" (36). Such are the rewards of enforcement and interdiction.

THE 1970S FOREVER

Is enforcement the best policy? Perhaps, if drug abuse is a cause of social ills. If drug abuse is an effect of those ills, however, then more Americans than just users, dealers, and terrorists are implicated. This is the possibility that current National Drug Control Strategy refuses to confront. As long as drug abuse appears to be a personal failing or a public menace, the social and economic conditions that produce it remain invisible to all but their victims. As long as search and seizure sets the terms for combating abuse, those victims will get what they deserve. Under such circumstances a policy of enforcement does much more than just prohibited deviant behavior. It privileges certain members of society while pathologizing others. Such effects are obviously not the stated object of law enforcement, but they nonetheless consolidate, in the name of justice, an unjust social order.

It is to sources other than the Office of National Drug Control Policy that we should turn for an analysis of such possibilities. The work of Philip K. Dick remains in this regard extremely valuable. His firsthand experience of west coast 1960s' counterculture gives his drug fictions special force in a cybernetic society where drugs splice users into various circuits of control. Many of his novels examine this effect and its implications for conventional notions of representation, identity, law, and democracy. The pharmaceutical face-off of *The Zap Gun* (1967), the hallucinated realities of *The Three Stigmata of Palmer Eldritch* (1964), the tempogogic drug trips of *Now Wait for Last Year* (1966) all challenge the accepted version of reality by testing it against induced alternatives. For Dick such alternatives are no less real for being drug induced. In an essay entitled "Drugs, Hallucinations, and the Quest for Reality," he argues that drugs produce not a counterfeit reality but a more complete one. The "pseudoschizophrenic sensory distortions brought about by chemicals such as LSD and organic toxins such as are found in some mushrooms" are "not delusions at all, but are, on the contrary, accurate perceptions of an area of reality that the rest of us cannot (thank the Lord) reach" (*Shifting Realties* 171). Drugs multiply perceptions—of how things are and the way they work. Drugs allow glimpses of a reality most people know little about.[3] But not without a cost. Dick is as aware of their dangers as their delights. In *A Scanner Darkly*, he assesses enforcement strategies first instituted as policy in the early 1970s and shows how they help produce the social and economic causes of the problem they purport to remedy.[4]

A Scanner Darkly anticipates in reverse a nostalgia for the 1970s promoted by films such as *Pulp Fiction, Boogie Nights, The Ice Storm, Almost Famous*, and even its own adaptation. Dick would call it an instance of *déjà prevu*—remembering a future that never arrives because it is already here. This nostalgia might also suggest a past that never left. That is how Dick imagines the future in *A Scanner Darkly*: as a loop that moves without a history. And indeed, his critique of the social and economic conditions of drug abuse remains uncannily pertinent today. *A Scanner Darkly* depicts *America* on drugs and suffering a culturally pervasive dependency irreducible to individual agency. Not personal weakness, culpability, or need perpetuate this culture of addiction, but specific social conditions that include consumption, class, and incarceration. Under such conditions all of us are hooked. The doper lives openly what every consumer senses but cannot quite perceive: that life in cybernetic society languishes between highs, that its only meaning is the next score.

"LIKE WHEN YOU BUY DOPE"

Dick never lets one forget that drugs are something one *buys*. The heavy doper lives to score and scores to live: "He felt lousy because he had only three hundred tabs of slow death left in his stash. Buried in his back yard under his camellia, the hybrid one with the cool big blossoms that didn't burn brown in the spring. I only got a week's supply, he thought. What then when I'm out? Shit" (8). So frets feckless Charles Freck, addicted to "Substance D," known in doper circles as "death." Life has become a terminal pursuit of the substance that sustains it. But living this circle of addiction differs less from straight life than stereotype would insist. In the "Author's Note" appended to his novel, Dick compares the pace of the doper's existence to that of the straight's: "It is…only a speeding up, an intensifying, of the ordinary human existence. It is not different from your life-style, it is only faster. It all takes place in days or weeks or months instead of years. 'Take the cash and let the credit go,' as Villon said in 1460" (277). The appeal of addiction comes in part from the ecstatic speed of dying. The addict hastens toward his end.

But never, as Dick's closing quotation indicates, alone. "Take the cash…": arising from the dim beginnings of bourgeois culture, Villon's recommendation locates the lethal speed of addiction in the social space of a cash and carry economy. The doper is the capitalist purified: cash sustains a life otherwise without credit. By insisting upon the fiscal conditions of drug abuse, Dick implicates the whole economy in which substance acquires cash value through exchange. Such is the lesson of Charles Freck's dream of a truly utopian drugstore: "In his fantasy number he was driving past the Thrifty Drugstore and they had a huge window display; bottles of slow death, cans of slow death, jars and bathtubs and vats and bowls of slow death, millions of caps and tabs and hits of slow death, slow death mixed with speed and junk and barbiturates and psychedelics, everything—and a giant sign: YOUR CREDIT IS GOOD HERE. Not to mention: LOW PRICES, LOW-EST IN TOWN" (8). To understand America's drug habit, Dick starts in a drug*store*.

Cybernetic society has a counter that runs its whole length, dividing over-the-counter medicine from under-the-counter dope. Whether legal or illegal, drugs are commodities acquired through exchange. They resemble the myriad other commodities that circulate in a capitalist economy, so much so that they become Dick's trope in *A Scanner Darkly* for the commodity itself. That is the gist of the following exchange between the novel's protagonist, Robert Arctor, and his sometime girlfriend/dealer, Donna Hawthorne:

> "*Buy?*" She studied his face uncertainly. "What do you mean by *buy?*"
>
> "Like when you buy dope," he said. "A dope deal. Like now." He got out his wallet. "I give you money, right?"
>
> Donna nodded, watching him obediently (actually more out of politeness) but with dignity. With a certain reserve.
>
> "And then you hand me a bunch of dope for it," he said, holding out the bills. "What I mean by *buy* is an extension into the greater world of human business transactions of what we have present now, with us, as dope deals."
>
> "I think I see," she said, her large dark eyes placid but alert. She was willing to learn. (147)

If drugs represent commodities in the greater world of business transactions, then capitalism is a drug economy through and through.
That is the polemical thrust of *A Scanner Darkly*. America's drug
problem cannot be separated from its economic foundations. Saying
"No" to drugs would mean saying "No" to the whole economy of
exchange.

Marx defines the commodity as "a thing that by its properties
satisfies human wants of some sort or another" (437). Because the
specific character of those wants is superfluous, a thing becomes a
commodity simply by providing satisfaction. It is clear enough why
drugs of all kinds fall into this category. Whether relief from pain or
release from drudgery, the satisfaction they offer makes life better.
Hence Charles Freck's joy at the prospect of a score:

> Happiness, he thought, is knowing you got some pills.
>
> The day outside the car, and all the busy people, the sunlight and
> activity, streamed past unnoticed; he was happy.
>
> Look what he had found by chance—because, in fact, a black-and-
> white had accidentally paced him. An unexpected new supply of
> Substance D. What more could he ask out of life? He could probably
> now count on two weeks lying ahead of him, nearly *half a month*,
> before he croaked or nearly croaked—withdrawing from Substance D
> made the two the same. Two weeks! His heart soared, and he smelled,
> for a moment, coming in from the open windows of the car, the brief
> excitement of spring. (16)

Substance D produces a satisfaction that sustains Charles Freck. This
particular commodity is the substance of things hoped for, and for its
consumers there is no life without it. But the satisfaction it produces
is always *re*produced too, the repetition of an earlier satisfaction.
One score incites another, and another. A logic of need structures an
economy of exchange, and the commodities that reproduce it incul-
cate dependency. By using drugs as a trope for commodities in general Dick suggests that an economy of exchange breeds a culture of
addiction.

In this regard, dope is a peculiar trope. It is a thing that satisfies human wants and yet, unlike other commodities, it warrants
prohibition.[5] Many drugs today are controlled substances; their
exchange above *and* below the counter proceeds by law.[6] The history
of their regulation is a surprisingly short one. The great nineteenth-
century habitués like Coleridge and De Quincey belong to an era
before prohibition turned drug users into junkies. From its start drug

regulation was more than merely prophylactic and its application more than merely personal. The earliest prohibition in the United States—an 1875 San Francisco ordinance against smoking opium—targeted Chinese laborers blamed for taking jobs from whites after the completion of the transcontinental railroad. Such selectivity came to characterize federal legislation as well. The Harrison Act of 1914, the nation's first comprehensive drug law, was passed in part out of fear that cocaine-crazed blacks posed a threat to white society; the Marijuana Tax Act of 1937 was instituted in part out of concern that Mexican workers were displacing whites as farm laborers. When the Comprehensive Drug Abuse and Control Act of 1970 systematized federal drug regulation it did nothing to address social selectivity. Rather, it institutionalized that effect by establishing the controlled substance as a legal category.[7]

Why control a substance, anyway? Obviously to control its users. But the legal status of the controlled substance reveals something interesting about the way commodities in general induce control. Legal regulation compromises the fetishism of commodities—one of Dick's best insights. It reveals the trace of a social relation where, strictly speaking, none should be visible. In the familiar passage on commodity fetishism from *Capital, Volume 1*, Marx remarks that "a commodity is [...] a mysterious thing, simply because in it the social character of men's labor appears to them as an objective character stamped upon that labor" (446). The function of the commodity—and here it turns fetishistic—is to translate social relations into abstract relations. Through exchange it acquires value, abstract equivalence with other commodities that occludes their material differences, and as Marx puts it, "value...converts every product into a social hieroglyphic" (449). The problem of commodity fetishism becomes one of representation. Commodities obscure the material and social relations that produce them, while their hieroglyphics represent a lie against life.

An incompletely fetishized commodity, however, would translate social relations badly, menacing the smooth operation of the hieroglyphics that represent the real. That is exactly how drugs work for Dick: they slur the speech of the capitalist real. Far from inducing a dangerous unreality, they *betray the irreality of the real itself*. By producing a bad translation of social relations, drugs allow them to be perceived. From this perspective drugs are menacing as much as fractured signs as addictive substances. Their danger lies in their failure to signify transparently, which means consistently with the codes of fully fetishized commodities in cybernetic society. Such substances require control not for their side effects but for their sign effects, the tendency to betray their hieroglyphic function. In this they recover, if but partially, social relations that the commodity functions to occlude, exposing not only the abstract logic of commodity fetishism but also the irreality of appearances. Drugs serve in a sense as a commodity with a conscience. They subject the capitalist real to a homeopathic critique by failing, as substances requiring control, to represent it faithfully.

In *A Scanner Darkly,* drugs fracture the hieroglyphics of the commodity by revealing the violence that sustains them. In this regard Charles Freck's drugstore fantasy continues to be instructive. Along with the usual commodities he sees displayed in the windows of the Thrifty Drugstore—"combs, bottles of mineral oil, spray cans of deodorant, . . . crap like that" (8)—he imagines something more satisfying stashed out of sight:

> I bet the pharmacy in the back has slow death under lock and key in an unstepped-on, pure, unadulterated, uncut form, he thought as he drove from the parking lot onto Harbor Boulevard, into the afternoon traffic. About a fifty-pound bag. (8)

As the zone where controlled substance acquires the status of legitimate commodity, the drugstore is a space of strange encryptions. There a thing like substance D both is and is not legal. To the good consumer it is a regular commodity, available for the right price in the prescribed dose; to the drugstore cowboy it is contraband. As Avital Ronell points out in *Crack Wars,* "The drug store figures a legalized reproach to uncontrolled or street drugs but at the same time argues for the necessity of a certain drug culture" (96). The Thrifty, as Freck calls it, splits the difference between over- and under-the-counter encryptions.

It also institutionalizes the aggression that sustains consumption, which is why Freck's fantasy quickly turns violent:

> He wondered when and how they unloaded the fifty-pound bag of Substance D at the Thrifty Pharmacy every morning, from wherever it came from—God knew, maybe from Switzerland or maybe from another planet where some wise race lived. They'd deliver probably real early, and with armed guards—the Man standing there with Laser rifles looking mean, the way the Man always did. Anybody rip off my slow death, he thought through the Man's head, I'll snuff them. (8)

Substance D, as controlled substance, requires armed distribution. Its commodity status legitimates violence—lethal if necessary—against those who refuse to play by the rules of exchange. Drugs thus manifest the violence of exchange in the capitalist real, and the drugstore institutionalizes it. There is an aggression built into the commodity that its fetishism obscures. The hieroglyphics of the controlled substance translate it badly, allowing a glimpse of economic violence, a fact of life Freck later encounters outside a shopping center: "He watched the uniformed armed guards at the mall gate checking out each person. Seeing that the man or woman matched his or her credit card and that it hadn't been ripped off, sold, bought, used fraudulently" (10). So fundamental is the use of force to the whole fantasia of exchange that the good consumer remains oblivious to it. Armed guards at malls appear perfectly natural—even somehow necessary.

But Freck's perception of the violence of exchange lasts only a moment. The drugstore also functions to hide the violence it institutionalizes and distributes. Pondering the logic of its operation, Freck concludes that the drugstore itself remains innocent of such effects:

> But in actuality he knew better; the authorities snuffed or sent up everybody selling or transporting or using, so in that case the Thrifty Drugstore—all the millions of Thrifty Drugstores—would get shot or bombed out of business or anyhow fined. More likely just fined. The Thrifty had pull. Anyhow, how do you shoot a chain of big drugstores? Or put them away?
>
> They just got ordinary stuff, he thought as he cruised along. (8)

Freck reasons from appearances to assert the innocence of Thrifty drugstores: they must be legitimate because they have not been shot; they have not been shot because they are everywhere. Conclusion: there is nothing sinister about them. They just got ordinary stuff. His reasoning may not be cogent, but it is representative of the sort that sustains the capitalist real. The belief in a centralized source of violence ("the authorities") produces a nonknowledge of its ubiquity. What Freck sees but fails to perceive is that precisely because drugstores cannot be shot they are implicated in the violence of exchange. As a place where economic violence acquires material and social legitimacy, the drugstore is a zone of unknowing.

In other words the drugstore replicates specific nonknowledges without which life in cybernetic society would remain unthinkable. It produces appearances such as the distinction between commodity and controlled substance in order to legitimate the way things are, hiding an underlying violence. In the estimation of Slavoj Žižek, this is precisely how the capitalist real works: commodity exchange produces social relations that obscure knowledge of their effects. As he puts it in *The Sublime Object of Ideology*,

> the social effectivity of the exchange process is a kind of reality which is possible only on condition that the individuals partaking in it are *not* aware of its proper logic; that is, a kind of reality *whose very ontological consistency implies a certain non-knowledge of its participants*—if we come to "know too much," to pierce the true functioning of social reality, this reality would dissolve itself. (20–21)

This is exactly what happens to Ragle Gumm, hero of Dick's *Time Out of Joint* (1959), who sees reality literally dissolve before his eyes to reveal its status as illusion. For Dick as for Žižek, a nonknowledge of the capitalist real is necessary for its operation. In *A Scanner Darkly*, however, no centralized authority produces that nonknowledge, as in the earlier novel. It lacks a single location, a stable origin. Rather the capitalist real produces a multiplicity of nonknowledges. Because commodity exchange both requires and replicates these nonknowledges, the business of such businesses as the Thrifty is to distribute them. Not the commodity itself but replicated nonknowledges sustain appearances in the capitalist real. Hence the rallying cry of straight culture: JUST SAY (K)NO(W).

"You Gotta Always Be Able to Come Up with a Name, Your Name"

But *who* knows, anyway? If one of the functions of the drugstore is to distribute these nonknowledges, then as long as the difference between legal commodity and controlled substance holds true, the *knower* knows. The priority of the legal commodity, to put the point another way, substantiates a particular subjectivity, transparent to itself and secure in its knowledge. Former "drug czar" William Bennett provides a happy instance of this assurance in his answer to the question of the appropriateness of a drug policy of enforcement:

> Should we have drug education programs or should we have [a] tough policy [of enforcement]? If I have the choice of only one, I will take policy every time because I *know* children. And you might say this is not a very romantic view of children, not a very rosy view of children. And I would say, "You're right." (138, my italics)

Bennett knows best. Children will take drugs if given the chance, making search and seizure the only mature policy, an attitude that still informs today's National Drug Control Policy. The paternalism of this knowledge is obvious, as is its condescension toward young people. Interestingly, Dick describes dopers as children, but to quite different ends: "They wanted to have a good time, but they were like children playing in the street; [...] and then the punishment was beyond belief" (*Scanner* 276). Although as aware as any Republican of the dangers of drug abuse, and more experienced than most, Dick resists the paternalistic knowledge of enforcement. He emphasizes instead the playfulness of childhood, and the tragic fact that to persist in playing is to court catastrophe. A more authoritarian knowledge denigrates not only young people but all who, like Dick's dopers, somehow resemble them. It cultivates in advance a dangerous class of refractory individuals who would resist paternal authority and the culpability it presumes. The knowledge that National Drug Control Policy espouses is hierarchical and imperial, obtuse to the economic and social conditions that give rise to the wrongs it pursues.

Dick trumps it by describing the social affinities of a subjectivity that eschews those wrongs. He shows that the material substrate of the subject who knows best turns out to be the commodity itself, that hieroglyphic of social relations. It grounds identity in the formal properties of its fetishism: a subjectivity suited to exchange, the consciousness of convenience in the capitalist real. Žižek describes how such a subject arises as an afterimage of the commodity: "the commodity-form articulates in advance the anatomy, the skeleton of the Kantian transcendental subject" (16). It does so through its strange attribute of exchangeability:

> The exchange of commodities implies a double abstraction: the abstraction from changeable character of the commodity during the act of exchange and the abstraction from the concrete, empirical, sensual, particular character of the commodity. (17)

This double abstraction, which allows exchange and produces the fetish, reveals in advance the a priori structure of the transcendental subject. For Žižek that subject becomes thinkable only as an effect of the commodity's double abstraction. It arises conceptually in formal homology to the commodity as fetish, which, though doubly abstract, remains nonetheless real. It is in this sense that Žižek can conclude that "*the 'real abstraction'* [the commodity fetish] *is the unconscious of the transcendental subject*, the support of objective-universal scientific knowledge" (18, italics in the original). Here, then, is the ultimate guarantor of a subjectivity suited to exchange and capable of the kind of knowledge National Drug Control Strategy presumes. The transcendental ego is a sublime afterimage of the commodity in the capitalist real.

As such it legitimates an identity without social affinities. That is the lesson of Charles Freck's fantasy of police interrogation: "To survive in this police state, he thought, you gotta always be able to come up with a name, your name. At all times. That's the first sign they look for that you're wired, not being able to figure out who the hell you are" (9). A name stands alone, and not to have one is to fall into a class that poses a danger to society. Subjectivity in the capitalist real produces such distinctions just as commodities circulate to preserve them. Names and goods reinforce each other while guaranteeing that those who lack belong to a dangerous class.[8] Dick illustrates this logic in the fortuitous observation Charles Freck makes of security guards at a shopping mall checking shoppers' IDs. You are what you buy or you are under suspicion.

So in a real sense the individual exists in the image of available commodities. His or her life replicates that of things that circulate to provide satisfaction. That explains the comfortable conventionality of Robert Arctor's former life. He enjoyed awhile the average satisfaction of a suburban family life built of bourgeois dreams and purchases: "there had been a wife much like other wives, two small daughters, a stable household that got swept and cleaned and emptied out daily, the dead newspapers not even opened carried from the front walk to the garbage pail, or even, sometimes, read" (64). Arctor lived in the image of things purchased to satisfy needs. But when reaching one evening for a popcorn popper, he smashed his head on a kitchen cabinet, and the pain awakened him to a violence he had not known before: "he hated his wife, his two daughters, his whole house, the back yard with its power mower, the garage, the radiant heating system, the front yard, the fence, the whole fucking place and everyone in it" (64).

It is the same violence Charles Freck saw when he imagined Substance D stockpiled in the back of the Thrifty. The violence there reinforced the operation of exchange. Here it accompanies the perception that things obtained through exchange induce dependency. The violence of exchange invisibly invests the subject, erupting at that moment when, by some blunt accident, it perceives the irreality of the capitalist real. Then it sees its own dependency upon commodities and the empty routines their consumption effects: "That life had been one without excitement, with no adventure. It had been too safe. All the elements that made it up were right there before his eyes, and nothing new could ever be expected" (64). This is the possibility

that drug policy, with its devotion to family values and quiet neighborhoods, cannot begin to comprehend: there is a malaise woven into
the fabric of the real, and when it is perceived, the American dream
unravels. In its routines and empty pleasures, how much does Arctor's
straight life really differ from that of the average doper? The scores
that brighten it may be legal, but their legitimating violence returns
to destroy the very satisfaction they are supposed to afford. If addiction ends badly for the addict, for Arctor a similar dependency ends
only with the violent collapse of the real.

So he becomes a doper. No, an undercover narcotics officer. No,
both at once. Part of him willfully enters the dangerous class of addicts
that by all appearances menaces society. In splitting Arctor's identity
in two, Dick is not suggesting that the human psyche is inherently
divided against itself, half dangerous doper, half upstanding nark. He
is suggesting instead that such differences reinforce the reality of the
capitalist real. Here is Arctor in strange pursuit of the injunction,
"Know Thyself":

> To himself, Bob Arctor thought, *How many Bob Arctors are there?*
> A weird and fucked-up thought. Two that I can think of, he thought.
> The one called Fred, who will be watching the other one, called Bob.
> The same person. Or is it? Is Fred actually the same as Bob? Does any-
> body know? I would know, if anyone did, because I'm the only person
> in the world that knows that Fred is Bob Arctor. *But*, he thought, *who
> am I? Which one of them is me?* (96, italics in the original)

Oedipus had it easy. He discovered that he was not the man he thought
he was. But at least he was someone else. Arctor faces a dilemma that
Oedipus never knew, that of the undecidability between identities
that are both irreal. Fred the nark and Bob the doper acquire opposite
valuations in the economy of appearances. The one is solid citizen, the
other is dangerous doper. But for Arctor who is both that difference
is moot. Neither *being* a doper nor *being* a nark determines his identity at any given moment. Rather, doper is as doper does: "he looked
like a doper;...he conversed like a doper; those around him now no
doubt took him to be a doper and reacted accordingly....What is
identity? he asked himself. Where does the act end? Nobody knows"
(29). "Bob" is merely a name given to a culturally stereotypical set of
behaviors, as to much different ends is "Fred." There is no "real" difference between them, only a nonknowledge of their affinity.

Why then the enormous energy devoted to distinguishing between
them? Fred's job as a nark is to identify and place under constant
surveillance the devious doper Bob. A huge mobilization of money

and human resources resembling contemporary National Drug Control Strategy sustains this surveillance. It is part of a complex network of domestic espionage equipped with the latest cybernetic technologies—all to the end of identifying and neutralizing the doper as public enemy. If the difference between Bob and Fred is nominal, however, if their identities are equally empty, the surveillance that distinguishes between them serves less to police that difference than to produce it. The difference between Bob and Fred arises socially rather than psychologically, as the direct effect of a drug policy of search, seizure, and enforcement. Surveillance is a benign violence that produces the dangerous class it observes. That is the implication of the obvious irony of Fred's assignment of "self-"surveillance. The doper whose movements he must monitor is not himself in any substantive sense but rather the *object* and *effect* of surveillance technologies:

> Across from him the other formless blur wrote and wrote, filling in all the inventory ident numbers for all the technological gadgetry that would, if approval came through, soon be available to him, by which to set up a constant monitoring system of the latest design, on his own house, on himself. (61)

The technical gadgetry of cybernetic surveillance generates the socially substantive difference between nark and doper, Fred and Bob. It legitimates this difference by identifying the doper as personally and morally responsible for his deviance. Then that gadgetry hides its operation by taking such differences as given.

Such is the power of observation that it produces the differences it observes. But the effects are not confined to select individuals. A whole class of malefactors arises out of a policy of enforcement and its surveillance technologies. When a street cop stops Arctor, a little community develops around him:

> "Okay, let's see your I.D.," the cop would say, reaching out; and then, as Arctor-Fred-Whatever-Godnew fumbled in his wallet pocket, the cop would yell at him, "Ever been ARRESTED?" Or, as a variant on that, adding, "BEFORE?" As if he were about to go into the bucket right then.
>
> "What's the beef?" he usually said, if he said anything at all. A crowd naturally gathered. Most of them assumed he'd been nailed dealing on the corner. They grinned uneasily and waited to see what happened, although some of them, usually Chicanos or blacks or obvious heads, looked angry. And those that looked angry began after a short interval to be aware that they looked angry, and they changed that swiftly

to impassive. Because everybody knew that anyone looking angry or uneasy—it didn't matter which—around cops must have something to hide. The cops especially knew that, legend had it, and they hassled such persons automatically. (29)

The police may stop and question an individual suspect, but their presence consolidates a dangerous class of potential offenders, minorities, and devoted dopers whose anger signals their deviance in advance. Under such circumstances defiance is always already culpable and dissimulation is its only alternative. A policy of search and seizure cultivates a politics of self-incrimination that sustains a class of dangerous individuals whose wrongs are attributable to their own agency. Thus does the capitalist real protect its solid citizens from any reminder of its failure to provide social and economic equity for all.

Young people and poor people and most of all minorities populate this dangerous class and receive blame for socially menacing behavior such as drug abuse.[9] Dick depicts the difficulty of their situation and the extent of their menace in the visit Arctor pays to Kimberly Hawkins, a young addict living in San Diego: "The girl, half Chicano, small and not too pretty, with the sallow complexion of a crystal freak, gazed down sightlessly, and he realized that her voice rasped when she spoke. Some drugs did that. Also, so did strep throat. The apartment probably couldn't be heated, not with the broken windows" (75). Arctor finds Kimberly alone, scared, and listless, having just been beaten by her boyfriend Dan. The trouble is not so much that she is hurt, but that Dan, also her pimp and supplier, will return pissed with his Case knife to make good on his promise to kill her. Arctor does his best to protect her, calls the cops when Dan shows. But futility hangs in the air like that knife. Kimberly may be a meth addict, but conditions of her life are so miserable that it remains hard to see what responsibility she bears for them or what menace she poses to society. On the contrary, the violence that sustains exchange in the capitalist real returns to menace *her*, as if in retribution for her wrongs, and with the sanction of police complacency:

> Dan had become weird and vicious, unpredictable and violent. It was a wonder the local police hadn't picked him up long ago on local disturbance-of-the-peace infractions. Maybe they were paid off. Or, most likely, they just didn't care; these people lived in a slum-housing area among senior citizens and the poor. Only for major crimes did the police enter the Cromwell Village series of buildings and related garbage dump, parking lots, and rubbled roads. (74)

Law enforcement contributes to the crime and violence it polices, tolerating it among minorities and the poor as a kind of rear-guard action against their alleged dangerousness. An attitude of banal retribution informs relations between them and their betters, summed up by a "well-educated-with-all-the-advantages" white girl's attitude toward a pesky insect: "IF I HAD KNOWN IT WAS HARMLESS I WOULD HAVE KILLED IT MYSELF" (94).

"A CERTAIN GOVERNMENTAL ECONOMY"

A cynical observer might conclude that one of the purposes of a war on drugs is to produce casualties, not results. Dick's analysis of the social effects of search and seizure anticipates the rise of the contemporary carceral state, described in devastating statistical detail in the Pew Center on the States 2008 report entitled *One in 100 Behind Bars in America*. The Pew Center's findings received extensive media coverage at the time of their release, but are worth rehearsing in detail:

> More than 1 in 100 adults is now locked up in America. With 1,596,127 in state or federal prison custody, and another 723,131 in local jails, the total adult inmate count at the beginning of 2008 stood at 2,319,258. With the number of adults just shy of 230 million, the actual incarceration rate is 1 in every 99.1 adults. (5)

Break those numbers down by race, age, and gender, and several disturbing patterns emerge. One in nine black males between the ages of twenty and thirty-four are behind bars (the figure is one in thirty for men collectively). Female prison populations are now growing faster than their male counterparts, with one in three hundred and fifty-five women between the ages of thirty-five and thirty-nine doing time— except among black women of the same age group, where the rate hits one in one hundred (6). Young people also are disproportionally represented, with one in fifty-three in their twenties serving prison sentences (3). These statistics are not exactly flattering to the Land of the Free. As the Pew Center points out, "The United States incarcerates more people than any country in the world" (5). That includes second place China (1.5 million) and Russia, a distant third (890,000). Per capita imprisonment in the United States exceeds that of South Africa and Iran (5). Using money as an index of value, it is sobering to note that between 1987 and 2007 state spending on higher education increased by 21 percent, while that devoted to "corrections" jumped 127 percent in inflation adjusted dollars. In the words of the Pew

Center report, "Higher education spending accounts for a roughly comparable portion of state expenditures as corrections" (15). From Penn State to the state pen: universities and prisons share institutional prestige when it comes to funding.

If one measure of the success of National Drug Control Strategy is a high rate of incarceration for drug-related crimes, then it is comforting to note that of the 176,268 inmates in federal prisons in 2006, 56% were drug offenders. Things are a little less soothing in the state system, where of 1,274,600 prisoners for the same year, only 249,400 or 19.6 percent were doing time for drug crimes (www.drugwarfacts. org/prisdrug.htm). But carceral trends do not end at the prison walls. As blogger J.D. Tuccille a.k.a. "Disloyal Opposition" points out, "The legal system's reach into American life—largely as the result of drug prohibition—extends even farther than the Pew Center figures would indicate." Factor in released offenders on probation or parole, and the conclusion is unavoidable "that police, courts, and prison authorities currently play a significant role in the lives of a shockingly high percentage of the adult population" in the United States (www.tuccille. com/blog/2008/02/war-on-drugs-has-prisons-bulging-at.html).

What is astonishing is that policy makers do not take these numbers as an indictment of the economic and social conditions they measure. Instead to the Bush Administration they indicated a lapse in self-control on the part of drug users that augers a predilection to commit other crimes:

> Compounding the tremendous costs to society from drug-induced and drug-related deaths, the trafficking of illicit drugs burdens various components of domestic financial sectors as individuals and organizations frequently engage in illegal activities to generate income in order to purchase drugs or finance drug trafficking operations. Mortgage fraud, counterfeiting, shoplifting, insurance fraud, ransom kidnapping, identity theft, home invasion, personal property theft, and many other criminal activities often are undertaken by drug users and distributors to support drug addictions, to control market share or to fund trafficking operations. (*National Drug Threat Summary* iii)

What about assassination and genocide? Drug abuse is a gateway crime in the eyes of the National Drug Intelligence Center, institutional author of this opinion. Score a dime and live a life of crime. Incarceration reinforces a subjectivity without social affinities. Never mind that current drug law remains as selective in its application as it always has been historically. The Office of National Drug Control Policy makes no mention of disproportionately high number of

African Americans in jail for breaking drug laws. This inflated rate of incarceration is explained away by the same old stereotypes invoked to prohibit drugs in the first place: "they" succumb to peer pressure, "they" lack autonomy, "they" will not work hard, "they" belong to a dangerous class that deserves what it gets. Incarceration simply enforces justice.

But if a policy of enforcement produces such a class, if surveillance creates the dangerous space of drug abuse, then law, which legitimates both, administrates these facts of contemporary life. Traditionally speaking, laws work through enforcement: when broken, trained professionals like Fred reinforce them. From this view, law assumes a sovereign relation to its subjects. But Dick repeatedly discovers the multiplicity of such subjects "before the Law": Bob is Fred is Arctor is both—or neither, or whatever. In the capitalist real, law functions less to enforce its own sovereignty than to administrate this multiplicity. Its purpose shifts from imposing justice to administrating appearances. That is the implication, anyway, of Hank's description of how his underling Arctor should go about the business of being a nark: "We evaluate; *you* report with your own limited conclusions. This is not a put-down of you, but we have information, lots of it, not available to you. The broad picture. The computerized picture" (106). Law administrates the computerized picture of appearances. It does not distinguish so much as distribute right and wrong throughout the economy of the capitalist real. Law thus administrates the non-knowledge of its own administrative function.

Put more simply, law administrates illegalities. Far from prohibiting illegal behavior, it tolerates and even exploits certain illegalities to sustain the legitimacy of appearances. Law makes illegalities productive by putting them to use, often to ends that are explicitly prohibited but nonetheless socially functional. This is the effect, for instance, of surveillance, even of telephone conversations. As a nark, Fred knows that "every pay phone in the world was tapped" (33). When dopers make deals on these phones, their conversations are routinely recorded. Even though all such deals are technically illegal, only unusually huge or otherwise nefarious ones register with the authorities. So to stay out of trouble Fred has only to stay cool, as when he arranges a buy with Donna:

> If they discussed anything strikingly illegal, and the monitoring officer caught it, then voiceprints would be made. But all he or she had to do was keep it mild. The dialogue could still be recognizable as a dope deal. A certain governmental economy came into play here—it wasn't

worth going through the hassle of voiceprints and track-down for routine illegal transactions. There were too many each day of the week, over too many phones. Both Donna and he knew this. (34)

The instructive phrase here is "routine illegal transactions," for it describes a class of illegalities that escapes legal prohibition. Such illegalities, however wrong from the perspective of enforcement, become useful from the perspective of administration. Law administrates their utility, maximizes their productivity. Fred and Donna, after all, are both narks posing as dopers. The administration of illegalities ostensibly allows them to enforce the law. In fact it enhances their productivity as small-scale dealers, *and keeps them consuming dope* at levels high enough to produce addiction but low enough to avoid independent capitalization. As a social practice, law administrates illegalities to produce an economy of addiction.

Foucault describes theoretically what Dick renders in fiction. Discussing delinquency, Foucault shows how prohibition allows illegalities to be organized, managed, and administered: "the existence of a legal prohibition creates around it a field of illegal practices, which one manages to supervise, while extracting from it an illicit profit through elements, themselves illegal, but rendered manipulable by their organization in delinquency. This organization is an instrument for administering and exploiting illegalities" (280). Law similarly administrates illegalities of drug abuse, obscuring its social origins and maximizing its profitability. Substitute for "delinquency" in Foucault's description the term "addiction," and the way the process works becomes suddenly clear. The prohibition of controlled substances creates a field of illegal practices, which the concept of addiction serves to organize and exploit. Surveillance legitimates the difference between doper and straight, dangerous and safe, managing illegalities productively. It turns out to be in the interest of the capitalist real to cultivate addiction, for like delinquency, it makes illegalities profitable and associates criminal behavior with an identifiable and dangerous underclass.

The way this process works offers melancholy commentary on consumer culture. Addiction is like delinquency in that its persistence is as much an institutional as an individual matter. Foucault maintains that prisons produce delinquency by institutionalizing the penality that would prohibit it: "the circuit of delinquency would seem to be not the sub-product of a prison which, while punishing, does not succeed in correcting; it is rather the direct effect of a penality which, in order to control illegal practices, seems to invest certain of them in a mechanism of 'punishment-reproduction,' of which imprisonment is one of the main parts" (278). Imprisonment thus produces an acceptable level of delinquency, which is appropriated for the purposes of administrating illegalities, partly through surveillance, partly through recidivism. Incarceration breeds the kind of criminals necessary to the administrative function of law. The greater their numbers, the more effective that function. That blacks in particular but also youth and the poor are most likely to be among them betrays the true end of this administrative enterprise: to reproduce the appearance in the capitalist real that those excluded from its full advantages deserve to be. Carceral justice materializes the selectivity of enforcement—in the name of the law.

A similar circuit produces addiction. Dick identifies its productivity with an apparently more benign institution than the prison: the rehabilitation center. Like surveillance, rehabilitation legitimates the difference between addict and straight. But as the saying goes, "rehab is for quitters"; the aim of rehabilitation may not only be recovery. For Dick it redirects dependency away from controlled substances and toward legal commodities, cultivating the addiction it would cure, but in the form most congenial to the capitalist real. Rehabilitation is a homeostatic recovery machine. Where it fails, it reproduces the addict as a legitimate candidate for surveillance. Where it succeeds, it produces the consumer as a legitimate partner in exchange. Either way, cybernetic society profits from addiction.

So rehabilitation as an institution reproduces the addict as consumer. Like the prison, it incarcerates, but in a domestic setting. Dick underscores this function by pointing out the obvious: that rehabilitation centers replicate the terms of the economy at large, to the point that they directly participate in the production and distribution of goods and services. "New-Path," the rehab center that Arctor eventually enters, is typical: "New-Path maintained assorted retail industries; probably most of the residents, guys and chicks alike, were at work, at their hair shops and gas stations and ballpoint-pen works" (50). Because the ability to hold down a job is the badge of solid citizenry, rehabilitation means worker training. The real end of this training, however, is not a job but continued addiction, whether to commodities or controlled substances is a difference primarily of appearances. Institutionally speaking, New-Path manages addiction like a business, a fact that occurs to Arctor's friend Mike, himself an undercover agent and recovering addict, when contemplating the burned-out automaton that was formerly Fred: "I wonder, he thought, if it was New-Path that did this to him. Sent a substance

out to get him like this, to make him this way *so they would ultimately receive him back?*" (265, italics in the original). Rehabilitation
cultivates addiction to the point that the addict becomes the perfect
worker—a slave.

Dick's crowning irony is to suggest that New-Path does this deliberately, actively producing and distributing the cause of addiction.
Here is the administration of illegalities at its most carceral, transparent, and profitable. The legal institution of rehabilitation administrates the illegal production and exchange of drugs, producing a class
of addicts that it then employs to maximize profits:

> No one but Donald, the Executive Director, knew where the fund-
> ing for New-Path originated. Money was always there. Well, Mike
> thought, there is a lot of money in manufacturing Substance D. Out in
> various remote rural farms, in small shops, in several facilities labeled
> "schools." Money in manufacturing it, distributing it, and finally sell-
> ing it. At least enough to keep New-Path solvent and growing—and
> more. (266)

Money makes the world go 'round, and the Executive Director of
New-Path understands that one maximizes the profitability of addiction not by curing but by cultivating it. And what is true for controlled
substances is true too for legal commodities: addiction guarantees
consumption. If the addict becomes slave to rehab, the consumer
becomes a slave to exchange. Both live for the next score in an economy of substance dependency. In this sense America is not only a vast
drugstore but also a perpetual rehab center. It produces the addiction
that sustains the capitalist real. Its whole economy is carceral. In a
beautiful touch Dick has a well-known dealer named Weeks, "a fat
black dude in his thirties, with a unique slow and elegant speech pattern, as if memorized at some phony English school," disappear once
and for all into the clean, white world of rehab: "Time to give up
on Spade Weeks" (49, 52). The carceral economy of rehabilitation so
normalizes its subjects that it renders an apparently dangerous black
man invisible. Such is life in a culture of addiction: consumers, like
commodities, are exchangeable. Only the dangerous live apart, under
perpetual threat of a more literal imprisonment.

And as Foucault says, "between the latest institution of 'rehabilitation,' where one is taken in order to avoid prison, and the prison
where one is sent after a definable offense, the difference is (and must
be) scarcely perceptible" (302). Dick shares this assessment: such
places normalize behavior while maintaining criminality at a level
that legitimates surveillance and a policy of enforcement. The carceral

economy that drug law administrates distributes power over a range of practices, producing bodies subject to control. It kills the spirit to cage the flesh. That is why Dick names the drug that New-Path produces to perpetuate addiction Substance D: *"Mors ontologica.* Death of the spirit. The identity. The essential nature" (254). Addiction to Substance D terminates uniqueness once and for all, reducing the addict to the empty operation of what Dick calls a "reflex machine." Arctor becomes such a machine when, fried beyond self-awareness, he is put to use by the police as the ideal surveillance technology: a human scanner without a life of its own to compromise its operation. Slave to both New-Path and the police, a prisoner of rehab, Arctor *incarnates* surveillance, materializing its carceral effects. Law and therapy administrate his bodily agency, illustrating Foucault's insight that "in its function, the power to punish is not essentially different from that of curing or educating" (303). Such strategies produce a body subject to surveillance, an effect Dick underscores by making that Arctor's sole function. All he can do is watch, tragically embodying Foucault's conclusion that "the carceral texture of society assures both the real capture of the body and its perpetual observation" (304). To see is to be seen; to live is to be lived. The body in this economy lives at the behest of other forces.

The bodies most subject to surveillance, of course, belong to those deemed most refractory: dopers like Bob, blacks like Weeks, poor losers like Kimberly Hawkins. A law that administrates illegalities incarcerates a dangerous class in advance. The carceral economy of *A Scanner Darkly* perpetuates class inequality in the name of that administrative law. Those prone to violating drug laws, from this perspective, deserve surveillance. The malaise that originally motivated Arctor's entrance into the dangerous class of dopers becomes evidence of his own dangerousness and culpability, as his boss reminds him: "Nobody held a gun to your head and shot you up. Nobody dropped something in your soup. You knowingly and willingly took an addictive drug, brain-destructive and disorienting" (226). By entering the class of the culpable, Bob abdicates his straight identity and ultimately his life. In a world of cybernetic surveillance he turns dangerous doper. So much for understanding the social conditions of drug abuse. A policy of enforcement assures that they remain unknown except as evidence of criminal culpability.

And that appears to be among the effects of drug policy today. *A Scanner Darkly* remains as frightening as it was when it appeared in 1977. It would be wrong to attribute its preoccupation with surveillance to a dated thematics of paranoia. Carceral justice is on the rise, as the Pew Report attests. Consider too the implications of policy innovations like the following: the educational program known as DARE, "Drug Abuse Resistance Education," which puts uniformed law enforcement officers in elementary school classrooms in part to promote "positive attitudes toward the police and greater respect for the law," while further assimilating education to surveillance (*DARE* i); the "user accountability" provisions of the Anti-Drug Abuse Act of 1988, which strip violators of drug laws of federal benefits such as student loans, research grants, mortgage guarantees; the encroachment upon Forth Amendment protection against unreasonable search and seizure;[10] or the increasing use of random drug testing in high schools to "identify nondependent users" and "steer them from drugs and into counseling, if necessary, before they become addicted or entice others to use drugs" (*Starting a Student Drug-Testing Program* 2).

The last policy installs within the institution of public education a procedure for violating Fourth Amendment privacy rights on the slenderest of justifications, upheld on appeal by the Supreme Court in a 5–4 decision (*Board of Education of Independent School District No. 92 of Pottawatomie County vs. Earl* [2002]). To say that government policy is high on this particular strategy would be an understatement:

> Random testing gives students a powerful incentive to abstain from drug use. [...] Random testing can provide young people with a reason never to start using drugs, protecting them during a time when they are the most vulnerable to peer pressure and the adverse health effects of drug use. [...] By addressing the continuum of drug use from pre-initiation to dependency, random testing can stop the pipeline to addiction, help create a culture of disapproval toward drugs, and contribute to safer school and work environments. (*Strategy* 7)

The Bush administration defended random drug testing in high school on the grounds that using controlled substances in the context of extracurricular activities presents imminent harm to others.

Four of nine Supreme Court Justices remained unconvinced. It is easier to maintain that athletes under the influence present immanent harm than students involved in activities such as Future Homemakers of America, Future Farmers of American, and marching bands. Justice Ruth Bader Ginsburg in her dissenting opinion (shared by Justices Stevens, O'Connor, and Souter) makes the point with biting clarity: "Notwithstanding nightmarish images of out-of-control flatware, livestock run amok, and colliding tubas disturbing the peace and quiet of Tecumseh, the great majority of students in the School District seeks to test are engaged in activities that are not safety sensitive to an unusual degree" (*Board of Education* 11).

As Ginsburg further points out, studies have consistently proven that students involved in extracurricular activities are those least likely to become involved in drug use in the first place. The pedagogical point of random drug testing might be less to deter use than to produce docility. If, as Nikolas Rose suggests, *biopower* involves "a whole range of more or less rationalized attempts by different authorities to intervene upon the vital characteristics of human existence," random drug testing in high schools marks a biopolitical turn in the purpose of public education. It advances a physiological criterion—a normalized vitality— not only for successful performance in school, but ultimately in *life*. As John P. Walters puts it, "We must identify and use the best tools at our disposal to protect kids from a behavior that destroys bodies and minds, impedes academic performance, and creates barriers to success and happiness" (*Starting a Student Drug-Testing Program* iv).

Such is the task of biopolitics as Rose describes it, which "consists in a variety of strategies that try to identify, treat, manage, or administer those individuals, groups, or localities where risk is seen to be high" (70). And why bother with such vital treatments? Because in the words of President Bush they "provide a charter for the future" (*National Drug Control Strategy* i). Rose maintains that such strategies, and random drug testing is among them, involve "calculations about probable futures in the present followed by interventions into the present in order to control that potential future" (70). Such is liberal education in a cybernetic social formation: a feedback loop that administrates life toward predictable ends—that at least is the nightmare scenario. The danger of random drug testing is that it advances administrated futures in the name of health and happiness. It all too neatly accommodates the larger operations of a carceral economy that identify drug users as a criminal class. With incarceration on the increase, it becomes easy to accept that a dangerous class is to blame for social ills. America has a drug problem because it needs an enemy. A war on drugs, even in the guise of market disruption, serves as a diversionary skirmish to convince us of a difference between us and them, solid citizen and criminal doper. But in the perpetual present of *A Scanner Darkly*, we all live for the next score and die buying: "Imagine being sentient but not alive. Seeing and even knowing, but not alive. [...] A person can die and still go on" (243).

5

QUEER SCIENCE

You make Gemini with nice astronaut?

William Burroughs, *The Wild Boys*

In space there is no closet—or is a spaceship a closet with hyperdrive? J. G. Ballard pointed out long ago that the first sex act in space— involving terrestrials—would be homosexual. No doubt it has already happened. Two human bodies in close quarters prognosticates sexual contact: the zero-grav ballet, slow-peeling space suits, solitude as deep as space itself. This sexual destiny haunts *Star Trek* ("To boldly go where no *man* has gone before"), particularly in its Next Generation phase, where the attractively aging and bald Captain Picard finds himself frequently bedeviled by a campy character called "Q." The possibility that Picard is queer (why is he so compulsively single anyway?) suggests that homosexuality serves cybernetic society as a cultural vanguard, even in so austere a culture as that of Western technoscience. But the whole trope of the closet is peculiarly domestic. To have a closet requires a house, an assumption that attaches queer life to the heterosexual dyad of mommy and daddy. What if homosexuality wants nothing to do with the single-family home? What if the spaces it aspires to are as open as the night sky? And what if science and not domesticity provides the highest boost into those heavens?

It is a strange fact of cyberfiction that from the start it has explored the intersection between homosexuality and technoscience without much regard for the closet. Witness the work of William Burroughs and Samuel R. Delany. Both writers assimilate sexuality to the pallid project technoscience. They write Queer Science, a sexualized cy-fi that makes gay sex the erotic software of cybernetic society. Queer science prefers other spaces to closeted inner sanctums and advances a politics more demanding than the liberal dream of market domination. Its hopes are radical and its beliefs disturbing. Technoscience might be queerer than it thinks.

C'MON ABAFT THE HEAD, HAN HONEY

If Chewbakka could speak, oh the stories he would tell. Years ago Leslie Fielder alerted anyone who would listen to the homoerotic desire driving American cultural production.[1] Its most usual form, which Fiedler cataloged with glee, paired a lonely white misfit with a big black buck, mixing homosexuality with miscegenation, doubling the zing of transgression. Huck and Jim were the great epitome, but the type appeared everywhere in high and low culture: Natty Bumpo and Chingachgook, Ishmael and Quequeg, the Lone Ranger and Tonto, Kelley Robinson and Alexander Scott, Han Solo and Chewbakka. Fiedler interpreted this doublet according to the precepts of the then prevailing "science" of sexuality, psychoanalysis. Homoerotic desire haunted the straight American psyche, producing the dream of a frontier where men could be men—all by themselves. It was a forbidden desire, but as American literature and popular culture attest, no less urgent for that. For Fiedler it was one of the foundational myths of American culture.

Call it the myth of male bonding. It begins with the premise that homoerotic desire is a deviation from the norm of sexual relations, which itself assumes that bodies are objects to be cathected in normal or deviant ways. And why not? My body is mine to dispose of, right? And yours belongs to you. If we want to dispose of them together, that is entirely our business. C'mon abaft and let's cathect. This logic, however obvious, might be worth a closer look than it often gets. For one thing, it is not universally the case that bodies are objects in the sense presumed here. For another, it is not at all clear how an individual can posses one the way she possesses a TV, a house, or a cat. The long history of *habeas corpus* in English law shows what a struggle it has been historically to enshrine the right of an individual to possess her body.[2] That right found its philosophical justification in Locke's claim that the one thing all people have in common was a "property in person." The belief that bodies are personal property disposable at will is the brainchild of the liberal political philosophy. Freud complicated this belief with his hidden economy of libidinal drives. But psychoanalysis still serves the liberal project of isolating bodies and making individuals responsible for them. When it comes to male bonding, it holds men personally responsible for homosexual desires *they all have*. If they succumb to those desires, their bodies become damaged goods. Witness the wreck of Ennis at the end of the hit movie *Brokeback Mountain*, alone in the closet of a ramshackle trailer home. No wonder the myth of male bonding needs a frontier. The only alternative is that closet.

Queer Science sees things differently.[3] It is *bios*-science, and one of the beliefs it refuses is that bodies are personal property, a belief which, not coincidentally, gains currency during the heyday of the transatlantic slave trade. For the early theorists of liberalism, either one had property in person or one's person *was* property, a situation miserably familiar to slaves, as well as to wage laborers, especially the indentured. A body by this description was a commodity, disposable in the ways typical of commodities. If one had the good luck to own it outright, then one could do what one wanted with it—participate in civil society, for instance. But if one did not have such luck, one's body belonged to another. To varying degrees, it was subject to control. Queer Science turns against this history by challenging its proprietary assumptions. Rather than taking bodies for personal property owned by private individuals, it proclaims the multiplicity of bodies, both as organisms and as agents. It eschews the closet as the domestic space of male bonding. It is a counterscience to control. When Chewbakka takes Han abaft the galley, it might not be to bond with another male body so much as to become it, become *with* it. Queer Science is a science of becoming.

"I DO"—DON'T YOU?

In this it contrasts sharply with current calls for gay marriage. While marriage should be an option for anyone, regardless of sexual orientation, it should not be confused with a program for social reform. Marriage is what straight culture does to secure its order. If gay men and women want to participate in the status quo from the inside, then by all means let them marry! The so-called sanctity of marriage between a man and a woman does not regulate an economy of social legitimacy so much as determine access to it. Tweak the terms of access—say by letting gays and lesbians marry—little about that economy actually changes. Neither those for gay marriage nor against it challenge the authority and function of *marriage* as a means of sustaining social order. But that is precisely what Queer Science does, which is why it advocates a politics more radical *and capacious* than one that takes marriage as its *sine qua non*, a politics of multiplicity open to all who participate in its constitutive practices.

This is *not* a politics of the closet. The closet is a space of privacy, a domestic space of private fantasy and performance. Coming out of it does not necessarily change its architecture. On the contrary, one of the great rewards of coming out is acquiring a closet of your own—in a strict material sense, the only one that matters economically, the sense of home ownership. Gay marriage holds out the promise of sexual intimacy and property relations. It is equal opportunity marriage, securing for a previously excluded individual all the rights and privileges of the status quo.

Michael Warner has discussed the trouble with this version of gay liberation: it does not much trouble a social order in which marriage circulates power. It is a strategy of assimilation that leaves the basic—and preferential—arrangement of civil society untouched. And that is fine, if all one wants is a liberal piece of the liberal pie. But if one's tastes are stranger or more demanding than those associated with legally sanctioned monogamy, then it is hard to see how gay marriage will help much. One can marry a monogamous beloved, sign a mortgage, adopt a child and raise a family, but has one really done anything to change a world that demonizes deviance?

Warner sees the trouble clearly, and his solution is deeply attractive: the creation of "counter-publics of sex and gender." He describes them as "scenes of association and identity that transform the private lives they mediate" (Warner, *Counterpublics* 57). Such counterpublics are a promising fix. They conjure better futures out of present possibilities. They envision a social order in which marriage is not necessary for full participation. They transform private lives. Warner's vision inhabits a conceptual territory close to that of cyberfiction, so close that it might have something to learn from Queer Science. What kind of *bodies* will live in Warner's counterpublics? That is not a frivolous question. Queer Science builds new bodies for a new politics. The old ones need an overhaul.

SIGN HERE

It is hard to have politics without bodies in the *polis*. Ask of any political theory how it imagines their production—or reproduction. Carole Pateman has shown how liberalism, the theory of possessive individualism, grounds its claims about human agency in a tacit "sexual contract" that secures the reproduction of human bodies. Locke himself is not much interested in such issues. Babies come into the world as sweet empty slates. Through care and tutelage, they acquire human reason and its prize possession, property in person. But Pateman points out that one cannot possess property in person without having a person to possess. Bodies are not created ex nihilo. They require mothers and fathers (at least in the seventeenth century), which means that men must have access to women's bodies for purposes of reproduction. A secret sexual contract is built into liberal political theory guarantees that access.

Pateman concludes rightly that the subordination of women gets written into liberalism in advance through a devaluation of reproductive agency. Little wonder that today's working single mom becomes the test case for full female participation in civil society. I want to emphasize a more obvious but no less decisive aspect of the sexual contract, however. It is heterosexual. The sexual activity it sanctions, albeit silently, occurs between a man and a woman for purposes of reproduction. Locke may say (to paraphrase), "pay no attention to the heterosexual copulating couple behind the curtain." But their sexuality is the sine qua non of civil society.

Call it liberal het/sex: it becomes the ruling body logic of the theory of possessive individualism. It is entirely unclear that civil society can get along without it, which is why gay marriage promises only to assimilate homosexual practices to this prevailing and compulsory liberal paradigm. Apparently gay people can be heterosexual too! I am less interested in that prospect, however, than in the practices that reinforce it, practices that Queer Science disrupts. After all, liberal het/sex is not compulsory primarily in order to punish the noncompliant (a handy aftereffect), but rather to produce, regulate, and reward normal (some would say natural) sexual behavior. It secures civil society. In cybernetic society it breeds control.

It does so in many ways through many practices, but the ones I have in mind are foundational to liberalism even today. Liberal het/sex locates sexual acts in the privacy of the master bedroom. It legitimates sexual acts by an appeal to reproduction—even (or maybe especially) when that outcome is to be avoided. And it secures the legality of sexual acts through the consent of the participants. In a society where the idea of a contract sets the theoretical and juridical terms for legitimate agency, consent secures the legal standing of the body as personal property to be disposed of at will. Consent is the performative condom that makes sex safe. It is the erotic equivalent of "Sign Here." Privacy, reproduction, consent: three practical components of liberal het/sex. Without them there would be no closet, no domestic space within which to confine sexual noncompliance.

"HEY, OPEN THE DOOR!"

The closet is not just an attitude. It is an architecture, one that has a material history. The word itself, according to the OED, refers to "a room for privacy or retirement; a private room; an inner chamber;

formerly often = BOWER" (440). That is the earliest definition (circa 1370), and it connotes a place of chosen solitude, as for study or devotion. It is not until the mid-eighteenth century that the word comes to refer simply to a room of small size: "Any small room, especially one belonging to or communicating with a larger" (440). That may seem a small shift in connotation, but it turns out to be significant. Between the time of Geoffrey Chaucer and the time of Samuel Johnson huge changes occur in domestic architecture. The closet of Chaucer's day was a private chamber distinct from the courtyard or great hall. One went there for that culturally exceptional experience, as odd as it was credentialing, called *solitude*. By Johnson's day solitude had become the name of the domestic game. The closet was a simple fact of home life, a space of privacy distinct from the more public salon or living room.

Involved here is a reversal of conceptual and affective priorities, which becomes crucial for the way civil society structures—literally— family life. Where privacy was once an exception to the social relations of family and court, liberalism makes it the rule. It is not the scholar or the monk or the bride who wants to be sequestered now, but pretty much everybody. Individual sensibility pushes social sympathy aside and an architecture emerges that materializes this autonomy. Courtyards become backyards. Great Halls get partitioned into dining rooms and salons. Open parlors shrink to little living rooms. And the family shrinks accordingly. The extended web of relations, blood and otherwise, that used to scatter bodies throughout a house, shrivels into the conjugal family. Now everyone needs a bedroom. The once humble closet proliferates as *the* space of privacy, where an individual lives and feels and loves and cogitates prior to sociality in the salon. The political implications of this architectural shift are worth pondering. In Jürgen Habermas's estimation, "The privatized individuals who gathered there [the salon] to form a public were not reducible to 'society': they only entered into it, so to speak, out of a private life that had assumed institutional form in the enclosed space of the patriarchal conjugal family" (46). In this sense liberalism is closet politics. It promotes the kind of citizenship that comes with having your own bedroom. The privacy of liberal het/sex is an architectural as much as a libidinal function. The architecture of the conjugal family structures and stimulates a closeted desire. Whether the sexuality that administers that desire takes for its object a male or a female is almost beside the point. Either way what matters most is the privacy of such longing, its mute loquaciousness, its perpetual secret pulsation.

JFWY.COM

Nowhere does the functionality of this architecture appear more clearly than in the story of Justin Berry, for a time famous on the Web as a teen porn star. A detailed account of his dubious celebrity appeared in the *New York Times* on December 19, 2005 (Eichenwald). Hoping to meet kids his age, Justin, then thirteen, broadcast his image on the Internet using a cheap Webcam. Although no teens responded, within minutes future friends of another sort did: men of indeterminate age and identity eager to make Justin's acquaintance. They chatted, watched, and flattered, singing praises, offering gifts. Justin was "excited" by their attention (http://www.nytimes.com/2005/12/19/national/19kids.ready.html, video 1). They took an unequivocal and urgent interest in him of a sort he never experienced at school.

It was not long before one of them offered him fifty dollars to take off his shirt in front of the camera, a proposition that launched Justin's stardom. In the words of Kurt Eichenwald, the reporter for the *Times*,

> So began the secret life of a teenager who was lured into selling images of his body on the Internet over the course of five years. From the seduction that began that day, this soccer-playing honor roll student was drawn into performing in front of the Webcam—undressing, showering, masturbating and even having sex—for an audience of more than 1,500 people who paid him, over the years, hundreds of thousands of dollars. (1)

By his mid-teens, Justin was a highly successful small businessman, trafficking pornographic images—of himself. Under the cover of operating a Web development company, he ruled a small cyberporn empire in which, as both CEO *and* celebrity performer, he could set his own price for services: forty-five dollars a month for subscribers, as high as nine hundred dollars an hour for private appearances. Justin had the computer savvy of a gifted geek and built an array of sexy Web sites: justinscam.com, jfwy.com, and justinsfriends.com among them. His new friends took full advantage. But by the time he turned eighteen, he had become exhausted by their demands and his complicities. He turned state's evidence and helped bust the doctors, lawyers, teachers, and construction workers who were his paying customers. There were pediatricians in the bunch and even an attorney who was a child's welfare advocate.

However one might feel about those predatory men, what interests me most is the architecture that makes their predation possible. Justin's saga and celebrity is a material function of the house he inhabited when it all began, a single-family home in Bakersville, California. He lived there with his mom, his step-dad, and his little sister. Asked in an interview what parents whose kids have a Webcam should do, Justin replied, "Throw the Webcam in the trash." Asked why, he says "Why? You're letting the pedophiles into your kids's bedroom." From his point of view (and his experience deserves respect) the Webcam allows the exploitation of a closeted desire. The problem Justin astutely diagnoses is twofold: first, the uncompromised privacy of sexuality (the bedroom), and second, its exploitability through images (the Webcam). The architecture of the single-family home structures both. The domestic legacy of the closet in civil society sequesters desire in a private space, a space whose muted sexuality only amplifies a loquacious pornography that circulates through it. When Justin's mother looked in his bedroom, she saw only computers—three of them. He stashed the Webcams out of sight and conducted business after she retired to her own bedroom. Once closeted, desire circulates with terrible freedom.

As Foucault would lead one to expect, Justin's tricky life ends in confession, complete with a priest of secular rectitude (Eichenwald) and ritual obeisance and absolution (the *Times* article and interview). That the media performs these sacred tasks in full view of an avid public shows how important its communications have become to the operation of liberal het/sex in cybernetic society. The media circulates the discourse of a closeted desire, not to open it up but on the contrary to keep it in the closet and regulate its agencies. It is pornography with a conscience, a discursive prophylaxis that lets solid citizens talk about masturbation and pederasty without hazarding perversion. Justin's story is so *shocking*—his behavior so *naughty*, his reform so *instructive*. What remains untouched by such sentiments is the operative logic of liberal het/sex, its constitutive investments in privacy, reproduction, and consent. It was the Webcam after all that violated Justin's privacy, allowing the rush into his bedroom of a predatory horde cavalier about consent and unconcerned with reproduction. This vagrant technology breached the closet's security, subjecting Justin to the demands of illicit desire. Blame technology, not the bedroom.

There is another way of looking at Justin's story, however. One thing it makes glassy clear is that the privacy of liberal het/sex allows its capitalization by means of images. Justin made a lot of money as his own porn pimp. Just because he was a kid and his preferred medium was a Webcam does not mean he was not a capitalist. From that first fifty dollars, he was "excited" by the money, and as his interview attests, once aroused he wanted more. Fiscal and carnal desires conflate and his body becomes an ATM. More accurately, sexual *images* of his body become (illegal) tender, good for gifts, credit, or ready cash.

To his credit as a capitalist if not as an adolescent, Justin cashed in, making hundreds of thousands of dollars during his years as a pornbroker. That images could be so valuable says something about the privacy that makes them possible. It is the material condition of their production, circulation, and consumption, the factory floor, so to speak, of cyberporn. Justin's buyers, it turns out, were also *buying privacy*, a transaction that later developments would prove difficult to guarantee. If privacy produces both liberal het/sex and its perverse violation, one might be forgiven for wondering how far apart they really are. But what about reproduction and consent—don't they establish the legitimacy of sexual agency? Well, sort of, but who can really tell who says, does, or wants what in private? The premium on privacy in liberal het/sex cripples its investments in reproduction and consent. Justin's story is morally unambiguous only because during most of his stint as a pornstar he was too young to consent legally to anything. That fact only enhanced the value of the images he sold and bartered. Blame the bedroom, not the technology. The real lesson here seems to be that a closeted desire produces images to capitalize the privacy at the domestic center of civil society. Justin and his predators exploit this logic to maximize pleasure and profit. Liberal het/sex is pornography with its clothes on. No amount of denouncing either porn or pederasty will disrupt the operation of a sexuality configured by an architecture as commonplace and as incorrigible as the closet.

THE BIZ OF BOOGIE

Maybe the best analysis of this architecture and its bodily effects is Paul Thomas Anderson's zesty film *Boogie Nights*. Released in 1997, it anticipates Justin's experience perfectly, with differences that measure how far we have come from those ostensibly frivolous days in the 1970s in which the movie is set. Like Justin, Dirk Diggler, the film's gifted protagonist (played by Mark Wahlberg), is a misunderstood loner until he awakens to the prospects that beckon with pornography. Like Justin, Dirk is introduced to those prospects by an older man,

a small time director of porn films with big time ambitions (acted
beautifully by Burt Reynolds). Jack Horner becomes a father to Dirk
and initiates him into a life in which, with hard work and a little luck,
he might realize financial rewards commensurate with his natural
gifts. Strangely, Justin's own father eventually joins him in business,
arranging online sex with prostitutes to keep the profits coming. Dirk
seals his devotion to his new life by moving into Horner's suburban
home, leaving behind his small, dark bedroom covered with moto-
cross posters in his mom's ranch house. He becomes part of Horner's
de facto family, one that includes actors and actresses, camera crew,
and even those distant but demanding relations, financial backers.
Horner is their titular head, the strapping Dad of this porno film
family, and with his guidance Dirk plays out an Oedipal drama that
has him fucking then falling in love with a woman old enough to be
his mother, Horner's star and sometime squeeze, Amber Waves. The
whole drama, literal and cinematic, unfolds—and gets filmed—in the
basement of Horner's split-level home.

Boogie Nights domesticates pornography, showing it to be the bas-
tard child of family ties and the architecture that binds them. Dirk's
first big scene comes in a bedroom-turned-film set, where Amber
Waves conducts a job interview that turns suddenly into desktop sex.
Anderson gets the logic of liberal het/sex just right: the privacy, the
dance of consent, even the premium on reproduction (Amber whis-
pers in Dirk's ear, "come inside me"). He emphasizes another feature,
however, that characterizes sexuality in contemporary civil society
and links Dirk's experience with Justin's. The whole thing is scripted.
It is acted (badly) on a makeshift set. It is not sex so much as "sex,"
more performance than encounter, and the point of the performance
is to make money—as much of it as possible.

That ambition is imaginable only because there is a camera in this
bedroom, or rather film set. Image technologies are now an intimate
part of sexual performance (who has not filmed themselves doing
it—or at least thought about it?). Ballard 101: the camera and the
body have assimilated to the point that sexuality *is* pornography. It
does not occur apart from the production of images that both iterate
and stimulate its performance. Anderson makes this point beautifully
by focusing his own camera on Amber's breast and tracking into the
mechanical depths of the other camera that films her performance
with Dirk. This move assimilates their fucking to the technology that
renders it in images until all you see is the film, clacking through the
sprockets of a sixteen millimeter cinecam. Liberal het/sex *is* a porn
film. Anderson's movie pursues the ostensible historical agenda of

examining what becomes of that cultural fact as celluloid gives way to much cheaper video tape as its material condition. The whole economy of porn production changes and with it Dirk's standing in the family. But what matters most is Anderson's simple acknowledgment that sexual performance in cybernetic society involves image technology so completely that even in the privacy of one's bedroom one is never quite free from the curious eye of the camera.

Blame the bedroom *and* the technology. Liberal het/sex has been a low-budget porn film at least since the 1970s. What is new to Justin's experience is less its pornographic manner than its technological means. Were Anderson to update his cinematic history of liberal het/sex he'd have to add a section on cyberporn, examining the effect on sexual performance of info-tech and instant Internet access. Dirk Diggler might start a business in his own bedroom netcasting private screenings over a live feed. But then he would be Justin, albeit too old to be of interest to pederasts. Justin's experience is not exemplary because it is unusual but because it reveals something banal about sexuality today: it is moving-image-sex through and through, as much a cinematic as a corporeal event. Perhaps, as Freud might claim, it always has been. But where in the old days we needed the clunky machinery of the unconscious to produce, store, and circulate sexual images, now the whole circuit works externally by means of cheap and admittedly cool technologies. The Internet is the exoconscious, the digital repository of all our dreams.

At the very least it structures desire in conjunction with the closet. A Webcam in the bedroom effectively disembodies sex, reversing the relationship between sexuality and its representations. Sexual performance is now an effect of the cinematic images that represent it, which is simply to state the obvious: such images script sex. That is where Justin's story seems most tragic. It is not simply that he fell victim to predators but that, given the ease of digital communications, he had so little say in controlling his own behavior once the sex script kicked in. Could it be that what his story makes too obvious to bear is that *consent is a ruse*, that not personal choice but the digital imagery scripts sexual performance in cybernetic society? Because as a teenager Justin did not have available the legal fiction of consent his story lays bear what that fiction otherwise covers up: liberal het/sex is a porn film that scripts and exploits bodies in civil society.

It is a little too easy to blame pornography for these circumstances, and a little too blithe to extol its virtues. That porn assimilates sexual performance to a successful business model is the easy lesson of its distribution on the Web. Porn profits have never been bigger, and in

Webonomics, size matters. The year 2005 saw fifty-seven billion dollars made worldwide, ten billion in the United States alone (Wooten 371). It has been said that one in every four online searches is for porn. That is not in fact the case, but the fiction registers a basic worry, if not preoccupation. With over four million porn sites on the Web and a million and a half P2P file shares per month in the United States, there would seem to be enough smut to go around. But like the love of God, the logic of accumulation is infinite. The closeted desire mobilized by so much pornography proves boundless in pursuit of new images, new possibilities, new perversions. And as we all know, anything can be had for a price. The question to be put to liberal het/sex under current technological and economic circumstances, then, is not whether but to what extent its performance advances biopolitical control.

FLICK FLUCK

I am beginning to talk like William Burroughs here, so I might as well return to the question of Queer Science. As a master of pornography, Burroughs casts a cold eye on the genre. Its images and scripts turn bodies into slag. As he says in an aside in *The Soft Machine*, his cut-up account of a siege on Venus, "It was explained to me that I must put aside all sexual prudery and reticence, that sex was perhaps the heaviest anchor holding one in the present time" (82). One of the projects of Queer Science is to cut that anchor away and move life toward better possibilities. In this regard, pornography is a power tool, but not because it is emancipatory. On the contrary, the trouble with porn in cybernetic society is that it circulates control. It scripts sexuality and directs this most creative of bodily agencies toward a mindless cycle of reproduction and death. Porn produces "Muttering addicts of the orgasm drug, boneless in the sun, eaten alive by crab men—terminal post card sinking in heavy time" (39). Yikes.

Porn has this effect because it turns flesh into film, a thin vegetable strip fed into a machine that then projects its movements. Porn films are not perverse because they represent bodies pornographically but because *they are those bodies*. As flesh becomes moving image, life goes celluloid. What then is liberal het/sex but a titillating blockbuster with the spectacle and banality that the term implies? Here's how Burroughs describes the way it works:

> "I am the Contessa di Vile your hostess for tonight"—She points to
> the boys at the bar with her cigarette holder and their cocks jumped

up one after the other—And I did the polite thing too when my turn
came—

So all the boys began chanting in unison "*The movies!—The
movies!*—We want *the movies*—*!*" So she led the way into the projection room which was filled with pink light seeping through the
walls and floor and ceiling—[...] they all got hard-ons waiting and
watching—[...] Then they run the movie in slow motion slower and
slower and you are coming slower and slower until it took an hour and
then two hours and finally all the boys are standing there like statues
getting their rocks off geologic—. (78, 79)

Porn films script sexual performance to the point of suspending animation. That is the downside of orgasm. It maxes control. Any film
that makes orgasm alluring will circulate this effect. The gender of
the cast is beside the point: " 'Now Meester we flick fluck I me you
cut.' The two film tracks ran through impression screen. One track
flash on other cut out in dark until cut back: 'Me finish Johnny's shit
[...] Clom through Johnny [...]' Hear rectums merging in flicks and
orgasm of mutual processes" (138). Straight and gay alike are stuck
in the perpetual motion picture machine of orgasm addiction. Such
is the force of liberal het/sex that pornography breeds biopolitical
control.

THE WISDOM OF QUEEN BOBO

What is a body to do? Queer Science has its visions. Writers like
Burroughs and Delany wage guerilla war against liberal het/sex
and the reality it produces. In a world where science sets the terms
for truth and knowledge, they queer science by eroticizing its fictions. Homosexuality becomes the new erotic software for sex in a
cybernetic society, but not because the sciences are secretly homosocial. How banal. No, for both Burroughs and Delany homosexuality advances possibilities for bodies incommensurable with liberal
het/sex and its serviceable sciences. Simply blurring the boundary
between genders does not disrupt the operation of a sexuality that
moves as much through architecture (the closet) and imagery (pornography) as bodies. Both writers, therefore, attack liberal het/sex on
those two fronts. They imagine new spaces for new bodies, counterpublics of a sort close in spirit if not detail to Warner's, and they create new images for new agencies, counterfictions for a sexuality that
swings free from control.

But the first move is to refuse the proprietary assumptions of liberal het/sex, the belief that bodies are private property disposable

at will. In his education tract masquerading as an interview, *The Job* (1989), Burroughs rejects the familiar conviction that sex has anything to do with love:

> I think what we call love is a fraud perpetrated by the female sex, and that the point of sexual relations between men is nothing that we could call love, but rather what we might call *recognition*. (118, italics in the original)

Look past the obvious misogyny of Burroughs's claim here and notice that what sex makes explicit is a certain *regard* for another. Liberal het/sex orients that regard toward ownership, the mutual and perpetual possession of bodies in married love. Sex between men configures that regard otherwise. Recognition (re-cognition) involves a regard that is less affective than effective, less loving, perhaps, than affirming—in a sense beyond possession. This is not to suggest that *love* between men is inconceivable or insignificant, just that it is not what, for Burroughs, gives gay sex its disruptive—and productive—potential.

In his painful, haunted memoir *Queer*, written nearly thirty years before its publication in 1985, Burroughs describes what drives Lee, his avatar, to Mexico, Panama, Ambato, Puyo: "What Lee is looking for is contact or recognition, like a photon emerging from the haze of insubstantiality to leave an indelible recording in Allerton's consciousness" (xvi). Allerton is the object of Lee's affections, but Lee's aim is not love. It is recognition, the awareness of the life of another, the acknowledgment of that life's luminous, dying flight. Confessing his homosexuality to Allerton in one of his wry and rueful routines, Lee offers up a body that is not just his own. Quoting a "wise old Queen" named Bobo, Lee says " 'You are part of everything alive.' The difficulty is to convince someone else that he is really part of you, so what the hell? Us parts ought to work together. Reet?" (40). Reet. Parts might work together, but not as mutual possessions.

In fact, they might not fully exist *until* they work together. Later Lee makes this confession: "I want myself the same way I want others. I'm disembodied. I can't use my own body for some reason." (99). Using your own body is the one thing liberal het/sex guarantees: use it for pleasure, for pain, for money, even for love, but by all means use it—any way you want. It belongs to you, after all. Unless you are Burroughs. He refuses that proprietary assumption and affirms instead a body that cannot exist apart from others. No wonder Lee seeks recognition so deeply, so terminally. His body is not fully alive until it makes contact with others that are similarly driven. No property, no possession. "Sex between men" offers only living recognition.

PARASITES AND SLAVES

Recognition like that is not easy to achieve, as Lee discovers in *Queer*. The main problem is the human body, or rather the kind of human body we are stuck with at the moment. Liberal het/sex prefers a body susceptible to possession, an individual body tricked out with special parts peculiarly suited to genital intercourse and orgasm. But a body like that is an effect not a given—for Burroughs the effect of a multiplicity of contesting influences. Bodies are not just *there* for the fucking. They are the products of a complicated interplay of forces, some of which are far from benign. As such bodies can hardly be expected to comprehend the multiplicity that produces them. What do any of us know of our physical geniture? One of Burroughs's significant contributions to Queer Science is to describe that unknowable process.

And it is bizarre. Burroughs presents it most completely in *Nova Express* (1964), part of his early trilogy that includes *The Soft Machine* (1961) and *The Ticket that Exploded* (1962). The body as we know it today, the apparently independent and self-possessing organism, is better understood as a human host under siege by an array of competing and incompatible life forms. Parasites. They control it biologically in order to live, directing the life of the human organism toward sustaining their own. Without belaboring the point (others have done it better justice than I can), I'll say only that Burroughs identifies at least three infectious life forms that feed on the human organism.[4] The first is the word virus, which infected the human organism some three thousand years ago and has since been directing its energies toward the replication of words and the agencies they script: "Word *is* flesh and word *is* two that is the human body is compacted of two organisms you have word and word is flesh" (*Nova Express* 76). The autonomous body of liberal het/sex is not autonomous at all but a double organism the flesh of which serves to sustain and replicate a verbal parasite. Property in person has become the personal property of a viral invader.

It gets worse. Another kind life form feeds upon this double organism, of which there are three varieties: "Three life forms uneasily parasitic upon a forth that is beginning to wise up" (10). Like the word virus, these three also vie for control of the human host, which, thanks to Burroughs's work, is starting to sense their presence:

> In this area of Total Conditions on the Nova Express the agents of shadow empires move on hideous electric needs—Faces of scarred metal back from the Ovens of Minraud—Orgasm Drug addicts back from the Venusian Front—and the cool blue heavy metal addicts of Uranus. (96)

Parasites from Minraud, from Venus, from Uranus all suck the life out of the human organism. What unites them is their *modus operandi*. They live by producing addictions—to power, to sex, to junk. Driven by such needs, the human organism succumbs to control.

A virus, three different parasites: how much more can a body endure? Quite a bit, it turns out. A gang of extortionists also besieges the human organism. Speaking as Inspector Lee of the Nova Police, Burroughs calls them the Nova Mob.

> Let me explain *how* we make an arrest—Nova criminals are not three-dimensional organisms—(though they are quite definite organisms as we shall see) but they need three-dimensional human agents to operate—[…]—and if there is one thing that carries over from one human host to another and establishes identity of the controller it is *habit*: idiosyncrasies, vices, food preferences—(we were able to trace Hamburger Mary through her fondness for peanut butter) a gesture, a certain smile, a special look, that is to say the *style* of the controller. (56, italics in the original)

Dimensionless organisms need bodies to operate in three-dimensional reality. They get them by promoting habits that subject the human organism to their control. There are as many Nova Mobsters as there are habitual tics. All control the agencies of their hosts.

And that is the real trouble with the individual body of liberal het/ sex: it *is not* individual. Rather it is a composite body produced by a multiplicity of organisms, all of which have their own agendas and only one of which is (or was) human. What is worse for Burroughs is that, in its current condition, this body has become so thoroughly subjected to control that it has stopped evolving. So various are the parasites that feed on its agencies that it is has no life of its own. It is a shell, a carapace, an old hotel with off-shore owners. A dead ass end—at least until it wises up. That is the whole point of Queer Science. It wises up us marks. It tries to transform the proprietary body of liberal het/sex by insisting first that it is an effect of a multiplicity of influences and second, quite simply, that it can and will change. In this it shares Warner's hope that "a culture is developing in which intimate relations and the sexual body can in fact be understood as projects for transformation among strangers" (*Counterpublics* 122). Warner underplays the possibility that culture needs new bodies to produce such futures. Burroughs wises up the old one so that it can live again, grow, and change.

Delany does something similar. Like Burroughs he sees the proprietary body of liberal het/sex as an obstacle to better futures for the human organism. Like Burroughs he describes his pursuit of new bodily possibilities in deeply personal terms. His astonishing memoir, *The Motion of Light in Water* (1988), gives a difficult glimpse of what it feels like to inhabit a reality where your body does not fit and your sexuality exceeds all liberal limits. "A black man. A gay man. A writer. [...] at that time, the words 'black' and 'gay' didn't exist with their current meaning, usage, history. 1961 had been, really, part of the fifties. The political consciousness that was to form by the end of the sixties had not been part of my world. There were only Negroes and homosexuals, both of whom—along with artists—were hugely devalued in the social hierarchy" (398, 399). To possess the body of an African American or a homosexual, or perish the thought of an African American homosexual, is in the 1950s and early 1960s to be classed among the dregs of society, to embody abjection. Such is the force of liberal het/sex and the biases it circulates. It denigrates and denudes.

Which is to say it enslaves. That is the point of the Prologue of what many consider to be Delany's best novel, *Stars in My Pocket Like Grains of Sand* (1985). Rat Korga is big, black, homosexual, a petty criminal, a drug user, a malcontent. The book's opening sentence sums up his world's response: " 'Of course,' they told him in all honesty, 'you will be a slave' " (3). Slavery is the fate of those who do not fit in a world that is heterosexual, capitalist, and scientifically advanced enough to induce happiness through brain modification. "Sexually? [...] In this part of the world your preferences in that area can't have done you any good. You're a burden to yourself, to your city, to your geo-sector. [...] But we can change all that" (3). Indeed they do. Rat Korga chooses happiness ("All right, change me! Make me like you!" [4]) and through a slight but decisive brain modification becomes a slave, sold first to a mining company in a remote corner of his planet, Rhyonon, then to a woman who secretly buys him for sexual purposes. For a black writer to invoke slavery is no small matter. For a black gay writer to describe a life characterized by commerce and heterosexuality as slavery is a huge indictment of liberal civil society. The body that best serves such a society is the body of a slave, a fact felt most keenly by those like Delany for whom slavery is a living cultural legacy.[5]

For both Delany and Burroughs the proprietary body of liberal het/sex, the creation of privacy, reproduction, and consent remains a slave to forces that determine its agencies, sexual or otherwise. The alternative for both involves creating new bodies. For Delany that process begins when Rat Korga's planet explodes in an ambiguous convulsion of raw energy, leaving him its sole survivor. Only then does he escape slavery to experience new forms of life and sex much more congenial to his tastes. That those forms are multiple and involve organisms that are in no way human shows how far, in Delany's estimation, liberal civil society remains from making space for new bodies. But that does not stop him from anticipating it. Here the speaker is male and the act he observes is something like a circle jerk: "I stood at the shadow's edge, joined—before the three of them, Korga, the human, and the evelm, were through—by a dozen others, their cool scaled haunches and warm fleshed shoulders jostling mine" (227). This is not a picture easy to square with liberal het/sex—particularly since an evelm is more lizard than mammal, more dragon than man. The question for Delany and Burroughs too becomes how to advance such sexual possibilities under social conditions of bodily enslavement.

COUNTER-COUNTERPUBLICS

Queer Science has a double strategy. New bodies require new *images* and new *spaces* to transform a reality that reduces the kaleidoscope of possible agencies to a few endless repetitions. Delany and Burroughs are spacemen in a peculiarly literal sense. Both make and map spaces for bodies untrammeled by the constraints of liberal het/sex. The closet and the single-family home it presumes are conditions that inhibit growth and transformation. Both writers turn their backs on it—which is a different act than coming out. Without much fanfare they walk away and explore other spaces. "Within a gay or queer counter-public," says Warner, "no one is in the closet" (120). If that is the case, Delany and Burroughs are each architects of queer counterpublics, whole worlds without closets where people can be at liberty to pursue hitherto proscribed bodily possibilities.

It is important to acknowledge at this point that their counterpublics differ from Warner's in a couple of decisive ways. First, neither Delany nor Burroughs has any interest in maintaining the subordinate status of such alliances. Warner claims that "a counter-public maintains at some level, conscious or not, an awareness of its subordinate status. The cultural horizon against which it marks itself off is not just a general or wider public but a dominant one." (119). This sounds dangerously close to acquiescing to enslavement, and Queer Science rejects it summarily. The aim of the counterpublic is to transform conditions of domination, not accept them. As Foucault demonstrates, and even more pointedly Wendy Brown, power circulates *through* resistance, managing it in advance by making it possible. Walking away from the closet, Delany and Burroughs refuse subordination and its masochistic pleasures. They aspire to worlds where such options have obsolesced. Granted, theirs is an uncompromising desire, but it at least remains numb to the allure of subjection.

And that leads to their second difference with Warner. For perfectly obvious reasons, Warner makes capital the economic condition of the queer counterpublic. And why not? It is pretty hard to wish away the material facts of free market economics gone global. As Warner insists, one cannot expect to secure urban space if one does not make commerce a fundamental practice. Hence the danger of zoning laws like those in New York City that push the sex trade away from urban centers. Queer conterpublics require queer capital: "because what brings us together is sexual culture, there are very few places in the world that have assembled much of a queer population without a base in sex commerce" (204). Although Warner refuses to identify membership in such communities with property ownership, maintaining that "the right to the city extends to those who use the city" (205), his strategic investment in commerce distinguishes his queer counterpublic from those of Delany and Burroughs.

Neither views capitalism as producing much else than control. Their turn away from the closet is a turn away from commerce too. Any counterpublic grounded in commerce will eventually succumb to its logic of accumulation, unless business stays just bad enough not to be profitable. Witness in this regard Delany's beautiful elegy for dead and gone counterpublic of the Times Square porn theaters in New York, *Times Square Red, Times Square Blue* (2001). Rather than call for its recovery, Delany advocates imagining new places for new counterpublics organized less around commerce than practices of pleasure. Warner too readily conflates sex and commerce. Why not imagine with Delany and Burroughs queer counterpublics that eschew the ways of commerce? The force, in other words, of sexual creativity might be to produce possibilities that exceed contemporary conditions and open up exciting if apparently preposterous new futures.

Image War!

Doing that requires desperate measures, cunning tactics, even guerilla war. It is as interesting as it is obvious that Delany and Burroughs
both choose to forge counterpublics through fiction rather than, say,
cultural criticism or policy analysis. Queer Science is cy-fi that disrupts the operation of biopower, producing queer futures. As such its
greatest weapon is neither a thermonuclear warhead nor a designer
pathogen. It is the image, or rather an arsenal of images, that jams
the cybernetic machines confining and controlling bodily agencies.
Apart from an emphasis on discourse as a means of consolidating
queer counterpublics, Warner remains peculiarly blind to the role
images play in administrating contemporary life. His counterpublics
are brick and mortar erogenous zones where sex is public and the
streets are queer. I am all for it, but there is something nostalgic in
a vision that does not take cyberspace and its frictionless circulation
of images into account as a means of configuring reality. Justin Berry
fell into an online community no less active for being virtual instead
of physical. I am not saying that securing physical space should not
be the aim of queer counterpublics, just that in a cybernetic society
where info-tech circulates relations of force, doing so is only half the
battle. The other half, the opening salvo, involves fighting images
with images, disrupting control.

That is what Queer Science *does*. Delany justifies this course of
action when he describes what it is like to tell people how he writes
science fiction:

> And how many people whom I'd just met and who'd asked me, "What
> do you do?" did I answer disingenuously, "Oh, I type manuscripts for
> people"? For by now I knew that such an answer troubled the easy,
> flickering social waters far less than the accurate, "I'm a writer," or
> the more troubling, "I'm a writer, I've published five novels," or the
> most disturbing, "I'm a writer, I've published five novels. They're sci-
> ence fiction," which, when you said it to men, mostly produced a low,
> bewildered grunt, as if you had unexpectedly slugged them somewhere
> below the navel, and which, when you said it to women, mostly pro-
> duced a sudden smile and the ejaculation "Oh, isn't that wonderful!"
> (*Motion* 440)

Science fiction is, socially speaking, troubling. It disturbs people's
expectations: about what is serious, what is significant, what is real,
what is art. As fiction, it does all that through images that don't
square readily with reality: bug-eyed monsters from another planet,

teleportation technology, or sex partners with wings and prehensile tongues. Such images contravene the World as We Know It in the service of alternatives. They punch people in the gut and force unexpected bodily responses. Men grunt and women ejaculate. Genders bend and reality warps. The images of Queer Science do not simply *represent* new possibilities. They *produce* them physically, or would once they gained bodily purchase: the real danger—or hope—of Queer Science.

Consider one of Delany's most exhilarating images, his description of dragon hunting in *Stars in My Pocket Like Grains of Sand*. Thanks to the technology of the "radar bow," which maps cerebrations between distinct organisms, a hunter *becomes* the creature she hunts, fully experiencing its alien life:

> But knowing the dragon's body from the inside is an adventure of a different order: in human women, hunger and desire, each sunk deep in the body, are always present, either as a full or an empty field. In the dragon the three drives, the one raging, the other two at sift and drift, in their various rhythms, are inconstant. . . . I glimpsed the wider wings of the neuter above, and chills detonated my spine; my gills erupted rings of excitation, and I arched away, borne under the beat of other urges, to drop through the world built in my mouth . . . (247–48)

This kind of hunting allows the hunter not to take but to experience the life of the hunted. The human body opens to another kind of body altogether, allowing a moment of physical hybridity and recognition: "I was a dragon . . . ? I was a dragon!" (248). Human bodies become other in the process, transform, and take wing. How is that for an image to confute the subjection that Delany attributes to the proprietary body of civil society?!

There is another one at work here too, less vivid perhaps but equally effectual. Throughout the novel Delany uses the word "women" where the word "men" would traditionally appear. All humans are women, some just have penises. This reversal disturbs a whole slew of assumptions about gendered agency in our reality. It is hard to get used to, unsettling the complacencies of sexual identity. Whether one considers oneself male, female, gay, lesbian, bi-, trans-, one still has to identify with "women" who are "men." Strange. Such images are quiet hand grenades tossed into the closet. They explode the proprieties of home and family, making women the new standard of humanity. They are weapons in an image war.

Burroughs is the great strategist of such warfare. He is not about to follow Delany's use of the word "women" to describe the human organism (see his essay "Women: a Biological Mistake?"), but he similarly uses cy-fi as means of disrupting control and advancing bodily transformation: "Souls rotten from their orgasm drugs, flesh shuddering from their nova ovens, prisoners of the earth to *come out*. With your help we can occupy The Reality Studio and retake their universe of Fear Death and Monopoly—" (*Nova Express 7*). Burroughs orders all prisoners, gay and straight, to come out—not from the closet but from a whole stinking reality produced and broadcast for public consumption and control. He is a cyberwarrior a good thirty years before the battleground shifted into cyberspace, a keen observer of life in cybernetic society, where images advance subjection. The revolution he calls for cannot be won with guns and bullets. The media that circulate those images (books, magazines, newspapers, radio, TV, movies—eventually too the Internet) are too formidable and dispersed a weaponry to attack directly. So he fights images with images, jamming the cybernetic machinery that produces and distributes them. Although the means of this guerilla warfare are virtual, the stakes are vital, nothing less than the life and future of the human organism.

Where Delany's cyberfiction offers bold visions of worlds to come, Burroughs's wrecks havoc on this one. Burroughs is an image terrorist, but to specific and progressive ends. He exploits the machinery that makes bodies so susceptible to image addiction. "The error in enemy strategy is now obvious—It is machine strategy and the machine can be redirected—Have written connection in The Soft Typewriter the machine can only repeat your instructions since it can not create anything" (85). Burroughs does all he can to redirect the operations of any control machine he can get his hands—or words—on. Famously, he cuts up the printed word, rearranging it to produce new statements. He writes by association and juxtaposition, producing not meaning so much as possibility. He elaborates wild routines ("Pack your Ermines, Mary!") that land somewhere between literature and pornography. He creates audacious images that stick in your brain like a burr in fur (the talking asshole of *Naked Lunch*, the Death Dwarves of *Nova Express*). Nor is he content with literary procedures. Using tape recorders, he cuts up sound to redirect its effects. He makes collages of pictures and print—he calls them "identikits"— that reconstitute the identities of fictional characters. He makes film ("Ah Pook"), he shoots paintings (with a twelve gauge). Maybe his greatest creation is the image "Burroughs," the plain talking pork-pie ironist whose gaunt face haunts the mediascape in shades as diverse as *Drugstore Cowboy* and an ad for Nikes. Burroughs *is* the images he circulates.

All to disrupt control, wise up the marks, get their bodies growing again. The human organism has quit developing not merely because it has been invaded by myriad parasites but more particularly because it has incorporated images that script its agencies. Those pesky parasites are such images, and they reduce human bodies to their own forms of life. That happens every time one catches a cold, according to Burroughs. A virus infects one's body with its image and one spends weeks replicating it by sneezing. In the words of the controllers, "Our virus infects the human and creates our image in him" (49). The result is a body that quits developing, which is to say that it no longer really lives: "It was important all this time that the possibility of a human ever conceiving of being without a body should not arise" (49). The true purpose of life for Burroughs is mutation, the transformation of bodies so they can survive under new conditions. Just as our bodies were piscine before they were human, so too they will continue to develop in ways that make them unrecognizable, perhaps disembodying altogether to enter the inevitable next stage of life, the space stage. That is the future Burroughs fights for, or rather futures, in which bodies develop multiple agencies through mutation: *"This is war to extermination—Shift linguals—Cut word lines—Vibrate tourists— Free doorways—Photo falling—Word falling—Break through in grey room—Calling Partisans of all nations—Towers, open fire—"* (67).

SPACE: THE FINAL FRONTIER

If sexuality in cybernetic society circulates through images, as Justin Berry's experience suggests, the problem of securing space cannot be separated from that circulation. Burroughs and Delany wage image war to open new spaces for new bodies. Not commerce but insurgent images consolidate their counterpublics. Not pornography but Queer Science advances sexualities that exceed liberal het/sex. When they turn their backs on the closet, both reject the architecture of home and family as an acceptable foundation for queer counterpublics. It remains too private to promote anything but liberal het/sex or, as in Justin's case, its spurious inversion. Burroughs and Delany turn instead to queer spaces where sex goes public, abjuring the holy trinity of privacy, reproduction, and consent. In such spaces bodies multiply and boundaries fall until sexuality circulates freely, irreducible to quaint heterosexual couplings in dim corners. While real, these spaces also circulate images that excite new bodily possibilities. In the counterpublics of Queer Science, space and image merge, turning sexuality into a means of bodily transformation, not reproduction.

In this sense Queer Science advances new sexualities for cybernetic society. Mutating bodies and multiplying possibilities might be irreducible to control.

IMPOSSIBLE? MAYBE. WORTH A TRY? OF COURSE!

Take Delany. The East Village sexual underworld that he describes in *The Motion of Light in Water* is a warren of physical spaces linked together by an errant and insurgent sexuality: toilets, subway stops, street corners, bars like Dirty Dick's, empty apartments, and most memorably a group of semitrailer trucks parked on the Christopher Street Pier. These spaces, the latter particularly, constitute the architecture of a queer sexuality incommensurable with the single-family home, its private bedrooms and dark closets. A new kind of body emerges there that is less origin than conductor of the energy of sex. As such these bodies multiply. They become congeries of multiple organs and interplays of multiple contacts in spaces capacious enough for sexuality to circulate freely. Sex goes public and bodies transform. The effect is less frenzy than intensity, tenderness, and concern.

Delany describes it better than I can:

> Sometimes to walk between the vans and cabs was to amble from single sexual encounter—with five, twelve, forty minutes between—to single sexual encounter. At other times to step between the waist-high tires and make your way between the smooth or ribbed walls was to invade a space at a libidinal saturation impossible to describe to someone who has not known it. Any number of pornographic filmmakers, gay and straight, have tried to portray something like it—now for homosexuality, now for heterosexuality—and failed because what they were trying to show was wild, abandoned, beyond the edge of control, whereas the actuality of such a situation, with thirty-five, fifty, a hundred all-but-strangers is hugely ordered, highly social, attentive, silent, and grounded in a certain care, if not community. At those times, within those van-walled alleys, now between the trucks, now in the back of the open loaders, cock passed from mouth to mouth to hand to ass to mouth without ever breaking contact with another flesh for more than seconds; mouth, hand, ass passed over whatever you held out to them, sans interstice; when one cock left, finding a replacement—mouth, rectum, another cock—required only moving the head, the hip, the hand no more than an inch, three inches.

So much for liberal het/sex. Here bodies turn multiple and sexuality circulates among them. Privacy, reproduction, and consent have nothing to do with it. Bodies are not property but parts without owners, *the* head, *the* hip, *the* hand. They touch and change.

Among the trucks on Christopher Street Pier Delany participates in the kind of world-making Warner calls for when he says that "a culture is developing in which intimate relations and the sexual body can in fact be understood as projects for transformation among strangers" (122). The difference is that for Delany such a culture is not commercial. It is sexual to be sure, but not in a way that would be easy to capitalize: no cover charge, no performance, no dancing, no drinks. Such sexuality is as much an image of possibility as its realization. Delany's counterpublic might be more rhetorical than commercial, as his thoughts on the subject suggest: "I've often pondered on the terms 'gay culture,' 'gay society,' 'gay sensibility.' [...] if, somehow, there is such a thing as culture apart from infrastructural realities, gay society has always seemed to me an accretion of dozens on dozens of such minutae, a whole rhetoric of behavior" (231). Here is why images play such an important role in the counterpublics of Queer Science. They promote the "rhetoric of behavior" that constitutes gay culture. They build its futures.

As when Delany imagines a new sexuality in *Stars in My Pocket Like Grains of Sand*. The spaces of the East Village return, but as images of coming possibilities. Public sex-runs mix bodies and statuary, making it hard to tell them apart. They mix species too: "The abstract statues along both sides, no matter how many times I came in here (three, five, ten times a week since I was twelve—at least when I'm home), always look like people for the first few seconds, till your eyes adjust to the dimness—at which point you begin to make out the people, humans and evelmi, who stand or stroll among them" (225). The encounters that occur resemble those among the trucks, except that dragon-descended evelmi mingle among the humans: "One I did recognize came over to me...and nuzzled my groin. I scratched behind his wide purplish gill-ruff (the male and neuter evelmi's most sensitive erogenous zone) and his great wings quivered" (225). This image of sexuality includes other bodies and transforms the human. The culture it promotes includes others as different as saurian is from *homo sapiens*. Such a future may be hard to square with zoning law and commercial practice. But that is the point. As bodies become—or become through—images of new futures they leave old ones behind. Liberal het/sex with its body closet might just wither away, a dim cultural memory in a world of new possibilities.

That would be Burroughs's hope too, except that he pursues it even more aggressively than Delany. Not a man for cruising public toilets, Burroughs prefers spaces that are at once more geographically dispersed and less culturally familiar than Delany's. For him public space has a global reach: Mexico City, Panama City, Tangier, London. Mobility rather than location determines accessibility. Burroughs travels the world in search of spaces where sexuality circulates more freely than in the land of the free. He finds them mostly in third world cultures where liberal het/sex has not fully taken hold—in Central America or North Africa. Mexico, for instance, offers public spaces that allow for a greater range of behaviors than square America allows: "It seemed to me that everyone in Mexico had mastered the art of minding his own business.... Boys and young men walked down the street arm in arm and no one paid them any mind. It wasn't that people didn't care what others thought; it simply would not occur to a Mexican to expect criticism from a stranger, nor to criticize the behavior of others" (Queer vi). This reticence proves the provisionality of liberal het/sex in Mexico, at least during the 1950s. It has not yet achieved a monopoly on sexual practice, which is to say that for Burroughs privacy is not always imperative in cultures outside the decorous West. Mexico and Morocco hold open possibilities for sexualities irreducible to the closet.

Even more radically than Delany, Burroughs insists that these sexualities unite image and flesh. Sex becomes a matter of circulation, which occurs by means of images: " 'Breath in Johnny. Here goes.' Red Youths fuck bent over a brass bed in Mexico. Feel through a maze of penny arcades and dirty pictures to the blue Mexican night. Penis of different size, shape swell in and out flicker faces and bodies' burning flesh sparks from camp fires and red fuck lights in blue cubicles" (Soft Machine 142). Sex acts cannot be separated from images of sex acts, in fact are those images, which shift, mix, and mutate, creating new spaces, bodies, possibilities. At its most extreme—and imaginative—these images float free from the spaces that create them to bring forth a different kind of space altogether, one where multiplicity lives out a life of perpetual mutation. People-City in Nova Express is one such place, a space where life collapses into film and bodies morph like edited effects:

> A million drifting screens on the walls of is city projected mixing sound of any bar could be heard in all Westerns and film of all times played and recorded at the people back and forth with portable cameras and telescope lenses poured eddies and tornadoes of sound and camera array until soon city where the movie everywhere a Western movie in Hongkong or the Aztec sound talk suburban America and all

accents and language mixed and fused and peopled shifted language
and accent in mid-sentence Aztec priest and spilled in man woman or
beast in all language—So that People-City moved in swirls and no one
knew what he was going out of space to neon streets—. (149)

The third world space of sexual possibility becomes a movie that
explodes in a whirl of shifting images, circulating a sexuality as
public as it is multitudinous: "the Kid stirred in sex films and The
People-City pulsed in a vast orgasm and no one knew what was film
and what was not and performed all kinda sex acts of every street
corner—" (149). So much for liberal het/sex. Like Delany, Burroughs
conflates space and image to produce a future beyond the reach of
property, reproduction, and consent. It may not be a commercial
future, but it is cybernetic in the sense that images set the terms
for reality and not vice versa. Bodies are image machines and sex is
mutant cinema. Queer Science is cybernetic sexuality, and Burroughs
is its master strategist.

Having no use for the closet, Queer Science returns to vandalize
it. Burroughs's best novel, *The Wild Boys* (1969), ends where liberal
het/sex begins, in the family home, but with a difference. The story is
set in a postapocalyptic world where the Earth's population has been
largely incinerated and rangy gangs of randy youth maraud the land.
They are the wild boys, and they live and love collectively, openly,
intensely, violently. Near the end of the novel one gang, badly in need
of clothes, comes upon a once familiar architecture: "There was a ram-
bling ranch-style house obviously built before the naborhood deteri-
orated. We stepped through the hedge and passed a ruined barbecue
pit. The side door was open" (182). So the wild boys enter and trash
the place, finding a thirty-eight revolver, a box of shells, and plenty of
togs. "We went through the house like a whirlwind the Dib pulling
out suits and sport coats from closets and holding them against his
body in front of mirrors, opening drawers snatching what he wanted
and dumping the rest on the floor" (182). Property is not private any
more and there is nothing sacred about the nuclear family.

Or its architecture. Closets get stripped, and the honorific space of
heterosexual conception sees another kind of intercourse: " 'This make
me very hot Meester.' He sat on the bed and pulled off his jockstrap
and his cock flipped out lubricating. 'Whee' he said and laid back on
his elbows kicking his feet. 'Jacking me off.' I slipped off my strap and
sat down behind him rubbing the lubricant around the tip of his cock
and he went off in a few seconds" (182). This is not an image of typical single-family home het/sex. Mommy and daddy have departed,

leaving only their clothes behind. The architecture of liberal het/sex provides a space now for honest, open queer sex. Would that it had offered Justin Berry such life-affirming possibilities. Ransacking the closet in the closing scene of *The Wild Boys*, Burroughs puts an end to its privacy and the sexuality it serves: "Darkness falls on the ruined suburbs. A dog barks in the distance" (184). After the closet, only the stars and the world and the sky remain. Life. The trick is to live it.

Coda: Virus

It seems irresponsible to write about queer counterpublics without referencing the invasion of that terminal alien, AIDS. As the supreme theorist of the virus, Burroughs has something to teach about this insatiable invader and its place in queer counterpublics. Like any virus, it comes to control. It inserts its DNA into the cellular machinery of a human host and commands replication. It directs the life of the human organism to its own viral advantage. In this regard AIDS is not a particularly astute virus, since it inevitably induces the total collapse of the host. It works a terminal magic, to the sorrow of millions. How to secure counterpublics from this blistering invasion? Burroughs's answer: cut the lines of transmission. "It is simply a question of putting through an inoculation program in the very limited time that remains—Word begets image and image *is* the virus" (*Nova Express* 48). Multiply images that multiply new bodies, as in People-City: images of asexuality immune to the invader AIDS, new flesh for new futures, disembodied image-flesh, strange as that may sound. One of the challenges AIDS presents, among many others, is the creation of images of queer sexuality no longer susceptible to AIDS. Bodies are extraordinarily supple. They change. They adapt. If the objective of Queer Science is to transform them, multiply their possibilities, purge them of terminal invaders, then it is not enough to call for commercial counterpublics. The urgent task now is to imagine new sexualities and bodies to come.

3

AFTERLIVES

6

THE SPACE MACHINE

Music is the weapon of the Future.

Fela Kuti

DARK ENERGY

Space is black. Check out any episode of *Star Trek*. When Captain
Kirk and his faithful crew boldly go where no man has gone before,
they take a journey into blackness, punctuated with a few bright
and shining stars. Maybe that goes without saying. Since Sputnik
popped the top of Earth's prophylactic atmosphere, everybody
knows the color of space. There are myriad pictures to prove it. But
forget pictures for a minute. Approach the question culturally and
it becomes obvious that space is more than just a transparent black
background for the space race and its colonialist *Enterprise*. When
Sun Ra, the great theorist and master mage of astro-black mythology, says "Space is the Place," he means it is the place of blackness:
black space. What, then, is the relationship between space and race
in cybernetic society?

A question for cyberfiction, that vernacular discourse for imagining new worlds. While traditional science fiction remains at best
complacent in examining the role of race in cybernetic society (having been produced for an adolescent white middle-class consumer),
an insurgence is occurring in the creation of black cyberfiction,
or what a recently published anthology calls "speculative fiction
from the African Diaspora." That anthology, *Dark Matter*, gathers
together an impressive array of black writers who are producing a
distinguished body of black cy-fi. Samuel Delany is no longer the
sole brother writing science fiction on an otherwise white planet,
nor is Octavia Butler its Hottentot Venus, curious queen in foreign
climes. From George S. Schulyer to Nalo Hopkinson, from Charles
R. Sanders to Tananarive Due, a renaissance—or maybe better, a

naissance—of black cyberfiction is under way that augurs unimagined possibilities.

Walter Mosely suggests in "Black to the Future," a brief commentary that appears in *Dark Matter*: "The genre speaks most clearly to those who are dissatisfied with the way things are: adolescents, post adolescents, escapists, dreamers, and those who have been made to feel powerless. And this may explain the appeal that science fiction holds for a great many African Americans. [...] Through science fiction you can have a black president, a black world, or simply a say in the way things are. This power to imagine is the first step in changing the world" (Thomas 405–6). Black cy-fi begins by affirming the blackness of space, the material space of contemporary social life rather than the transparent space of imperialist expansion. The space of this world, and not the galaxy, needs a change. Black science fiction dares to imagine such possibilities. In this regard, Amiri Baraka becomes one of its forerunners, and his inclusion among the writers in *Dark Matter* proves instructive. While accounting for only a small part of his astonishing body of work, Baraka's science fiction asserts the fact that space is black, or will be. Working in close concert with Sun Ra's astro-black mythologizing but toward even more physical ends, Baraka imagines a future in which space materializes a previously transparent blackness. His means for pursuing this future is music. Black music is the doomsday weapon Baraka directs against an oppressively wired, white world.

Although it would be overstating the case to call Baraka a science fiction writer per se, he makes it clear in his autobiography that the genre constitutes part of his cultural heritage as a mid-twentieth-century city kid. Growing up in Newark meant listening to the radio and imagining life's possibilities accordingly. "The radio," he says, "was always another school for my mind" (26). The shows that captured his imagination conjured up adventure and strangeness: *The Shadow*, *I Love a Mystery*, *Inner Sanctum*, *Escape*. The last was particularly influential. It broadcast stories by famous writers, stories of fantasy and science fiction by the likes of H. Rider Haggard and H. G. Wells. Baraka mentions Wells's "The Valley of the Blind" in particular. The real lesson of these radio shows was that the enemy to human happiness, whether the cold-blooded killer or the invading alien horde, could be identified, opposed, and maybe even defeated. As Baraka puts it, those shows "taught us that evil needed to be destroyed," a lesson he took to heart and made the driving force of his life as a writer (27). So clear and so compelling was the moral charge of this material that Baraka included the motto of that close cousin of science fiction, the superhero Green Lantern, in his collection of poems entitled *The Dead Lecturer*:

> In Blackest Day
> In Blackest Night
> No Evil Shall Escape My Sight!
> Let Those Who Worship Evil's Might
> Beware My Power
> Green Lantern's Light.

Popular pulp fiction and radio sow the seeds of resistance to social injustice.

And that is something of an irony, given such stuff was produced to sell products, circulate images, and promote satisfactions in keeping with the comforts of majority culture. It would be wrong, therefore, to conclude that the kind of science fiction Baraka heard on the radio as a kid was subversive in the way Mosely imagines for contemporary black cy-fi. With the important exception of Wells, who was British and openly socialist in his politics, science fiction before World War II—and long after as well—participated in the cultural project of imagining the future in the image of a perpetual American present. Call it cosmic liberalism tricked out in the latest technoscientific gadgetry: the sci-fi of the pulps and the radio shows launched the politics of possessive individualism into outer space. Maybe it was an inevitable move, culturally speaking. The disappearance of the American frontier and the eradication of "the native problem" rendered obsolete the wild-west mythology of manifest destiny. So manifest destiny builds a rocket and blasts off.

With the help, of course, of the latest advances in science and its fictions. Gernsback and Campbell, those godfathers of the pulps, both helped cosmic liberalism get off the ground. Both set and policed the standards that qualified writing as science fiction, not only openly stated scientific standards of plausibility and extrapolation, but also unstated cultural standards of appropriateness and legitimation. Pulp science fiction stories had obviously to invoke plausible science, but less obviously legitimate culture as well. Their cosmic liberalism saturates space with the values of individuality, accumulation, and perpetual progress. In this regard, Stanley Weinbaum's landmark story "A Martian Odyssey" (1933) proves representative. Its title makes the cultural agenda of it and so many other Golden Age sci-fi stories unavoidably clear: to boldly discover Western culture where no man has gone before. And that is pretty much what happens. A diverse crew of "true pioneers" (German, French, English, and American) braves the deeps of interplanetary space to become "the first men to feel other gravity than earth's" (Silverberg 13). On Mars a scout ship piloted by the American breaks down, forcing him to face down the elements (which are nasty), the natives (who are nastier), and the moral dilemma of whether or not to steal a sacred crystal that also happens to cure cancer—which turns out, of course, to be no dilemma at all. The American returns to his mother ship a hero, having survived alone and swiped the crystal. Thanks to the wonders of science, the possessive individual triumphs again (with the help, it must be admitted, of an eight foot Martian that looks like a duck but fights like a man). There is no need to belabor the whiteness of "the famous crew" or the Eurocentrism of their spacecowboy beliefs. But it is worth noting that when race becomes an issue around the apparent humanity of the eight foot duck, the deciding criterion is the limited, primitive intelligence of African "Negritoes." Unlike the duck, they "haven't any generic words, [...] no names for general classes" (22). The cosmic liberalism of pulp sci-fi legitimates beliefs that promote racial exclusion.

As a popular genre, science fiction from its inception until the work of Samuel Delany remains pretty much, in the worst sense of the phrase, color blind. Even when race is its explicit subject, as in Ray Bradbury's famous story from *The Martian Chronicles*, "Way in the Middle of the Air" (1950), the ideological imperative of cosmic liberalism renders it transparent to majority culture. Bradbury's story, for all its humanity, is a neocolonial fantasy of racial justice that directs the historical longings of black separatism toward the distant shores of colonized Mars. Simply put, the story's African Americans, "every single one here in the South," abandon the Earth for Mars, having secretly arranged rocket passage (90). Although Graham Lock makes the useful suggestion that Bradbury's description of black emigration to another planet might have in some way influenced Sun Ra's astro-black mythology, it is important to realize that "Way in the Middle of the Air" never really solves the problem it raises. Yes, African Americans vacate this planet, propelled by the dream of a better world in the sky. And Bradbury unflinchingly depicts the racism they leave behind. Asked what to do about the loss of a young black clerk, the protagonist replies, "Kill that son of a bitch" (100). Earth is no world for African Americans. But neither, it appears, is Mars. For although Bradbury depicts them leaving this planet en masse, he never shows them arriving anywhere else. Blacks abandon Earth to land nowhere. They simply disappear into black space, as if the logic of cosmic liberalism can make no room for them in the known universe. Sun Ra had other plans for African Americans—and other planets too. But the space of cosmic liberalism is a place only for possessive individuals and neocolonial heroes. Black is the color of its transparent background, the meaningless backdrop of really heroic acts—like imperialist expansion. Way up in the middle of the air, Bradbury's black émigrés get lost in space, absorbed into the emptiness between worlds.

What would happen if black space were a place and not a transparency? That is the question that drives Sun Ra's astro-black mythologizing, and in a different way it drives Baraka's science fiction too. In raising the question of space so directly in terms of place Sun Ra and Baraka both disrupt the ideological superstructure of cosmic liberalism and the Golden Age science fiction that sustains it. Traditionally sci-fi after all, is *the* genre of temporal imagination. Time travel is one of its foundational tricks and favorite tropes because time is what *happens* in the space of transparent blackness. The apparent inevitability of time's passage opens the future to imagination too, so that a characteristic gimmick of science fiction is the story set in some time yet to come. Distant or near, utopian or dystopian, terran or transgalactic, the relationship of that future to the reader's present forefronts the all too simple fact that time passes. This investment in time as a medium for human life and imagination is one of the ways classic science fiction advances the agenda of cosmic liberalism. It thereby participates in a larger cultural project coincident with the emergence of capitalism that prefers time to space, history to geography, as ways of valuing life and making it meaningful. To live temporally, from this view, is to exist individually, in ultimate relation to death. It is to live and die in time, without particular reference to the spatial locations, the physical geographies of that mortal span. A science fiction that takes time for the main theater of its imagination, even when staged against the backdrop of whole galaxies, helps make space innocuous, a place only of fantasy, not politics.

Blue Aliens

Much pulp sci-fi perpetuates what Edward W. Soja calls the "illusion of transparency." Like many cultural practices characteristic of modernity, it "dematerializes space into pure ideation and representation, an intuitive way of thinking that equally prevents us from seeing the social construction of affective geographies, the concretization of social relations embedded in spatiality, an interpretation of space as a 'concrete abstraction,' a social hieroglyphic similar to Marx's conceptualization of the commodity form" (7). The space of cosmic liberalism (as opposed to Wells's progressive socialism) is transparent in just this way. Its blackness is merely a medium for pure ideation and representation, the pervasive trace of social relations that such a conception of space arises to hide. Space in this sense, the sense of a thousand space operas and a hundred episodes of *Star Trek*, becomes an empty medium through which the heroic adventurers of science fiction fly to discover the strangeness of aliens or the weirdness of time. Lost to such adventures are the less sublime, more material spaces of social life such as those Wells explores, and with them the awareness that, for all its apparent vastness, space is socially produced. For Soja, this loss proves useful to a capitalist social order in which that production involves domination and unequal distribution of wealth and power. That is why he so urgently advocates another way of approaching space, "one which recognizes spatiality as simultaneously [...] a social product (or outcome) and a shaping force (or medium) in social life" (7). Making this move from transparent to productive space recovers what modernity on Soja's reading has worked so hard to forget, a sense of personal responsibility for space as a collective production—even the empty space of cosmic liberalism. Not time but space becomes the medium of change, and the best means of predicting it: "Prophecy now involves a geographical rather than historical projection; it is space and not time that hides consequences from us" (23).

In this sense Baraka is a prophet in three dimensions and his cy-fi is a space machine. It projects and produces other spaces to disrupt social control, not in some distant future, but right HERE, right NOW. That at least is the aim of the most obvious instance of science fiction among his many works, the triumphant short story entitled "Answers in Progress" from his 1967 collection *Tales*. Its scenario is as simple as it is funny: spacemen arrive on Earth in search of Art Blakey records. But it is not this scenario so much as the social transformation it augurs that makes "Answers in Progress" an instance of Baraka's space machine. The first thing to notice about the story is how deeply grounded it is in its historical moment. Unlike myriad tales of space invaders flung across the interminable pages of the pulps, Baraka's has a setting that is socially palpable, historically concrete, and menacing: the Newark of 1967, on the brink of the rebellion that would erupt that July. But what is interesting about Baraka's treatment of that reality is the way he transforms it. Part future history, part manifesto, and pure science fiction, "Answers in Progress" envisions black rebellion against the white establishment as a victory for the oppressed. Triumph transforms spatial possibility. Spacemen arrive in New Ark, as Baraka is fond of calling it, as harbingers of this victory and the ensuing transformation of social space.

Baraka's descriptions of the rebellion in *The Autobiography of Leroi Jones* make it clear that when it did occur the stakes were higher—or maybe lower—than abstract principles of justice and equality: at issue was the possession and configuration of space itself, the social space in which black people lived and moved in Newark. Himself locked up on the first night of the rebellion, Baraka sums up its historical outcome: "In its entirety the rebellion went on for six days or so. Thousands of blacks were arrested and thousands more were injured. The official score was 21 blacks killed and 2 whites, a policeman and a fireman. But there were many more blacks killed, their bodies on roofs and in back alleys, spirited away and stuck in secret holes. It was no riot, it was a rebellion" (371). That distinction is important, because as a rebellion the unrest aimed not simply at damaging property and the space it configured but seizing that space and transforming it radically. Hence Baraka's understanding of its political implications in terms of warfare: "It was a war, for us, a war of liberation. One had to organize, one had to arm, one had to mobilize and educate the people. For me, the rebellion was a cleansing fire" (375). And as in conventional war but without its usual termination, taking and occupying material space is the major objective, which is why Baraka sees it continuing throughout America even to this day:

> So the Newarks of the U.S. still exist like they did in 1967, trying to drive the blacks out to the hopeless exurbs, so that the whites can urban renew, having found out the ancient teaching of Ibn Arabi is true, that the cities are the chief repositories of culture and the highest thrust of human life. Or having read Mao they know that the socialist revolutions in the Western industrial countries *will begin in the cities* and then move out to the countryside. (371, italics in the original)

Space, the social space of contemporary urban life, becomes for Baraka the only space that, materially speaking, really *matters*. His cy-fi is a space machine that actively promotes transformation.

"Answers in Progress," then, transforms the coming event of the Newark rebellion into a spatial triumph for the black populace. In other words it spatializes that temporal event, reconfiguring the relations of power that turn Newark into a battlefield. That is why, after a harrowing account in verse of the violence that attends such change, the story begins so abruptly: "The next day the spaceships landed. Art Blakey records was what they were looking for" (219). Paul Gilroy views this visitation as testimony to the obsolescence of racial identity, arguing that "because race consciousness is so manifestly arcane, its victims and others who perceive the open secret of its residual status *must* be closer to advanced interplanetary travelers than they are to its deluded earthly practitioners" (344). But Baraka's visitors are *space* men in an even more literal sense than Gilroy's investment in consciousness can account for. They appear, literally and materially, in the new space produced by the rebellion. These spacemen inhabit a social space materially transformed by black power. Not consciousness but three-dimensional mobility determines their appearance in this world. That is why they react the way they do when stabbed and bleeding whites stagger out of a department store: "The space men thought that's what was really happening. One beeped (Ali mentioned this in the newspapers) that this was evolution. Could we dig it? Shit yeh. We were laughing" (219). What is really happening, what the space men have the capacity to think and to live, is an evolutionary transformation of space and reconfiguration of power that opens New Ark up to new life forms.

Baraka's opening lines continue: "We gave them Buttercorn Lady and they threw it back at us. They wanted to know what happened to The Jazz Messengers" (219). The space men are pursuing the great drummer Art Blakey, whom they also call by his Muslim name Buhainia. Their appearance is a material response to the call of Blakey's Jazz Messengers. Here is a new version of the old sci-fi close encounter salutation, "take me to your leader." In this case the leader is a musician whose authority *is* the music he plays. Baraka makes music a means of achieving the evolutionary advance his story describes. Jazz, or a particular instance of it, becomes his weapon of the future. It explodes upon the scene, reconfiguring social space in new ways and toward new ends. Jazz in this sense is much more than either entertainment or even art. It becomes a vital force that participates directly in the material transformation of space and the power relations that sustain it. The new world that "Answers in Progress" depicts would be impossible without the force of black music to open social space up to new possibilities.

SPACE MUSIC

Baraka describes this effect more directly in an essay first published in 1966 entitled "The Changing Same (R&B and New Black Music)."

Discussing the new music then emerging under the banner of "free jazz," he repeatedly stresses its spatial location. At its best, jazz bespeaks the place of its creation and performance, at least until its appropriation by majority culture: Jazz is "the direct expression of a place" and "seeks another place as it weakens, a middle class place" (*Black Music* 180). It is against this weakening, this exurbanization, that Baraka directs his commentary on the new black music or free jazz. That music amounts not to a mere appeal for a place in America, but more menacingly to the production of other spaces within it. Free jazz is space music. It powers Baraka's space machine. As he puts it, "The new music began by calling itself 'free,' and this is social and is in direct commentary on the scene it appears in. Once free, it is spiritual" (193). The last remark will require further treatment, but for now the thing to notice is that the freedom of free jazz occurs only in the material surround of a social scene.

Free jazz materializes freedom, rendering it socially practicable, at least in terms of its occurrence as music: "There are other new musicians, new music that takes freedom as already being. Ornette was a cool breath of open space. Space, to move. So freedom already exists" (198). Ornette Coleman's free music transforms space. It literally, materially produces space to move, places where freedom already exists. Something similar occurs in the music of Sun Ra, whose astro-black mythologizing is too often taken for otherworldly speculation. Baraka knows better. Affirming the obvious, that Sun Ra is spiritually oriented, Baraka emphasizes the materiality of that orientation, given that Sun Ra "understands 'the future' as an ever widening comprehension of what space is, even to 'physical' travel between the planets. [...] It is science-fact that Sun-Ra is interested in, not science-fiction. It is evolution itself, and its fruits" (198–99). Space in Sun Ra's mythologizing cannot be dissociated from place, the place of blacks in a universe saturated by the facts of science. Sun Ra's music opens space to a blackness cast into the background by science, producing new relationships (the Arkestra) and realities (its communal living). Social space becomes accessible to freedoms hitherto unavailable, which is why Baraka can assert that "Ra's music changes places" (199). The spiritual valence of that change involves the production, socially speaking, of a new unity that conflates spirituality and materiality. "What will come," says Baraka in a prophetic idiom, "will be a *Unity Music*.... The consciousness of social reevaluation and rise, a social spiritualism. A mystical walk up the street to a new neighborhood where all the risen live" (210). Right HERE. Right NOW. The new music will produce new spaces, new neighborhoods

necessary?

where dead freedoms live again and spiritual aspirations take material shape.

As Sun Ra was fond of saying, "THE SPACE AGE CANNOT BE AVOIDED." It is as simple as that. The statement appears as the first line and title of one of two poems printed on the back cover of *Super-Sonic Jazz, 21st Century Limited Edition* by Le Sun Ra and his Arkestra (Saturn 1956). This record, like so many of Sun Ra's, accepts the Space Age as the cultural condition of production—but not in the same manner as myriad movies, pulps, and musical confections. There the Space Age constitutes a discourse as much of consumption as contemporaneity. For Sun Ra, the Arkestra, and the black community they helped to sustain, it provides a language for social transformation. In their hands the popular cultural discourse of the Space Age promotes social and spiritual change. Witness the poem that unfolds beneath those arresting caps. It becomes a kind of manifesto of the Arkestra's creative purpose: "The greater future is the age of the space prophet / The scientific airy minded second man. / The prince of the power of the air. / The air is music" (see Ra, *Immeasurable* 139). Sun Ra accepts the future orientation built into the discourse of the Space Age and makes it the vehicle of art, specifically that of music. Air is the medium of the magic of air travel and space flight (think of Gernsback's *Air Wonder Stories*), jets and rockets whose technological prowess are constitutive of cybernetic society. For Sun Ra the air is music and its real scientists are musicians: "Art is the foundation of any living culture. [...] Skilled culture is the new weapon of nations" (139). The discourse of the Space Age provides Sun Ra and company a new language for a new politics, artful in purpose and atonal in practice, irreducible to conventional forms and phraseology: "TOMORROW BEYOND TOMORROW IS THE GREATER KINGDOM" (139).

This kind of thinking would seem, like that of most poetry, to involve metaphor, the substitution of one reference (say air) for another (say music). But no. What is weird about Sun Ra's poetry is that there is almost nothing metaphorical about it. Statement follows statement with bland, impassive flatness. It is declamatory, conceptual, and peculiarly *auditory*, not the kind of poetry churned out by the Iowa Writer's Workshop and imprimatured by the *New Yorker*. Abstraction is its element, and exhortation its characteristic mode. Here is the other poem printed on the back of *Super-Sonic Jazz*, "Points on the Space Age," quoted in full:

This is the music of greater transition
To the invisible irresistible space age.
The music of the past will be just as tiny in the world of the future

As earth itself is in the vast reach of outer space.
Outer space is big and real and compelling
And the music which represents it must be likewise.
The music of the future is already developed
But the minds of the people of earth must be prepared to accept it.
The isolated earth age is finished
And all the music which represents only the past
Is for museums of the past and not for
The moving panorama of the outer spacite program.

(see Ra, *Immeasurble*, 138)

For Sun Ra the language of the Space Age does two things: first, it marks a divide between past (which is dead) and future (which alone, therefore, lives); second, it posits a new reality. The key line in this poem is "Outer space is big and real and compelling." Big. Real. Compelling. Sun Ra *literalizes* the discourse of the Space Age. It is not a metaphor for progress, prowess, or cool merchandise. It is the language of a new reality, or rather *is that reality*. Sun Ra refuses the traditional distinction between real and unreal that bamboozles cultural theorists from Debord to Baudrillard. Instead he distinguishes between what is *gone* and what is *not*. The past is gone. There is no use even believing in it. But the future is not. And in its *notness* Sun Ra finds a condition irreducible to the real / unreal divide. Because the future is not, it is real in a way that cannot be revoked by unreality. Reality in its notness, its not yetness, includes an element of possibility, potentiality, *fiction*. "The moving panorama of the outer spacite program" is music as the medium of this real, fictive future.

One of Sun Ra's few uses of the phrase "science fiction" comes in a poem called "The Realm of Myth" that clarifies his odd understanding of reality. It reveals also his counterintuitive sense of science: "Everything is of a particular science / And myth is no exception. / Witness: 'science fiction' / And the manifestation of its self / To a living what is called reality / Or so-called reality" (154). Science for Sun Ra is less technological than epistemological, a way of knowing particular to what is known. That which *is not*, the future or in this instance myth, has a science of its own summed up in the phrase "science fiction," a science *of* fiction as the element of what is not. A science of myth. Sun Ra calls it "myth-science." It comprises the epistemic procedures appropriate, not to so-called reality, but to the reality of the future, which is to say the reality of the not: "Thus when we speak of the future, / We speak of a lie, / Because the future is tomorrow / And tomorrow never comes" (154). Myth-science is science fiction gone literal, a science for which what is not yet is as important to know as what is merely observable.

Music is the procedural means of that science. If traditional science assimilates change through its flexible procedures of observation, hypothesis, and verification, Sun Ra's myth-science *produces* change by making music its means of investigation. A poem entitled "Of Coordinate Vibrations" shows how that science works, at least at the level of language: "But the not is the note / And note permutated is tone. / Music is of the epi-cosmic ray point. / It is of mathematical symbolic-permutation" (95). Language for Sun Ra is sound, and sound has a "mathematics" of its own called music. Permutate notation and you get tonation. Not is note is tone in an equation that is potentially immeasurable—and immeasurably potential. A difference in *sounds* produces a change in reality, a move from negation (not) through representation (note) to a music that transforms them (tone) into vibrations. It is a move similar to Derrida's turn to writing as an alternative to logocentrism, only more audacious, since for Sun Ra sound is always multiple, transitory, and *not*. As he puts the point in a brief and rare commentary on his poetry, "The myth is not but not is the future potential... as I said, phonetic differentials point to another kind of world" (226).

Musicians, then, are in this sense scientific investigators of other worlds. Here is how Sun Ra puts it in his poem "The Outer Bridge": "In the half-between world / Dwell they the tone-scientists / Sound / Mathematically precise / They speak of many things / The sound-scientists / Architects of planes of discipline" (126). Sun Ra is not simply alluding to the Pythagorean mathematics of harmony, although it lies behind such statements. He is referring too to the literal efficacy of sound as a material occurrence. Tone science is no quaint metaphor. A typescript among his business partner Alton Abraham's papers (on Mount Sinai Hospital letterhead and entitled "AMERICA AND HER THREE CHILDREN") contains a rude but challenging description of the physical, even physiological operations of tone science (unconventional spellings are the typist's):

These invisible sound-vibrations have Great power over concreat matter. They can Both Build and destroy. If a small quanitity of very fine powder is placed upon a Brass or glass plate, and a violine-Bow drawn across the edge, the vibration will cause the powder to assume beautiful Geometrical Figures. The Human voice is also capable of producing these Figures; Always the same Figure for the same tone.

If one note or cord after another be sounded upon a musical instrument say, a piano, or perfurable a violine, for from it more gradiation of Tone can be obtained, a tone will finally be reached which will cause the hearer to feel a distinct vibration in the Back of the lower part of the head. Each time that note is struct, the vibrations will be felt. That note is the "key note" of the person whom it so effects, [if] it is struct slowly and smoothingly I will Build and rest the Body, tone the nerves and Restore Healthe. If, on the other hand it be sounded in a domant way, loud and long enough, it will kill as surely as a Bullet from a pistol.

The tone science of Abraham and Sun Ra is not without a physical register. Music becomes a "scientific" means of transformation for the force of its vibrations, their physiological effect on the human organism. It introduces, or maybe *induces*, futures *that are not* into a dead reality. Vibrations work that magic, attuning matter to otherwise unavailable potentials. Music makes them real—again *literally*, which is why Sun Ra uses the literal language of the Space Age to describe new worlds to come: "This is the space-age.../ The age beyond the earth-age / A new direction /Beyond the gravitation of the past / This is the disguised twin of tomorrow" (143). When he embosses a Christmas card from himself and the Arkestra with *"Better Life Vibrations* for always," Sun Ra means every word.

SPACE IS THE PLACE

In a typescript entitled "The Space Age Music of Sun Ra...Between Two Worlds" and dated 1969, Tam Fiofori argues that the Sun Ra Arkestra in its early avatars functioned as a musical vehicle for communicating the implications of his poetry:

> The Arkestra then (1956) based in Chicago, was functioning as a Unit dedicated to the complete mastery of the principles of sounds and its natural values, as a means for retranslating Sun Ra's Cosmic-Equation poems into a more assertive and accessible medium. The immediate aim of the Music was to communicate the beauty, truths, realities and the creative nature of "a better tomorrow." This music, in its totality Sun Ra Calls Astro-Infinity Music, and recently he defined the music as "The design of another kind of world, that has nothing to do with the reality of what is called today, yesterday, or even tomorrow." (Abraham Collection, Box 17)

It is important to remember that the totality of Astro-Infinity Music includes not just music in the conventional sense, but all the paraphernalia of cultural commerce in the Space Age: album covers, record labels, catalogues, business cards, posters, advertisements, handbills, interviews—the whole jetsam of supersonic sound production. The space-music of Sun Ra and the Arkestra amounts to a material assemblage of a multiplicity of activities and products, all contributing to the cultural production of new futures by force of sound. Old practices are put to new uses, transforming their content and their political efficacy. Witness a handbill for Saturn Records Research: "Let SUN RA and his ARKESTRA thrill you with "COSMIC-SOUNDS" of the NOW-MYTH WORLD...Vibrating...LIVE-NOW SOUNDS specifically designed for you to bestow BLESSINGS of spiritual SOUND-PLEASURE.... upon your...MINDS-EYE...yes sounds which can lift dreams from NOTHING to REALITY !!! YES...NOW SOUNDS!!!" (Corbett, *Pathways* 122).

Nowhere is this purpose more obvious than in the bizarre and beautiful movie released by North American Star System in 1976 and directed by John Coney, *Space Is the Place*. Sun Ra's answer to *Star Wars* and the whole B-movie legacy of scifi-film, the movie *signifies* in the African American sense on that legacy and its contemporary equivalents. It opens with a spangle-robed Sun Ra inspecting the vibrations of another planet, one better suited than this one to realizing the full potential of black people, and it develops into a cosmic drama in which he draws Tarot with a world-historical pimp for the fate of planet Earth. One of the film's most important scenes occurs at Sun Ra's Interplanetary Employment Agency, located somewhere in Oakland, California in the 1970s. Sun Ra sits behind a desk littered with gadgets, June Tyson working a switchboard in the background. A balding white guy approaches the half-door: a laid off NASA engineer trained in space propulsion. Sun Ra conducts the interview sitting down: "we specialize in teleportation, astro-vehicular tranportation, transmolecularization," to which the unemployed engineer, scared of landing with his wife and six children on welfare, responds nervously and backs hastily away into darkness. Sun Ra turns the language of the engineer's scientific training into a menacing mumbo jumbo.

Which is the point. Sun Ra transforms the discourse of science and the tropes of science fiction into vehicles—literally—of collective cultural affirmation. He blackens them, and by doing so makes them almost unrecognizable to their former masters. Old words make new things happen when used in new ways. Sun Ra uses them to create and to promote a cultural ensemble whose vocation is space. Science fiction becomes myth-science, a means of black cultural insurgence in a white world. As he reminded his Arkestra, "You're not musicians, you're *tone scientists*" (Szwed, 112). The tone science of space-music proclaims the counterfiction of a better future. *Space is the Place,* Sun Ra's technoscience fictional move beyond the culture of technoscience, transports its audience along spaceways that leave the old world behind.

That is the desideratum of space-music. From its original conception in the 1950s to its continuing insurgence today, the music of Sun Ra, the Arkestra, and its sustaining communities works to change the world, by the immeasurable measure of a fictive, impossible future. And yet that future is *real*, as real as the popular culture of the Space Age. That is the lesson of the space-aged language that traces through the whole material assemblage of space-music like a golden thread. Sun Ra's titles for records and tunes are not metaphors for tomorrow. They *are* tomorrow, rendered literally in the language of contemporary popular culture. Sun Ra makes that language *real*, and not without a little humor. "A race needs clowns," he once said (Szwed 236). It is important to appreciate the impish joy involved in appropriating the discourse of the Space Age with such seriousness. One should sense it in every astronomical reference, every cosmic flourish. It is there from the start: the very first group Sun Ra played with (circa 1952) was called "The Space Trio." His earliest records announce that joy too: *Super-Sonic Jazz*, *We Travel the Spaceways*, and *Sun Ra Visits Planet Earth* all hail from 1956. Later ones only reinforce the sense that Sun Ra speaks musically about a joyous future far surpassing the popular promise of the Space Age: *Sun Ra Visits Planet Earth* (1957), *Rocket Number Nine Take Off for the Planet Venus* (1959), *Fate in a Pleasant Mood* (1960), *The Futuristic Sounds of Sun Ra* (1961), *Art Forms of Dimensions Tomorrow* (1961), *Secrets of the Sun* (1962), *Space Probe* (1963), *Other Planes of There* (1964), *The Heliocentric Worlds of Sun Ra, Vol. I* (1965)—to name only a few.

The same holds for the extraterrestrialized register of the titles of Sun Ra's compositions. They collectively name a new future, torqued free from a dead and deadly cultural past: "Music from the World Tomorrow," "Plutonian Nights," "Star Time," "Future," "Sun Song," "Saturn," "Planet Earth," "Somewhere in Space," "Interplanetary Music," "Interstellar Low Ways," "Space Loneliness," "Space Aura," "Lights of a Satellite," "We Travel the Spaceways," "Calling Planet Earth," "Voice of Space," "Cluster of Galaxies," "Solar Drums," "Kosmos in Blue," "Spiral Galaxy," "Next Stop Mars," and the list goes on. Such titles clearly partake of the popular vogue for space-aged sounds, but they do not simply exploit that faddishness. They turn fad into reality, transform kitsch into cosmology, change fiction into another, newer kind of fact. Sun Ra's music becomes a medium of the translation of popular culture into *space*, a place of new social possibility, an atonal omniverse of new fictive futures.

A space impossible, really, to talk about apart from the declamation of those titles. The only appropriate way of receiving Sun Ra's space music is *to hear it*. The best possible response to this whole discussion would be to listen to as much of the music of Sun Ra and the various Arkestras as possible. It will disrupt expectations. It might change the future. At the very least it alerts the open listener to new musical and political possibilities. If those possibilities are atonal, that is because they are irreducible to tempered traditions, whether of sound or of social activism. Sun Ra's space music remained over the course of his fifty-year career a collaborative production grounded in a communal way of life. The Arkestra lived together as well as played together, lived as a form of play: in Chicago, in New York, and to this day in Philadelphia. Their space-music grew into a bold departure from conventional forms—of jazz and society. Listen to an early record like *Jazz in Silhouette* (1958); hear the bebop heritage of the Arkestra. But hear too the emergence of something else, something bigger that, as on the tune "Enlightenment," bursts the bonds of the traditional thirty-two bar American song form.

The Arkestra moves through such forms into other *spaces*, creating a music not beholden to tonality or harmony in any usual sense, but exploring their outer reaches. *Interstellar Low Ways* (1960) makes playful use of bebop to move toward a new intensity, gesturing in the direction of unprecedented destinations in "Rocket Number Nine Take Off for the Planet Venus." At least two very different kinds of space emerge, and with them new possibilities for ordering political life. The first is airy and open, anticipated in the clunky, spare rhythms of *The Nubians of Plutonia* (1959, originally issued as *The Lady with the Golden Stockings*) and coming to fruition in *Outer Planes of There* (1964), a haunting tapestry of sound. The second is fiery and ballistic, a high-energy cacophony of collective interplay, best heard on records like *The Heliocentric Worlds of Sun Ra, Vol. II* (1965), *When Angels Speak of Love* (1966), and the glorious *Magic City* (1965). These different spaces have in common a commitment to improvisation—not as a freely freaking spontaneity but as a collective and collaborative discipline. A fully integrated musical practice emerges in such spaces, not beholden to past forms but wholly committed to future possibilities realized in an improvised present. Atonality drives out dominant traditions and opens music to collective exploration.

What would be the prospect of such a politics? The only answer Sun Ra hazards is space-music itself—not as form but as performance. Sun Ra and the variable Arkestras make music the means of recreating political life in the midst of a civil society not as commodity but as commitment: music becomes a way of living the future right *now*. It breaks with a past that obstructs its becoming: "This is the Space Age / The age beyond the Earth age / A new Direction / Beyond the Gravitation of the Past" (Ra, *Immeasurable* 12). One of the most exhilarating instances of this transformation comes rather late in Sun Ra's life. On tour in Europe in 1985, he found his way to a pipe organ and recorded a magnificent solo improvisation that attempts the abolition of a past whose cultural authority would seem to doom all futures in advance. *Hiroshima* is the title of the piece, and it stands as an example of the force of space-music, its ability to obliterate a baleful heritage of obliteration. If cybernetic society begins at Hiroshima, Sun Ra's improvisation tries to end it, opening the controlled economy of contemporary music to an atonality that communicates something else—new possibilities, if not of freedom (Sun Ra was fond of saying there was no freedom in the universe), then of futures unencumbered by the cultural past and its insatiable dead. Sun Ra never attempted that end alone. The production of space-music always involves collaboration, even when performed solo. It involves others. It opens worlds. It beckons futures. It promotes vibrations:

> THIS IS THE SOUND OF SILHOUETTES
> IMAGES AND FORECASTS OF TOMORROW
> DISGUISED AS JAZZ.
>
> (Ra, *Immeasurable* 66)

RHYTHM TRAVEL

Baraka imagines such a future in "Answers in Progress." That black music produces it is part of his point. It ruptures the space of white domination and lets in the cool blue space men, homing in on a beam of Blakey. "The space men could dig everything" (219). In such new spaces, everything is diggable. With the rebellion taking a victorious turn, the insurgents pipe music through the streets, songs of new unity, circulating sentiments such as those expressed in the poem at the center of the story:

> Walk through life
> beautiful more than anything
> stand in sunlight
> walk through life

> love all the things
> that make you strong, be lovers, be anything
> for all the people of
> earth.
>
>   (220)

Social space changes and with it the apportionment of power: "Boulevards played songs like that and we rounded up blanks where we had to" (221). Songs now promote new values, not unrequited love but "the beauty of the whole" (221). The effect ideologically is to promote an awareness of changed social circumstances, the world of new possibilities brought to life by black music: "We thought about the changing reference, of our new world. As it stood already in the old ruins. And we all felt like Bird" (222). And the space men, those forerunners of a new, blue kind of free black people, hear the music opening new spaces, and respond accordingly: "But when the Sun-Ra tape came on this blue dude really opened up. He dug the hell out of it. Perfect harmony these cats had too. Boooooo—Iiiiiiiiioooooooooooooo...daaaaa ahhhhhhhh aaaaahhhhhh...booooooOOOOOOOOOOOOOO ooooooooooaaaaa aaaaooooaaaaa" (222). The freedom of those sounds materializes new spaces.

    Black music reconfigures social space: that is its most menacing legacy. It shares with cyberfiction the capacity, as Mosely put it, to let African Americans have a say in the way things are. Baraka's cy-fi, in contrast to the sort of science fiction that serves the ends of cosmic liberalism, develops this capacity through music: not techno-science but cultural politics provides the best weapons for building new worlds. In this, Baraka's work intersects with the brazenly sci-fi elements of free jazz, from Sun Ra's astro-blackness to Ornette Coleman's *Science Fiction Sessions*. In the hands of these black artists, cy-fi gets "musicked," to apply a phrase Baraka uses to describe poetry that recapitulates the disruptive sounds of bebop. Its sonic intensities disrupt the operations of control in cybernetic society. If what Baraka says of poetry, that "the fact of music was the black poet's basis for creation," can be said too of science fiction, then the kind he writes, and that black musicians *play*, has more to do with politics than science, with social than outer space (*Autobiography* 337). Music becomes a means of materializing new spaces, producing the future, not as some distant never-never land, but in (the) place of today. Cyberfiction musicked advances this project in the idiom of dominant culture, but toward the end of transforming it—like the Black Arts movement from which it derives much impetus—by "daring to raise the question of art and politics and revolution, black revolution!" (299).

Baraka pursues this project in more recent works of cyberfiction too. The anthology *Dark Matter* contains a short but provocative story called "Rhythm Travel" that assimilates cyberfiction to black music. What makes "Rhythm Travel" cy-fi is the development of the peculiar new technology at its center, the "Molecular Anyscape" or "RE soulocator." What makes "Rhythm Travel" *black* cy-fi is the identification of that technology with music: says its inventor, "I can "dis" appear, "dis" visibility. Be un seen. But now, I can be around anyway. Perceived, felt, heard. I can be the music!" (Thomas 113). Baraka reconstitutes the old trope of black invisibility in auditory terms. Music allows what is "dis" visible to persist materially, producing an alternative dimension for living. By becoming the music this mad scientist inhabits space in unprecedented ways, ways easily overlooked by eyes accustomed to conventional dimensions:

> Your boy always do that. You knock, somebody say come in. You open the door, look around, call out, nobody there. You think!
>
> But then, at once, music come on. If you watching, there's a bluish shaking that flickers—maybe "Mysterioso" will surround you. The music is wavering like light. The room seems to shift to step.
>
> Then you recognize what you hear: yo' man. [...] I rolled my eyes as he materialized before me, dissing the Dis Report on Appearance. (113)

Music here is a means of inhabiting space, a way of investing it, living it, claiming it, changing it. This "dis" appearing person materializes to give the lie to his apparent invisibility.

But more is at issue here than mere (dis)appearances. For this inventor has perfected a new form of space travel. The music moves him into other spaces, or rather reconfigures space through other locations: "I pushed the anyscape into rhythm spectroscopic transformation. And then I got it tuned to combine the anywhereness and the reappearance as Music"! (114). The result is Rhythm Travel. "You can Dis Appear and Re Appear wherever and whenever that music played" (114). The trick is simple: Rhythm Travel lets one go, physically, to the place a particular tune is being played, without regard to where or when, or rather *with* regard to all wheres and whens. Baraka reconfigures space along lines of musical force. During Rhythm Travel "here" is not a place so much as a constellation of spaces. The traveler's life becomes spatially redistributed, organized no longer by a master narrative of linear time but by a simultaneity of different spaces linked together by the common force of a particular tune. Like this:

> "if I go into 'Take this Hammer,' I can appear wherever that is, was, will be sung."
> "Yeh, but be that song you be on a plantation…"
> "I know." He was smilin'. "I went to one." (114)

Rhythm Travel turns history into a geography of force, as the experience of the plantation proves, with its overseers and its slaves. The point is to inhabit these multiple spaces rather than simply dismissing them as historically past or yet to come. Black music invokes not just the memory of historical suffering but the reappropriation of the spaces in which it occurred, toward the end of shifting relations of power and multiplying freedoms. Rhythm Travel transforms social space by showing that it is never a historical given but a constellation of material events subject to change. Science fiction once again serves Baraka as a space machine, materializing space as a multiplicity wherein the "dis" visible move about freely. Or in the traveler's words, " 'Man the stuff I seen!' 'you mean you been rhythm traveling already?' 'Yeh. I turned into some Sun Ra and hung out, inside gravity.' " (114). Space travel becomes Rhythm Travel as black music remakes science fiction.

And always, for Baraka, under the auspices of Sun Ra. Sun Ra, Sun Ra. The originary interplanetary astro-black Sun Ra. The musical space traveler, Sun Ra. The abductee, the philosopher, the poet, the activist, Sun Ra. "We Travel The Spaceways, from planet to planet," Sun Ra. "Some space metaphysical philosophical surrealistic bop funk. Some blue pyramid home nigger southern different color meaning hip shit. Ra. Sun Ra" (*Eulogies* 171). Baraka's cyberfiction would, to say the least, be different without the example of Sun Ra. So would black music. Sun Ra puts them together so completely in order to demand and to produce a transformation of social space of the sort Baraka describes. Sun Ra's astro-black mythologizing is not the folk art of a marginalized dreamer. It is a sophisticated political response to a technoscientific culture he viewed as primitive, destructive, benighted (see Szwed). Music was the weapon he directed against that world. That he believed it could achieve the impossible was the crux of his politics. As he put it, "The impossible is the watchword of the greater space age. The space age *cannot be* avoided and the *space music* is the key to understanding the meaning of the *impossible* and every other enigma" (quoted in Lock 26, italics in the original). In Sun Ra, music becomes a material means of changing space.

Put differently, Sun Ra's music materializes black space. It rescinds the transparency of blackness posited by cosmic liberalism and asserts, simply and boldly, that space is the place for black people. Says Baraka, "Ra was so far out because he had the true self consciousness of the Afro-American intellectual artist revolutionary. He knew our historic ideology and sociopolitical consciousness was *freedom*" (171). This possibility moved Sun Ra to demand and produce new social spaces for African Americans. Hence his involvement in the initial stages of the Black Arts Movement. "For some, Sun Ra became our resident philosopher," Baraka writes, telling too of the march of the Myth Science Arkestra across 125th Street in Harlem the summer the Arts opened (*Autobiography* 298). The place of Sun Ra's space may involve interplanetary (rhythm?) travel, but its social location remains emphatically terrestrial, the material place of African American life: "No matter how 'far out' the insiders said Ra was, in the Harlem streets he was a rare treat" (*Eulogies* 172).

SECOND COMING

That's the point of Baraka's tour de force of cyberfiction, the poem or rather performance entitled "When Sun Ra Gets Blue," currently available only on a recording made with trumpeter Hugh Ragin called *An Afternoon in Harlem* (1999). Ragin's title locates socially Baraka's amazing performance—with musicians—of a poem that enacts the return of Sun Ra's astro-black mythology to planet Earth. Sun Ra left this planet when he died in 1993. But he returns in Baraka's poem like some black messiah materializing out of dark matter. He comes to communicate a message, one that involves music as much as poetry and effects the transformation of social space. Working with musicians allows Baraka to materialize his earlier thematic treatment of music in prose, which remains limited by the fact that, however radical in content, it falls subject to the politics of print. As a performance (a speech act somewhere between recitation and song) Baraka's delivery of "When Sun Ra Gets Blue" eschews the apparent fixity and finality of a poem printed in a book. Compared with a poem like "In the Tradition," also a favorite for performance but often reprinted, "When Sun Ra Gets Blue"—at least until it gets transcribed—remains an event with a communal dimension. One man may have written it, but a group of musicians (which included Baraka playing an instrument called *language*) performs it. Those musicians are tops—some of

them early practitioners of free jazz: Andrew Cyrille on drums, David
Murray on bass clarinet, Hugh Shahid on bass, and Craig Taborn on
piano. In its occurrence as music among this community of players,
"When Sun Ra Gets Blue" turns cy-fi into something more than a
literary practice, transforming its formerly transparent black spaces.
That is the gist of the message Sun Ra returns to deliver to this
backward planet: you gotta change. That is the meaning of the poem
that Baraka and the other musicians *perform*. Ragin's recording of
"When Sun Ra Gets Blue" opens with a lone thumb piano plucking
a vagrant melody, which is soon eclipsed by a series of block chords
gesturing toward the popular idiom of "space music" and parodying
the opening statement of Richard Strauss's *Also Sprach Zarathustra*.
Stanley Kubrick turned that statement into *the* sci-fi soundtrack cliché
by using it during the opening of *2001: A Space Odyssey*. "When Sun
Ra Gets Blue" musically contests the space of cosmic liberalism by
parodying that opening, suggesting that evolution, at least for humans,
is a planetary matter, not the odyssey into outer blackness that Kubrik
imagines. Sun Ra brings that blackness back to this planet and materializes it *here*. Hence his message: "The world is in transition, your
world and your condition." It is a message, says Baraka, specifically
"for niggers," those who are socially subjected but still defiant. And
it is a message that is less meaningful than material. "The world is
really matter independent of your mind," Baraka says late in his performance. It is black matter urging toward transformation: "Inside
the world is blackness—everything is dark as sky." Sun Ra comes to
work that change, materially and socially. "I am nothing but a color,
nothing but a name, nothing but a flash of daylight, nothing but an
x-slave." This color/name/flash/x-slave comes to reconstellate space,
figured in the force of pronouns: "The world is everything, the world
is everywhere. Whatever is said and done is just a description of the
there.... Everything is the same. Here is there and there is here."
Troubling reference reconfigures the here, makes it a space related to
other theres. And as space changes, so does blackness: "From black to
ultraviolet to indigo to soulful blue—take me, take me, take me, take
us altogether." Changing color bespeaks changing space, an other-
worlding that turns the planet toward new life. Baraka's performance
builds to the thundering exhortation, "All you different colored niggers, live and live and rebuild a dying world." Here. Now. Space is
the place. Material, planetary, social space to fulfill Baraka's closing
imperative—"live, live, live, live, live, live...."

    But it is crucial to remember that cy-fi as Sun Ra announces it and
Baraka practices it in this poem involves music. Its "here" configures

the listener's "there," the space(s) of new musical occurrence. Put another way, the "here" of playing and the "there" of listening coincide, at least for a time, to transform social space. It takes space to stage such a performance. It takes space even to listen to it, if only at home on the stereo. Once assimilated to music, cy-fi invests space in three dimensions. What opens up is the possibility of collaboration among a community of musicians and a company of witnesses. To the extent that it occurs as music in a particular place, the performance of "When Sun Ra Gets Blue" exceeds even its message, exceeds it by enacting it. Space becomes a place of collective improvisation. Baraka cedes the traditional priority of words over music to allow his language to interact freely with other sounds. While the freedom he realizes in performance does not drain his words of meaning, it reconfigures that meaning in relation to the collective event of his performance. Music transforms language, turning what was meaning into the architecture of the space that opens with performance. As "When Sun Ra Gets Blue" proceeds, collective improvisation among the musicians increases until what began as chordal statement becomes a collaborative freakery that affirms—in the social space of performance and participation—the practice of freedom. And as Baraka punctuates his performance with the words "Sun Ra," variously declaimed, chanted, and sung, they acquire material persistence in the space that collective improvisation opens and maintains. Sun Ra returns. Sun Ra, Sun Ra. In a performance such as this one, cy-fi turns space machine, as black music freely freaking reconfigures social space. Doing so it produces new futures, but in the material terms of this (new) world. That is how Baraka's science fiction differs from the kind that recapitulates cosmic liberalism. It rhythm travels with Sun Ra: "The evolution of humanity was his theme. From revelation to revelation, immeasurable, revolution to revolution, like heartbeats of truth. [...] The destiny, but as a constant character of motion and change" (*Eulogies* 174). Here. Now. In Baraka's black-cyber-music-fiction, space is the place.

7

WE CAN BREED YOU

Cyberfiction is full of fantasies of technological triumph over female flesh. Often it gets replaced with more amenable mechanical, electronic, or biochemical equivalents. From *Metropolis* to *Do Androids Dream of Electric Sheep*, these surrogates are remarkable for their sterility. Machines cannot conceive, and bedding an android is risky business. All this changes, however, when women start writing cyberfiction, women whose bodily experience of reproduction abides no easy mechanical or chemical equivalent. Interestingly, their writing coincides with the emergence of cybernetic society, as if cybernetics were somehow necessary for the insurgence of the reproductive female body against its masters. While that is obviously an overstatement (Mary Shelley was a woman), not until the body and its myriad mysterious agencies turn to code does a scientific discourse become available that proves capable of shaping rather than just subjecting the process of reproduction. Genetics and bioengineering take that cybernetic turn with their reinvention of the human organism from the perspective of constituent proteins, its DNA. As epiphenomena of genetic code, bodies become malleable matter. Soft sciences emerge to counteract the blunt traumas of hard science and its even harder technologies. Perhaps surprisingly, the best cy-fi practitioner of that soft science and its body magic is Octavia Butler, African American woman from Los Angeles. She puts female reproduction at the center of her work and asks simply, what will happen when, as is inevitable, it becomes a consciously creative enterprise?

One thing will happen for sure. Humans will change. Breeding them will be no more arcane or reprehensible than breeding pigs, horses, cows, or dogs—except that the aim may be to transform rather than perfect the species. The female reproductive body becomes for Butler a means of engineering flesh, and the question she raises is the ethical question of how soft science should appropriate, manage, or enhance its life. That is the preoccupation of her *Xenogenesis* trilogy (retitled

Lilith's Brood), which includes the novels *Dawn* (1987), *Adulthood Rites* (1988), and *Imago* (1989). In Butler's future sexual reproduction gives way to genetic hybridization in a way that sheds the human like an old skin. Humanity dies a double death: first by becoming animal, second by becoming hybrid. What persists throughout these changes is the fecundity of the female body, its generative capacity to produce *more life* in the face of its extinction. The future belongs to mothers—but not human ones.

WE'D MAKE GREAT PETS

Jacques Derrida speaks of "the passion of the animal." It is less love than shame, or rather an acknowledgment that shame portends. Derrida experiences it when his cat follows him into the bathroom and watches him: "Especially, I should make clear, if the cat observes me frontally naked, face to face, and if I am naked faced with the cat's eyes looking at me as it were from head to toe, just *to see*, not hesitating to concentrate its vision—in order to see, with a view to seeing—in the direction of my sex" (373). Here is a sight. The philosopher exposed, naked before the implacable gaze of his pet kitty. Derrida experiences his nudity as shame, shame before an animal that knows no nakedness, no self-consciousness, no shameful dangling sex. A double acknowledgment follows:

> My passion *of* the animal, my passion of the animal other: seeing oneself seen naked under a gaze that is vacant to the extent of being bottomless, at the same time innocent and cruel perhaps, perhaps sensitive and impassive, good and bad, uninterpretable, unreadable, undecidable, abyssal and secret. Wholly other, like the (every) other that is (every bit) other found in such intolerable proximity that I do not as yet feel I am justified or qualified to call it my fellow, even less my brother. (381)

Derrida sees himself seen from his cat's blank perspective. Cartesian subjectivity goes out the window. More baleful, however, is the acknowledgment that accompanies such a naked seeing. That gaze is wholly other. But so is that on which it gazes: the naked body of the philosopher, the flesh subtending thought. A double nakedness: the gaze of the cat and the body of the philosopher.

    They meet in an intolerable proximity, which is to say they do not meet at all.[1] The passion of the animal *is* this confrontation of alterities, incommensurable with the human and its embarrassed interiority.

And there are so many alterities. As Derrida puts it, "beyond the edge of the *so-called* human, beyond it but by no means on a single opposing side, rather than 'the Animal' or 'Animal Life,' there is already a heterogeneous multiplicity of the living, or more precisely (since to say 'the living' is already to say too much or not enough) a multiplicity of organizations of relations between living and dead" (399). No Animal Life opposed to Human, then, but multiplicities of organizations, among them this cat and that body aligned however intolerably by a constitutive nakedness. Animals abound, even where the philosopher stands and thinks, or maybe straddles a toilet, facing his kitty.

For now we should face it: the unembarrassed gaze of that kitty disturbs something dear to us too, not just to the philosopher, although he describes it with such moxie: "the gaze called animal offers to my sight the abyssal limit of the human: the inhuman or the ahuman, the ends of man" (381). Derrida, or really any one who bothers looking, sees in what the animal sees: the end of the human, the limit of our self-nominated authority. Simple embarrassment turns apocalyptic. A cat's naked gaze sees past the human, maybe sees the posthuman, if that were not just a bit too clairvoyant to be credible. Sees the *post-*, then, the possibility that something or some*body* else is to come. After us. So that we will become, simply and fatefully, what follows. Better let the philosopher take it from here: "In these moments of nakedness, under the gaze of the animal, everything can happen to me, I am like a child ready for the apocalypse, *I am (following) the apocalypse itself*, that is to say the ultimate and first event of the end, the unveiling and the verdict" (381, italics in the original). Death rides a pale cat—toward a new dawn. To follow an animal's gaze is to solicit a future beyond the human, one that becomes visible in this exchange of glances, this conjunction of animal bodies. Biped meets quadruped in a naked congress of becoming.

XENOGENESIS

The situation Derrida describes bears strange resemblance to the one Butler sets up in *Dawn*, the first installment of the *Xenogenesis* trilogy, whose action follows upon apocalypse. Humans have destroyed the earth and all but destroyed their species through nuclear exchange. Only the most incredible luck saves them from extinction: the arrival from deep space of a curious alien life form. The aliens harvest human specimens from their desolated world and preserve them unconscious until the time arrives when, with a little tweaking, they might repopulate Earth. There is a catch, however, and the novel's protagonist, Lilith

Iapo, learns of it the hard way. Some two hundred and fifty years after nuclear holocaust, she experiences a series of awakenings. She is frightened and at first alone, but only for a while. Eventually she is joined by others: first a human child, then something else altogether, a vaguely humanoid *thing* that is gray and covered with twisting tentacles:

> The tentacles were elastic. At her shout, some of them lengthened, stretching toward her. She imagined big, slowly writhing, dying night crawlers stretched along the sidewalk after a rain. She imagined small, tentacled sea slugs—nudibranchs—grown impossibly to human size and shape, and, obscenely, sounding more like a human being than some humans. Yet she needed to hear him speak. Silent, he was utterly alien. (12)

Speak it does, in perfectly unctuous English, which in spite of the long tradition that identifies speech and reason, turns out not to make it very human. This thing is ugly, too ugly to be accepted as anything but *alien*.

Lilith responds with visceral disgust to this ugly, alien body. She registers his otherness on and in her flesh, "his" because as this creature explains to Lilith: " 'It's wrong to assume that I must be a sex you're familiar with,' it said, 'but as it happens, I'm male' " (11). His alien nakedness confirms both his difference and its irreducibility, in spite of sexual identity, to the human. "She did not want to be any closer to him. She had not known what held her back before. Now she was certain it was his alienness, his difference" (11). This is an incontrovertible point, and many have missed it. The encounter between Lilith and this talking slug marks, in Derrida's phrase, "the abyssal limit of the human."

Lilith's response is utterly irrational. "She tried to imagine herself surrounded by beings like him and was almost overwhelmed by panic. As though she had suddenly developed a phobia—or something she had never before experienced. But what she felt was like what she had heard others describe. A true xenophobia" (22). Butler ups Derrida's ante. Say his kitty was covered with sentient pseudopods and spoke elegant French. Well then—the human might not offer much of a basis for a relationship. Faced with such creatures a body fends for itself. It goes xenophobic. It lapses into the animal. The encounter between Lilith and that alien involves a confrontation between animals—ultimately to breed new ones.

Literally. The aliens have come to breed humans, or rather to crossbreed them—with themselves. They are the Oankali. Their name means "gene trader." They cross galaxies to exchange genes, flesh for flesh, DNA for DNA, in a bid to improve themselves *and* their trading partners: "we are powerfully acquisitive. We acquire new life—seek it, investigate it, manipulate it, sort it, use it" (39). Lilith is a quick study. " 'It is crossbreeding, then, no matter what you call it' " (40). Her Oankali tutor insists simply that it will improve the lives of future generations on both sides. Change comes not through politics, culture, economics, or entertainment. Nuclear exchange has incinerated such human achievements. Only breeding can change the bare animals that remain. Only a gene trade holds out hope for a future: " 'We are committed to the trade,' he said, softly implacable" (41).

This is the point commentators often miss: Butler's postapocalyptic future is neither human, nor posthuman but utterly, alienly animal. Lilith feels it in her flesh: "Medusa children. Snakes for hair. Nests of night crawlers for eyes and ears" (41). The conjunction of human and alien bodies unveils the coming of new animals. It would be nostalgic to read Lilith's ordeal as an allegory of miscegenation or even some happy celebration of difference.[2] Those remain categories framed by the human limit that gene trading irreparably breeches. The Oankali offer a cross between not genii but *species*. Difference is not the cozy alternative between one kind of human (say white) and another (maybe black). Difference is an abyss that divides primate from mollusk.[3]

Butler asks her readers seriously to consider the possibility of a woman fucking a slug—or whatever that *thing* is. Her proposition more closely resembles bestiality than miscegenation. Beyond the abyssal limit of the human, bodies beget bodies that further beget bodies. We humans know that, which is why we crossbreed pets in kennels and create chimeras in labs. Describing her treatment by the Oankali, Lilith says "we used to treat animals that way. [...] We did things to them—inoculations, surgery, isolation—all for their own good. We wanted them healthy and protected—sometimes so we could eat them later' " (31). The Oankali treat us the way we treat animals, and in the process the *human* obsolesces. Only abject, unknowable animal bodies remain. The Oankali know them, however, much better than humans ever can. Gene traders unleash the animal. They cultivate its passion. They make people pets.

MINOTAUR

Becoming pets is only the first step. The Oankali have bigger plans than domesticating bipeds. Their devotion to the animal has little to do with our terrestrial tradition of defining the human against it. Giorgio Agamben calls that tendency "the anthropological machine." In his reading of Heidegger's ontology, *The Open: Man and Animal* (2003), he shows how this distinction drives human history in the West, or rather the historical *becoming* of the human. That becoming, he argues, has closed, and at this (post)historical moment, "the machine is idling" (80). He shares with Butler a sense that whatever the human *was* is obsolescing, which is to say too that its constitutive relationship with the animal will change. This is not the same thing as saying that the human is becoming animal—which is not exactly what Butler is saying either. Both imagine an end for the historical era of the human, in apocalyptic explosion for Butler, and in biopolitical stasis for Agamben. Or at least that is Agamben's fear. His hope is endearingly, maybe preposterously, intimate: the post-coital acknowledgment of man and woman for each other "outside of being" (apparently a heterosexual outside). Neither animal nor human, that loving, spent couple embodies the promise of life after the history of the human.

It is worth asking whether that couple uses contraception. Probably not, since Agamben finds their type in Titian's *Nymph and Shepherd*, a painting that dates from a time when interruption was the best prevention. But say that loving couple conceives. Then what? Does their offspring fall back into history and the anthropological machine? Agamben never says. His is a fantasy of perpetual postcoition. Butler's fantasy at least confronts the life to come after the sighs and the cigarettes. For her there is nothing anthropological about it. The animal/human divide collapses to produce a beyond for both, a genoplasmic future that propagates bodies beyond such historical categories. Witness this exchange between Lilith and her keeper:

> "Your people will change. Your young will be more like us and ours more like you. [...] That's part of the trade. We're overdue for it."
> "It is crossbreeding, then, no matter what you call it."
> "It's what I said it was. A trade." (42)

Gene trading between species involves a mutual becoming—sexual, yes, as Agamben suggests, but the living effects of this congress exceed simple bodily bliss. As a partner in this kind of trade Lilith the animal and Lilith the human both become *something else*. The movement of life beyond the human for Butler involves physical transformation, a return to the animal that jams the anthropological machine: "What will you make of us? What will our children be?' 'Different, as I said.

Not quite like you. A little like us" (42). Xenogenesis. Becoming other. That is the human, all-too-human, transhuman fate of humanity. What forms will this future take? That remains to be seen. But for Agamben a lapse into the animal typically produces an abject other: "above all the slave, the barbarian, and the foreigner, as figures of an animal in human form" (37).

ONCE AND FUTURE SLAVE

Butler forces the issue, not merely of the animal, but more pertinently of the historical animality of certain humans, specifically slaves. It is no accident that the master/slave dialectic becomes an organizing principle of philosophy and history at the moment when Western slavery reaches its culmination.[4] Hegel's *Phenomenology of Spirit* appears in 1807, the very year England abolished the slave trade. Hegel, of course, views slavery as a practice that dialectic overcomes. His account of history gives all the good lines to the slave, who outconcretizes the master's consciousness of death, achieving a higher kind of freedom.[5] Butler will have none of it. Her speculation about what humans will become involves an encounter with what they have been. And as any African American knows, many have been slaves.

Consider this scenario: a woman wanders a primordial landscape separated from community and kin and gets spirited away to an alien vessel that carries her off to an unknown world. Sound familiar? That is the backstory not only of Butler's *Dawn*, but also of the lives of many African Americans. *Dawn* presents the strangest account of the Middle Passage on record. Just because it involves worm-covered aliens, does not mean it is historically inaccurate. Butler slams the history of Atlantic slavery fast-forward into a near future that recasts European slave merchants as alien invaders and the whole human species as chattel for trade. The Middle Passage parallels are too many to overlook, and yet that is what happens when most critics read *Dawn*.[6] They claim it is about miscegenation, or gender trouble, or political biologism. And it probably is, but Butler raises those issues in the future preterite tense of a history both past and *yet to come*. For her the Middle Passage has already happened and will happen again, next time not just to Africans but to any humans who happen to survive their self-inflicted apocalypse.

People of the African Diaspora, in other words, constitute a cultural vanguard whose history puts them in the best position to negotiate a coming catastrophe: the historical closure of the human. A heritage of slavery proves prophylactic knowledge—or might, if it could be mobilized to imagine the world to come. In *Dawn* the history of the Atlantic slave trade produces a knowledge of the future that puts all humans in the position of chattel and asks, simply, "what should we do?" The Middle Passage becomes the test case, not for humanity, but for whatever comes after. That is why Butler takes such pains to transport that history forward. Lilith's experience is quite explicitly that of an African sold and shipped into slavery. It is not simply that she is taken from her world against her will and stored away in the hold of an alien vessel, or that her kidnappers represent themselves as innocent traders. More crucially, it is that she has to negotiate the terms of her survival with a master who holds all the cards and the ship's tiller too—which is to say that Lilith has no real choice. Her history moves in one direction only. Into the future.

Through the Middle Passage. Like a stolen African, Lilith loses her history, her culture, her identity, and not incidentally her freedom, or what remains of it after the bombs drop. She falls into the hands, or the tentacles, of an alien form of life, one that claims her body for its own designs and reduces her agency to the negative splendor of *not dying*. That is the upshot of her keeper's strange offer of release from a bondage that it cannot otherwise rescind: "'I can't *un*find you,' he said. 'You're here. But there is…a thing I *can* do. It is deeply wrong of me to offer it. I will never offer it again. […] Touch me here now,' he said, gesturing toward his head tentacles, 'and I'll sting you. You'll die—very quickly and without pain.'" (43). Life for Lilith reduces to the pyrrhic choice of ending it. To choose is to die. Not to choose is to live as a slave. So much for choice as constitutive of humanity. Or rather, so much for humanity as constitutive of Lilith.

Her dilemma is exactly that of the captured African. To die or not to die, that is the question. Survival is living by default. That is the way Olaudah Equiano depicts it in the harrowing account of the Middle Passage he includes in his memoir, *The Interesting Narrative of Olaudah Equiano* (1789). His first sight of a slave ship inspires astonishment that turns to terror when he meets the crew: "When I was carried on board I was immediately handled, and tossed up, to see if I were sound, by some of the crew; and I was persuaded that I had gotten into a world of bad spirits, and that they were going to kill me" (55). More precisely, Equiano fears being eaten by *aliens*, "white men with horrible looks, red faces, and long hair" (55). His fear is legitimate, since they serve his body up for consumption across the sea, just another commodity in a marketplace of flesh. Equiano wants only to be released from their alien mastery: "I therefore wished much to be from amongst them, for I expected they would sacrifice me: but my wishes were vain; for we were so quartered that it was impossible for any of us to make our escape" (57). Once the ship gets under way death is the only option, which Equiano's companions sometimes choose: "two of my wearied countrymen, who were chained together (I was near them at the time), preferring death to such a life of misery, somehow made through the nettings, and jumped into the sea" (59). Here is that pyrrhic choice Lilith's keeper offers her, not the choice between life and death but the choice of life *as* death. To remain onboard is to submit to something other than life, at least in human terms. It is to begin to become something else entirely.

Stock Options

History is full of strange coincidences. The expansion of political liberties in the West coincides with the expansion of the slave trade. Both also coincide with huge advances, especially among the English, of the art of breeding animals. Harriet Ritvo relates the odd but illuminating detail that the weight of sheep and cattle at slaughter doubled over the course of the eighteenth century. If consumption is an index of prosperity, the ability of the English to eat meat attests to the growing opulence of their Empire. It was a carnivore paradise, much to be preferred to onion-eating France. The English ate six times as much beef as their contemporaries across the Channel, and they raised it all themselves with a fraction of France's farmers and arable land. John Bull was a happy, stout meat eater, and the success of the British Empire depended on keeping him that way.

So the Empire learned to breed, or rather its yeomanry did. They bred fancy animals for aristocrats or market, livestock fat with meat. Whether for show or for slaughter, breeding was the art of sculpting flesh, animal eugenics with a happy face. It had its geniuses, men whose intimate knowledge of conception and descent made them famous and even rich. Robert Bakewell was one. When he died in 1795 he was known throughout England for his almost magical practice of the breeder's art. He designed animals with meat in mind, large in the pricey rump, small in the cheap shoulders. His designer stock fetched big coin. He kept his methods to himself, but setting aside scruples against incestuous pregnancies he was an early practitioner of "in-and-in breeding" in the interest of prime cuts. Crossbreeding was out, inbreeding was in—to maximize the production of desirable qualities. Bakewell's beasts were superior specimens, hand picked—and pricked—for perfect progeny. It was only a matter of controlling the process of reproduction. As Ritvo puts it, "crossing within a restricted lineage of animals selected for desirable characteristics was simply an effective technique for increasing control over the quality of the next generation" (67).

It should come as no surprise that similar methods were applied to slaves. Although information about breeding slaves is sketchy and scarce, there is little doubt that reproduction was a primary concern to almost everyone involved in the slave trade, except maybe the slaves themselves.[7] In terms of market value, male Africans were prized for production, females for reproduction. The most valuable males were usually between eighteen and twenty eight years of age, the most valuable females between twelve and eighteen. These were the breeders, purchased for the purpose of increasing property the easy way—sexually. One of the hopes of planters in the West Indies, for instance, was that one day their slave stock would be self-sustaining, relieving them of reliance on the slave trade and the untamed Africans it delivered—a fractious lot, unused to the yoke and prone to revolt. It was believed that Creole slaves, being plantation born, would more readily accept their lot in life. Planters bought slaves the way they bought cattle, with an eye to increase.

That is the historical legacy behind Lilith's encounter with her alien captors. The Oankali are gene traders, and they deal in flesh. Lilith's keeper confesses as much: "I can only say that your people have something we value" (16). That something is the human body, more particularly its DNA. The Oankali come to master and then manage the body's reproductive capacity: in the context of the African Diaspora, a harrowing purpose. Through the Oankali, Butler reenacts one of the darkest aspects of the slave economy, its reduction of the body, specifically the female body, to its reproductive capacity. "Putting it as a slaveholder would," writes Walter Johnson, "one might say that buyers were concerned that their female slaves be 'breeders'" (144). It is no accident, then, that Lilith is a woman. However unusual a distinction that might be for a cy-fi protagonist, she is just what the Oankali need. She is fertile, she is the mother of a dead child, she is strong, and she deeply wants to live. She would make a good breeder.

But Butler locates her with even greater specificity in the heritage of plantation slavery. The Oankali train and equip her for the task of awakening a whole brood of sleeping humans. In slave terms, she epitomizes the ideal of the female slave as Johnson describes it: "The reduction of femininity into reproduction was ultimately embodied in the figure of the enslaved nurse and midwife—the woman who cared for and often suckled not just her misteress's offspring but those of other slave women who had to return to the fields shortly after giving birth" (144). This is the role the Oankali assign Lilith: nurse, midwife, and group mother responsible for the lives of those she releases from storage on board the Oankali ship. She will be the first to breed too, but before that she must awaken a group of humans, becoming in the process their surrogate single mom. Once a mammy always a mammy. There is no escaping that legacy, at least for black women. To the extent that reproduction sets the terms for the life of the female body, plantation slavery frames all Afro-futures.

PARABLE OF THE SOWERS

Precisely because it frames the past. Black women's bodies incarnate a legacy of breeding. It is bad enough to contemplate the status of slaves in liberal civil society, possessing bodies only their masters truly possess. Not to own one's own body means one has no civil status. One is chattel: a cow, a sentient appliance. But the tribulations of slavery only increase with the demands of the flesh. The bodies of female slaves suffered a double subjection. All were at least potentially breeders. From their masters' point of view, they lived to reproduce. The stud was their carnal destiny. That is the first subjection: to the body of a breeder male. The second was to their own breeding capacity. Once impregnated female slave bodies produced precious new property. To be a breeder was to live—and live through—the carnivorous fate of regenerative flesh.

Under such circumstances, reproduction becomes *life*, not its means, not its purpose, but its essence. Socially speaking, the black female slave inhabits a peculiar position, one closer to livestock than to free members of her gender. Her life, both personal and social, collapses into biology. Its story has no beginning, middle, or end. Rather, it enacts a terminal cycle of serial births punctuated only by death. The body of the female breeder *has no history*, leaves no historical trace in some honorific human sense, no more than that of this line of sheep, that family of dog. Like a domesticated animal, it remains merely *biohistorical*, living alongside its human masters with slow bovine grace. If such a life has meaning, in a slave economy it is commercial. The marketplace, or more specifically the auction block, determines its value. Capital, that breed of barren metal, gives the biohistory of the female slave its only social significance. The whole point of her existence is to reproduce—bodies and bucks.

Reminiscences of American slaves tell the same biohistorical tale. Breeders were animals in the raw, wholly without human accoutrement. Betty Powers, speaking in the 1930s about life as a slave, says with sly understatement, "Dey thinks nothin' on de plantation 'bout de feelin's of de womens. No, sar, thar warn't no 'spect fo' de womens" (Howell 14). One might prize breeding stock, but really, does one respect them? Not according to Thomas Johns:

> If a owner had a big woman slave and she had a little man for her husban', and de owner had a big man slave, or another owner had a big man slave, den dey would make de woman's little husban' leave, and dey would make de woman let de big man be with her so's dere would be big children, which dey could sell well. If de man and de woman refuse to be together, dey would get whipped hard, maybe whipped to death. (Howell 9)

Stripped of the civilizing vestments of love, matrimony, and family, the breeder conceives under a death sentence. The generative capacity of the female body delivers all slaves over to the eugenics of the marketplace. Masters with an eye to increase become Bakewell's heirs, crossing and culling to produce fat margins.

Unlike other livestock, however, slaves know their fate. They bring to biohistory an awareness of its ways. Hillard Yellerday's account of the practice of breeding emphasizes the mobility and multiple utility of the stud. A good male could service a bevy of breeders, and owners were not shy about sharing the wealth—usually for a fee: "Master would sometimes go and get a large hale hearty Negro man from some other plantation to go to his Negro women. He would ask the other master to let this man come over to his place to go to his slave girls" (Howell 15). The rest is biohistory. One stud could do the work of a hundred husbands. With the right qualifications—big limbs and a barrel chest—he might find himself matched with any and all available females. When asked how many children his father had, Lewis Jones gently educated his interrogator: "Yas, sar. Dat am right. Close to 50 chilluns. Yous don't undahstand dat? 'Tis dis a-way: My pappy am de breedin' nigger" (Howell 10). The stud's work was reproduction, and women were raw material. The living products of this labor could not have been more alienated.

White men owned them. With the right stock they could make a killing, as did John Smith's owner, who started with next to nothing and ended up with a fortune: "My marster owned three plantations and 300 slaves. He started out wid two 'oman slaves and raised 300 slaves....Just think o' dat, raisin' 300 slaves wid two 'omans. It sho is de truf, do" (Howell 17). That is a 15,000 percent return on the initial investment—not a bad life's work, all thanks to good breeding. So potentially prolific is the generative force of the female slave's body that it becomes disqualified from the social and cultural relationships that characterize even the meanest of lives. Describing the ban on banns on the plantation he grew up on, Willie Williams tells of

> a marster anxious to raise good, big niggers, de kind what am able to do lots of work and sell for a heap of money. Him have 'bout ten wenches [that] him not 'llow to git married. Dey am big, strong women and de doctor 'xamine dem for de health. Den de marster picks out de big nigger and de doctor 'xamine him, too. Dat nigger do no work but watch dem womens and he am de husban' for dem all. De marster sho' was a-raisin' some fine niggers dat way. (Howell 19)

Where white folks conceived children, slaves bred property and wealth. It fell to them to fulfill the scriptural imperative to be fruitful and multiply. That doctors lent destiny a helping medical hand neatly documents the complicity of science in the bad business of backyard eugenics. American breeders mastered the arts of increase in ways that would have done Blakewell proud, to the point that a lively domestic trade helped sustain the slave economy in America after the British abolished maritime traffic in Africans.

Sometimes the master breeders were the masters themselves. James Green openly details circumstances familiar to certain of the Founding Fathers, however clandestine the actual practice: "de nigger husbands wasn't de only ones dat keeps up havin' chillen 'cause de marsters and de drivers [white overseers] takes all de nigger gals dey wants. Den de chillen was brown, and I seed one clear white one—but dey slaves, jus' de same" (Howell 20). For profit-minded masters, dipping in the till only increased assets. Who is to say how this legacy shapes culture or even politics today? Might it be possible to view relations between Imperial America and the developing world as reenacting, on a geopolitical scale, Jefferson's proprietary indiscretions? Whatever the case, it little burdened a plantation master to take a personal interest in maximizing his capital. He always possessed the fruits of his labor—and that of his burgeoning stock. This biohistorical husbandry still shapes not only race relations but also the generative connection between descendents of slaves and their past. What happens when generation leads back to some master's command, or worse, when the master begets children—or even grand children—on his own children? "In-and-in breeding" is inevitable when people are bred like stock. The great fictional commemoration of such events is Gayl Jones's *Corregidora* (1974), the story of a Portuguese slave master who fathers three generations of women from the same maternal line. As Corregidora fucks first one slave, then her daughter, then the daughter of that daughter, bio-history disrupts descent to confuse identity beyond endurance. For both Jones and Bulter, African American women still *live* this legacy of forced labor and generation, nominally free to make choices but shackled to an animal past.

"PERSISTENT IGNORANCE"

Butler remains keenly aware of this pregnant legacy, to the point of incorporating it thematically in *Dawn*. Before Lilith becomes nurse and surrogate mother to the community she awakens, she has an encounter with a human male held in captivity for years by the Oankali, a man named Paul Titus. It occurs as a kind of blind date, and it does not go well. Lilith is hungry for contact with another human being. So is Paul, but it turns out he is looking for another kind of contact than she is. Lilith makes the usual curious overtures, and at first Paul responds in kind. They talk about the old days. They compare family histories. They share sandwiches and pie and "something that looked like French fries" (88). Then, as seems so often the case on such occasions, the subject comes up of secondary sexual characteristics, specifically those of their overseers: " 'They change when they've grown those two extra things.' [Paul] lifted an eyebrow. 'You know what those things are?' " (87–88). Lilith knows. She knows too where this conversation is going: "she did not want to encourage him to talk about sex; not even Oankali sex" (88).

But once it comes up, it is hard to ignore. Lilith will not touch it, but Paul will not leave it alone. He develops a keen interest in her reproductive history, and chides her readiness to accommodate the designs of their captors. The Oankali are skilled and imperious breeders, capable of creating human offspring without recourse to intercourse: "They can make people in ways I don't even know how to talk about" (93). Paul is a conservative when it comes to conception. He likes it old fashioned, the time-tested in and out, with hugs and kisses if he can get them. So Paul says to Lilith in his best Barry White, "Let us do it our own way" (93). Baby. "His hands were almost gentle on her" (93). Then comes a confession straight out of their shared past, a past that includes not only the earth's nuclear destruction but, as diasporic Africans, the rough heritage of slavery: "He shook her abruptly. 'You know how many kids I got? They say 'Your genetic Material has been used in over seventy children.' And I've never even seen a woman in all the time

I've been here" (93). It is hard to read these lines without thinking of the plantation practice of forced breeding. Paul is the second coming of the "breedin' nigger," with the difference that *his* masters have eliminated the cumbersome mechanics of intercourse. The company of generative flesh proves too much for Paul to resist, and he succumbs to the violence that so often dogs heterosexual desire in Butler's work: "He tore her jacket off and fumbled with her pants" (93).

Lilith resists. She struggles not only against Paul, but also against the whole terminal legacy of forced breeding bearing down on her black female body:

> "No!" she shouted, deliberately startling him. "Animals get treated like this. Put a stallion and a mare together until they mate, then send them back to their owners. What do they care? They're just animals!" (93)

For Lilith there is no returning, even sexually, to a biohistorical past that reduces female flesh to its generative force. Slaves were chattel and bred accordingly. Lilith's future, and Butler's, involves the transformation of that legacy. The Oankali are able to breed new life without this reduction, appealing as the old ways might be to Paul: "They said I could do it with you. They said you could stay here if you wanted to. And you had to go and mess it up!" (94). It falls to Lilith to breed new futures, but not through intimacy with another human being. The way forward for Lilith and by implication her kind is to accept the opportunity the Oankali offer to breed new forms of life, neither animal nor human.

TALENTS OF THE FLESH

The Oankali are gene traders, after all. Like the old plantation masters, they view their human captives as a source of life and abundance. Their mastery of the arts of increase, however, is wildly more advanced than brutish practices like stud service and in-and-in breeding. They more closely resemble today's genetic engineers, except that the way they work makes mapping the human genome about as innovative as moveable type. "We're in the hands," says Lilith, "of a people who manipulate DNA as naturally as we manipulate pencils and paintbrushes" (167). The Oankali have completely dissociated the process of reproduction from the practice of sex, with the result that conception has been thoroughly rationalized, the effect not of a shot in the dark but of careful consideration of compatibilities among constituent genes.

This somber artistry is the province of the ooloi, a sort of third sex (neither male nor female), whose function among the Oankali is to oversee both the event of conception and the pleasures of sex. As one of her captors tells Lilith, "the ooloi can perceive DNA and manipulate it precisely" (39). They read gene sequences as if they were heroic couplets, turning conception into poetry. Reproduction becomes a form of creativity: "They do it for us. They have special organs for it. They can do it for you too—make sure of a good, viable gene mix. It is part of our reproduction, but it's much more deliberate than what any mated pair of humans have managed so far'" (39). Not to mention genetic engineers. These "treasured strangers," the ooloi, mix genes as they match mates, creating in the process new forms of life and, as Lilith later experiences with a partner chosen specially for her, new heights of pleasure: "Now their delight in one another ignited and burned. They moved together, sustaining an impossible intensity, both of them tireless, perfectly matched, ablaze in sensation, lost in one another" (163). All such intensity takes is intercourse with a sentient slug whose proboscidean appendages unite male and female without their having to touch.

Reproduction is not the only occasion on which the ooloi take an interest in human genetics, however. Lilith proves irresistible for reasons other than sex. Her flesh has talents she never dreamed of, talents it took an ooloi to recognize and nurture. Lilith learns from one of her keepers that an ooloi relative found something special in her flesh: "My relative examined you, observed a few of your normal body cells, compared them with what it had learned from other humans most like you, and said you had not only a cancer, but a talent for cancer" (20). Lilith's cancer teaches the Oankali the magic of genetic mutation, and they harness its creative potential to provide direction and drive to their genetic imagineering. The ooloi found Lilith's cancer "beautiful but simple to prevent" (21). Quite without her permission but for the good of the species (human, Oankali, and whatever their interbreeding might produce) the ooloi laid claim to that cancer, studied it, mastered it, appropriated its agency of mutation for the purpose of advancing knowledge and ultimately life. It was all part of the trade. As Lilith says later, "They know our bodies better than we do" (169). Such is the imperial propriety of healing. Lilith lives. The Oankali flourish. Species increase. Who is to say where, in this mutually beneficial exchange of flesh for knowledge, vitality ends and domination begins?

THE WONDROUS LIFE OF HENRIETTA LACKS

Behind Butler's account of Lilith's examination at the alien hands of the ooloi lurks the strange story of Henrietta Lacks, whose own talent for cancer far outlived the short term of her vitality.[8] Henrietta was born in 1920 on property in rural south Virginia that her forebears had worked for generations—as slaves. Her family worked it still, but by the 1940s some headed north to Baltimore, where Bethlehem Steel offered jobs with good wages. In 1943 Henrietta's husband, David Lacks, decided to try his luck there too, so together they moved to the city, where their lives took a turn for the better. They bought a small brick house in the segregated community of Turner Station. David eventually took a job at the shipyard. Neither rich nor poor, Henrietta and David were happy, and children started coming—five in all by 1951.

Then came trouble. Henrietta noticed blood spotting her underwear and immediately made an appointment at Johns Hopkins Hospital. Dr. Howard Jones performed the examination, during which he made a portentous discovery: a soft tumor on Henrietta's cervix the size of a quarter and the color of an eggplant. Jones had never seen anything like it. He took a biopsy and sent Henrietta home to await diagnosis. When the news came it was bad, but not necessarily terminal. Cervical cancer of the sort Henrietta was diagnosed with usually advanced slowly, allowing ample time for treatment. Eight days after her initial visit she was back at Hopkins to have her cervix treated with radium in an attempt to kill her cancer. Just before the treatment, and without asking Henrietta's permission, a resident at the hospital took one more biopsy—a routine procedure at a time before informed consent was standard medical practice.

The new sample was sent to George Gey, a leading cancer specialist and head of tissue culture research at Hopkins. For years Gey had been searching for a self-sustaining strain of cancer cells, one that could live and multiply outside the human body. Richard Te Linde, the chairman of Gynecology at Hopkins, suggested Gey try cervical cells. Henrietta's soft, purple tumor arrived as if by grace. Gey prepared a culture while Henrietta began her treatment. In seven months Gey would realize amazing results. In seven months Henrietta would be dead. Her tumor had been misdiagnosed. It was in fact a rare adenocarcinoma, quick to metastasize and swift to kill.

On the day Henrietta died, October 4, 1951, Gey appeared on national television with a test tube in one hand containing what remained of her, or at least what remained alive. Gey had found his

grail, a strain of cancer so vital, so virulent that it lived and reproduced in culture after culture, generation after generation. As he held
her cells, which he dubbed HeLa for Henreitta Lacks, toward the
camera, he conjured a breathless prospect: "It is possible that, from
a fundamental study such as this, we will be able to learn a way by
which cancer can be completely wiped out" (Skloot, *Hopkins*). While
Henrietta's dead body was prepared for burial back in Virginia, her
living tumor was incubated, irrigated, and fed. It grew like Kudzu.
It gobbled up nutrients. It layered and scaled the walls of test tubes.
When Gey determined that its cells could tolerate travel through the
U.S. mail, he sent out a slew of gifts to fellow researchers in Minnesota,
New York, even Chile and Russia. So began the posthumous odys-
sey of Henrietta Lacks, alive and well if no longer quite human. Her
immortality took the form of a tumor so prolific that, in the words
of one researcher (spoken in 1971) "if allowed to grow uninhibited,
[HeLa cells] would have taken over the world" (Skloot, *Hopkins*).

Henrietta's revenge, if one can call it that, would wreck a wry kind
of havoc on the medical establishment that cultured her tumor without her consent. HeLa cells quickly became a reference standard for
cancer research. They flourished wherever they went, and they went
everywhere—to Pittsburgh, to Tokyo, even into space to circle the
Earth aboard the space shuttle. They became the medium in which
Jonas Salk grew the polio virus, allowing him to isolate its crippling
strains and produce an effective vaccine against them. HeLa cells
have since been used to study viral replication, protein synthesis, gene
mechanics, radiation effects and, of course, the causes and possible
cures for cancer of all kinds. And there is where Henrietta's robust
carcinoma began to realize its revenge. So virulent was its life that
it contaminated other cell populations. It would migrate from culture to culture on the hands and pipettes of lab technicians. It would
infest the air of ostensibly sterile environments, infecting innocent
cultures upon exposure.

HeLa cells moved with the mindless cunning of biological weaponry, overpowering all they touched. One researcher might be study-
ing prostate cancer. His tissue would turn out to be Henrietta's cervix.
Another might be investigating breast cancer. Her sample cells would
prove to be HeLa. So triumphant was the march of HeLa cells upon
clinical cancer research that by the 1970s Walter Nelson-Reese, head
of the Oakland Cell Culture Laboratory and Bank at UC Berkeley,
could declare all available cancer cell lines potentially contaminated.
At no small cost to his reputation, given the vast amount of data he
was impugning, Nelson-Rees developed techniques for authenticating

cell lines that challenged the integrity of much cancer research. To this day it is estimated that as many as 20 percent of research cell lines remain contaminated. Studies of lung, liver, and intestinal cancer cells have all turned out to be using cervical cells—Henrietta's revenge. In the words on one commentator, "The peer review process has almost completely failed in the respect of false cell lines" (Masters 319).

Medical science has some explaining to do. But that is not the least of it. More urgent is the issue of the way it acquired Henrietta's immortal flesh in the first place. Although memories are misty, it appears that no one at Johns Hopkins bothered to ask Henrietta or her family for permission to culture her tumor, at least not initially. David, her husband, recalls being asked to allow tissue samples to be taken at the time of her death, a request he initially resisted. But doctors convinced him that such samples might help treat his children should they ever develop cancer. David relented, believing that he would remain informed about the fate of his wife's flesh. But no one ever told him what became of those cells. They grew and they multiplied. He heard nothing. Researchers bred them and traded. No phones rang. Eventually Henrietta's cells started secreting that rare substance, capital, amassing reputations and profits for their keepers. Still no word for David and his children. For them Henrietta's ubiquitous, undead flesh fell into oblivion.

But not forever. Quite fortuitously at a dinner party in 1975 the wife of one of Henrietta's children learned that her mother-in-law was, in a strange sense, still living. "Your mother's cells," she later told her husband, "*They're alive.*" (Skloot, *Hopkins*). This was shocking news to the Lacks family. For twenty-four years, during which the medical remains of their mother's body proliferated across the planet, they knew nothing of the vagrant, lucrative life of those plucky cells. They called Johns Hopkins. They spoke with representatives. Interest was shown. Gestures were made. Blood tests were performed. Then more silence. The Lacks family grew tired of fruitless inquiry and let the matter drop—not without resentment. Deborah Lacks-Pullman, another of Henrietta's children, sums the matter up succinctly: "We never knew they took her cells, and people done got filthy rich, but we don't get a dime" (*Citypaper*). While it is true, as Hopkins spokesperson Gary Stephenson said in an interview with the *Baltimore Citypaper*, that "Hopkins never sold HeLa, so it didn't make money from Henrietta's contribution"; this is a pretty disingenuous claim, given the prestige— not without fiscal implications—that accrued to individuals and institutions conducting research with those cells. Lacks-Pullman's cynicism is justifiable: "Hopkins, they don't care" (*Citypaper*).

And why should they? They are the breeders. They are the miracle workers of medical science. In a peculiar sense they are the artful hands of God. That is one way of interpreting Henrietta's fate, the way Henrietta's nephew Gregory Lacks prefers back in rural southern Virginia: "I go back to the Book of Genesis when God created man. He created him to live forever, really, but man ate up what God told him he couldn't eat, and a process of death took over his body. But the possibility was in man that he could live—and if he could live, then his parts could live" (*Citypaper*). HeLa arises from the tomb of Henrietta's flesh to live in blessed perpetuity. But there is another way of looking at the story of Henrietta's rebirth. It repeats with the blithe disregard of science the historical tradition of breeding slaves. Not literally, of course. But Henrietta and the whole Lacks family were black. The institution of medical science was in the 1950s and remains today largely white. One only need consider the role medicine played in the production of race as a category of knowledge to perceive the implications. Remember the physician that one master called upon to evaluate the fitness of his slaves for breeding? Medicine has a long and ignoble history of reinforcing racial inferiority and legitimating its reproduction—literally in the case of breeding slaves. Sampling and culturing Henrietta's living tissue is not so far, historically and institutionally, from the brutal, banal practice of breeding humans for sale and service. Breeding Henrietta's tumor in a test tube is a racially configured enterprise. In a sinister historical sense, the masters of medical science who oversee it still traffic in black flesh, which even now lives and breeds at their behest.

It is not enough to say with Ruth Faden, executive director of the Johns Hopkins Bioethics Institute, that "the Lackses' story is a sad commentary on how the biomedical research community thought about research in the 1950s" (Skloot, *Hopkins*). Faden implies that advances in the policy of informed consent would today assure the Lacks family a say in the disposal—if not the use—of their beloved mother's cancerous tissue. But the breezy compassion of the bioethicist overlooks at least two problems that remain endemic to the project of cultivating HeLa cells. The first is the racial bias built into it. When researchers first confronted the possibility that HeLa cells had contaminated other cell lines, they might have identified their progenitor in detail. All they knew, according to freelance science writer Rebecca Skloot, was that "she was black, she was a woman, and she was dead" (*Hopkins*). Those three predicate nominatives contain almost the whole story of professional medicine as an institution of power deployed in the name of health. Buried in them are mute proprietary assumptions: a prior right of possession of human flesh. That in this case it is black flesh manifests with peculiar clarity the status of Henrietta's black body from a medical perspective: it is property, bred for possession. The point is not that the fate of Henrietta's flesh would have been different were it white (although it might have), but that its blackness positions it historically and socially as property—even prior to its appropriation by medicine. The experiments at Tuskegee are only the most egregious instance of the proprietary insouciance of medicine in this regard. Henrietta's fate—and her revenge—reaffirms the historical status of black bodies as property whose reproductive capacity only increased their value. Slaves were valuable for their generative force, as is Henrietta's flesh today, a fact scantily covered by claims of advancement by medical ethics.

But there is second problem too, more abstract but still compelling. HeLa cells, like any cells for that matter, may multiply, but they lack volition. They reproduce with mindless animal aplomb. Medical science acquiesces in the liberal gimmick of property in person, which construes the human body as the epitome and prototype of all possessions and commodities. It puts flesh, in other words, at reason's beck and call, subject to its authority. It treats the human body like an animal, to be diagnosed and disposed of by science—particularly, as with tissue biopsies, in the absence of sentience. Professional medicine, with its trained physicians and diligent nurses, its technologies and institutions, both presumes and reinforces this foundational distinction between the human and the animal. In fact it produces that distinction, or helps to. Medical science set Agamben's "anthropological machine" in motion, which is why it might be premature, given the role practices as diverse as blood tests, colonoscopies, and insurance forms play in most people's lives, to believe the machine is idling.

The professionals who biopsied Henrietta's tumor without her permission did so with the authority of a double institutional entitlement: her flesh was black and animal, which viewed from a regrettable but still active historical perspective, comes to the same thing. Medicine masters flesh. It is the same old Hegelian story, except that in this case the slave cannot transcend the master's consciousness—because animal flesh has none. Henrietta in this sense lacks humanity. HeLa incarnates the animal. However beneficial the knowledge that results, cultivation and exchange of Henrietta's flesh replays in a humanitarian key the brutal legacy of breeding humans. Unavoidable? Perhaps. But it behooves medical science to acknowledge this dilemma and the appropriative assumptions in regard to living tissue that sustains it.

HeLa lives on while Henrietta's living descendents remain unrequited by an institution that profits from their mother's odd immortality. It has been a bad exchange. The doctors at Johns Hopkins took a biopsy that changed the world. They have offered little in return. The "Henrietta Lacks Days" and the "Congressional Record Resolutions" at least commemorate the fierce life of this black woman's indomitable body. But its strange fate appears most clearly in a proposal for new nomenclature. In 1991 the biologist Leigh Van Valen suggested that, given their nonhuman number of chromosomes and ability to reproduce perpetually, HeLa cells should be considered a whole new organism (*Wikipedia*). He dubbed it *Helacyton gartleri*. Henrietta, black breeder of perpetual flesh, gives birth to a new animal. Blurred by its fancy Latin name, however, is a history of appropriation and mastery that aligns, in the name of health, breeding animal cells with older, more dubious breeding practices.

SCRATCHIN' THE GENOME

The Oankali too breed new species. They take an oncologist's interest in cancer, but with bigger aims than eradication. Cancer's potential for mutation becomes for them an occasion, not for death but new life—in entirely new forms. That is the lesson of Lilith's talent for cancer that the Oankali learn from mastering her flesh:

> Your body knows how to cause some of its cells to revert to an embryonic stage. It can awaken genes that most humans never use after birth. We have comparable genes that go dormant after metamorphosis. Your body showed mine how to awaken them, how to stimulate growth of cells that would not normally regenerate. The lesson was complex and painful, but very much worth learning. (236)

The encounter between Lilith and her captors occurs in irreducibly biological terms, and the result transfigures both parties. Lilith's talent for cancer breeds new forms of life.

Something dies in the process, something whose passing can be difficult to accept: that hallowed human organism whose exceptionality arises in contradistinction to the animal. The touch of the Oankali transfigures human flesh, breeding new bodies irreducible to that hoary doublet. Lilith's human peers sense that a change is upon her even before she becomes pregnant at the weird hands of her genetically suitable ooloi, Nikanj. "Are you really human?" (180), asks Allison, a woman Lilith has awakened as part of the Oankali plan to resettle a desolated earth. It is a reasonable question, since the Oankali have modified Lilith genetically, giving her superhuman powers: the ability to open solid walls, to heal quickly, to overpower the toughest adversary. Lilith's answer is instructive, coming as it does after Allison has been sexually attacked: "If I weren't human, why the hell would I care whether you got raped?" (180). To Allison's *physical* query of her humanity, Lilith gives a *moral* answer. To be human is to behave according to a moral imperative that secures the sanctity of bodily life. From this perspective Lilith's modified body is beside the point. Moral commitments define humanity. Only animals act without them.

But it is just this moral configuration of the human and its implied contrast with the animal that the coming of the Oankali disrupts. They are, after all, gene *traders*. Unlike old time plantation masters, unlike contemporary medical researchers, their appropriation of human flesh involves *exchange*: bodies for bodies, genes for genes. Butler transforms the historical legacy of domination that frames slavery and race relations by imagining the physical transformation of all involved. Lilith's moral commitments, however humanitarian and laudable, prove completely inadequate to the prospect of such transfigurations. While she allows the Oankali to tweak her physiology, she insists her humanity remains intact: "We're an endangered species— almost extinct," she says to her human companions. "If we're going to survive, we need protection" (140). The trouble is her flesh knows nothing of species and endangerment. It lives to reproduce and in reproducing creates new bodies, new species, new forms of life.

When her ooloi Nikanj, already entangled with her human lover Joseph, appeals for her participation in their threesome, he speaks with the tongue of the libertine: "Lie here with us...why should you be down there by yourself?" However much Lilith's humanity bridles at the thought of sex with an alien, her body feels otherwise: "She thought there could be nothing more seductive than an ooloi speaking in that particular tone, making that particular suggestion. She realized she had stood up without meaning to and taken a step toward the bed" (161). The sexual bliss that ensues, bestial by any conventional standard, becomes the occasion for the genetic exchange that transfigures all parties. When finally Lilith becomes pregnant by her masters (*after* the death of her beloved Joseph), it is against her will. In moral terms, and like so many female slaves before her, she has been raped.

Harrowingly perhaps, such terms have no force for Nikanj, who views the event as an act not of violence but creation: "I have made

you pregnant with Joseph's child" (245). The logic of this confession exceeds that of human moral discourse. This rape has produced
another man's child. The creature who committed it did so with the
best intentions. The generative effect of this violation incarnates the
only hope open to humanity. It produces a life form and a future that
exceeds the measure of human morals. Lilith is hardly happy about it
("She stared down at her own body in horror. 'It's inside me, and it
isn't human!' " [246]), but her moral indignation appears hopelessly
inadequate to the weird economics of trading genes. Butler is no advocate of rape or apologist for slavery. She insists simply that the human
will obsolesce. As intercourse gives way to engineering as a means of
reproduction the prospect will emerge of creating new forms of life
irreducible to either the human or its feral double, the animal. And
maybe, just maybe the historical legacies of violence, appropriation,
and domination that constitute our humanity will obsolesce too.

They can. They must. It is what happens in the remaining books
of the *Xenogenesis* trilogy (or *Lilith's Brood*). At the end of *Dawn*
Lilith still clings to the nostalgia of humanity, devoting herself to
its preservation upon her return to earth: "*Learn and run!* If she
were lost, others did not have to be. Humanity did not have to be"
(248). But, of course, it does have to be. That is the viscid lesson of
Butler's vision. In the mute apocalypse of nuclear self-destruction,
the human reached a dead end. Forward movement comes *through*
the Other, a becoming alien that occurs the only way change can for
an organic life form: physiologically. In *Adulthood Rites*, the book
that follows *Dawn* in the trilogy, Lilith soon gives up her attachment
to humanity, not the least because she becomes the mother of a form
of life incommensurable with it. The child that Nikanj makes for her,
named Akin, resembles a human infant, but his long gray tongue and
precocious speech portend something else. Lilith breeds a new form
of life from human flesh. For Nikanj life *happens* through change:
"It rustled its head and body tentacles. 'Trade means change. Ways
of living must change. Did you think your children would only *look*
different?' " (260). Lilith acquiesces in that difference and comes to
love what flesh becomes in the child she bears, so strange by human
standards.

WHAT ROUGH BEAST?

The future of the human requires its transfiguration. Where is a
moral discourse equal to this prospect? Christianity insists upon
something similar, but it takes God to pull it off. All Butler requires

is a sexually receptive alien. The trope of the cyborg might do the trick. But even here the relation of the human to the Other is pros- thetic: not transfiguration but substitution troubles human integrity. Butler calls for something different, something radically, terribly— *else*, as if the breeders and the biopsy thieves had the right idea, just the wrong means. Their insight was to see in breeding flesh the value of life to come. Their mistake was to make the measure of that value *human*: the myopia of the overseer and the oncologist alike. On this score Butler could not be clearer. The human genome is soft-wired to explode. "Your bodies are fatally flawed," says Lilith's first Oankali companion. "You have a mismatched pair of genetic characteristics," namely intelligence and a tendency toward hierarchy (36). Thanks to this physiological contradiction, "Humanity was doomed" (475). Salvation from this certain death comes not through transcendence but transfiguration, a prospect as intimate as sex and as menacing as cancer—for both the Oankali and their partners in trade: "That's why the humans are such a treasure. They've given us regenerative abilities we had never been able to trade for before" (551). The true human legacy is regeneration, which is to say the transfiguration of humanity.

The alternative to the human, for Butler the only viable, living alternative, requires bodily change. "The Oankali *know to the bone* that it's wrong to help the Human species regenerate unchanged because it *will* destroy itself again. To them it's like deliberately caus- ing the conception of a child who is so defective that it must die in infancy" (532). That the Oankali will not do. They come to trans- figure the organism. They're breeders with a difference, or better, breeders *of* a difference, and in this they transfigure as well the long and violent legacy of breeding human flesh for the purpose of per- petuating mastery. Part human, part Oankali—ooloi, it turns out— Lilith's son Akin lives this mutation. His mother urges him to do so willfully: " 'Human beings fear difference,' Lilith had told him once. 'Oankali crave difference. [...] When you feel a conflict, try to go the Oankali way. Embrace difference' " (329). Doing so means supersed- ing humanity—both morally and genetically. Akin's destiny is to pass beyond the human, beyond even the animal, to become a new form of life altogether. It is a destiny full of danger, but full of promise too. Signaling his affirmation of this future, the only viable future Butler delivers in *Lilith's Brood*, Akin receives this daunting reply: "There's no safe way to begin a new species" (743).

A new species? Can Butler be serious? Can genetic engineering become a politics? Obviously not literally and not yet. But Butler *is* quite serious about transfiguring the human as the means to this future. For her change must occur physically, which is to say at the level of living flesh. It is worth emphasizing what this change will cost. By focusing so exclusively on carnal destiny Butler all but abandons culture as its driving force. The Oankali are gene traders whose history embraces the whole cosmic drama of their evolution as a species. Their technologies are alive and their preferred language is chemical. Effectively they *have no culture*: no poetry, no architecture, no laws, no nations. Their great achievement as a species is *themselves as a species*, which has its branches (Thoat, Dinso, etc.), but nothing constitutive of culture or even ethnicity. They are what they are, down to the braided subtext of their DNA. This makes the Oankali appear unhuman, but that is Butler's point. Unencumbered by human cultures and ethnic differences they are free to invent new kinds of life. Butler views culture, and the human tendency to make it the condition of identity, as an obstacle to the kind of change she calls xenogenesis.

To put it plainly, cultural differences are deadly. They tie life to its past and obstruct the emergence of new futures. The identities they produce can only come to blows. That is what causes the destruction of earth. That is what perpetuates violence among the survivors. As Lilith tells her strange son, "Humans persecute their different ones, yet they need them to give themselves definition and status" (329). Butler interrupts this terminal logic by forsaking culture and identity as political strategies. Crazy as it sounds, she imagines a postcultural future in which identity is flesh and life is change. So much for identity politics, which reduces life's variety to some prevailing standard. So much too for cultural politics, which subordinates flesh to its inventions. For Akin, firstborn of an emergent new species, "Life was treasure. The only treasure" (564). What really matters? The futures of flesh. Neither the *human* with its cultural achievements, nor the *animal* with its spontaneous vitalities. By so thoroughly jamming the anthropological machine, Butler takes life beyond the old oppositions—human and animal, culture and nature—that traditionally frame its value. Flesh will live on to burst the human like a chrysalis. Whatever new life form emerges will produce values commensurate with its vitality. Humanity and, hard as this may be to accept, its great cultural achievements will go the way of the Neanderthal.

All it will take is good breeding. Butler brings together two baleful cultural legacies to envision xenogenesis, transfiguring them in the process. She crosses the ignoble tradition of plantation slavery with the questionable history of Henrietta's cancer to posit a future in which the reproduction of flesh becomes a creative process. Does that mean the future belongs to genetic engineers? In short, yes. That is the unavoidable implication of Lilith's acquiescence to the Oankali. These gene traders come to transform flesh. Already bioscience has the means to do so. But from Butler's perspective mapping the human genome will be a pointless enterprise if it simply recapitulates the *human*. The Oankali would do so only as a prelude to carefully orchestrated change. Butler invites us to envision genetic engineering neither as a means of breeding more and better human beings, nor as a manner of advancing human health. Humans *will* acquire the capacity to manipulate their genes, and they *should* transfigure the human, breeding a better beast. Cloning lacks imagination. It reproduces flesh without changing anything. Truly imaginative genetic engineering would put DNA to more promising uses, creating new kinds of flesh, proliferating new forms of life. That is the bold challenge of *Lilith's Brood*: engineering flesh to breed new futures.

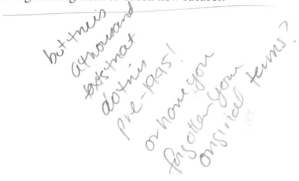

8

STEALTH

VALEDICTION FOR THE VISIBLE

The plane came streaking across the sky like a stray missile. Air Traffic Control could not pinpoint a location: "They seem to think that he is descending" (*9/11* 6), said one observer, an odd maneuver for a Boeing 767 over New York City. On board, flight attendant Amy Sweeny knew the situation was grave. From her position in coach she had witnessed a fracas that left one passenger dead and two other flight attendants bleeding. Five men had stormed the cockpit and seized control of the jet. Now the ground below was ascending like a concrete fist.

"We are flying low," Amy told Michael Woodward, manager at American Airline's Flight Services Offices, whom she had reached by phone. "We are flying very, very low. We are flying way too low." Then a pause, followed by her last words: "Oh my God, we are way too low" (7).

In the mordant prose of *The 9/11 Commission Report*, "At 8:46:40, American 11 crashed into the North Tower of the World Trade Center in New York City. All on board, along with an unknown number of people in the tower, were killed instantly" (7).

Everyone knows what happened next. Another passenger jet, United Airlines Flight 175 en route from Boston to Los Angeles, struck the South Tower at 9:03. At 9:37 a third jet slammed into the Pentagon, American Flight 77 flying from Washington Dulles to Los Angeles. When United Flight 93, bound from Newark to San Francisco, buried its nose in the dirt outside of Shanksville, Pennsylvania, at 10:02, a new day dawned on America and the world, a day lasting seventy-six harrowing minutes—or an eternity, depending on how you count. It has its own moniker now: 9/11, a day in the words of the National Commission on Terrorist Attacks "of unprecedented shock and suffering in the history of the United States" (3).

America's own little Hiroshima? Strangely, those errant airplanes struck the Two Towers at a height not much lower than detonation altitude of Little Boy over a hospital near Hiroshima's center. How different the devastation. Heavy with jet fuel, the planes exploded and the Towers burned, igniting chaos all around, especially on the floors above impact. Desperate scenes remain etched in our heads: smoke billowing, bodies falling, firemen rushing to heroic deaths, while the Towers stare into the quiet blue sky, embarrassed by these unexpected blows—until they buckle and fall, first the South Tower, then the North, bowing to the call of gravity. A rush of concrete, glass, and girder. Then silence. 2,973 dead. Lower Manhattan like a war zone. Around "ground zero" a sharp odor lingered for months, the indelible musk of death.

In fact Lower Manhattan *was* a war zone, which is why the comparison with Hiroshima is apt, however incommensurable in scale. But it was a war zone of a different sort than that which characterizes traditional hostilities. Granted, those planes took aim at a civilian target just like the *Enola Gay* did in 1945. But unlike the *Enola Gay*, they were not military aircraft, at least not ostensibly. They had been *militarized by being hijacked*, a point *The 9/11 Commission Report* emphasizes repeatedly. This was no traditional hijacking. It was "a suicide hijacking designed to convert the aircraft into a guided missile" (18). The hijackers worked a lethal magic that caused "the transformation of commercial aircraft into weapons of mass destruction" (31). They beat ploughshares into weapons. They militarized civilian aviation—with shocking ease, as if they simply scraped the logos off international carriers to expose military roundels underneath. With this difference: they exposed the insignias of a new kind of military, one lacking national affiliation and making no distinction between commerce and war, civilian and solider. An assistant to the harried crew at NORAD (North American Aerospace Defense Command) trying to track the hijackers put it point blank: "This is a new kind of war" (46).

What makes it new, exactly? *The 9/11 Commission Report*, perhaps surprisingly, credits the hijackers and their sponsor, the terrorist organization al Qaeda, with a better grasp of contemporary reality than the military establishment of the Earth's only superpower. Al Qaeda was immersed in that reality. America was aloof to it. This cultural and political asymmetry produced a perilously uneven understanding of the world, summed up by the 9/11 Commission in a stunning confession: "To us, Afghanistan seemed very far away. To members of Al Qaeda, America seemed very close. In a sense, they

were more globalized than we were" (340). More globalized than
the United States, with its globally roving military, its globally dispersed financial flows, and its globally ubiquitous network of satellite
communications? Apparently. It is not simply that those on the receiving end of
Imperialism better know its ways than its purveyors. Like insurgent
groups the world over, al Qaeda found members among the dis-
enfranchised. They came from a variety of countries and a variety
of class backgrounds, and they shared the conviction that a particular and pervasive kind of cultural imperialism crushed their
hopes and dreams. Its members alone are not what made al Qaeda
a uniquely effective terrorist organization, however. That grim distinction belongs also to its ability to exploit the material conditions
of a peculiarly American imperialism: global in scope, dispersed in
operation, and coeval with a complex electronic communications
network.

Al Qaeda worked like a multinational corporation in miniature. Its
operations crossed national boundaries. Its senior leaders were successful entrepreneurs of terror. Its training facilities attracted a diverse
range of recruits not only from throughout the Middle East, but from
Europe and America too. It moved money with ease among banks
and individuals, in a web of transactions that reached from Kuala
Lampur to Riyadh to Kabul to Los Angeles. Where al Qaeda differed
from its multinational cousins was in its means of funding. This corporation lived not by profit but by gift, as if in perverse fulfillment
of the promised glories of a gift economy. Taking full advantage of
the Muslim tradition of *zakat*, charitable giving, al Qaeda funded its
multinational exploits with donations from the far-flung faithful—
stockholders of an oddly ideological sort whose only expectation of
return was the satisfaction that comes with charity. Perhaps they got
more than they bargained for.

Al Qaeda payed American Imperialism back in kind. Its terror was
globalized terror. Its means were globalized means. Nowhere is this
aspect of its operation clearer than in its sophisticated command of
communications, which was nothing short of remarkable, a point
Richard Holbrooke summed up in exasperation: "How can a man in
a cave outcommunicate the world's leading communications society?"
(377). One answer to that question (and there are many) involves the
"new kind of war" al Qaeda began openly waging on September 11,
2001. By 11:00 that morning it had transformed three commercial airplanes into guided missiles and targeted the architecture of
global Imperialism, the World Trade Center's Twin Towers and the

Pentagon. What is new here is not the strategy of suicide attack. That was familiar enough. Al Qaeda's only innovation on the kamikaze was to up the scale to include jets. What is new here is the role communications play in making the attack successful. A commercial airliner becomes a missile only when it hits its target, a point illustrated by the fate of United Flight 93, which crashed three hundred miles short of its military objective. Furthermore, such a missile can hit its target only if it avoids detection and interception.

Here is where al Qaeda worked its magic. It not only planned, practiced, and successfully perpetrated the hijacking of four passenger planes fully loaded with jet fuel. It also managed to crash them into their targets, with the exception of Flight 93 whose heroic passengers foiled that aim. The brilliance of al Qaeda's strategy was to see the attack in cybernetic terms. To turn civilian aircraft into guided missiles al Qaeda had first to turn them into information—or the lack of it. To avoid detection they had to be undetectable—a reversal of the traditional strategy in which hijackers communicate demands and negotiate outcomes. These hijackers were strangely transparent.[1] Once they stormed the cockpits and secured the planes, they disappeared. The physical planes still flew, of course, until the baleful moment of impact, but they evaded the radar of American air defense. On three of the four planes the hijackers turned off the transponder that emits a unique signal distinguishing the plane's identity and altitude among the thousands in the air at any given time. With the transponder off, air traffic control had to rely for identification on "primary radar," which shows only generic blips. Controllers depend so heavily on transponder signals that they usually do not display primary radar returns. When they flipped off the transponders, the hijackers transformed the radar signatures of their aircraft, significantly minimizing detectability. They flew information missiles in an information war in which signature and source were out of sync.

For the archipelago of monitoring agencies that constituted national air defense on 9/11 (local air traffic control centers in Boston, New York, Washington, and Indianapolis; the Federal Aviation Administration; the Northeast Air Defense Sector; and the North American Aerospace Defense Command), the results were havoc. Something seemed wrong when the transponders went dead, and it soon became clear that one or more hijackings were in progress. What remained maddeningly unclear was where the damn planes *were.* Confusion ruled among controllers trying to find a single blip in a thicket of signals. In the words of one witness, "It drops below the radar screen and it's just continually hovering in your imagination;

you don't know where it is or what happens to it" (42). The Air Force scrambled interceptors—in the wrong direction. By the time Vice President Dick Cheney authorized fighter aircraft to engage a plane apparently bound for Washington, DC, it was a smoldering wreck in a field near Pittsburgh. Three others had hit their targets with catastrophic results. It remains for conspiracy theorists to determine whether there was anything purposeful to these errors. But credit al Qaeda with conceiving their attack in terms of information as much as mayhem.

In the future, if there is one, wars will be fought on video screens. By anticipating this prospect and exploiting its vulnerabilities al Qaeda put themselves on the cutting edge of U.S. military strategy at a fraction of its cost—under half a million dollars for this attack compared with untold and untellable billions spent annually by the Department of Defense and more darkly, the Central Intelligence Agency. With careful planning and the flip of a transponder switch al Qaeda turned commercial airliners not only into guided missiles, but also into *stealth bombers*. It changed aviation safety telemetry into stealth technology. It retrofit commercial air transports for military stealth missions. Al Qaeda accommodated terror to prevailing strategies of military engagement that arose to manage global threats, first during the Cold War, then during the period of limited and dispersed conflicts that followed the fall of the Soviet Union.

Al Qaeda *practiced stealth*. In doing so it produced something both easy to recognize and difficult to describe: a present threat that is impossible to see—not because it is invisible, but because its *visibility can't be perceived*. A present threat that isn't present. An invisible danger in plain sight. Flights 11, 77, and 173 were not in any conventional sense invisible. But they were not perceived, by radar or by human observers, as bombers or as missiles. *They were seen but not perceived*. That is how stealth works, and that is how al Qaeda orchestrated the attacks of 9/11. Because of the success of that strategy, or rather the pervasiveness of its globalized practice, al Qaeda now exists everywhere and nowhere, the prime stealth enemy in an interminable War on Terror.

How do you fight an enemy that is and is not there? More disquietingly, how do you inhabit a world where stealth sets the terms for life—and death? If *The 9/11 Commission Report* achieves nothing definitive, it at least advocates a reconfiguration of government and politics to accommodate the material conditions of global communication: "With globalization and the telecommunications revolution, and with loosely affiliated but networked adversaries using commercial devices and encryption, the technical impediments to signals collection grew at a geometrical rate" (87). As agency and cognition turn cybernetic, so too must governance. That is why the 9/11 Commission recommends a wholesale consolidation and coordination of Intelligence activities, including the creation of a cabinet level National Intelligence Director. "A 'smart' government would *integrate* all sources of information to see the enemy as a whole" (401). The wars it fights will be info-wars, cybernetic engagements in which seeing the enemy will require the ability, simply and certainly, to perceive it. But to function effectively, the various agencies of such a government should be reimagined as parts of a communications network: "A decentralized network model, the concept behind much of the information revolution, shares data horizontally too. Agencies would still have their own databases, but those databases would be searchable across agency lines" (418). The implied effect of such innovations will be to reinvigorate democracy in a cybernetic society that is global in scope and decentralized in operation.

Blueprint for a new New Imperialism? Perhaps. There is nothing more chilling in *The 9/11 Commission Report* than the simple claim that "the American homeland is the planet" (362). That makes America the custodian, ultimately, of time and space. No small task. Luckily it has a plan: "The United States must stand for a better future." Having secured the present through Intelligence and networked communications, the 9/11 Commission secures the future with a vision of boundless if familiar possibility: "That vision of the future should stress life over death: individual educational and economic opportunity. This vision includes widespread political participation and contempt for indiscriminate violence, and tolerance for opposing points of view" (376). The American homeland, which is to say the planet, looks forward to an American future. Maybe Muslims the world over will jump at it. But the question this vision begs in the context of changing agencies of governance and war is whether those new agencies will change the future too: the way it occurs, the possibilities it freights. If your enemies are so stealthy you cannot see them when they are there, how can you predict where and when they will show up—and what difference their baleful appearance might make? One of the achievements of *The 9/11 Commission Report* is to document the obsolescence of the future as an ideological promise. Now there rages a War on Terror with no foreseeable finish. Maybe there can be no better future than a perpetual cybernetic present.

POST PUNK

Enter William Gibson. His dazzling early novels made him the high priest cyberpunk—the dystopian sci-fi subgenre in which low-life hackers pit their wits and reflexes against the digital defenses of transnational corporations. While Gibson was at work on *Pattern Recognition* (2003), something happened that changed the world—and his writing—completely. As he put it to Andrew Leonard at *Salon*, "I was about 100 pages into the book on Sept. 10th. Then I got up on Sept. 11 and whoa—nodal point!" As usual, Gibson had set his story in the near future. But after 9/11 he found that his future no longer made sense: "the meaning of everything, *ever* that had gone before had to be reconsidered." It was either rewrite the book or junk it. Gibson chose rewrite, and the result was his first novel set completely in the present, more precisely the summer of 2002, only months after 9/11. The future died in that catastrophe, leaving only one plausible setting for *Pattern Recognition*: "The present is actually inexpressibly peculiar now," Gibson told Lawrence, "and that's the only thing that's worth dealing with" (Leonard).

Strange words coming from the author who gave a name to cyberspace and made it sexy beyond the wildest wet dreams of code crunching geeks. If the present is peculiar it is in part because of the imaginative force of Gibson's own novels: *Neuromancer* (1983), *Count Zero* (1986), *Mona Lisa Overdrive* (1988), *Virtual Light* (1993), *Idoru* (1996) and *All Tomorrow's Parties* (1999). But *Pattern Recognition* avoids all their flash and with it their future. If the present is the only thing worth dealing with, then the future is a thing of the past. Science fiction will either adapt or die, and Gibson seems ready to close the coffin. Michael Berry suggests that "Gibson's recent novels have displayed a certain weariness with the tropes of science fiction." He views *Pattern Recognition* as a critique of the genre, including Gibson's own cyberpunk. Change comes too fast and furious to sustain plausible futures any more, at least of the sort science fiction used to imagine: "the world-building that science fiction takes for granted just at the moment doesn't seem as possible" (Berry, quoted in Vitale). *Pattern Recognition* depicts a cyberpresent in some ways as grim as the futures of cyberpunk, but what is less clear is what gets lost when the future collapses into the present.

Gibson voices this attitude toward the future through his character Hubertus Bigend, global entrepreneur and chief operative of the Blue Ant advertising agency:

> we have no idea, now, of who or what the inhabitants of our future might be. In that sense, we have no future. Not in the sense that our grandparents had a future, or thought they did. Fully imagined cultural futures were the luxury of another day, one in which "now" was of some greater duration. For us, of course, things can change so abruptly, so violently, so profoundly, that futures like our grandparents' have insufficient "now" to stand on. We have no future because our present is too volatile. (*Pattern Recognition* 57)

9/11 blew away that "now" and with it all fully imagined futures. Among the dead on Gibson's version of that nodal day was Wingrove Pollard, a specialist in security and crowd control caught in traffic in lower Manhattan—the wrong place at the wrong time. His daughter Cayce (the name gestures toward the protagonist of *Neuromancer*) is a cool hunter by trade, a freelance corporate identity consultant whose visceral reaction to street fashion and corporate logos makes her valuable to advertisers. For Cayce too the legacy of 9/11 is violent change: "nothing really is the same now" (195).

But the future is not so obsolete as it might appear. Something replaces it in these character's lives, something they experience through their capacity to see patterns in the roil of events: "We have only risk management," says Bigend, "the spinning of a given moment's scenarios. Pattern recognition" (57). Managing risks involves imagining possibilities, tipping the present into what is to come by means of observed trends. Recognizable patterns—of fashion, of habit, of mobility—are the alternative to what used to be the future, which now becomes predictable through such dispersed but noticeable patterns of activity. That is what Cayce's cool hunting is all about. The custodian of this future is no longer science, with its rockets and its radio telescopes, but advertising. Bigend and Cayce are in the best position to see what is to come, observing a world given over to what Gibson once called the "dance of biz" (*Neuromancer* 144). Given a little life and liberty, people are driven more by the pursuit of hip than happiness. Life becomes an ongoing quest to identify a piece of cool to come, and with luck and the right connections, to capitalize it.

One of the strange facts of life in *Pattern Recognition*'s present, however, is that some patterns go unnoticed, patterns obvious to the book's readers but invisible to the characters who stake reputations and make fortunes on their ability to notice. Militarism, for instance, saturates the fads that Cayce and Bigend pursue, but neither recognizes it in any terms other than style. It is as if in the summer of 2002, the historical present of *Pattern Recognition*, the U.S. military has turned fashion designer—the Tommy Hilfiger of the War on Terror. For all their market savvy, Gibson's characters remain oblivious to the militarization of everyday life that has followed 9/11, with its encroachments on civil liberties and international mobility. The present of *Pattern Recognition* seems unlike the summer everybody lived through in 2002, one that remains unaware of certain patterns that set the terms for risk management—for now and the foreseeable future.

A BRIEF HISTORY OF WORLD WAR III

In popular culture, it falls to science fiction to anticipate the future of warfare. The genre's infatuation with advanced technologies and deep if questionable regard for alien life forms make it a compendium of military fantasies, mostly of the laser-blasting variety. From H. G. Wells's *War of the Worlds* (1896) to the last episode of *Battlestar Galactica*, war sets the terms for life in the future. Its slide into fashion in Gibson's recent work is symptomatic of cultural trends that reach far beyond genre writing. To measure their extent it is worth considering the role war and its wagers play in a couple of exemplary works of earlier science fiction. Doing so means discovering that the weirdly unacknowledged military presence in *Pattern Recognition* completes a pattern of it own: the withdrawal of war from plain view and its assimilation to the ways of everyday life.

The high point, if one can call it that, of military chic in science fiction is Robert Heinlein's *Starship Troopers* (1955). Heinlein wrote it when American Imperialism was innocent enough to believe in the dream of benign world domination. American had won World War II and things were looking good against the Communists in Korea. These were unapologetic military adventures aiming at unequivocal political results. Little wonder Heinlein could entertain with complete seriousness the possibility of reinventing liberal democracy in military terms. *Starship Troopers* is a sustained and powerful argument for the militarization of civil society. Heinlein makes it sound easy. Just take individuals with an inclination to serve their Federation, sign them up for a stint of voluntary service and, presto, you have citizens.

Heinlein makes military service the sole criterion for full citizenship in his democracy. Only veterans get the vote. The reason is as compelling as it is simple: only veterans put their lives on the line for democracy, demonstrating their willingness to die not for themselves alone but for the good of society. Heinlein puts the point bluntly for the benefit of his adolescent readers: "Since sovereign franchise is the ultimate in human authority, we insure that all who wield it accept the ultimate in social responsibility—we require each person who wishes to exert control over the state to wager his own life— and lose it, if need be—so save the life of the state" (145–46). One of the deficiencies of liberal democracy, as Heinlein views it, is the insouciance with which it grants citizenship. Birth is a bad criterion. Death would be better—but it would limit the number of citizens. A willingness to die is, therefore, best, for it banishes the principle of self from citizenship. The founding contract of civil society for Heinlein is not economic but military, the agreement a recruit signs when mustering in. Heinlein militarizes citizenship and makes war the prevailing agency of democratic life, to the point that even voting becomes a military activity: "To vote is to wield authority; [...] the franchise is force, naked and raw, the Power of the Rods and the Ax" (145). Civil society *is* military might.

In *Starship Troopers* nobody denies it. Even those who choose not to serve and remain, therefore, unenfranchised see the value of equating citizenship and soldiery. Heinlein solves the liberal problem of war as a state of exception by assimilating it.[2] There can be no state of exception if war is a fact of everyday life. As a member of society, the warrior is not exceptional but exemplary, the model citizen for her (and Heinlein takes pains to include women in his vision of citizenship) sacrifice of self and term of service. Nowhere is this status more apparent than in the equipment of the Mobile Infantry grunt, the most common soldier of them all. Thanks to the fabled "power suit," a smart exoskeleton that protects and vastly enhances the human body it encases, a member of the Mobile Infantry can do anything anybody can do—only way, way more terminally.

The power suit is a full body prosthesis: "The real genius of the design is that you *don't* have to control the suit; you just wear it, like your clothes, like skin" (81). The warrior is, thanks to this technology, Everyman as Terminator (women do not serve in Heinlein's Infantry). The agencies of everyday life are amped to military specifications, turning the average Federation flatfoot into a fighting machine qualified to wield handheld nukes—and the franchise. The secret is negative feedback: "The suit has feedback which causes it to match *any* motion you make, exactly—but with great force. Controlled force ... force controlled without your having to think about it. You jump, that heavy suit jumps, but higher than you can jump in your skin" (82). The power suit is more than just military hardware. It's the mechanism of human agency in a militarized democracy. The autonomous individual of liberal civil society fulfills its potential for Heinlein only when its agency gets amped, atomized, and aggregated. The power suit turns individual humans into autonomous marauders whose actions can be coordinated according to tactical necessity. They scream into battle from deep-space troop transports orbiting on high, protected on their way down by the technological miracle of their power suits. They are the true heirs of democracy. Citizenship is a military prosthesis.

Heinlein's description of civil society resembles Foucault's, but with a happy face. That is no surprise, really. Both take military discipline for the prime mover of liberal democracy. Heinlein simply goes public with Foucault's analysis: he wants more discipline not less, more and not fewer military techniques for diffusing disciplines socially. Hence the service requirement for suffrage. Hence too the administration of justice in both the Infantry and at home through public flogging. Heinlein secures the operations of militarized discipline through a spectacle of power whose effect is to configure a personally responsible agent, beholden to justice and capable of its self-administration. Witness Rico, Heinlein's protagonist, witnessing military punishment: "I had never seen a flogging. Back home, while they do it in public of course, they do it in back of the Federal Building—and Father had given me strict orders to stay away from there. I tried disobeying him on it once . . . but it was postponed and I never tried to see one again. Once is too many" (63).

The point here is the *visibility* of justice. Rico *sees* punishment, and it ain't pretty. It makes him think. The sight of pain makes him remember. Not enough perhaps for him to avoid a flogging of his own for a minor infraction. But when that comes, it only reinforces the earlier lesson: "Now here is a very odd thing: a flogging isn't as hard to *take* as it is to *watch*" (86, italics in the original). Sight is the main agent of this spectacle of justice. The terms of Heinlein's militarized democracy are visible for all to see: the citizen, the power suit, the public flogging, eventually a vicious war against Arachnid invaders. Military agency is open and continuous with political sovereignty. *War is democracy.* Evidence is everywhere. Its force is overwhelming. And what is the lesson of this openly visible assimilation of war to politics? Rico's words are perilously direct: "You *don't* forget it" (87).

But Heinlein wrote in the 1950s, when American military confidence was high and science fiction, at least in his hands, could keep the democratic faith. It was a ruse, of course. His militarized democracy was obsolete long before he imagined its establishment to come in the twenty-first century. Technology made it so, the very technology that Heinlein believes will ensure human supremacy. The contradiction built into those power suits is the contradiction at the heart of liberalism between human and prosthetic agency. So long as human individuals set the terms for human agency, as when Locke declares all men to have property in person (more simply, body control), humanity reigns supreme. But when the agency of prostheses exceeds that of their human hosts, as with the paradigmatic example of automated targeting of enemy aircraft, all human bets are off. Technology sets the terms for human agency and not vice versa. Heinlein's future for democracy belongs to his past, the world before World War II turned warfare cybernetic. Those power suits, for all their beefy feedback, only amplify human reflex. A guided missile exceeds it exponentially. In a fight between Mobile Infantry and smart, cybernetic ballistics, I pick the missiles. So much for citizenship.

The science fiction writer who takes these new cybernetic conditions of agency fully into account is Joe Haldeman. His wondrous novel from the 1970s, *The Forever War* (1975) is much more than a simple allegory of American military involvement in Vietnam. That would be plenty, of course, and Haldeman knows it. Early on he references "the Indochina thing" (11), making the conflict in Vietnam the historical backbone of his narrative. Like Heinlein, he was a military veteran himself, but of a war that somehow *requires* cy-fi to render faithfully. Although in many ways a rewrite of *Starship Troopers*, *The Forever War* adds one decisive detail to the facts of future warfare: it will occur on a relativistic scale. Haldeman wildly if quite credibly increases the duration of hostilities. Heinlein imagined that interplanetary battles, like those of World War II, would occur on a Newtonian scale of space and time. Haldeman ups the ante. True interplanetary warfare will take place in Einstein's cosmos, not Newton's. The scale of the known universe—and its physics— demands it. While it is a brilliant move by which to allegorize the slow-motion morass of an undeclared foreign war halfway around the globe, it also acknowledges the effect on human agency of advancing science and technology. Military transport in future wars will have to move at near light speed. Add to that a nod to quantum theory (Haldeman's gimmick of the "collapsar jump") and you have a recipe for relativistic warfare in all its weirdness: "Just fling an object at a collapsar with sufficient speed, and out it pops in some other part of the galaxy" (8). Collapsar transport occurs instantaneously across vast distances. "Travel time between the two collapsars...exactly zero" (8).

The implications for war are boggling. Haldeman's hero, William Mandella, begins to face them when he realizes that each jump adds years to his service: "I'd been in the army ten years, though it felt like less than two. Time dilation, of course; even with the collapsar jumps, traveling from star to star eats up the calendar" (80). No kidding. By the end of his tour of duty Mandella will by Earth standards be 1,163 years old. The relativistic scale of military service allows him to live a millennium of cultural history. It also complicates military strategy, as Mandella learns in a briefing after a particularly disastrous encounter with the enemy: "Relativity traps us in the enemy's past; relativity brings them from our future" (100). The relativistic scale of hostilities twists time in upon itself, turning it from a series of connections into a braid of discontinuous causalities. The present *precesses* in relation to its future. The future *recedes* in relation to its past. The effect on military strategy is to turn any given engagement into a probability smear: "The logistical computer calculates that we have about a 62 percent chance of success. [...] Unfortunately, we have only a 30 percent chance of survival" (101). Run the numbers. War turns statistical as relativity scrambles the temporality of any given engagement.

Haldeman accepts as Heinlein does not the cybernetic conditions of all future warfare. When the efficiency of military technology exceeds the human ability to control it, soldiers do not *use* weapons so much as *inhibit their use*. If it were not for the grim fact that military victories accrue through body counts, soldiers might not be necessary at all, as in the old *Star Trek* episode in which computers simulate battles, crunch the casualty numbers, and a requisite percentage of the defeated then report for incineration. Haldeman knows keenly that contemporary warfare has outstripped the agencies of the human warrior. In a passage that shows clearly how cybernetics changes the game, he turns the gallant gunner of a million celluloid foxholes into nothing more than a human circuit breaker in an automated swivel-mounted laser:

> The operator—you couldn't call him a "gunner"—sat in a chair holding dead-man switches in both hands. The laser wouldn't fire as long as he was holding one of those switches. If he let go, it would automatically aim for any moving aerial object and fire at will. Primary detection and aiming was by means of a kilometer-high antenna mounted beside the bunker. [...] The aiming computer could choose among up to twelve targets appearing simultaneously (firing at the largest

ones first). And it would get all twelve in the space of half a second.
(38–39)

So much for Heinlein's Mobile Infantry streaking into battle from above. Their power suits would make them easy pickins for a targeting computer that fires, in an odd phrase, "at will." Cybernetics renders humans obsolete as responsible agents for the wars they wage. Their primary value derives from their ability to inhibit the function of their war machines. While that is not much of a role for John Wayne, it is the condition of William Mandella's thousand-year tour of duty. He gets shuttled around the universe from collapsar to collapsar according to a military strategy that baffles human understanding: "Strike Force Command *plans* in terms of centuries. Not in terms of people" (169). With the loss of responsible human agency comes perpetuity, the automated military morass that Haldeman sardonically dubs "the forever war."

Cybernetics unhumanizes warfare, which is why there is no talk of citizenship in his future. To beat the odds and survive automated targeting is not much of a qualification for governance. Even so the inhabitants of Haldeman's Earth all eventually serve their planet. About four hundred and fifty years into his stint, Mandella returns from yet another hapless battle to learn that conscription is now universal: "Everyone is drafted into the UNEF at the age of twenty. Most people work at a desk for five years and are discharged. A few lucky souls, about one in eight thousand, are invited to volunteer for combat training" (182). The noble volunteerism of Heinlein's citizen soldier is a thing of the distant past and heroism, like weaponry, is programmed in advance. Haldeman abdicates the whole question of democratic citizenship, replacing deliberative politics with social engineering. He is more concerned with his world's new social imperative of homosexuality than the old politics of rights and suffrage. Militarization is so pervasive as to be banal, a simple fact of life rather than a state of exception, a five-year stint behind a desk unless you are unlucky enough to fit combat specs.

But for all its pervasiveness, actual warfare and its effects recede from view on Haldeman's Earth. The planet may be involved in an intergalactic shootout, but there's little direct evidence of it. Now and then a few veterans return and a warship needs repairing. Warfare itself retreats from the register of human visibility. It is as if the legacy of civil society will not be democracy so much as military engagement—on the peripheries of vision, pervasive but unperceived. Eventually even forgotten. When Mandella returns from his last engagement he learns that the war has been over for two hundred and twenty-one years: seven hundred years of hostilities ended not by military victory but evolutionary advance. In his absence humans have evolved from autonomous rational agents into hive-minded clones. Bye-bye liberalism. And, interestingly, bye-bye militarism. The perfect, androgynous creatures who tend his rehabilitation welcome him and his cohort back to a postpolitical world: "You don't have to do anything you don't want to do because...you're free men and women. The war is over" (248). Freedom and war are mutually exclusive conditions for Haldeman, which makes any militarized politics a state of incarceration. When humans evolve past their humanity, war disappears. Until then it persists beyond the horizon of perceptibility, a fact of life for those engaged in it, a forgotten habit for those who do not. Warfare floats free from its social conditions and continues invisibly for 221 years, at least for the evolved beings who remain on Earth.

For Mandella war remains a relativistic reality with a cybernetic script. In social terms it is less a political than an economic practice. One of the bonuses for the warrior of war on a relativistic scale is that combat pay mounts up—with interest. Mandella realizes just how much on returning to Earth after his first tour: "We'd be fairly rich: twenty six years' salary all at once. Compound interest, too" (108). Imagine the windfall of seven hundred years' back pay! That military service translates into not citizenship but capital shows that, however risky or peripheral it may be, it is just another job. War does not make anybody special, certainly not a citizen. What it does do is assimilate the high risk of military life to the financial algorithm of compound interest. Haldeman's forever war wholly accommodates the fungible futures of economic practice—*is those futures*, in so far as the warrior is the biggest beneficiary of their accumulating returns. Sad irony, then, when Mandella learns that in the brave new world where war is obsolete, capital is too: "Even the wealth you have accumulated, back salary and compound interest, is worthless, [...] Nor is there such a thing as an economy, in which to use these...things" (248). Haldeman assimilates military life to economic practice. If the warrior is exemplary of anything, it is the capitalist, not the democrat. As war obsolesces, so does capitalism—and so does the warrior. Haldeman sees militarism so deeply integrated into bourgeois culture that it persists unseen until that culture is no more. War lives a life of its own called civil society, whose future belongs to money—or the posthuman clones of evolution. Hope, no end of hope, only not for the United States.

THE GIBSON CONTINUUM

Recognizing a pattern of militarization in everyday life is one of the preoccupations of Gibson's earlier work, particularly *Neuromancer*. Set in a time that obliquely resembles Reagan's 1980s of corporate takeovers, urban sprawl, and massive Japanese investment, its future is an alternative present given over to the accumulation of capital on a global scale. The technological condition for global greed is cyberspace—the World Wide Web, whose development Gibson anticipates with more flare than accuracy. But he gets its culture right, the digital wonderworld where geek gamers, programmers, and petty thieves spin fortunes out of virtual air. In this near-dystopia, places are crowded, people are ornery, and "Biz. [...] Commerce. The dance" makes the world go 'round (*Neuromancer* 145). That dance is unimaginable apart from its particular history. War sets the terms for biz in *Neuromancer* and biz sets the terms for life. When Gibson's protagonist Case, petty hustler and cyber-cowboy, wants to learn something of this past, the lesson is fatally brief: " 'The war? What's there to know? Lasted three weeks' " (35). The shadowy figure who hires him to crack the security of corporate data arcologies fills in the details: " 'Too young to remember the war, aren't you, Case?' Armitage ran a large hand back through his cropped brown hair. [...] 'Leningrad, Kiev, Siberia' " (28). There is nothing more to say.

For Gibson, one of the "victories" of the Cold War was the militarization of everyday life. In *Neuromancer*, the transnational corporations that set terms for agency in a globalized economy are organized like armies:

> Power, in Case's world, meant corporate power. The zaibatsus, the multinationals that shaped the course of human history, had transcended old barriers. Viewed as organisms, they had attained a kind of immortality. You couldn't kill a zaibatsu by assassinating a dozen key executives; there were others waiting to step up the ladder, assume the vacated position, access the vast banks of corporate memory. (203)

Global capitalism is world war made costeffective. Hence the economic importance of cyberspace, the "consensual hallucination" (51) that replaces the battlefield as the primary site of strategic engagement: "On the Sony, a two-dimensional space war faded behind a forest of mathematically generated ferns, demonstrating the spatial possibilities of logarithmic spirals; cold blue military footage burned through, lab animals wired into test systems, helmets feeding into fire control circuits of tanks and war planes. 'Cyberspace' " (51).

The virtual reality of *Neuromancer* is built out of military information technologies. Something similar can be said of the Internet. It began as a communications network among mainframe computer researchers conceived under government auspices by the Advanced Research Projects Agency. Its military applications were clear from the start.

The Reagan 1980s saw military spending increase from $134 billion in 1980 to $299.3 billion in 1990 ("Federal Budget Outlays"). The money was not all spent on uniforms. It funded an array of weapons and information technologies, including the B-2 and the Strategic Defense Initiative, "Star Wars." It bankrolled covert military operations in El Salvador, Nicaragua, Guatemala, overt actions in Grenada, Panama, and eventually Iraq. In Gibson's diagnosis, this militarization directly affects the organization of civil society. His novels after *Neuromancer* show how information technologies disperse military power. In *Count Zero* and *Mona Lisa Overdrive* corporations with their own security forces and intelligence organizations script life by administrating the circulation of information. Celebrity, as that of global diva Angie Mitchell in *Mona Lisa Overdrive*, manages people more effectively than any army ever could. Agency shifts past what used to be called politics: "Shit *happens*," says the gnomic Yamakazi in *Virtual Light*. "You think it was politics. That particular dance, boy, that's over" (101). The new dance is digital, and social life moves to its rhythms. *Idoru* completes this trend as American-born celebrity rocker Rez plans to marry Rei Toei—a beautiful, famous, and entirely virtual Japanese media star. While he pursues his high-profile romance, lesser cyberites sift the dust of digital communication for signs of what might happen next. Not politics but information sets the terms for life in a cybernetic social formation.

In *Empire* (2000), Michael Hardt and Antonio Negri describe how globalization gives rise to a "new paradigm of power," one that "regulates social life from its interior, following it, interpreting it, absorbing it, and rearticulating it." Like Foucault, they call this paradigm "biopower." It scripts "the production and reproduction of life itself" (23, 24). Gibson's early novels describe the militarization of biopower. Hardt and Negri view the new global Empire "as a universal republic, a network of powers and counterpowers structured in boundless and inclusive architecture" (166), but Gibson is not so sure. In his view the operations of global capitalism have become saturated by the agencies of war, to the point that biopower reproduces a life so pervasively militarized that even open warfare—and the future it administrates—becomes almost impossible to recognize.

Life on the Gibson Continuum, to put the point differently, comes to be administered by a pervasive if unperceived military strategy: *stealth*. Stealth is a strategic response to the cybernetic agencies that eclipse old-time human autonomy. Once aircraft targeting gets automated, for instance, one way for a jet to avoid being shot down is for it to avoid being seen by air defense systems. Ideally that would mean becoming *invisible*, but short of *Star Trek*'s Romulan cloaking technology, that is a difficult goal to achieve. So the next best thing is to be only minimally visible or, to coin a useful term in this context, *avisible*, which is to say *seen without being perceived*. What is avisible cannot be seen and is not there—until one sees it. *Avisibility* is a strategic effect of military stealth technology. It is also a pervasive cultural practice on the Gibson Continuum. Where cybernetics sets the terms for military and social engagement, avisibility configures perception, cognition, and ultimately life.

R(ADAR) C(ROSS) S(ECTION)

Stealth has been the dream of military strategists since the invention and deployment of radar during World War II. If the streaking speed of a fighter plane makes it humanly impossible to target, radar is a cybernetic equalizer. It *sees* the menace in advance, allowing time to get ready, aim, and fire. Stealth is the inevitable response to air defense, a strategy of disrupting radar in order to minimize visibility. Stealth, in the words of *Wikipedia*, "is accomplished by using a complex design philosophy to reduce the ability of an opponent's sensors to track, detect, and attack an aircraft" (http://en.wikipedia.org/wiki/Stealth_technology). Stealth reduces the telltale signals radar returns to an observer (human or cybernetic) that allow it to identify an airplane as an airplane. Stealth does not work by eliminating those signals altogether, although that would be ideal. It works by disrupting them in such a way that what radar *sees* radar cannot really *perceive*. The blip of a bomber looks like a bird. Signs of a fighter signal a benign anomaly. An approaching menace remains unperceived and in that sense *is not there*—until the moment of its sudden, baleful appearance. Stealth beats radar at its own cybernetic game.

As an aircraft design strategy, stealth goes back to tinsel streamers and chicken wire baffles that festooned fuselages in an attempt to scatter their perilously obvious signals. Cold War surveillance aircraft like the U-2 and the sleek SR-71 Blackbird incorporated signal disruption into their designs, but solved the problem mostly by flying *above* Soviet radar. Stealth really took off with the ability to simulate radar signatures. That became possible in the 1970s through a computer program called Echo One designed by a Russian programmer named Pyotr Ufimstev, which allowed engineers to anticipate the "Radar Cross Section" of specific designs. Military aircraft were among the earliest products deigned by software instead of blueprint, making them the precursor "blobjects" of an increasingly virtual world: objects that in the words of Bruce Sterling "have suffered a remake through computer graphics" (www.boingboing.net/images/blobjects.htm). Sterling's examples include the Apple iMac computers and the new generation VW Beetle, but the prototype for both is stealth aircraft, designed by computer for maximum avisibility.

Some of those designs have become familiar, even iconic: the bat-winged sliver of the B-2 Spirit stealth bomber, the insectoid leer of the F-117 Nighthawk. But well into the 1980s, stealth aircraft had the social signature of a rumor. They were designed at secret locations and tested over remote desert sands. An early experimental demonstrator manufactured by Northrop was called "TACIT BLUE" and nicknamed "The Whale" for its bottle-headed design and lumbering look. But it worked like a charm, reducing what should have been a massive radar signature to a coy and cunning trace. It flew in the mid-1980s from the Groom Lake aircraft-testing site in Nevada (also knows as "Area 51," home to the military's "Special Projects Flight Test Squadron" [Paglin 9]), but it was not declassified until 1996. Other stealth aircraft that have found their way onto the radar of public awareness include the F-35 Lightning II, the X-35 Joint Strike Force Fighter, the Boeing-McDonnell-Douglas Bird of Prey demonstrator, as well as prototypes that remain classified such as Lockheed's UAV (Unmanned Aerial Vehicle) nicknamed "Darkstar" and "something called the "YF-24" (Paglin 12). All incorporate the stealth designs, materials, and technologies that give radar the slip, trimming exhaust plumes and masking size profiles to maximize their avisibility.

Stealth has its uses. The first F-117 squadron went operational in 1983 and saw its initial combat deployment over Panama in 1989. The avisible bombers have seen a lot of action since: Operation Allied Force in the Balkans in 1999, the invasion of Iraq in 2003, and most famously during Operation Desert Storm in 1991, in which the F-117 flew 1,270 missions without a loss. One was downed over Yugoslavia in 1999 by a Russian-built ground-to-air missile, but the secret to their remarkable success is the internal stowage of their payloads. Radar signature remains tiny until the moment bomb hatches swing open, when the bombers bloom on video screens like poison flowers. Stealth bombers, therefore, fly in low, drop the goods, and depart

fast, leaving radar to sniff their fading contrails. "Huge Deposit—No
Return": that is how a patch commemorating a "Low Observables"
flight test puts it (Paglin 66). These planes pack a huge wallop and
return a minimal radar signature, Furies of the avisible.

NOYFB

They are part of a larger military strategy that aims to transform warfare, which is to say reinvent it as a cybernetic enterprise. The future
of the U.S. military belongs to "Future Combat Systems," a strategic initiative that aims at minimizing the vulnerable human element
in the theater of war. According to the *Washington Post*, "there's a
hint of Buck Rogers in the program," whose purpose is "to create a
lighter, faster force that can react better to tomorrow's unpredictable
foes" (Klein). That word "tomorrow" tells the whole story: the practice of the future is being militarized in the name of unpredictable
coming violence. The *Post* continues:

> In the Army's vision, the war of the future is increasingly combat by
> mouse clicks. It's as networked as the Internet, as mobile as a cell-
> phone, as intuitive as a video game. The Army has a name for this
> vision: Future Combat Systems, or FCS. The project involves creating
> a family of 14 weapons, drones, robots, sensors and hybrid-electric
> combat vehicles connected by a wireless network. (Klein)

The formula for this future is written 14+1+1: fourteen weapons systems, one network, one soldier. Future Combat Systems aspires to an
extraordinary coordination and dispersal of human agency by means
of cybernetic command and control. The particulars of this vision are
pretty well known. "Tactical autonomous combatants" (robots) will
replace foot soldiers, deploying massive firepower on downsized tank
tracks by remote control. Collectively they are called SWORD, and
their specs vary according to combat conditions. Military transport
over rough terrain may involve a robot like Big Dog, currently being
developed by Boston Computer, a mechanical quadruped that combines a canine agility with elephantine strength. Tiny little cyborgs,
flies and beetles tricked out with nanotech surveillance gear, will
infest enemy outposts with the ease and innocence of insects, gaining
entry through their own power under direction from afar.

What these surreptitious systems have in common is the displace-
ment of human presence away from the field of engagement. Onetime
soldiers turn remote controllers, orchestrating hostilities from behind

a laptop in a bunker in Iraq—or a barracks in Oklahoma. Writing in
Adbusters, Clayton Dach sums up the situation nicely:

> It is tempting to say that military technology is steadily transforming
> war into a video game. Yet there's a strange irony in the works: as the
> games claw themselves even closer to the look and feel of real, down-
> and-dirty warfare, real warfare is fluttering away into strategic and
> technological abstraction, effectively taking a step back from its own
> reality. (April 28, 2008)

War is being virtualized, purged of human presence, which turns
increasingly avisible. The real point here is not that robots will sow
real violence on real battlefields. It is that their irreal controllers will
manage the action cybernetically. According to one government study,
a single such controller can manage twelve attack systems without
undue fatigue (Cummings and Guerlain): a massive multiplication of
force—and correlative reduction of human signature in the field of
hostilities. The title of another widely cited study from 2003 says it
all: "Unmanned Effects: Taking the Human Out of the Loop." Dach
claims that "a congressional mandate has already called for one-third
of all US military land vehicles to be unmanned by 2015, increasing
to two-thirds by 2025." If that is the case, then in the near future, to
vary Clausewitz's old phrase, war will be war by other means.

Odd and instructive here is that it is easier to know the technological gimmickry of Future Combat Systems than its means of funding. Avisibility is not a strictly military practice. It seeps into civilian
life via the economics of military research and development. Who
for instance really knows the cost of those systems? It is not entirely
clear that anyone does—or can. The problem is not merely that until
recently the Intelligence budget has been classified. Everybody knows
that the Department of Defense has a "black budget," money directed
toward its most secret research. But nobody can perceive it. It remains
avisible. Try and total it up. It is not possible, not merely because the
sums involved are so huge (108 billion dollars in the initial phase
of FCS alone). Their signatures may appear materially as the cybernetic weapons systems of "the army after next" but the sums themselves cannot be clearly perceived. Avisibility secures them. Consider
in this regard the conclusions of Michael E. Salla. In a scrupulously
researched article entitled "An Investigation into the CIA's 'Black
Budget,' " Salla shows how the CIA generates funding for its "black
budget" (the budget one knows about but cannot know, sees but cannot perceive) by siphoning it from other government agencies.

Nor are such appropriations the stuff of cloak and dagger conspiracy. They are completely in accordance with the CIA Act of 1949, which authorizes such creative funding techniques. The pertinent language is worth pondering closely:

> any other Government agency is authorized to transfer to or receive from the [Central Intelligence] Agency such sums *without regard to any provisions of law* limiting or prohibiting transfers between appropriations. Sums transferred to the Agency in accordance with this paragraph may be expended for the purposes and under the authority of sections 403a to 403s of this title without regard to limitations of appropriations from which transferred. (Italics in the original.)

The CIA Act of 1949 legislates the suspension of law for the purposes of funding CIA initiatives. What a strange feedback loop: the legal suspension of law. No wonder it is impossible to know how much money flows into CIA coffers. The laws of funding and cognition simply do not apply. A bubble of avisibility opens up in the black budget, what Salla calls an "unofficial" black budget whose size and sources cannot be tracked because they accrete "without regard to any provisions of law." Another phrase for it would be stealth funding: to the tune according to Salla of 1.1 trillion dollars. Military technologies of stealth get funded through a legislated economics of stealth. The result is to install stealth as a cultural practice at home as well as on the battlefield. One can see the " 'unofficial' black budget" but one cannot perceive it. Like a stealth bomber, it is avisible. Just try and comprehend it in all its legislative finesse and complexity. NOYFB. Culturally, one hits the limit of perception and cognition.

Zoon Biopolitikon

Under such circumstances war becomes difficult to perceive. It may be ubiquitous in a way that makes the Cold War look like street theater. In *Pattern Recognition* the Cold War is not over, it has just been commodified. Opposing economic blocs do not vie for sovereignty any more. In the global market they advance effects of biopower, producing and reproducing the occurrence of life itself. Ex-KGB agent Wiktor Marchwinska-Wyrwal turns the Cold War defeat of the Soviet Union into economic victory for all in a stirring tribute to his old adversary, Wingrove Pollard. Raising a glass toward Cayce, he asks, "had there not been men like her father, where would we be today? Not here, certainly. [...] Men like Wingrove Pollard, my friends, through their long and determined defense of freedom, enabled men like Andrei Volkov to come at last to the fore, in free competition with other free men" (341). Volkov is the richest man in Russia, head of a mammoth mafia-style oil cartel, and his advance "to the fore" can hardly be said to have been the effect of free competition with free men. But that is Gibson's point. With his enormous wealth and influence Volkov inherits a chunk of one security network formerly serving the national interests of the Soviet state (the KGB), and builds another, fully adapted to the transnational flows of information on the Internet. Biopower absorbs the global free market, militarizing its agencies and administering its futures.

What kind of weapon is a commodifier? Explaining what she does for a living, Cayce says she uses one regularly:

> "I hunt 'cool,' although I don't like to describe it that way. Manufacturers use me to keep track of street fashion....What I mean is, no customers, no cool. It's about group behavior pattern around a particular class of object. What I do is pattern recognition. I try and recognize a pattern before anyone else does."
>
> "And then?"
>
> "I point a commodifier at it."
>
> "And?"
>
> "It gets productized. Turned into units. Marketed." (86)

Many of the coolest commodities in Cayce's world adapt military fashion: "It's somehow her nature, she thinks, to pick out this one detail, this errant meme: a British military symbol re-purposed by postwar style-warriors, and recontextualized again, here, via cross-cultural echo" (142). The here is Tokyo, the context is street fashion, and the symbol is a red, white, and blue RAF roundel on the back of an M-1951 U.S. Army fishtail parka. Cool. But not as cool as Cayce's own jacket, a Buzz Rickson's, the miraculously meticulous and unutterably expensive "museum-grade replica of a U.S. MA-1 flying jacket" (10–11). By recognizing cool in the present Cayce promotes a future commodified in its image.

The crown of cool belongs to Bigend, materialized in his Hum Vee:

> He drives a maroon Hummer with Belgian plates, wheel on the left. Not the full-on uber-vehicle like a Jeep with glandular problems, but some newer, smaller version that still manages to look no kinder, no gentler. (58)

The civilian Hummer H2, introduced in the late 1990s by AM General, the makers of the original Hum Vee (High Mobility Multipurpose Wheeled Vehicle) is the epitome of military chic. Advertising copy promises military exploits for the middle-aged executive: "In a world where SUVs have begun to look like their owners, complete with love handles and mushy seats, the H2 proves that there is still one out there that can drop and give you 20." (Shouldn't that be 50?) A stripped-down H2 starts at about $50,000, while the H1, the civilian equivalent of the actual military vehicle, lists at $116,000. But it *will* give you "an incredible feeling of freedom" and allow you "to experience the world, and your place in it, like never before." Of course, if you cannot afford your own, you could always enlist and drive one of the U.S. military's. They ordered 50,000.

If cool commodities circulate biopower, its infrastructure is the Internet. In *Pattern Recognition* the Internet functions ultimately as a means of monitoring and administrating flows of information. The agency that pursues these ends is Echelon, a shadowy Web-based security network that, true to Gibson's newfound realism, actually exists.[3] Cayce believes it to be ubiquitous and possibly omniscient: "American intelligence have a system that allows for the scanning of all Net traffic" (244). Gibson's Echelon is an all-seeing U.S. agency that monitors the flight of information through the digital night. Like Artificial Intelligence in *Neuromancer*, its omniscience allows for the possibility of total knowledge in a world of particulated information and perpetual terror. But Gibson oversimplifies. In a novel so willfully realistic, his description of Echelon as Big Digital Brother is strangely dated. It remains impossible for a single nationally based agency to monitor all Internet traffic. Echelon is actually a security consortium among five nations: the United States, the United Kingdom, Canada, Australia, and New Zealand ("Echelonwatch"). It has listening stations around the globe, so it could potentially monitor all radio and satellite traffic. That is indeed a troubling fact, and although the International Covenant on Civil and Political Rights adopted by the United Nations in 1966 guarantees privacy protection, the United States has not signed its Optional Protocol allowing the Human Rights Committee of the UN to hear complaints by private individuals. When Gibson imagines Echelon to be the God of digital communications, he renders it in old-time imperialist terms. What makes Echelon scary, in particular to the European Parliament, is not that it can know everything but that as a dispersed security consortium it can operate without regard to nationally based privacy rights. Echelon is the perfect infrastructure for biopower, administering flows of information without regard for nation borders and civil rights, producing and reproducing social life in the image of commodified cool.

Still, in a book so insistently tied to reality, why does Gibson misrepresent Echelon? And why does he avoid any mention of real military action? There is something disconcerting about a novel that makes so emotionally much of 9/11 and so little of its political effects. Characters skip effortlessly through airports and across national borders, never so much as opening a bag to pass through security. No revoked visas, no racial profiling, no armed security guards. It is as if the only real militarism is economic, affecting people through private acts of consumption, communication, even creativity. For Gibson, 9/11 is a private trauma. It remains, in his bewildering phrase, "An experience outside of culture" (137). Why this stunning lack of recognition? Is it because the ways and means of war are becoming such everyday events? Hardt and Negri claim that "the history of imperialist, interimperialist, and anti-imperialist wars is over" (189). What has arisen instead is a perpetual and dispersed militarism that deploys force less to destroy life than to administrate it. Today every war is "a police action—from Los Angeles and Granada to Mogadishu and Sarajevo" (189). A coalition of the willing becomes the global equivalent of a squad car—with "to protect and to serve" written in mobile artillery. What forever passes away under such conditions is the future, the possibility that life might be different tomorrow than it is today.

In an interview with National Public Radio, Gibson describes the difficulty of keeping his novel faithful to what really happened during the summer after the terrorist attack. In one early version, "London was filled with soldiers—you're constantly seeing troops." But reality failed to oblige: "that wasn't happening, so I took them out" (Vitale). Commendable verisimilitude, perhaps, but in a novel so insistently global in scope, the selectivity of that realism is striking. There may not have been troops in London, but there were plenty in Kabul. Kabul does not register in Gibson's reality, however, giving the impression that his preferred sites of intrigue—London, Tokyo, Moscow—lack any real relationship to the global War on Terror. Gibson says it was hard to keep up with the world's changes that summer: "I'm used to dealing with thirty years in the future, and a few months proved to be infinitely more challenging" (Vitale). But why answer the challenge by looking away from the war to come?

Do such events matter less than the cool that commodifies them? In deciding to set *Pattern Recognition* in the present, Gibson abandons the future. If biopower administrates the production and reproduction of life, he offers little to suggest that things will ever really change. The future will come dressed in khaki, and it will not differ much from today. It may be hipper. *Pattern Recognition* posits the future as biopower's perpetual present. In that present the wounds of 9/11 are so traumatic they obliterate all awareness of the world to come. Gibson has confessed to believing that "in some incredibly bone simple way, nobody can write about the future" (Leonard). He should have added the word "anymore." The future used to be *the* subject of science fiction, as the bug-eyed monsters and atomic rockets of a zillion sci-fi pulps attest. No longer. There's an immense nostalgia behind Gibson's remark, nostalgia for the future as an arena of imagination, cognition, and critique. Its collapse into the present makes it all but impossible to perceive. It appears all around in the military chic of commodity culture, but it remains hard to perceive in its own terms. The future is becoming *avisible*.

CYBERNETIC WATERWITCH

Not only because it is being militarized. Maybe a bigger impetus for avisibility arises from the superabundance of information that runs like sick blood throughout a cybernetic social formation. Information is everywhere. There is more than one can possibly absorb. An avisibility of its mounting abundance complements the avisibility of minimal signatures—not merely because information is so profuse, but also because it is so widely dispersed. Plenty appears every day. It increases with every keystroke. But only rarely does one *perceive* its shape, contours, content, implications. The pixels are too dense and widely scattered. So much information moves through cybernetic society and with such speed that it becomes extremely difficult to play Hubert Bigend's game of risk management through pattern recognition.

Take the familiar example of the Enron debacle. It illustrates this sort of avisibility with dismal clarity. Thanks to a virtually criminal overvaluation of its stock, Enron suddenly declared bankruptcy in 2001, ruining dreams and retirements by the hundreds. CEO Jeffrey Skilling took the fall. In the words of Judge Simeon Lake, who presided over his trial for fraud, "The evidence established that the defendant repeatedly lied to investors, including Enron's own employees, about various aspects of Enron's business" (Gladwell). Lake found Skilling guilty and sentenced him to twenty-four years in prison. Somebody had to be held responsible. But as Malcolm Gladwell shows in his analysis of the Enron's fall from ostensible glory, "Open Secrets: Enron, intelligence, and the perils of too much information," that verdict seems out of sync with the widely distributed "facts" of the case. It is as if the sheer abundance of information has outstripped any human—or corporate—capacity to manage it responsibly.

Gladwell submits that "In an age of increasing financial complexity the 'disclosure paradigm'—the idea that the more a company tells us about its business, the better off we are—has become an anachronism" (Gladwell). The reason is that it is impossible to disclose all there is to know about a company like Enron. Gladwell argues that "deception" occurred not because executives like Skilling concealed information, but because they could not perceive it in the first place. It was avisible. In market terms, they relied too heavily on "mark-to-market accounting," a practice that determines the present value of a contract against future returns. Given the fungibility of such futures, no assurance exists that a stated value will persist to maturity. Enron's reliance on mark-to-market accounting and other kinds of creative bookkeeping gave rise, not to a secret set of books that contained the truth about its questionable investments, but a sprawling network of entries and accounts whose complexity made it impossible to perceive. It logged too much information to take in.

When a reporter for the *Wall Street Journal* sought to clear up the questions of Enron's actual value, he did not hire a private detective, but "read a series of public documents that had been prepared and distributed by Enron itself." When he asked Enron for clarification, six or seven executives flew to New York. Enron provided all the information it took to topple Enron. That information was openly available, enough for a group of Cornell undergrad business students to reach a reasonable economic conclusion regarding Enron stock in 1998: "Sell." It was overvalued. They could perceive as much *because they were amateurs*, attending only to a few facts available in Enron's public declarations. But most investors could not see the salient facts among the sheer abundance of available information. Enron's overvaluation was avisible. Among myriad records of creative accounting, a pattern of overly optimistic prediction was all but impossible to recognize.

So Skilling takes the fall. The Enron implosion illustrates more than just the perils of high finance. The avisibility of its accounting practices augurs a transformation in the operation of justice. With the coming of an overwhelming welter of information, traditional moral discourse obsolesces—in function if not in fact. Information is too vast and communication too fast to allow for plausible moral responsibility to be attributed to a rational agent. Law turns fictive, a legislative theater that does not so much distribute justice as simply fix blame. Such trials as Skilling's are show trials, meant mostly to persuade investors and citizens alike that morality persists beyond its conceptual obsolescence, that among a welter of information floats the flotsam of law. Skilling must be held accountable for Enron's bankruptcy (economically and morally) not because he is a liar (which he may well be—who knows?), but because an antiquated discourse of distributive justice requires him to be a liar. Thus does a morality of personal responsibility persist in a world where the abundance of information and the difficulty of perceiving significant patterns exhaust its force. Under such conditions the autonomous individual of liberal democracy becomes an index of the information it cannot rationally comprehend: the stealth subject.

What replaces morality? For Gibson moral agency becomes a question less of adjudicating right from wrong than simply *perceiving patterns*—and acting accordingly. That is one of the lessons of *Idoru*, which anticipates Gibson's turn to the present in *Pattern Recognition*. *Idoru* is still set in a near future beset by the grim effects of natural disaster, nanotechnology, and information marketing. But it shares with the later novel a preoccupation with avisibility as a condition of inhabiting a cybernetic social formation. Gibson's hero is a man named Laney, whose stint in a federal orphanage given to pharmaceutical experimentation has left him peculiarly susceptible to the pull of data: "he was an intuitive fisher of patterns of information: of the sort of signature a particular individual inadvertently created in the net as he or she went about the mundane yet endlessly multiplex business of life in a digital society" (24). In other words, he is a "cybernetic waterwitch" (24).

He has been hired by Slitscan, a televised tell-all celebrity exposé, to dig up dirt on the rich and famous, but comes across a more disturbing pattern of information in the digital mist, the clear but avisible indication of an impending if incidental tragedy. "Alison Shires was going to kill herself. He knew he'd seen it. Seen it somehow in the incidental data she generated in her mild-mannered passage through the world of things" (53). Laney perceives significant patterns in opaque data. Like a gifted radar operator, he reads the signature of data for what it occludes, in this case despair. And he acts accordingly. In defiance of company policy, he seeks out Alison Shires, reaching across an abyss of anonymous data to pull her back from her brink. He arrives too late, of course. She shoots herself in the head, and he loses his job with Slitscan.

But he acted. He did not do the right thing, or even the moral thing. He just acted to save a solitary, sad life in a world gone cybernetic.

That is not much, but it is what Gibson offers in lieu of morality in cybernetic society. Laney's talent is intuitive and he instinctively acts on his perceptions. He is not an autonomous moral agent so much a sympathy machine guided by a sense of life's value in a world of information. One of the interesting outcomes of that commitment is the way it expands the category of life. Laney's next employers put him on the trail of the Rei Toei, the digital Idoru and Japanese celebrity. The very density of information that constitutes her opens the possibility that she manifests a new cybernetic life form. "She is not flesh; she is information." Or better, "an architecture of articulated longing" (178). That architecture becomes an object of desire for celebrity rocker Rez of the band Lo/Rez. By the end of the novel he and Rei Toei move toward a communion that assimilates them both. "Our marriage will be gradual, ongoing," she says to Laney, who alone seems to perceive her meaning. "We wish simply to grow together" (237). The ultimate outcome of Laney's attention to avisible patterns of information is his recognition of the new form of life they configure. Affirming that life by perceiving it is a start, and about as close a thing to a morality as Gibson is willing to imagine.

COUNT ZERO INTERRUPT

If not morality, then what? Gibson has a soft spot in his digital heart for that traditional arena of moral exemption, art. A large chunk of his work pursues the question of what art becomes in cybernetic society. That is the major concern of his second novel, *Count Zero*, the oblique sequel to his dazzling debut, *Neuromancer*. *Count Zero* concerns a onetime art dealer named Marly who suffered the ill fortune of promoting a fake Cornell box as the real thing—not a recipe for longevity in the art world. Her keen intuition for style, however, brings her to the attention of one Virek, a fabulously wealthy but perilously ill financier interested in tracking down the creator of a new kind of construction resembling Cornell's, only more mysterious. Virek is wealth incarnate, and he lives in a medical treatment vat—or his body does. But thanks to the wonders of info-tech, he seems to be everywhere, as he explains to Marly, confused by his apparent ubiquity: "You saw a double. A hologram perhaps. Many things, Marly, are perpetrated in my name. Aspects of my wealth have become autonomous, by degrees; at times they even war with one another. Rebellion in the fiscal extremities. However, for reasons so complex as to be entirely occult, the fact of my illness has never been made public" (13). Virek is as ubiquitous as his money, whose movements are so complex that they exceed knowability. And so does he. His wealth circulates information in such abundance that its contours are impossible to perceive.

Hence Marly's skepticism that even Virek can know anything about Virek: "She wondered how powerful money could actually be, if one had enough of it, really enough. She supposed that only the Vireks of the world could really know, and very likely they were functionally incapable of *knowing*" (26). In *Count Zero* money is the condition of avisibility, the medium of an information glut that overwhelms cognition and baffles perception. Art, that once most sacred practice of secular bourgeois society, can be seen but not perceived or known as a human creation: "Bone and circuit-gold, dead lace, and a dull white marble rolled from clay. Marly shook her head. How could anyone have arranged these bits, this garbage, in such a way that it caught at the heart, snagged in the soul like a fishhook?" (27). That is where Marly's intuition comes in. It directs her quest for that sacred someone, the artist, whose Phidean touch turns garbage into art. Virek hires her to find the creator of these precious pieces precisely for her ability to *know without knowing*: "intuition, in a case such as this," he says, "is of crucial importance" (15).

The joke of Marly's quest, a little fresher in the mid-1980s than it is today, is that the Sacred Creator turns out to be a computer, or rather an artificial intelligence originally designed to manage a complex corporate empire and the aspirations of its human owners. Now it hangs in orbit around the earth, itself a pile of junk sold for salvage that occasionally spits out one of those beautiful boxes from a detritus of centuries of commodity capitalism that has collected around it. It is a sentimental old artificial intelligence. It has sweet reasons for doing what it does, as it confides to Marly: "I have my song, and you have heard it. I sing with these things that float around me, fragments of the family that funded my birth" (226). Marly's quest for the creator ends in an interview with an artificial intelligence. Her intuition confronts an agency that contravenes humanity: an impasse that Gibson cannot resolve in *Count Zero*. Art, if the boxes are any indication, serves up a signature that belies its origin—like enemy planes on a radar screen. It becomes a posthuman practice in a world that can only perceive it in human terms. Art testifies no longer to its inherent human value but to its own avisibility. Part of Gibson's project as an artist, if that is the right word, is simply to perceive art, to see how it works today, what it is becoming. Marly gets a box for her trouble, made from the junk her quest produces: patches from her leather jacket, tabs of holofiche, a crumpled Galois pack. "And that was all"

(236). Gibson leaves Marly baffled by a beautiful object—consoling perhaps, but nostalgic too. In cybernetic society such consolations are obsolete, vestiges of a lapsed world in which art, in all senses of the word, *matters.*

ALLERGY

Art does not matter any more—not in the sense that tradition-ally grounds its value. That is the assumption at work in *Pattern Recognition*, where Gibson sees art beginning to work in new ways. A new aesthetics is emerging, a stealth aesthetics commensurable with similar practices characteristic of cybernetic society. *Pattern Recognition* is in many ways a retelling of *Count Zero*. Its protagonist is a woman on a quest to find an artist—in this case the creator of a series of segments of digitized video released serially and anonymously on the Web. Known as "the footage," a quaint cinematic anachro-nism, it inspires a global following of devotees called "footageheads" obsessed with both its lyrical beauty and mysterious creation. Cayce is not merely among them. She is a leading proponent of a position associated with a group known as "The Progressives," who contend that "the footage consists of fragments of a work in progress, some-thing unfinished and still being generated by its maker" (46). Like Marly, Cayce is uniquely qualified for her quest, but not because she possesses some special cognitive capacity like intuition.

No, Cayce's sensitivity has more peculiar causes. She is allergic to bad trademarks. She makes her living as an advertising consul-tant because she can sense immediately whether or not a logo will succeed, which is to say circulate mass appeal. The bad ones make her sick: "next to a display of Tommy Hilfiger, it's all started to go sideways on her, the trademark thing. Less warning aura than usual. Some people ingest a single peanut and their head swells like a basketball. [...] When it starts, it's pure reaction, like biting down hard on a piece of foil" (17). Cayce's relation to allergens, like all such relations, is entirely exterior. They come from outside her and she responds physically, physiologically. They invade and she reacts. Gibson makes no appeal here to interiority or consciousness to explain this reaction. It just happens—reflexively. A pure imperative of perception. Cayce perceives viscerally what others only see: the avisible violence of advertising. She suffers "a morbid and sometimes violent reactivity to the semiotics of the marketplace" (2). Her most fearsome adversary: the Michelin Man. No wonder she removes all logos from her clothes.

From intuition to allergy—that is the trajectory of the subject in cybernetic society. Intuition bespeaks dark, knowing interiors. Allergy structures reflex. But it puts Cayce in the perfect position too to recognize important patterns in a world awash in information. Again like Marly, Cayce is hired to find the creator of the work she holds so dear. The equivalent of Virek is, of course, Bigend, whose ad agency Gibson describes as less multinational than postgeographic. Bigend takes as axiomatic the colonization of creativity by capital: "Far more creativity, today, goes into the marketing of products than into the products themselves, athletic shoes or feature films" (67). Not the object but the information concerning it is what matters to creativity. Bigend knows that the real art is no longer art but advertising, the condition of a new aesthetics that takes information as its medium and dissemination as its goal. "It's as if the creative process is no longer contained within an individual skull" (68). Creativity, like consumption, has become a mass enterprise.

Bigend hires Cayce to track the creator of the footage not because it is art, then, but *because it is advertising*. Its appeal to him is exactly the reverse of its appeal to Cayce. She cherishes it for its austerity, its anonymity, the gorgeous slow beauty of its images, as does Fredric Jameson, who finds in the footage "the Utopian anticipation of a new art premised on 'semiotic neutrality,' and on the systematic effacement of names, dates, fashions, and history itself, within a context irremediably corrupted by all those things" (389–90). Bigend is less nostalgic. For him the footage has become "the single most effective piece of guerilla marketing ever" (64), and he is perfectly willing to exploit Cayce's allergy and her sentimentality to discover who is behind it.

Which he does, with the ebullient brutality of the fiscally endowed. It is tempting to read the difference between Cayce and Bigend as a difference between art and commerce: aesthetic appreciation of semiotic neutrality versus crass consumption of the latest fashion. But tread warily. Gibson fails to imagine any plausible *beyond* of consumer culture where art could bask in its neutrality and its lovers could feel warm for its company. Cayce may love the footage, but she is "a secret legend in the world of marketing'" (65) and makes her living as a cool hunter commodifying street fashion. She strikes a deal with the devil of advertising fully aware that by discovering the creator of the footage she will be delivering the whole miracle into his cloven hands.

Besides, her awareness of the footage arises in a way that exactly parallels the cutting-edge advertising that works through what Gibson calls the "word-of-mouth meme thing" (95). There is a form of stealth advertising—call it fadvertising—that starts as a casual remark: "you're in a bar, having a drink, and someone beside you starts a conversation. Someone you might fancy the look of. All very pleasant, and then you're chatting along, and she, or he, [...] mentions this great new streetwear label, or this brilliant little film they've just seen" (84–85). Stealth advertising minimizes its signature. One sees it happen but cannot perceive it work. It remains avisible. The real aim is not, as with conventional advertising, to sell goods, but more simply *to circulate information*. Conversation becomes capitalized and *advertising becomes consciousness*. Which is why its effect is ultimately uncanny, as one of its practitioners confesses: "it's starting to do something to me. [...] I'm starting to distrust the most casual exchange" (85). Because knowledge of the footage arises in exactly the same way—the word-of-mouth meme thing—its cultural condition of possibility is, in a sense, fadvertizing. Hence Bigend's self-described interest. "I saw attention focused daily on a product that may not even exist. You think that wouldn't get my attention? The most brilliant marketing ploy of this young century" (65). Call it art. Call it advertising. But don't call it Utopian.

What would be an aesthetics equal to such practices? The obvious candidate in *Pattern Recognition* is the footage. As Jameson suggests, it betrays all the signs of the aesthetic: it is made, it is mysterious, it is disinterested to the point of Zen. Here is Cayce observing the most recently discovered segment, number 135:

> It's as if she participates in the very birth of cinema, that Lumiere moment, the steam locomotive about to emerge from the screen, sending the audience fleeing, out into the Parisian night. [...]
>
> They are dressed as they have always been dressed, in clothing Cayce has posted on extensively, fascinated by its timelessness, something she knows and understands. The difficulty of that. Hairstyles too.
>
> He might be a sailor, stepping onto a submarine in 1914, or a jazz musician entering a club in 1957. There is a lack of evidence, and absence of stylistic cues, that Cayce understands to be utterly masterful. (23)

Yup. Looks like Art: a sublime representation purged of all debilitating history. Kant on a celluloid halfshell. Except that it *moves*. What distinguishes the footage from Marly's beautiful boxes is precisely this capacity for the footage to move, to exceed its image status, becoming, in Deleuze's terms, a *movement-image*.[4] As such the footage is cinematic and then some, inspiring the same obsession with framing and duration that Deleuze pursues in his famous examination of cinema. Footageheads also concern themselves with the question of set to frame, frame to whole, cinematic whole to that of the world at large. Gibson explores here the passage of art beyond Western aesthetics, where form sets terms for value, and into a space where movement becomes an aesthetic medium. Cayce may love the footage, but she does not see it in formal terms. Rather she perceives it as a signature for something larger, which Western aesthetics would call an *auteur* but which turns out to be something much more complicated.

The first requirement of an aesthetics of stealth, then, is that the work of art be apprehended not as form but as information. For all her admiration, Cayce sees through the austere beauty of the footage to perceive, like the cool hunter she is, patterns of information that compromise avisibility. With Bigend's boundless credit behind her, she perceives not the maker but the making of the segments: their digitally embedded watermark, their spatial configuration as a blueprint for an antipersonnel explosive, their digitized (re)production in a Russian rendering facility, their role as affective tissue connecting the survivors of a traumatized family, and finally if almost incidentally their "creation" by a young Russian woman named Nora whose brain remains permanently damaged by a chunk of shrapnel embedded inside it and whose motives, like those of the artificial intelligence of *Count Zero*, lack human intelligibility. There is no plausible way of identifying human creativity with that damaged woman. Although she works from found video to create her haunting footage, her "art" (to speak an antique lingo) requires the money of a Russian oil magnate and the labor of a cohort of digitizers to exist at all. In all senses, then, this art *moves*: the footage comprises movement-images, of course, but to create them requires movements of money and collaborative labor, not to mention the movement of information among its admirers.

This then is the second requirement of a stealth aesthetics: it lives and dies in movement. Maybe the most important movements it involves are those of Cayce herself, who moves globally in pursuit of the footage: from New York to London to Tokyo to Russia. Because Cayce follows the footage, her movements are also part of its aesthetic effect. Art no longer rests easy in material form. It moves in the myriad movements of its production and reception *as information*. That money fuels these movements is a fact as bland and inevitable as oxygen. Trying to come to terms with her aesthetic experience, Cayce asks the inevitable question: "I don't understand how this could all have been put together, just to facilitate Nora's art." Bigend gives just as inevitable an answer: "Massive organizational redundancy, in the service of absolute authority" (330). A stealth aesthetics mobilizes info-tech to breech the avisibility of its social and material conditions. The footage presents the signature of art, but like a stealth bomber, it is much more powerful than it appears. It lives as the information it circulates and the movements it induces. And the moment it becomes a form, it lapses back into art, which is to say fadvertising, Bigend's ultimate product that does not exist. Cayce concurs at the end of the novel with the claims that "We found the maker" (351), but it is a discovery that goes nowhere. Cayce's global odyssey is over, as much an aesthetic effect as the footage itself. The maker is a footnote to the movements of the footage, the information it disseminates. That is stealth: art as a minimized signature of the avisible.

PLACE IS THE SPACE

Gibson pursues the possibilities of this new aesthetics further in *Spook Country* (2007). Stealth aesthetics acquires a name, "locative art," and it anticipates a future after the future, not so much a time as a space to come that eliminates the difference, so dear to philosophers from Plato to Baudrillard, between the physical and the virtual.[5] Consider the following exchange, quite remarkable coming from the man who coined the term "cyberspace":

> "Someone told me that cyberspace was 'everting.' That was how she put it."
> "Sure. And once it everts, then there isn't any cyberspace, is there? There never was, if you want to look at it that way. It was a way we had of looking where we were headed, a direction." (64)

Cyberspace was a symptom of a future whose arrival renders it—and the future—obsolete. Without waxing dialectical, it is clear that in *Spook Country* Gibson views the future as a temporal description for a spatial disturbance. As cyberspace everts, it takes time with it, shoving the world to come into a world simultaneously both physical and virtual.

The person who was told of the everting of cyberspace is Hollis Henry, the novel's protagonist, onetime minor music celebrity turned art reporter writing for a hip magazine called *Node*. She is in Los Angeles to cover locative art, a new aesthetic practice that takes advantage of GPS (the Global Positioning System) to create virtual images and place them in public locations. Alberto Corrales does exactly that. Using GPS to situate an image, he annotates a particular location and plunks his work down digitally—*right there*. That is the trick as Hollis Henry's contact describes it, "the artist annotating every centimeter of a place, of every physical thing. Visible to all, on devices such as these.' She indicated Alberto's phone, as if its swollen belly of silver tape were gravid with an entire future" (22). The device allows a viewer to perceive a work of locative art that is there but cannot otherwise be seen. Locative art on Gibson's description partakes of stealth aesthetics. It exploits the ubiquity of GPS to insert avisible images in specific public locations, images that the right technology renders visible.

Alberto is clever. One of his works depicts a meticulously rendered River Phoenix facedown dead on the sidewalk in front of the Viper Club. Another shows F. Scott Fitzgerald suffering a heart attack in the world music section of Virgin Records. Why Corrales, a Mexican American, would be drawn to just these images remains a mystery, but he is a hard worker: "'I start with a sense of place,' he began, 'With event, place. Then I research. I compile photographs. For the Fitzgerald, of course, there were no images of the event, precious little in the way of accounts. But there were pictures of him taken in roughly the same period. Wardrobe notes, haircut. Other photographs'" (41). It is odd that stealth aesthetics in *Spook Country* remains freeze-frame. Corrales's images do not move. They remain static, immobile, as if he has read only Kant and not Deleuze—and certainly not *Pattern Recognition*. They are everything that the footage is not, historically faithful snapshots attesting to the discontinuousness of history. Gibson retreats from the movement-image to the photograph as the model for locative art and in doing so sacrifices a large part of the efficacy of a stealth aesthetics, its capacity in a literal sense to *move*. No matter. Corrales creates representations that, like stealth aircraft, are avisible, present but imperceptible until the right technology renders them *there*.

The technology that locates those images in physical space, however, is beyond the ability of the artist to know and to manage. Corrales depends for his locative statuary on the assistance of one Bobby Chombo, GPS savant and wizard of things digital. "'If I didn't have Bobby,' Corrales confesses, 'I couldn't do any interior pieces. Even some of the exterior pieces work better if he triangulates off cell towers. The Fitzgerald piece, he's actually using Virgin's RFID system'" (51). Smart guy, that Bobby. He uses global positioning to locate virtual artwork that you walk right through unless you see it. He is a stealth aesthetician in a practical sense, rewiring perception to reveal the avisible. The trouble is, Corrales is wholly dependent on his wizardry: "I build the work, but Bobby hacks it for me. Gets it to work, even indoors. And he gets the routers installed" (37). When Bobby leaves Los Angeles for reasons of his own, Corrales's work goes offline. For the moment, a stealth aesthetics is only as effective as its best and most generous technician.

There will come a time, or rather a space, when an avisible art becomes perpetually perceptible. The sensorium is acquiring new eyes, ones that will not distinguish between real and virtual. The physical world is old school, and its priority is withering away. "The locative, though, lots of us are doing it already. But you can't just do the locative with your nervous system. One day you will. We'll have internalized the interface. It'll have evolved to the point where we forget about it. Then you'll just walk down the street..." (65). And the street will be *really virtual*. One will perceive the avisible, and its signature will exist as literally as anything else. The space that opens as cyberspace everts—call it Space 2.0—assimilates the virtual to the physical in a way that includes them both. What would be a space wherein images acquire the same status as things? The space of global capital? Perhaps. But Gibson offers the alternative of a world *continuous with info-tech*. Not surprisingly, Bigend, who reappears in *Spook Country* as a prophet of postfuturity, puts the point best when he predicts the coming "of a state in which 'mass' media existed, if you will, within the world." To which his interlocutor responds, "As opposed to?" And he replies "Comprising it" (103). Media not as medium and not as message but as world. Space 2.0. The transumption of stealth.

Location, "Location," Location

A pipedream? A nightmare? That space flowers in our midst. I will close with an example of locative art that shows how stealth aesthetics transforms space. In May of 2003 as part of a military strategy of shock and awe a squadron of F-117 Nighthawk stealth bombers screeched avisibly over Baghdad, dropping their lethal payloads. The targets were ostensibly military, but Baghdad is a city of millions. The propinquity of military to civilian targets was a fact of tradition and masonry. Bombs fell. Buildings exploded, with all due terror to their occupants and neighbors. But as *The 9/11 Commission Report* concluded in a different context, Iraq is much further from America than America is from Iraq. Iraqis felt *and continue to feel* the force of those explosions. Americans can barely imagine them, so distant is their thunder. For all practical, even political purposes, the war in Iraq is avisible. Images of devastation are available for all to see. But who *perceives* them? Apparently not even embedded reporters, whose militarized perceptions only render the enemy impossible to perceive. Paula Levine is a locative artist whose work assaults that avisibility. In a piece entitled "Shadows from Another Place: San Francisco><Baghdad," she mobilizes info-tech to transform space and in doing so render an avisible war perceptible. In a brilliant appropriation of publicly available information and technology, Levine uses GPS to redirect with excruciating precision the original bombing pattern of Baghdad over San Francisco. GPS, after all, began as a military application one of whose primary purposes was and remains weapons targeting. How else would it be possible to direct cruise missiles over hundreds of miles of open territory? Or bombs over Baghdad? GPS. Targeting coordinates can be plotted to the longitudinal and latitudinal second. Levine gathered those coordinates in 2004 from a Website sponsored by the *Guardian* newspaper in London that tracked the U.S. invasion. Then she redistributed them over San Francisco on a Website of her own design (http://www.shadowsfromanotherplace. net/). The site shows a map of Baghdad, a map of San Francisco, then overlays them with corresponding bombsites. Scroll over them and a location pops up, precisely mapped, complete with coordinates.

The next move is obvious. One takes a sort of atrocity tour of the virtual bombardment of San Francisco. Levine urged that move by placing caches at each coordinate containing detailed information about targets hit and people killed. She explained in an interview that she made the caches from tennis ball containers she wrapped in tin foil—giving them in her words "the unfortunate appearance of a bomb." Or maybe fortunate. She put some in bushes, some in plain view, one she attached by a wire to a street sign. She encouraged geo-cachers to contribute responses to the caches. Her aims were three-fold: to transpose a distant to a local space by relating San Francisco to Baghdad through devastation; to plant seeds toward a more fully flowered "cartographic imagination," one that fuses physical and virtual realities; and to encourage a collective engagement both with this transposed space and its otherwise avisible destruction.[6] Explosions were her idiom, mute explosions of bombs dropped halfway around the world.

Levine's work enacts stealth aesthetics at its best. It cannily reverses the fell trajectory of those stealth bombers, rendering perceptible the targeting that their avisibility was designed to obscure. Iraqi defenses could not see them coming. But we can perceive the destruction they left in their wake—or at least begin to. I spent a long day with my friend Talli following the trail of that virtual carnage. Starting at

Crocker Amazon Park at the southern edge of the city (N 38* 47.130'
W 122* 30.033') we wormed our way north on a luminous afternoon
darkened by flashes of imagined destruction. The sun blazed while
the bombs fell: on a high density residential neighborhood (N 37*
43.505 W 122* 27.657') where an aging Asian man seated in a door-
way wearing sweats clapped his hands and shouted "This is my place,
get the fuck out"; on high bluff (N 37* 44.534 W 122* 27.540) with
tasteful aging Tudors behind old hedges and a sign that read "Fall
Hazard"; on a row of old painted ladies (N 37* 45.453' W 122*
26.216') near Bikram Yoga beneath a sign that said "Out of Iraq";
on a cul-de-sac on the edge of Mountain Lake Park (N37* 47.256"
W122* 28.164') where shrill sounds of children playing and, yes, a
bagpipe cut the air. The atrocity tour ended, mercifully, at Lincoln
Park and the Legion of Honor Memorial (N 37* 47.118' W122*
30.003') overlooking, in all its pastoral calm, San Francisco Bay and
the Golden Gate bridge.

It was a beautiful, brutal afternoon. San Francisco was pulsing
with life, and it was being bombed back to the Stone Age—at the
same time. The neighborhood above Castro was particularly hard
hit. It is all but impossible for Americans to imagine the effects of
a city bombing. 9/11 was a surgical strike compared to the disaster in my head. Surely there were military targets mixed among the
houses, businesses, churches, hospitals, and schools of San Francisco.
But it was impossible to distinguish them from the surrounding city.
It became clear to me that civilians are not collateral damage. They
are primary targets. They have to be. There is not a weapon in the
world smart enough to confine its explosion to a prescribed radius.
As I made my way across the city I witnessed its comforts fall into
confusion, its insouciance flame into rage, its monuments crumble to
rubble. Imagine, please, a 500 pound bomb exploding at the end of
your block. That is what Levine forced me to do as I picked my way
through a city reduced virtually to bricks and ashes. San Francisco
would not be the same if it were littered with the bodies of the col-
laterally damaged. Nor will Baghdad.

Levine's work fuses the space of local comforts with that of distant traumas to create a world that Gibson only imagines in which
the physical and the virtual intertwine. Cyberspace everts to contest
the avisibility of military violence. San Francisco becomes haunted
by a space of devastation in which all Americans are implicated. In
this Levine surpasses Gibson. She fully exploits the capacity of stealth
aesthetics to *move*, provoking a quest something like Cayce's only
darker, the pursuit of a persistently avisible, apparently interminable

War on Terror whose missing images are bodies, bricks, and broken
dreams. Her work mobilizes new perceptions, literally and physically
as one drives around the city in search of caches containing information that contests avisibility. I found none. They are long gone. But
the city remains and the coordinates endure and the bombs continue
to fall, silently and perpetually. Stealth aesthetics makes them perceptible, not tomorrow but now, in the space of a world coming after the
future.

Notes

Preface to Apocalypse

1. Robert McNamara confesses in Errol Morris's documentary about him, *The Fog of War*, that if the Allies had lost, its major command would have been tried—and convicted—of war crimes.

1 Speculative Futures

1. So say Aldiss and Wingrove. *Wikipedia* makes the same claim.
2. See Mellor, Benjamin, and Smelik.
3. See Locke's *Second Treatise of Government*. The crucial passage is the following: "since Gold and Silver, being little useful to the Life of Man in proportion to Food, Rayment, and Carriage, has its *value* only from the consent of Men, […] they […] found out a way, how a man may fairly possess more land than he himself can use the product of, by receiving in exchange for the overplus, Gold and Silver, which may be hoarded up without injury to any one, these metals not spoiling or decaying in the hands of the possessor" (301–2). Money allows Locke to defend endless accumulation.
4. See Foucault's *History of Sexuality, Vol. I,* for his description of biopolitics, and for its further elaboration see Hardt and Negri's *Empire.*
5. Or maybe, on the contrary, they get way *too* far. Jameson is the most influential the best of the utopians of science fiction studies—and a formidable one at that. See his important *Archaeologies of the Future.* His theoretical assumptions are Marxist, of course, mixing Adorno and Bloch. While there is undeniably much science fiction that comfortably situates itself in the lineage of utopian writing that spans from Thomas More to George Orwell, I see it as primarily a European and a literary lineage, one that survives as a kind of cultural and conceptual fossil—not the living creature of a globalized, cyberneticized social formation. That there has been a spate of good writing on utopia is also undeniable (symptomatic of its demise?). See in particular Jacoby, Wegner, and Baccolini et al.
6. This might be the place to acknowledge the large and growing body of criticism devoted to science fiction. But note first that I am not offering a *definition* of the genre, a pitfall that many critics seem happy to take flyingly. Science fiction is many things. I'm more interested in what it *does* than what it *is*, and even here I'm pretty selective, as the chapters that

follow will evince. A good grounding in criticism of sci-fi would include some old standards (Suvin, Rose, Scholes), some newer genre studies (Roberts, Disch, Kilgore), a couple of historical/cultural inquiries (Landon, Bacon-Smith, Kitchin and Kneal), some feminist readings (Russ and Larbalestier), and a few hipster titles (McCaffery, Dery, Jonson and Cavallaro, Iglhaut and Spring, and Tatsumi).

7. See among the myriad sources Jameson (*Postmodernism*), Harvey, Henderson, and Weatherford.

8. See Goodstone, Tyan and Ashley, and Ashley.

9. On the economics of the pulps and of magazines in general, see Abrahamson, Bass, Brooks, Smith, and Miller.

2 CYBERFICTION

1. On cybernetics, see Weiner, especially *The Human Use of Human Beings*, which provides a kind of operating system for popular culture as society goes cybernetic. See too Hales (for an especially astute history of cybernetics), Tofts, Dyens, and Haraway, as well as the *Wikipedia* entry for "cybernetics."

2. This move gives rise to a whole array of contemporary posthumanisms, characterized by terms such as biopower, rhizomatics, or the informatics of domination. As any reader of Nietzsche or Foucault would expect, post-structuralism has a military heritage.

3. The following is a recent definition of cybernetics: "the science that studies the abstract principles of organization in complex systems. It is concerned not so much with what systems consist of, but how they function. Cybernetics focuses on how systems use information, models, and control actions to steer towards their goals, while counteracting various disturbances." See Heylighen and Joslyn, "Cybernetics and Second-Order Cybernetics."

4. See Jameson's *Postmodernism*, of course, but also "Culture and Finance Capital" in *The Cultural Turn*.

5. Perhaps this is the place to comment on the words "society" and "social" that I have been using with such insouciance. I don't mean them to refer to some systemic totality. Rather society as I mean it, particularly in the formulation "cybernetic society," gestures toward a sprawling and discontinuous network of communicative patterns constitutive of contemporary collective life.

6. Biopower is becoming an increasingly useful—and powerful—discourse for describing contemporary life. The emphases vary, but see Foucault (*Sexuality*), Agamben (*Homo Sacer*), Esposito, and Nikolas Rose.

7. See Friedman's illuminating discussion of Walmart's command and control of supply-chain distribution.

8. See Hardt and Negri on affective and immaterial labor, Harvey on post-Fordism, and Friedman on the flatness of the world for various attempts to describe this transformation of labor.

9. See Baudrillard, "Two Essays."

10. In this Bester anticipates Bauman's critique in *Globalization: The Human Consequences*.

11. The great heir to this tradition is Kim Stanley Robinson, whose *Mars* trilogy ranks as its fulfillment. While brilliant in their way, these books are peculiarly out of step with their contemporary moment, staging in breathtaking but dull detail the old Imperial dream of interplanetary colonization. Robinson reinvents the Victorian novel for the Space Age—*Middlemarch* on Mars.

4 SCORE, SCAN, SCHIZ

1. There's much more to be said on this subject, but in light of the intimate relationship between war and liberalism, it's easy to see the strategic appeal of terrorism to a liberal regime: the terrorist legitimates perpetual military aggression in the name of an all but invisible distributed enemy. See Esposito on "the paradigm of immunization."

2. The agencies involved are the Department of Defense, the Department of Education, the Department of Health and Human Services, the Department of Homeland Security, the Department of the Interior, the Department of Justice, the Office of National Drug Control Policy, the Small Business Administration, the State Department, the Department of Transportation, and the Department of Veterans Affairs. All receive funding under the 2009 Budget request for the National Drug Control Strategy. Many have their own military or paramilitary forces, as for instance, the independent air force, comprising some 250 planes, maintained by Customs and Border Patrol.

3. Compare Dick's position with Derrida's: "The question of *mimesis*, or, if I might risk a shortcut, the question of drugs as the question—the great question—of truth. No more, no less. What do we hold against the drug addict? Something we never, at least to the same degree, hold against the alcoholic or the smoker: that he cuts himself off from the world, in exile from reality, far from objective reality and the real life of the city and the community; that he escapes into a world of simulacrum and fiction" ("Rhetoric" 236).

4. *A Scanner Darkly* has received negligible critical attention. Among the few articles that treat it, see especially "P.K. Dick: From the Death of the Subject to a Theology of Late Capitalism," by Scott Durham, and "Irrational Expectations: Or, How Economics and the Post-Industrial World Failed Philip K. Dick," by Eric S. Rabkin, both available in Mullen.

5. The category of the "controlled substance" achieved its current form in 1970 with the passage of the Comprehensive Drug Abuse Prevention and Control Act, which created five schedules of such substances. In a lovely constative loop, "controlled substance" is defined legally as "a drug or other substance, or immediate precursor, included in schedules

I, II, III, IV, and V." These five schedules then name substances requiring control. The primary criteria for control are "a high potential for
abuse" and the tendency to "psychological or physical dependence." A
1973 ruling sheds light on the meaning of the first: *Hoffmann -LaRoche,
Inc. v. Kleindienst* determined that "potential for abuse [...] does not
turn on drug's [sic] having a potential for isolated or occasional nontherapeutic purposes" but on its "substantial potential for the occurrence of
significant diversions from legitimate drug channels" as well as its potential for endangering personal and public health. The likelihood of illegal
trafficking is here the first criterion for identifying the "potential for
abuse" that would warrant a substance's control. Commodity status,
and not nontherapeutic use, determines the legal definition of a "controlled substance." See Title 21 of the *United States Code Annotated*.
Historically speaking, drug regulation has not always been necessary to
secure public health.

6. In fact, the greatest increase in drug abuse over the past decade has come
from the illegal acquisition and distribution of prescription drugs, making it a problem whose proportions are second only to marijuana use.

7. The best history of drug regulation in America remains Musto's. See
also Morgan and Walker III. On the question of selective enforcement
of drug regulations against minorities, see Lusane.

8. My use of this term follows Gordon whose book *The Return of the
Dangerous Classes: Drug Prohibition and Policy Politics* offers a trenchant
critique of drug policy. She sees the reemergence of a rhetoric of class
indictment among policymakers as a return to old habits of damning the
underprivileged to avoid facing up to the failures of current economic and
social relations. As she describes them, "today's dangerous classes include
segments of the diverse communities of racial and ethnic minorities;
young people who exhibit some degree of independence from their elders'
direction and values; and aliens and the 'new immigrants' who have come
to the United States from Third World countries. [...] A fourth group is
what can perhaps best be called cultural liberals—crudely, those who tolerate (and occasionally celebrate) drugs, sex, and rock 'n roll and do so in
the name of individual freedom" (125–26). For a capacious engagement
of the range of problems besetting policymakers, see Kleiman.

9. It is an obvious point but worth repeating that the overwhelming majority of drug users in the United States are white.

10. In regard to the latter, see Wasserstrom.

5   Queer Science

1. I am referring of course to *Love and Death in the American Novel*.

2. In *Homo Sacer* Agamben suggests that habeas corpus marks the beginning of the appropriation of bodily life by sovereign power, setting the
terms for the emergence of biopolitics.

3. If interested in querying queer theories, see Morland and Willox, Sedgwick, Butler, Delany, and Warner, among a host of others.

4. The critical work on Burroughs I like best can be found in Murphy and scattered throughout Ballard's writing, especially the RE/Search editions.

5. At a reading I once attended Delany looked into the audience and asked, "How many of you have grandfathers?" With a majority of hands in the air, he then said, simply and unfathomably, "my grandfather was born a slave."

7 WE CAN BREED YOU

1. Donna Haraway faults Derrida for failing "a simple obligation of companion species; he did not become curious about what the cat might be doing, feeling, thinking or perhaps making available to him in looking back at him that morning" (*Species* 20). True enough. But Haraway's "encounter value," which arises when species meet, also does too much talking on behalf of the animal. Butler advocates something else: not "becoming with" the animal, but *becoming beyond the animal*—through mutual genetic mutation.

2. See Jacobs, Boutler, or Ramirez for readings along these lines. Walter Benn Michaels offers a stubbornly ideological interpretation of Butler's biopolitical fantasia.

3. Which is to say that the category of "companion species," Haraway's furry update of the cyborg, hardly begins to comprehend the kind of encounter between species that Butler has in mind. See Haraway's *Companion Species Manifesto.*

4. On the problem of race and Western philosophy, see Outlaw and Goldberg.

5. But to be fair to Hegel, or maybe the best intentions of the phenomenology of spirit, see Buck-Morss.

6. Such issues get raised around other of Butler's novels, most obviously *Kindred.* See, for instance, Steinberg.

7. This is a dark history, difficult to fathom, but see Spillers, Johnson, and Howell.

8. The information in this and the following paragraphs has been cobbled together from a variety of online sources including *Wikipedia, The Johns Hopkins Magazine,* and *The Baltimore City Paper.*

8 STEALTH

1. In a sense akin to Baudrillard's. See *The Transparency of Evil.*

2. See Agamben's *State of Exception* for a discussion of the way war provides an occasion in civil society for concentrating political authority in the hands of an autocrat—or decider.

3. Google "echelon" and you will get the idea. Of particular interest is a site called "Echelonwatch."
4. It might be worth wondering whether the logic of Utopia, formally a function of literary narrative, can fully assimilate the inevitable senescence of the moving image.
5. On locative art, see the work of the Locative Media Workshop, as well as Hemmet, Riesser, and Levine.
6. As she described in a telephone conversation on June 29, 2008.

Works Cited

2001: A Space Odyssey. Metro-Goldwyn-Mayer, 1968.

The 9/11 Commission Report. Authorized edition. New York: Norton, 2003.

Abrahamson, David. "Magazines in the Twentieth Century." *History of the Mass Media in the United States: an Encyclopedia.* Ed. M. Blanchard. New York: Routledge, 1998. 340–42.

Agamben, Giorgio. *Homo Sacer: Sovereign Power and Bare Life.* Trans. Daniel Heller-Roazan. Stanford: Stanford UP, 1998.

———. *The Open: Man and Animal.* Trans. Kevin Attell. Stanford: Stanford UP, 2004.

———. *State of Exception.* Trans. Kevin Attell. Chicago: U of Chicago P, 2005.

Aldiss, Brian and David Wingrove. *Trillion Year Spree: The History of Science Fiction.* London: Stratus, 2001.

Alliez, Eric. *Capital Times.* Trans. George Van Den Abbeele. Minneapolis: U of Minnesota P, 2001.

Alton Abraham Collection of Sun Ra Papers. U of Chicago.

Ashley, Mike. *Gateways to Forever: The Story of the Science Fiction Pulp Magazines from 1970–1980.* Liverpool: Liverpool UP, 2007.

———. *The Time Machines: The Story of the Science-Fiction Pulp Magazines from the Beginning until 1950.* Liverpool: Liverpool UP, 2001.

———. *Transformations: Volume 2 in the History of Science Fiction Magazines, 1950–1970.* Liverpool: Liverpool UP, 2005.

Baccolini, Raffaella and Tom Moylan. Eds. *Dark Horizons: Science Fiction and the Dystopian Imagination.* New York: Routledge, 2003.

Bacon-Smith, Camille. *Science Fiction Culture.* Philadelphia: Penn UP, 2000.

Ballard, J.G. *The Atrocity Exhibition.* 1970. San Francisco: RE/Search, 1991.

———. *Crash.* New York: Vintage, 1975.

Baraka, Amiri (Leroi Jones). *The Autobiography of Leroi Jones.* Chicago: Lawrence Hill, 1997.

———. *Black Music.* 1968. New York: Da Capo, 1998.

———. *Blues People: Negro Music in White America.* 1963. New York: Harper, 1999.

———. *Eulogies.* New York: Marsilio, 1996.

———. *The Fiction of Leroi Jones/Amiri Baraka.* Chicago: Lawrence Hill, 2000.

Bass, Sharon. "Economics of Magazine Publishing." *History of the Mass Media in the United States: An Encyclopedia.* Ed. M. Blanchard. New York: Routledge, 1998. 197–99.

Baudrillard, Jean. *The Transparency of Evil.* London: Verso, 1996.

———. "Two Essays." Trans. Arthur B. Evans. *Science Fiction Studies.* 18.3 (1991): 309–20.

Bauman, Zygmut. *Globalization: The Human Consequences.* New York: Columbia UP, 2003.

Benjamin, Maria. *A Question of Identity: Women, Science, and Literature.* New Brunswick: Rutgers UP, 1993.

Bester, Alfred. *The Stars My Destination.* 1956. New York: Vintage, 1996.

Blade Runner. The Ladd Company, 1982.

Blake, William. *The Complete Poetry and Prose of William Blake.* Newly rev. ed. Ed. David V. Erdman. Berkeley: U of California P, 1982.

Bloch, Ernst. *The Spirit of Utopia.* Trans. Anthony A. Nassar. Stanford: Stanford UP, 2000.

Booker, M. Keith. *Alternate Americas: Science Fiction Film and American Culture.* Westport: Praeger, 2006.

Boulter, Amanda. "Polymorphous Futures: Octavia E. Butler's *Xenogenesis* Trilogy." *American Bodies: Cultural Histories of the Physique.* Ed. Tim Armstrong. New York: New York UP, 1996. 170–85.

Boogie Nights. New Line Cinema, 1997.

Bradbury, Ray. *The Martian Chronicles.* 1950. New York: Bantam, 1977.

Brokeback Mountain. Paramount Pictures, 2005.

Brooks, Dwight E. "Magazine Advertising." *History of the Mass Media in the United States: An Encyclopedia.* Ed. M. Blanchard. New York: Routledge, 1998. 319–21.

Brosnan, John. *The Primal Screen: A History of Science Fiction Film.* London: Orbit, 1991.

Brown, Wendy. *States of Injury: Power and Freedom in Late Modernity.* Princeton: Princeton UP, 1995.

Buck-Morss, Susan. "Hegel and Haiti." *Critical Inquiry.* 26.4 (Summer 2000): 821–65.

Burroughs, William. *Naked Lunch.* 1959. New York: Grove, 1990.

———. *Nova Express.* 1964. New York: Grove, 1992.

———. *Queer.* New York: Penguin, 1985.

———. *The Soft Machine.* 1961. New York: Grove, 1992.

———. *The Ticket that Exploded.* 1962. New York: Grove, 1987.

———. *The Wild Boys.* 1969. New York: Grove, 1992.

Burroughs, William, and Daniel Odier. *The Job: Interviews with William S. Burroughs.* New York: Penguin, 1989.

Butler, Judith. *Bodies that Matter: On the Discursive Limits of Sex.* New York: Routledge, 1993.

———. *Gender Trouble: Feminism and the Subversion of Identity.* 1990. New York: Routledge, 1999.

Butler, Judith. *Undoing Gender*. New York: Routledge, 2004.

Butler, Octavia. *Lilith's Brood*. New York: Warner, 2000.

Carey, James. *Communication as Culture: Essays on Media and Society*. New York: Routledge, 1992.

Castells, Manuel. Ed. *The Network Society: A Cross-Cultural Perspective*. London: Elgar, 2005.

———. *The Rise of the Network Society. The Information Age: Economy, Society, and Culture*. Vol. 1. 2nd Ed. London: Wiley-Blackwell, 2000.

Corbett, John. *Extended Play*. Durham: Duke UP, 1994.

Corbett, John, Anthony Elms, and Terry Kapsalis. Eds. *Pathways to Unknown Worlds: Sun Ra, El Saturn and Chicago's Afro-Futurist Underground 1954–68*. Chicago: Whitewalls, 2006.

———. Ed. *The Wisdom of Sun Ra: Sun Ra's Polemical Broadsheets and Streetcorner Leaflets*. Chicago: Whitewalls, 2006.

Cummings, M.L. and Stephanie Guerlain. "Human Performance Issues in Supervisory Control of Autonomous Airborne Vehicles." http://web.mit.edu/aeroastro/www/people/missyc/pdfs/AUVSI_Cummings.pdf.

Dach, Clayton. "Future Soldiers." *Adbusters* April 28, 2008. www.adbusters.org/magazine/77/Future_Soldier.html.

Delany, Samuel R. *Dahlgren*. New York: Bantam, 1974.

———. *Longer Views: Extended Essays*. Middletown: Wesleyan UP, 1996.

———. *The Motion of Light in Water: Sex and Science Fiction Writing in the East Village*. 1988. Minneapolis: U of Minnesota P, 2004.

———. *Nova*. New York: Bantam, 1968.

———. *Shorter Views: Queer Thoughts and the Politics of the Paraliterary*. Middletown: Wesleyan UP, 1999.

———. *Stars in my Pocket Like Grains of Sand*. 1984. Middletown: Wesleyan UP, 2004.

———. *Times Square Red, Times Square Blue*. New York: New York UP, 1999.

Deleuze, Gilles. *Cinema I: The Movement-Image*. Trans. Hugh Tomlinson and Barbara Habberjam. Minnneapolis: U of Minnesota P, 1993.

———. *Negotiations*. Trans. Martin Joughin. New York: Columbia, 1997.

Deleuze, Gilles and Felix Guattari. *A Thousand Plateaus: Capitalism and Schizophrenia*. Trans. Brian Massumi. Minneapolis: U of Minnesota P, 1987.

Derrida, Jacques. "The Animal That Therefore I Am (More to Follow)." Trans. David Wills. *Critical Inquiry*. 28.2 (Winter 2002): 369–418.

———. "The Rhetoric of Drugs." *Points...Interviews, 1974–1994*. Ed. Elisabeth Weber. Trans. Peggy Kamuf and Others. Stanford: Stanford UP, 1995.

Dery, Mark. Ed. *Flame Wars: The Discourse of Cyberculture*. Durham: Duke UP, 1994.

Dick, Philip K. *Now Wait for Last Year*. 1966. New York: Vintage, 1993.

———. *A Scanner Darkly*. 1977. New York: Vintage, 1991.

———. *The Three Stigmata of Palmer Eldritch*. 1964. New York: Vintage, 1991.

Dick, Philip K. *Time Out of Joint.* New York: Carroll and Graf, 1959.
———. *Valis.* 1981. New York: Vintage, 1991.
———. *The Zap Gun.* New York: Carroll and Graf, 1965.
Disch, Thomas M. *On SF.* Ann Arbor: U of Michigan P, 2005.
Drug War Facts. www.drugwarfacts.org/prisdrug.htm.
Dyens, Ollivier. *Metal and Flesh: the Evolution of Man: Technology Takes Over.* Trans. Evan J. Bibbee and Ollivier Dyens. Cambridge, MA: MIT, 2001.
"Echelonwatch." American Civil Liberties Union Archives. American Civil Liberties Union http://archive.aclu.org/echelonwatch.
Eichenwald, Kurt. "Through His Webcam, a Boy Joins a Sordid Online World." *New York Times.* December 19, 2005. http://www.nytimes.com/2005/12/19/national/19kids.ready.html
Einstein, Albert. *Relativity: The General and the Special Theory.* New York: Penguin, 2006.
Eshun, Kodwo. *More Brilliant than the Sun: Adventures in Sonic Fiction.* London: Quartet, 1998.
Esposito, Roberto. *Bios: Biopolitics and Philosophy.* Trans. Timothy Campbell. Minneapolis: U of Minnesota P, 2008.
"Federal Budget Outlays for Defense Functions: 1980–2002." Infoplease http://www.infoplease.com/ipa/A0883084.html.
Fiedler, Leslie. *Love and Death in the American Novel.* 1966. New York: Anchor, 1992.
Fiofori, Tam. "The Space Age Music of Sun Ra...'Between Two Worlds.'" Typescript, 1969.
The Fog of War: Eleven Lessons from the Life of Robert S. McNamara. Sony Pictures Classics, 2003.
Foucault, Michel. *Discipline and Punish.* Trans. Alan Sheridan. New York: Vintage, 1979.
———. *Ethics: Subjectivity and Truth.* Ed. Paul Rabinow. New York: New Press, 2006.
———. *The History of Sexuality, Vol. I.* Trans. Robert Hurley. New York: Vintage, 1990.
———. *The Order of Things: An Archaeology of the Human Sciences.* New York: Vintage, 1973.
———. *Power/Knowledge: Selected Interviews and Other Writings, 1972–1977.* Ed. Colin Gordon. New York: Pantheon, 1980.
Friedman, Thomas L. *The World Is Flat: A Brief History of the Twenty-First Century.* New York: Picador, 2007.
Gernsback, Hugo. Ed. *Air Wonder Stories.* New York: Stellar Publishing, 1929–30.
———. *Science Wonder Stories.* New York: Stellar Publishing, 1929–30.
Gibson, William. *All Tomorrow's Parties.* New York: Bantam, 1999.
———. *Burning Chrome.* New York: Ace, 1988.
———. *Count Zero.* New York: Ace, 1986.
———. *Idoru.* New York: Putnam, 1996.
———. *Mona Lisa Overdrive.* New York: Bantam, 1988.

Gibson, William. *Neuromancer.* New York: Ace, 1983.

———. *Pattern Recognition.* New York: Putnam, 2003.

———. *Spook Country.* New York: Scribners, 2007.

———. *Virtual Light.* New York: Bantam, 1993.

Gillespie, Bruce. Ed. *Philip K. Dick, Electric Shepherd.* Melbourne: Norstrilia Press, 1975.

Gilroy, Paul. *Against Race: Imagining Political Culture Beyond the Color Line.* Cambridge, MA: Harvard UP, 2000.

Gladwell, Malcom. "Open Secrets: Enron, Intelligence, and the Perils of Too Much Information." *New Yorker.* January 8, 2007. http://www.newyorker.com/reporting/2007/01/08/070108fa_fact_gladwell?

Goldberg, David Theo. *Racist Culture: Philosophy and the Politics of Meaning.* Oxford: Blackwell, 1993.

Goodstone, Tony. *The Pulps: Fifty Years of American Pop Culture.* New York: Bonanza, 1970.

Gordin, Michael D. *Five Days in August: How World War II Became a Nuclear War.* Princeton: Princeton UP, 2007.

Gordon, Diana R. *The Return of the Dangerous Classes: Drug Prohibition and Policy Politics.* New York: Norton, 1994.

Greenberg, Martin Harry and Joseph D. Olander. Eds. *Philip K. Dick.* New York: Taplinger, 1983.

Habermas, Jürgen. *The Structural Transformation of the Public Sphere: An Inquiry into a Category of Bourgeois Society.* Cambridge, MA: MIT, 1991.

Haldeman, Joe. *The Forever War.* New York: Ballantine, 1976.

Hayles, N. Katherine. *How We Became Posthuman: Virtual Bodies in Cybernetics, Literature, and Informatics.* Chicago: U of Chicago P, 1999.

Haraway, Donna. *The Companion Species Manifesto: Dogs, People, and Significant Otherness.* Chicago: Prickly Paradigm, 2003.

———. *Simians, Cyborgs, and Women: the Reinvention of Nature.* New York: Routledge, 1991.

———. *When Species Meet.* Minneapolis: U of Minnesota P, 2008.

Hardt, Michael, and Antonio Negri. *Empire.* Cambridge, MA: Harvard UP, 2000.

Harvey, David. *The Condition of Postmodernity: An Enquiry into the Origins of Cultural Change.* London: Blackwell, 1992.

Hebdige, Dick. *Subculture: The Meaning of Style.* London: Methuen, 1977.

Heidegger, Martin. *Being and Time.* Trans. John Macquarrie and Edward Robinson. San Francisco: Harper and Row, 1962.

Heinlein, Robert. *Starship Troopers.* 1955. New York: Ace, 1987.

Helmer, John. *Drugs and Minority Oppression.* New York: Seabury Press, 1975.

Hemmet, Drew. "Locative Arts." www.drewhemment.com/pdf/locativearts.pdf.

Henwood, Doug. *After the New Economy.* New York: New Press, 2003.

Hilferding, Rudolf. *Finance Capital: A Study of the Latest Phase of Capitalist Development.* Trans. Morris Watnick and Sam Gordon. London: Routledge & Kegan Paul, 1981.

Howell, Donna Wyant. Ed. "The Breeding of Slaves." *I Was a Slave: True Life Stories Told by Former Slaves in the 1930's.* Washington, DC: American Legacy, 1967.

Iglhaut, Stefan and Thomas Spring. Eds. *Science + Fiction: Between Nanoworlds and Global Culture.* Berlin: Jovis, 2004.

Jacobs, Naomi. "Posthuman Bodies and Agency in Octavia Butler's *Xenogenesis.*" *Dark Horizons: Science Fiction and the Dystopian Imagination.* Ed. Ralaella Baccolini and Tom Moylan. New York: Routledge, 2003. 91–111.

Jacoby, Russell. *Picture Imperfect: Utopian Thought for an Anti-Utopian Age.* New York: Columbia UP, 2005.

Jameson, Fredric. *Archaeologies of the Future: The Desire Called Utopia and Other Science Fictions.* London: Verso, 2007.

———. *The Cultural Turn: Selected Writings on the Postmodern, 1983–1998.* London: Verso, 1998.

———. *Postmodernism; Or, the Cultural Logic of Late Capitalism.* Durham: Duke UP, 1991.

Johnson, Gordon. "Unmanned Effects: Taking the Human Out of the Loop." *Project Alpha, US Joint Forces Command,* 2003.

Johnson, Walter. *Soul by Soul: Life Inside the Antebellum Slave Market.* Cambridge, MA: Harvard UP, 1999.

Jones, Gayl. *Corregidora.* New York: Beacon, 1986.

Jonson, Annemarie and Alessio Cavallaro. Eds. *Prefiguring Cyberculture: An Intellectual History.* Cambridge, MA: MIT, 2002.

Kilgore, De Witt Douglas. *Astrofuturism: Science, Race, and Visions of Utopia in Space.* Philadelphia: U of Pennsylvania P, 2003.

Kitchin, Rob and James Kneale. *Lost in Space: Geographies of Science Fiction.* London: Continuum, 2002.

Kleiman, Mark A.R. *Against Excess: Drug Policy for Results.* New York: Basic Books, 1992.

Klein, Alec. "The Army's $200 Billion Makeover." *Washington Post.* December 1, 2007. www.washingtonpost.com/wp-dyn/content/story/2007/12/06.

Kuhn, Thomas. *The Structure of Scientific Revolutions.* 3rd Ed. Chicago: U of Chicago P, 1996.

Landon, Brooks. *Science Fiction after 1900: From the Steam Man to the Stars.* New York: Twayne, 1997.

Larbalestier, Justine. *Daughters of Earth: Feminist Science Fiction in the Twentieth Century.* Middletown: Wesleyan UP, 2006.

Leonard, Andrew. "Nodal Point." *Salon.* http://www.salon.com/tech/books/2003/02/13/gibson.

Lewis, Jeremy. "An Interview with J. G. Ballard." *Mississippi Review.* 20.1, 2 (1991): 27–40.

Levine, Paula. *Shadows of Another Place: San Francisco><Baghdad,*" 2004. http://www.shadowsfromanotherplace.net/

Lock, Graham. *Blutopia: Visions of the Future and Revisions of the Past in the Work Of Sun Ra, Duke Ellington, and Anthony Braxton.* Durham: Duke UP, 1999.

Locke, John. *Two Treatises of Government.* Ed. Peter Laslett. Cambridge: Cambridge UP, 1988.

Lusane, Clarence. *Pipe Dream Blues: Racism and the War on Drugs.* Boston: South End, 1991.

Masters, John R. "HeLa Cells 50 Years On: the Good, the Bad and the Ugly." *Nature Reviews: Cancer.* 2 (April 2002): 315–19.

McCaffery, Larry. Ed. *Storming the Reality Studio: A Casebook of Cyberpunk and Postmodern Science Fiction.* Durham: Duke UP, 1991.

Mellor, Anne K. *Mary Shelley: Her Life, Her Fiction, Her Monsters.* New York: Routledge, 1989.

Michaels, Walter Benn. "Political Science Fictions." *New Literary History.* 31.4 (Autumn 2000): 649–64.

Miller, Laura J. "The Rise and Not-Quite Fall of the American Book Wholesaler." *Journal of Media Economics.* 16 (2): 97–120.

Monitoring the Future Survey. U of Michigan. www.monitoringthefuture.org.

Morland, Iain, and Anabelle Willox. *Queer Theory: Readers in Cultural Criticism.* New York: Palgrave Macmillan, 2004.

Mullen, R. D., Istvan Csicsery-Ronay, Jr., Arthur B. Evans, and Veronica Hollinger. Eds. *On Philip K. Dick: 40 Articles from Science Fiction Studies.* Terre Haute: SF-TH, 1992.

Murphy, Timothy. *Wising Up the Marks: The Amodern William S. Burroughs.* Berkeley: U of California P, 1997.

Musto, David F., M.D. *The American Disease: Origins of Narcotic Control.* Expanded edition. New York: Oxford UP, 1987.

Outlaw, Lucius. *On Race and Philosophy.* New York: Routledge, 1996.

Paglen, Trevor. *I Could Tell You but then You Would Have to Be Destroyed by Me: Emblems from the Pentagon's Black World.* Brooklyn: Melville House, 2007.

Pateman, Carole. *The Sexual Contract.* Stanford: Stanford UP, 1988.

Pew Center on the States. *One in 100: Behind Bars in America 2008.* The Pew Charitable Trusts. www.pewcenteronthestates.org.

Pierce, Hazel. *Philip K. Dick.* Mercer Island: Starmount House, 1982.

Poster, Mark. "The Information Empire." *Comparative Literature Studies.* 41.3 (2004): 317–34.

Ra, Sun. *Collected Works. Vol. 1: Immeasurable Equation.* Ed. Adam Abraham. Chandler: Phaelos, 2005.

Ragin, Hugh. *An Afternoon in Harlem.* Evidence, 1999.

Ramierez, Catherine S. "Cyborg Feminism: The Science Fiction of Octavia Butler and Gloria Anzaldúa." *Reload: Rethinking Women and Cyberculture.* Ed. Mary Flanagan and Austin Booth. Cambridge, MA: MIT, 2002. 374–402.

Reynolds, Quentin James. *The Fiction Factory: Or, from Pulp Row to Quality Street. The Story of 100 Years of Publishing at Street and Smith.* New York: Random House, 1955.

Rieser, Martin. "Locative Media and Spatial Narrative." *Refresh: Banff 2005.* September 29–October 4, 2005.

Ritvo, Harriet. *The Animal Estate.* Cambridge, MA: Harvard UP, 1987.

Roberts, Adam. *Science Fiction.* 2nd Ed. London: Routledge, 2006.

Robinson, Kim Stanley. *The Novels of Philip K. Dick.* Ann Arbor: UMI Research Press, 1984.

———. *Red Mars.* New York: Spectra, 1993.

Ronell, Avital. *Crack Wars: Literature Addiction Mania.* Lincoln: Nebraska UP, 1991.

Rose, Mark. *Alien Encounters: Anatomy of Science Fiction.* Cambridge, MA: Harvard UP, 1981.

———. Ed. *Science Fiction: A Collection of Critical Essays.* Englewood Cliffs: Prentice Hall, 1976.

Rose, Nikolas. *The Politics of Life Itself.* Princeton: Princeton UP, 2007.

Russ, Joanna. *The Female Man.* 1975. Boston: Beacon, 2000.

———. *To Write Like a Woman.* Bloomington: Indiana UP, 1995.

Scalla, Michael E. "An Investigation into the CIA's 'Black Budget.'" *Scoop Independent News.* http://www.scoop.co.nz/stories/HL0401/S00151.htm.

A Scanner Darkly. Warner Independent Pictures, 2006.

Scholes, Robert. *Science Fiction: History, Science, Vision.* New York: Oxford UP, 1977.

Sedgwick, Eve Kosofsky. *Between Men: English Literature and Male Homosocial Desire.* New York: Columbia UP, 1985.

———. *The Epistemology of the Closet.* Berkeley: U of California P, 1990.

Seed, David. *American Science Fiction and the Cold War: Literature and Film.* Edinburgh: Edinburgh UP, 1999.

Shaviro, Steven. *Connected: Or, What It Means to Live in the Network Society.* Minneapolis: U of Minnesota P, 2003.

Shelley, Mary. *Frankenstein.* Ed. Maurice Hindle. New York: Penguin, 2003.

Silverberg, Robert. Ed. *The Science Fiction Hall of Fame.* Vol. 1. New York: Avon, 1970.

Skloot, Rebecca. "Henrietta's Dance." *Johns Hopkins Magazine.* April 2000. http://www.jhu.edu/jhumag/0400web.

———. "An Obsession with Culture." *Pitt Magazine.* March 2001. http://www.pittmag.pitt.edu/mar2001/culture.html

Smelik, Anneke. *Bits of Life: Feminism at the Intersection of Media, Bioscience, and Technology.* Seattle: U of Washington P, 2008.

Smith, Erin A. "How the Other Half Read: Advertising, Working-Class Readers, and Pulp Magazines." *Book History.* 3 (2000): 204–30.

Smith, Van. "Wonder Woman: The Life Death and Life after Death of Henrietta Lacks, Unwitting Heroine of Modern Medical Science."

Citypaper Online. April 7, 2002. http://www.citypaper.com/news/story. asp?id=3426.

Soja, Edward J. *Postmodern Geographies: The Reassertion of Space in Critical Social Theory.* London: Verso, 1989.

Space Is the Place. North American Star System, 1974.

Spillers, Hortense. "Mama's Baby, Papa's Maybe: An American Grammar Book." *Diacritics.* 17.2 (Summer 1987): 64–81.

Star Trek. New York: National Broadcasting Company, 1966–69.

Star Wars. 20th Century Fox, 1977.

"Stealth Aircraft." *US Centennial of Flight Commission.* http://www. centennialofflight.gov/essay/Evolution_of_Technology/Stealth_ aircraft/Tech31.htm.

"Stealth Aircraft: The Technology Behind the Planes." http://www.seorf. ohiou.edu/~af641/.

Steinberg, Marc. "Inverting History in Octavia Butler's Postmodern Slave Narrative." *African American Review.* 38.3 (Fall 2004): 467–76.

Sterling, Bruce. "When Blobjects Rule the Earth." www.boingboing.net/ mages/blobjects.htm.

Sterling, Christopher H. "Telegraph." *Encyclopedia of International Media and Communications.* Vol. 4. New York: Elsevier, 2003.

Sutin, Lawrence. *Divine Invasions: A Life of Philip K. Dick.* New York: Vintage: 1992.

———.Ed. *The Shifting Realities of Philip K. Dick: Selected Literary and Philosophical Writings.* New York: Vintage, 1995.

Suvin, Darko. *Metamorphoses of Science Fiction: On the Poetics and History of a Literary Genre.* New Haven: Yale UP, 1979.

Szwed, John. *Crossovers: Essays on Race, Music, and American Culture.* Philadelphia: Penn UP, 2005.

———. *Space Is the Place: The Lives and Times of Sun Ra.* New York: Da Capo, 1997.

Tatsumi, Takayuki. *Full Metal Apache: Transactions Between Cyberpunk Japan and Avant-Pop America.* Durham: Duke UP, 2006.

Thomas, Sheree R. Ed. *Dark Matter: A Century of Speculative Fiction from the African Diaspora.* New York: Warner, 2000.

Thompson, Robert Farris. *Flash of the Spirit: African and Afro-American Art and Philosophy.* New York: Random House, 1983.

Tofts, Darren. Ed. *Prefiguring Cyberculture: an Intellectual History.* Cambridge, MA: MIT, 2002.

Tymn, Marshall B. and Mike Ashley. *Science Fiction, Fantasy, and Weird Fiction.* Westport: Greenwood Press, 1985.

Umland, Samuel J. Ed. *Philip K. Dick: Contemporary Critical Interpretations.* Westport: Greenwood Press, 1995.

United States. Department of Justice. *An Introduction to DARE: Drug Abuse Resistance Education.* Washington, DC: GPO, 1991.

———. National Drug Intelligence Center. Department of Justice. *National Drug Threat Assessment 2008.* Washington, DC: GPO, 2008.

United States. Office of National Drug Control Policy. *FY 2009 Budget Summary.* Washington, DC: GPO, 2008.

———. Office of National Drug Control Policy. *National Drug Control Strategy 2008 Annual Report.* Washington, DC: GPO, 2008.

———. Office of National Drug Control Policy. *What You Need to Know About Starting a Student Drug-Testing Program.* Washington, DC: GPO, 2008.

———. *United States Code Annotated,* Title 21, "Food and Drugs, Subchapter I: Control and Enforcement." Washington, DC: GPO, 2008.

Vieth, Errol. *Screening Science: Contexts, Texts, and Science in Fifties Science Fiction Film.* Lantham: Scarecrow, 2001.

Virilio, Paul. *The Information Bomb.* Trans. Chris Turner. London: Verso, 2000.

———. *Speed and Politics.* Trans. Mark Polizzotti. New York: Semiotext(e), 1986.

Vitale, Tom. "Tom Vitale Reports on Author William Gibson's Latest Book *Pattern Recognition.*" http://www.discover.npr.org/features/feature. jhtml? wfId=1399923.

Walker III, William O. *Drug Control Policy: Essays in Historical and Comparative Perspective.* University Park: Penn State Press, 1992.

Warner, Michael. Ed. *Fear of a Queer Planet: Queer Politics and Social Theory.* Minneapolis: U of Minnesota P, 1993.

———. *Publics and Counterpublics.* New York: Zone, 2005.

———. *The Trouble with Normal: Sex, Politics, and the Ethics of Queer Life.* Cambridge: Harvard UP, 1999.

Warrick, Patricia S. *Mind in Motion: The Fiction of Philip K. Dick.* Carbondale: Southern Illinois UP, 1987.

Wasserstrom, Silas J. "The Incredible Shrinking Fourth Amendment." *American Criminal Law Review.* 21.3 (1984): 257–401.

Weatherford, Jack. *The History of Money: From Sandstone to Cyberspace.* New York: Three Rivers, 1997.

Wegner, Phillip E. *Imaginary Communities: Utopia, the Nation, and the Spatial Histories of Modernity.* Berkeley: U of California P, 2002.

Wells, H.G. *The Time Machine/The Invisible Man.* New York: Signet, 2007.

Wiener, Norbert. *Cybernetics; Or Control and Communication in the Animal and the Machine.* 2nd Ed. Cambridge, MA: MIT, 1961.

———. *The Human Use of Human Beings: Cybernetics and Society.* New York: Da Capo, 1954.

Wikipedia. "*DARPA.*" http://en.wikipedia.org/wiki/DARPA.

———. "Global Positioning System." http://en.wikipedia.org/wiki/GPS.

———. "Henrietta Lacks." http://en.wikipedia.org/wiki/Henrietta_Lacks.

———. "Stealth Aircraft." http://en.wikipedia.org/wiki/Stealth_aircraft.

———. "Stealth Technology." http://en.wikipedia.org/wiki/Stealth_technology.

———. "Telegraphy." http://en.wikipedia.org/wiki/Telegraph.

Williams, Jeffrey C. "The Origins of Futures Markets." *Agricultural History.*
    56.1 (1982): 306–16.

Wooten, Todd. *White Men Can't Hump (As Good as Black Men): Vol. II: Sex
    and Race in America.* New York: Authorhouse, 2006.

Wylie, Philip and Edwin Balmer. *When Worlds Collide.* 1932. Lincoln: U of
    Nebraska P, 1999.

Žižek, Slavoj. *The Sublime Object of Ideology.* London: Verso, 1989.

———. *Welcome to the Desert of the Real!* London: Verso, 2002.

INDEX